SEAN WILLIAMS

Based on a story by Haden Blackman

BALLANTINE BOOKS • NEW YORK

Star Wars: The Force Unleashed is a work of fiction. Names, places, and incidents either are products of the author's imagination or are used fictitiously.

2009 Del Rey Mass Market Edition

Published in the United States by Del Rey, an imprint of The Random House Publishing Group, a division of Random House, Inc., New York.

DEL REY is a registered trademark and the Del Rey colophon is a trademark of Random House, Inc.

Originally published in hardcover in the United States by Del Rey, an imprint of The Random House Publishing Group, a division of Random House, Inc., in 2008.

This book contains an excerpt from the forthcoming book *Star Wars: Death Troopers* by Joe Schreiber. This excerpt has been set for this edition only and may not reflect the final content of the forthcoming edition.

ISBN 978-0-345-50285-8

Printed in the United States of America

www.starwars.com
www.lucasarts.com
www.delreybooks.com

OPM   9 8 7 6 5 4 3 2 1

For my family:
Amanda, Xander, and Finn;
and Seb, always

ACKNOWLEDGMENTS

My sincere thanks go to Ginjer Buchanan, Christine Cabello, Leland Chee, Keith Clayton, Richard Curtis, Darren Nash, Frank Parisi, Lindsay Parmenter, Brett Rector, Sue Rostoni, Shelly Shapiro, John Stafford, Cameron Suey, and Dan Wasson, without whom this book would have been much less enjoyable—and probably impossible—to write.

Kudos to Haden Blackman for a killer script, and George Lucas for allowing the window onto the Dark Times to open . . . at last.

I would also like to thank Kevin J. Anderson, whose friendship, generosity, and creative energy have served as inspiration throughout my career, and will continue to inspire me, I am sure, for many years to come.

THE STAR WARS NOVELS TIMELINE

1020 YEARS BEFORE STAR WARS: A New Hope

Darth Bane: Path of Destruction
Darth Bane: Rule of Two

33 YEARS BEFORE STAR WARS: A New Hope

Darth Maul: Saboteur*

32.5 YEARS BEFORE STAR WARS: A New Hope

Cloak of Deception
Darth Maul: Shadow Hunter

32 YEARS BEFORE STAR WARS: A New Hope

**STAR WARS: EPISODE I
THE PHANTOM MENACE**

29 YEARS BEFORE STAR WARS: A New Hope

Rogue Planet

27 YEARS BEFORE STAR WARS: A New Hope

Outbound Flight

22.5 YEARS BEFORE STAR WARS: A New Hope

The Approaching Storm

22-19 YEARS BEFORE STAR WARS: A New Hope

**STAR WARS: EPISODE II
ATTACK OF THE CLONES**

The Clone Wars
The Clone Wars: Wild Space

Republic Commando
  Hard Contact
  Triple Zero
  True Colors
  Order 66

Shatterpoint
The Cestus Deception
The Hive*
MedStar I: Battle Surgeons
MedStar II: Jedi Healer
Jedi Trial
Yoda: Dark Rendezvous
Labyrinth of Evil

**STAR WARS: EPISODE III
REVENGE OF THE SITH**

Dark Lord: The Rise of Darth Vader

Coruscant Nights
  Jedi Twilight
  Street of Shadows
  Patterns of Force

10-0 YEARS BEFORE STAR WARS: A New Hope

The Han Solo Trilogy:
  The Paradise Snare
  The Hutt Gambit
  Rebel Dawn

5-2 YEARS BEFORE STAR WARS: A New Hope

The Adventures of Lando Calrissian

The Han Solo Adventures

The Force Unleashed

STAR WARS: A New Hope YEAR 0

Death Star

**STAR WARS: EPISODE IV
A NEW HOPE**

0-3 YEARS AFTER STAR WARS: A New Hope

Tales from the Mos Eisley Cantina
Allegiance
Galaxies: The Ruins of Dantooine
Splinter of the Mind's Eye

3 YEARS AFTER STAR WARS: A New Hope

**STAR WARS: EPISODE V
THE EMPIRE STRIKES BACK**

Tales of the Bounty Hunters

3.5 YEARS AFTER STAR WARS: A New Hope

Shadows of the Empire

4 YEARS AFTER STAR WARS: A New Hope

**STAR WARS: EPISODE VI
RETURN OF THE JEDI**

Tales from Jabba's Palace
Tales from the Empire
Tales from the New Republic

The Bounty Hunter Wars:
  The Mandalorian Armor
  Slave Ship
  Hard Merchandise

The Truce at Bakura

5 YEARS AFTER STAR WARS: A New Hope

Luke Skywalker and the Shadows of Mindor

6.5-7.5 YEARS AFTER STAR WARS: A New Hope

X-Wing:
  Rogue Squadron
  Wedge's Gamble
  The Krytos Trap
  The Bacta War
  Wraith Squadron
  Iron Fist
  Solo Command

Part 1

IMPERIAL

CHAPTER 1

THE LIFE OF DARTH VADER'S secret student took a strange and deadly turn the day his Master first spoke of General Rahm Kota.

He'd had no warning that a moment of such significance was approaching. During his nightly meditations, kneeling on the metal floor of his chamber while construction droids built the *Executor*, unaware of his existence, he had seen no visions in the pure, angry red of the lightsaber that he held like a burning brand in front of his eyes. Although he had stared until the world vanished and the dark side flowed through him in a bloody tide, the future had remained closed.

Nothing, therefore, prepared him for the sudden deviation from the day's punishing and unpredictable exercises. His Master was not a patient teacher; neither was he a talkative one. He preferred action to debate, just as he preferred recrimination to reward. Never once in all the days they had sparred together, with lightsaber, telekinesis, or suggestion, had the Dark Lord offered a single word of encouragement. And that was as it should be, he knew. A teacher's job was not to drag a student along a single, well-worn path. Rather it was to let the student forge his or her own way through the forest, intervening only when the student was hopelessly lost and needed to be corrected.

Even on the wrong paths, he knew, lay some wisdom.

What didn't kill him only made him more powerful in the dark side.

And there had been many, many times he had thought he might die . . .

Breathing heavily after a punishing round of blows, lightsaber lowered in submission, he knelt before his Master and prepared for the killing strike. He could feel the wrath radiating from the Dark Lord like heat—a visceral, angry heat that brought out his skin in gooseflesh. For a moment that seemed to stretch for years, all he could hear was the regular, implacable respiration that kept the man inside the mask alive.

"You were weak when I found you." The voice seemed to come from the far end of a long, deep tunnel. "You should never have survived my training."

He closed his eyes. He had heard these words before. They were the closest thing to a bedtime story he'd had as a child. The moral he had taken from them was burned into his mind: *Learn . . . or die.*

Behind his eyelids he pictured again the clean, cleansing heat of the lightsaber. He had brushed his skin against it many times, defying the pain, and taken numerous small wounds while dueling with his Master. He imagined that he knew what the blade would feel like when it struck him down. Part of him longed for it.

The lightsaber drifted so close to his neck that he could smell his hair burning.

"But now, your hatred has become your strength."

The lightsaber retreated. With a hiss it deactivated.

"At last, the dark side is your ally."

He didn't dare nod or look up. What was this? Some new ruse to lure him into overconfidence and failure?

His Master's next words made his heart trip a beat.

"Rise, my apprentice."

Apprentice. So he had always thought himself, but never before had it been said aloud! And that strange motion with the lightsaber . . . Could he possibly have just been knighted?

His lightsaber retracted. It was all he could do to balance on knees that felt suddenly made of rubber. The black shape looming over him was unreadable, limned with crimson from the light of the star shining through the wide viewport to their right. Metal, angular, and functional, the space around them was as familiar to him as the scars on the back of his hand, but suddenly, disconcertingly, everything seemed different.

The apprentice kept his eyes up and his voice level.

"What is your will, my Master?"

"You have defeated many of my rivals. Your training is nearly complete. It is time now to face your first true test."

A roll call of past missions sped through the apprentice's mind. Lord Vader had instructed him to dispatch numerous enemies within the Empire down the years: spies and thieves, mainly, with the occasional high-ranking traitor as well. He felt only satisfaction at having fulfilled his duty. His victims had brought their fates upon themselves, these vermin that gnawed at the footings of the Empire's magnificent edifice.

But this was different. He could sense it in more than his Master's words. Darth Vader wasn't talking about some low-life smuggler with no awareness at all of the Force. There could be only one foe he was worthy to fight now.

"Your spies have located a Jedi?"

"Yes. General Rahm Kota." The name meant nothing to the apprentice: just one of many in an archive of unconfirmed Jedi kills. "He is attacking a critical shipyard above Nar Shaddaa. You will destroy him and bring me his lightsaber."

Excitement filled the apprentice. He had trained and hoped for this moment as long as he could remember. At last it had come. He could never truly call himself a Sith until he had taken the life of one of his Master's traditional enemies.

"I'll leave at once, Master."

He had taken barely a step toward the door when Darth Vader's irresistible voice stopped him. "The Emperor cannot discover you."

"As you wish, my Master."

"Leave no witnesses. Kill everyone aboard, Imperials and insurgents alike."

The apprentice nodded, keeping his sudden uncertainty carefully clouded.

"Do not fail in this."

The lightsaber hanging back at his hip was a comforting, reassuring weight. "No, my lord," he said, back straight and voice firm.

Darth Vader turned away and gripped his hands behind his back. The red sun painted his helmet with lava highlights.

Thus dismissed, his secret apprentice hurried about his latest, darkest duty.

GENERAL RAHM KOTA.

The name ran through his mind as he hurried through the warren connecting his Master's secret chambers. They were sparse, functional spaces, consisting of a meditation chamber, a droid workshop, sleeping quarters large enough for one, and a hangar deck. All were on a concealed level of Darth Vader's flagship, a space long since written out of the floor plans; it would go unnoticed by the future crew.

The Emperor cannot discover you.

Excited though he was by the thought of hunting Jedi, the reminder of the goal his Master allowed him to share was instantly sobering. All his life he had been trained to turn fear into anger, and anger into power. It was no different, he realized, for Darth Vader. Where else could Lord Vader look for increased power than to the Emperor himself? People were either predators or prey. That was one of the most basic rules of life. Together, Darth Vader and his apprentice would ensure that their joint power only increased.

But first he had to survive an encounter with a Jedi. That his Master had found one at liberty was unsurprising. A handful were suspected to have survived the Great Jedi Purge, and none was more adept at finding them than Darth Vader. The dark side infiltrated every corner of the galaxy; nothing could remain hidden from it forever. Perhaps one day, the apprentice thought, he, too, could seek out his enemies by their thoughts and feelings alone, but like the visions of the future that were closed to him, that ability remained elusive. He had never met a Jedi. Their natures were mysterious to him.

Their history, however, was not. His Master set no lesson plans or written examinations, but Darth Vader did give him access to records surviving from the Republic and the Order he had helped unseat from its position of undeserved privilege. The apprentice had devoted himself to the study, understanding that knowledge of his enemy might mean the difference one day between life and death.

General Rahm Kota.

The name still brought forth no details of combat styles, character, or last sightings from his memory. He would access the records when he reached the *Rogue Shadow.* There would be time to research on the journey to Nar Shaddaa. If he dug deeply enough, he might find some small detail that would give him an edge when he most needed one. That was the only preparation he required.

Entering the hangar bay, he wound his way through the familiar maze of crates, weapons racks, and starfighter parts. The ambient lighting was dim, with shadows pooling in every corner. The air tasted of metal and ozone—a sharp stink that had by now become very familiar. For some, the underbelly of a Star Destroyer might have seemed a strange place to grow up, but for him it was a comfort to be surrounded by such unambiguous symbols of technological and political power. Ships like these had patrolled the trade lanes of the galaxy for years. They had put down insurrections and quashed resistance around hundreds of worlds. Where else would a Sith apprentice live and learn?

Kill everyone aboard, Imperials and insurgents alike. Leave no witnesses.

Even as he mulled over this new development, a familiar *snap-hiss* sounded to his right and a glowing blue-white blade sprang into life in a dark corner of the hangar. A brown-robed figure ran forward, weapon raised.

Instantly in a fighting crouch, the apprentice brought his own blade up to block the blow, teeth bared in a delighted snarl.

He and his adversary held the pose for a bare second, lightsabers locked across their chests. The apprentice quickly sized up the being who had attacked him. Human male, fair-haired and bearded, with calm, serious eyes and a firm set to his jaw. Anyone within living memory of the Clone Wars—or possessing free access to the Jedi Archives—would have recognized him immediately.

Jedi Master Obi-Wan Kenobi, High General of the Galactic Republic and master of the Soresu form of lightsaber combat, slid his deadly blade down and to the right, ducking at the same time to avoid the inevitable countersweep. Sparks flew as the apprentice Force-leapt high into the air and landed with perfect agility on top of a stack of crates. He reached out with his cupped left hand and swept a metal tool kit across the hangar bay, toward his opponent's head. Kenobi ducked and leapt up after him, deflecting a flurry of blows that would have left an ordinary man in pieces, then responding with a sweep of his own that sent the apprentice dodging backward, jumping from one stack to another in temporary retreat.

So the duel proceeded for almost a minute, with Kenobi and the apprentice dancing like acrobatic Gados from stack to stack, lightsabers spinning and clashing, racks and tools turned into temporary weapons as they hurled themselves from one to the other. The racket was enormous, and the threat very real. Kenobi slashed a new rip in the sleeve of the apprentice's combat suit with a move that would have taken his arm off at the elbow had he not moved in time. Twice he felt rather than saw the Jedi's blade sweep over his head.

The apprentice wasn't afraid of dying. His only fear was of failing his Master, and that fear he put to good use. The dark side rushed through him, made him strong and resilient. He felt more powerful than he ever had before.

Vader was sending him to hunt one of his old foes—and how better to warm up for the mission than by killing the man who had once been among the most famous Jedi in the galaxy?

Alive with murderous intent, the apprentice rushed forward, his red blade swinging, to finish the job.

CHAPTER 2

AT THE SOUND OF AN unfamiliar energy weapon activating nearby, Juno Eclipse looked up from her work and reached for the blaster pistol at her side. She had just about finished sealing up the hull of the *Rogue Shadow,* and her thoughts had already turned to testing the new systems she'd installed when this distraction had come along to ruin her concentration. Combat drills weren't unknown on large Imperial vessels, but she'd yet to see anyone on the secure deck—indeed, anyone anywhere on the ship—apart from Lord Vader. Her appointment was still so recent, and so soon after the catastrophe on Callos, that she felt compelled to treat any unexpected development with caution.

Two weapons were in play, humming and clashing, and the harsh, almost percussive sound was punctuated by noises of physical violence. Metal banged and crashed as though a dozen troopers were throwing armor at one another. There were many fragile components stored in the hangar, some of them actively dangerous if handled carelessly, but a cry of anger stalled on her lips. There was something about the sound of those weapons . . . something familiar that she couldn't quite place . . .

Putting down her welder, she disengaged the safety on her pistol and moved stealthily out from under the ship. At first glance, the *Rogue Shadow* wasn't much to look at: a twin-armed, long-bodied starship with the chassis of a small transport, two solar gather panels on the starboard side, and a larger weapons pod to port. That, however, was the point. A prototype intentionally designed to look common, unremarkable, it was in fact a combat vessel possessing the fastest hyperdrive Juno had ever worked with, plus a bona fide cloaking system. That, on top of first-rate scanners and sensors, competitive sublight engines, and powerful deflector shields, made the *Rogue Shadow* the most fascinating ship she'd flown.

Or would fly, if she survived her first day on the job.

"Your record impresses me, Captain Eclipse," Lord Vader had told her little more than a week ago. Barely scrubbed after her return from Callos and still shellshocked from what had happened there with the Black Eight, she had felt none of the pride she might ordinarily have taken. "Few pilots of your caliber also share your clear sense of duty."

"Thank you, Lord Vader."

"I have a new assignment for you. Some would consider it a reward, were they to learn of it. They will not. Is that understood?"

Although she didn't yet understand, not remotely, she had nodded. Darth Vader had given her directions to the flagship's hidden level and described the vessel that she would find there, which would be hers to pilot.

"You will be working with an agent of mine operating under the call sign *Starkiller*. He will make himself known to you shortly. I am placing a considerable amount of trust in you, Captain. Be sure you don't give me reason to doubt it. The price for failure has never been higher."

"I do understand, Lord Vader." To forestall his dismissing her, for he seemed about to, she asked, "But what is our assignment, sir? You have yet to explain."

"That will become clear." The masked figure had already turned away. She knew the conversation was over.

An obedient Imperial officer, Juno had done as she was told and gone to see her new command. The ship had impressed her, requiring only a small amount of tinkering to make it function at its full potential. But now this strange clamor, this rowdy duel had taken over the hangar and, by the sound of it, threatened to spill out of Lord Vader's secret spaces and into the wider ship.

Creeping around a cryo cylinder taller than she was, Juno finally caught sight of the combatants. Her blue eyes widened in surprise.

What struck her first were the weapons: glowing swords of a type she had seen only once before, on an old, forbidden holo her father had found in the depths of their new home's database. He had shown it to her before erasing it with a snarl. "Murderers," he had declared of the figures she'd glimpsed: brown-robed men and women of various species, fighting droids with shining swords of pure light. "Traitors, all of them."

"What did they do?" She had been younger then, not yet fully cognizant of the frustration and resentment her father kept bottled up inside him. It only fully manifested when she gave it reason, and it was only ever directed at her.

"What did they *do*?" He turned on her, tone harsh and disparaging. "The Jedi filth betrayed Palpatine—that's all they did. What rubbish do your teachers fill your head with if you don't even know that?"

The memory of his mockery still stung. Juno forced herself to put it aside while she assessed what was happening before her. Two men—one bearded and solemn, the other much the same age as her, stubble-haired and thin as a whip—were dueling with weapons identical to those of the hated Jedi. One blade was so bright and blue, it burned almost white. Its counterpart was red and just as deadly. When they clashed, sparks flew in all directions. The men leapt and tumbled with inhuman agility. When they gestured, metal walls buckled and engine parts flew like missiles.

She didn't dare make a sound. Every muscle was frozen as she crouched in the shadows, filled with a mixture of fear and awe. In all her years of service to the Empire, she had never seen anything like it. Heard rumors, yes—of Lord Vader's arcane powers and of the cylindrical hilt that hung at his side—but seen nothing. It had been easy to dismiss the rumors as scaremongering and propaganda disseminated to instill fear and encourage loyalty. She had never needed to be threatened into service, so she had happily ignored them.

Now she was wishing she had paid closer attention.

Things became stranger still when the younger of the combatants, with a look of wild satisfaction, rammed his crimson lightsaber through the chest of his opponent. Defeated, the older man dropped to his knees, a look of shock spreading across his face.

That expression was shared by Juno when the form of the older man began to spark and flicker like a hologram—which, she realized an instant later, was exactly what he was. Arms, legs, torso, and face sputtered and dissolved, revealing the bipedal form of a droid beneath. He stirred and fell forward with a clatter of metal on metal.

"Ah, master. Another excellent duel." The droid's words were muffled until the young man who had "killed" him rolled him over onto his back.

"You caught me by surprise, PROXY," the man said with an easy affection that belied his former ferocity. "I haven't fought that training program in years. I assumed you'd erased it."

The droid struggled to stand, but succeeded only in

losing his balance and almost falling again. His owner caught him in time and helped him straighten.

"Easy, PROXY. You're malfunctioning."

"It's my fault, master," the droid said with an electronic sigh, looking down at the smoking hole in his chest. "I had hoped that using an older training module would catch you off guard and allow me to finally kill you. I'm sorry I failed you again."

A concerned smile flickered across the young man's face. "I'm sure you'll keep trying."

"Of course, master. It is my primary programming."

Droid and master began moving through the maze of debris across the hangar. Juno remembered herself in time. Before they could see her, she ducked down behind cover and hurried back to the ship. Their voices were growing louder as they approached. She frantically reholstered the pistol and reached for her welder.

"Well, you won't be ambushing me again until we get your central stabilizer replaced—and that could take weeks, this far from the Core . . ."

She didn't look up as the odd pair rounded the cryo cylinder she had been crouching behind just seconds before, but she could feel the young man staring at her and hear in his sudden silence the double take he had performed. She kept her head down, hiding a flush of embarrassment—and a small amount of fear. What this unknown person might do if he found out that she'd been spying on him, she didn't know.

A faint patter of footsteps told her that he and the droid had pulled back out of sight. She fought to make out a furious exchange of whispers.

"PROXY, who is that?"

"Ah, yes. Your new pilot has finally arrived, master."

"But who *is* she?"

"Accessing Imperial records . . ."

There was a moment of silence during which she told

herself not to be so curious. That only ever got her into trouble.

But then she heard her own voice speaking in the hangar and her temper got the better of her.

"Captain Juno Eclipse," said the holodroid in Juno's clipped tones. "Born on Corulag, where she became the youngest student ever accepted into the Imperial Academy. Decorated combat pilot with over one hundred combat missions and commanding officer during the Bombing of Callos. Handpicked by Lord Vader to lead his Black Eight Squadron, but later reassigned to a top-secret project—"

She stormed around the cryo cylinder and caught the strange sight of herself standing directly in front of her—an exact doppelgänger supported by the man whom she now realized was Darth Vader's agent, the so-called Star-killer. Her face burned at the indignity and the invasion of her privacy.

"Is there a psychological profile in there, too?" she asked.

Young man and droid stared back at her. With a look of barely concealed embarrassment, Starkiller let go of the droid and stepped away. The droid, PROXY, wobbled on his feet, and then snapped to attention in a fair imitation of her—complete with neat blond hair, regulation uniform, tricolored insignia, and a smudge of grease just forming on her cheek as the droid updated his image files.

"Actually, yes," the machine told her, "but it's restricted." To Starkiller as an aside he added, "Master, I can tell you that she's going to be impossible to reprogram."

Juno suppressed an urge to take the welding tool and ram another hole through the droid's perforated chest. Coming face-to-face with herself was a disconcerting development, one for which she had been completely unprepared.

The young man gestured. The droid dropped his simulation of her and went back to being just a droid.

"You know why you're here?" Starkiller asked her.

Remembering herself, she lowered the welder and took a deep breath.

"Lord Vader gave me my orders himself," she said. "I am to keep your ship running and fly you wherever your missions require."

Starkiller seemed neither pleased nor displeased. "PROXY," he instructed the droid, "get the *Rogue Shadow* ready to launch."

The damaged machine stumbled off to do his bidding, while Juno and his master followed at a more sedate pace.

"Did Lord Vader tell you that he killed our last pilot?"

Juno studied him as closely as he was obviously studying her. He was dressed in a worn black combat uniform that looked as though it had been mended many times. His arms and hands were a mess of scar tissue. "No. But I can only assume he or she gave Lord Vader good cause to do so." She paused, then added, "I will not."

"We'll see. I'm sick of training new pilots." His eyes slid past her to where she had been working on the *Rogue Shadow.* His brows crinkled on seeing the new panels she had welded into place. "What's this? What have you done to my ship?"

Suddenly self-conscious, Juno wiped the smudges from her cheek. "I have taken the liberty of upgrading the *Rogue Shadow*'s sensor array. Now you will be able to spy on any suspect ships across an entire system." She waited for some sign of approval, but he only nodded. Her pride slightly stung, she said, "I assume that's part of your mission profile. You can only be one of Darth Vader's spies. Your ship has the most amazing long-range scanners *and* a cloaking device—"

"You don't need to know anything about my missions except where I'm going."

"Where *are* we going?"

"To Nar Shaddaa. Can you handle that?"

"Of course." She bit her lip on an angry retort and brushed past him to the ramp leading into the ship.

In the cockpit she found the droid fiddling ineptly at the controls. "Leave that alone," she snapped. "I'll do it."

"Yes, Captain Eclipse."

The droid backed away with a series of creaks and sparks from his damaged midriff. Only then did she remember his strange remark to his master—about ambushing and killing him—and wondered if she shouldn't perhaps have been more polite.

CHAPTER 3

THE *ROGUE SHADOW*'S SUBLIGHT ENGINES surged with smooth acceleration as its new pilot deftly manipulated the controls. The apprentice watched her closely as she worked, assessing her qualifications as well as her other qualities. Of the pilots he had worked with so far, none had been women. She was barely his age and very beautiful with it, but in the pilot's seat she was a consummate professional. Confident and precise, she moved as though she had been born in a cockpit.

Once he was certain that he and PROXY were in safe hands, he turned his attention to the details of his mission.

"PROXY, give me the target."

The droid who had been his sole continuous companion for most of his life was sitting in a jump seat at the rear of the cockpit, strapped carefully in place. Familiar distortions played across his metal skin and features as he activated the holoprojectors that made him unique. The appearance of a hardened human warrior took form in the droid's seat. Dressed in the familiar browns of the hated Jedi, he possessed high cheekbones and a strong, broken nose. His eyes were deeply recessed and revealed none of his thoughts.

"According to official Imperial records," PROXY said in a deep, commanding voice that was nothing like his own, "Jedi Master Rahm Kota was a respected general in the Clone Wars."

"The Clone Wars?" Juno half turned at the controls as she prepared the ship for its jump through hyperspace. Her expression was as grave as that of the man sitting where PROXY had been. "You're hunting Jedi."

The apprentice hadn't realized she was paying attention. "I bring Darth Vader's enemies to justice," he told her. "And now so do you." Before she could initiate a full-on discussion about it, the apprentice said, "Go on, PROXY."

"Of course. Master Kota was a military genius, but did not believe that the clone soldiers were fit for battle. Instead he relied on a small squad of his own personally trained troops. It's the only thing that kept him from being executed when the Emperor discovered the Jedi's plot against the Republic."

Juno nodded. "There were no clones in his squad to bring him to justice."

"Exactly, Captain Eclipse. After Order 66, he vanished. Imperial records actually claim he's dead."

The hologram of Kota faded, and PROXY returned to normal.

Juno still appeared more interested in the mission than plotting the hyperspace jump. "So why come out of hiding and attack the Empire now?"

The apprentice had been considering that very question himself. "Kota wants to be found."

"Then we are walking into a trap." She looked from the apprentice to PROXY and back again. "How many pilots have you lost before me?"

"Seven."

"Oh, excellent." She flipped a switch on the *Rogue Shadow*'s complicated console. "Coordinates for Nar Shaddaa are locked. Prepare for lightspeed."

The apprentice braced himself as the stars ahead turned into streaks and the familiar unreal tunnel opened up around the ship. With a well-tuned whine, the *Rogue Shadow* and its passengers rocketed into hyperspace.

NAR SHADDAA, AKA THE SMUGGLER'S MOON, the Vertical City, or even Little Coruscant: the apprentice had never been there before, but he had learned as much as he could from history and other educational holos. Its criminal classes and extensive underground networks were famous across the galaxy, with lowlifes by the tens of thousands flocking there in search of ill-gotten fortunes. Although dwarfed by noisome Nal Hutta, the large planet it orbited, it outshone every other world in the Y'Toub system in every conceivable spectrum. Dozens of different species called it home.

The apprentice couldn't hide a contemptuous sneer as the *Rogue Shadow* approached. Notorious for changing allegiances, the criminal capital was currently courting Imperial favor by inviting—or at least tolerating—the presence of a new TIE fighter manufacturing facility in its upper atmosphere. He could imagine the reasoning behind it: more money and resources flowing into the system; a new source of "legitimate" jobs for those few who required them; an influx of potentially corrupt officials to bribe. Sad for the locals, then, that the facility was staffed entirely by humans, with security maintained by a full legion of Imperial stormtroopers.

The sneer became a frown as the apprentice remembered Lord Vader's words: *Leave no witnesses.* He was more uncertain about that than he was about facing his first fugitive Jedi. Although his Master spoke of confronting the Emperor and taking over in his stead, the apprentice felt no disloyalty to the many troopers and officers working steadfastly in Imperial service. If they broke no laws or hatched no plots against his Master, he had no gripe with them. But now, for the first time, he would have to act against those whose only error would be to cross his path. Was this a test, he wondered, to see how far he would go in pursuit of his destiny? If so, he swore not to disappoint his Master. He would obey orders and follow his instincts. He would not fail.

Sometimes he despaired of ever attaining full mastery of the Force and thereby earning his Master's respect—but he knew well how to turn despair to his service, by using it to fuel his anger and thereby stoke the desire for power. In time, he would succeed. There was nothing he could not do, in this matter or any other, if he tried hard enough.

Yet his frown deepened as he watched Juno pilot the ship closer to the facility. What did he know about her? Nothing, really. In almost every respect, she seemed the perfect Imperial officer: neat, efficient, and human. That she wasn't afraid to speak her mind couldn't have bothered his Master overmuch, so he shouldn't let it bother him. He would trust her with the *Rogue Shadow* while he went about his duties, and the Emperor help her if she failed him.

The starfighter facility was much larger than it had seemed from a distance, looking like a stack of round plates hanging high above the Vertical City. What he had assumed were lights flashing across its irregular surface resolved into explosions when viewed from a nearer perspective. Vast balls of yellow-hot gas erupted at irregular intervals from shattered viewports, weakened bulkheads, and burst access tubes.

"The shipyard's sustained heavy damage," Juno said matter-of-factly as she looked for a place to dock.

"I can see that." The apprentice peered with her. Former general Rahm Kota had obviously been busy. "Get us closer."

The *Rogue Shadow* wove gracefully between gouts of flame. The apprentice was forced to admire Juno's deft hand at the controls. The only tension she showed as the ship rocked and slewed was in her jaw. It was clenched tight.

He rode out the turbulence with a calm, confident center, enjoying the sharp eddies and currents of the Force. Some craved peace and quiet in order to detach from the cares of the galaxy. He, however, had learned to find himself in any environment—the noisier, in fact, the better. In conflict it was easier to become one with the dark side. Violence was the ultimate meditation.

"Over there," he said, pointing. "That looks like an open hangar."

She nodded tightly. "It is defended."

"We don't have the time to talk to security." Or to explain that he was forbidden to let anyone know who they were. "Come in hot. Let me handle the defenses."

With well-practiced moves of his own, he activated the ship's weapons systems and took a bead on the cannon emplacements protecting the open hangar. He waited until automated targeting had registered their presence and they swiveled to take aim at the *Rogue Shadow*. Then, with two precise shots, he destroyed the emplacements and thus cleared the way for a landing.

Juno didn't waste any time. The starfighter streaked into the hangar and settled onto a flat space clear of debris. As thrusters brought the *Rogue Shadow* to a halt, the apprentice was already out of his seat.

"I will slice into the mainframe and guide you through the infrastructure," Juno said, slipping a commset over her right ear. "Your friend here can help me."

The apprentice didn't dissuade her, although he knew her efforts would be mostly unnecessary. He could already feel the presence of the Jedi radiating through the facility like a bright light after a snowstorm. Kota wanted to be found, all right.

"Just keep the ship safe," he told her, "and be ready to leave when I get back. We might need to move quickly."

"That is my specialty," she said through the comlink on his wrist as he glided through the ship to the exit ramp, which was fully extended before he arrived. He smelled smoke and spilled blood on the air. That and the faint stench of Jedi made his heart quicken. His eyes narrowed. He took a running jump out of the ship.

His lightsaber was lit before he hit the deck, ready to deflect the shots fired his way by the contingent of troopers sent to investigate their landing. The Force guided his arm—no, the Force *was* his arm. That was how it felt to him. During moments such as these, he was purely a vessel for the dark side. It rushed through him like wine down the neck of a bottle, joyous with release and the promise of more to come. His blade drew glowing lines through the air, casting energy bolts back at the troopers who'd fired them, sending them sprawling in a shower of sparks.

A dozen open-helmeted men and women in brown combat uniforms—Kota's insurgents, the apprentice presumed—came down the hangar's primary access corridor, sealing the blast door behind them. Baring his teeth, he ran to meet them, eager to take the offensive. Their rifles were no match for the power of the Force. A single, powerful push scattered them like dolls. One he blasted with lightning. A second he choked until all consciousness fled. A third he swept up and pounded against the nearest bulkhead. The rest he dismembered with graceful aggression, ignoring their cries of fear and pain.

The blast door opened, and both insurgents and Imperials retreated through it.

"All Imperial squads maintain offensive stance," blared a voice over the intercom. "All squads maintain offensive stance!"

The apprentice grinned and followed his welcoming committee up the corridor.

"Can you hear me?" Juno said through the comlink.

"Yes."

"Reports are showing that Kota's forces have stormed the command bridge."

"Then that's where I'm headed." He stepped over the bodies and followed her directions to the letter.

Her calm voice guided him level by level up a huge chasm leading to the top of the facility. Once he was out of her sight, he didn't have to worry about her asking questions about his harsh treatment of their supposed comrades. Lord Vader could fill her in on that point later, if he thought it necessary. For now Kota was the most important thing.

"The intruders may try using TIE fighter assembly lines as cover," she said. "And I am picking up explosives on my scanners. Be careful."

He assured her he would, even as he dodged a trap laid by Kota's insurgents at the top of a turbolift shaft. The voice over the station's intercom became progressively more alarmed.

"Threat status upgraded. Eliminate all unauthorized personnel."

"Unnecessary force is authorized."

"All K-Level squads report in!"

"Reinforce local security stations *immediately*!"

The walls shook from an explosion so close, it must have buckled every bulkhead on that level. Always he kept in mind Juno's echoing of his own observation: *We are walking into a trap*. Except he was doing the walking while she sat in the ship, safe from BlasTech E-11 rifles and the insurgents' ragtag weapons.

"Another stormtrooper squadron has reached Hangar Twelve," Juno informed him. "It looks like we will have some help in retaking the facility."

"The station is not our concern."

"But Imperial High Command will be quite upset if the TIE assembly lines are damaged—"

"I don't answer to High Command. Now cut the chatter. I'm trying to concentrate."

On the floor of a massive starfighter assembly rig, he stopped with his head raised and his lightsaber cocked. A prickling in the back of his neck warned him of a new threat just as a railgun charge exploded to his right, sending bits of TIE fighter in all directions. He deflected the main force of the explosion, but was still stung by tiny pieces of shrapnel down the back of his right hand.

"Give up!" the insurgents shouted. "We have the factory!"

"What is he?" called another to one of his fellows. "Some kind of shadow trooper?"

"Doesn't matter. Blast him!"

Anger rose up in him, pure and clean, sweeping all other concerns aside. He vaulted a stack of detached solar gather panels and sent a stream of machine parts raining down on the source of the weapons fire.

Screams sounded over the crashing of metal. Kota's insurgents scattered from behind the TIE cockpits they had been using as shelter. Some fired shots at him, employing a range of weaponry that displayed either a lack of organization or restricted resources, or both. He deflected every shot with controlled fury and poured his rage into retaliation. He felt no need to hold back. Those disloyal to the Empire deserved everything they got.

Only when the last was buried under a small mountain of titanium alloy hull plates and reactor shielding did he examine in more detail the equipment they had been carrying. As well as their motley weapons and mismatched armor, the fighters had brought explosive timer packs and had clearly been setting such charges elsewhere on the level. He'd best hurry, he told himself, before the whole facility went up in flames.

No sooner was this thought complete than another shock wave rolled through the structure, much stronger than the last. He barely kept his footing on the heaving deck as TIE fighter and body parts tumbled around him. Juno was shouting something at him, but it was a moment before he could hear her over the blaring of the intercom.

"—the stabilizers or the repulsor engines—can't tell which—not good at all."

"What's that?" he said. "Repeat."

"Kota's accomplices have hit the facility where it hurts," she summarized. "Finish up soon, or we're going down into the skylanes with it."

"Right." The deck was still moving underfoot as he made his way out of the assembly area, blocking the path behind him with a pile of ejector seats and unmounted ion engines. "Where did you say this control center was?"

Juno guided him through the quaking facility. Anyone unlucky enough to get in his way was unceremoniously pushed aside by telekinesis. Doors buckled shut and weapons mysteriously jammed. He didn't have time to play games anymore.

"Any available squadrons," blared the intercom, "defend the security stations at once!" Then: "They're breaching the security stations!" And finally: "Command bridge to all squadrons, we need your assista—"

The final broadcast ended with a rasp of blasterfire. Then relative peace fell.

Ambient gravity was noticeably lighter by the time he reached the doors that Juno assured him led to the control center. That meant the entire facility was falling at a faster rate than he cared to think about. Taking a moment to gather himself, to wrap his will like a cloak around the fiery heart of his anger, he prepared himself to face the Jedi whose presence he could feel through several centimeters of durasteel.

Then he gestured with one finger, and the heavy blast doors slid open. Beyond lay a room identical to hundreds in the galaxy: cold and metallic, with red display screens keeping staff updated on the facility's status. A long, elevated walkway led to a command post where General Rahm Kota stood with his back to the door, in a gesture deliberate in its commingled confidence and contempt. He hadn't even drawn his lightsaber, which hung diagonally across his shoulder blades in a custom-made sheath. A brown cloak hung from two metal shoulder pads that only added to the physical presence of the man. He was a warrior with every breath and wore his battle scars with pride.

The apprentice had been ready to attack, but now he felt a brief moment of hesitation. This wasn't what he had expected. Jedi were soft from a life of privilege, outdated, spent. He hadn't expected a *soldier*.

Kota's voice, when he spoke, was deep and commanding, as it had been during PROXY's impersonation of him. "So I've finally drawn you out of hiding." He turned at last. "I ordered my men to lower the containment field on your approach and—" On seeing the apprentice he stopped midsentence and looked visibly surprised.

"A *boy*?" With one blindingly fast movement, the lightsaber was in his hand and lit. "After all these months of attacking Imperial targets, Vader sends a boy to fight *me*?"

Grim and silent, the apprentice adopted a fighting crouch. So the trap had been directed not at him but at his Master. If Kota was disappointed, the apprentice swore that this would be the last emotion Kota ever felt.

He raised his left hand and with the power of the dark side unleashed a bolt of Sith lightning at the renegade Jedi.

Kota only laughed. Raising his left hand in a move that was a mirror image of the apprentice's own, he sent the lightning arcing back to its source. The energy struck both of them, hurling them apart.

The apprentice broke off the attempt, blinking smoke away from his eyes. His anger intensified. He was the first to his feet and running as soon as his boots touched the deck. He felt completely weightless, yet full of momentum, like a hurled spear. His red blade cut a blur through the air, aimed hard at Kota's throat.

The Jedi general ducked and swept his green lightsaber up and down in a lazy attempt to catch him as he went by. That was a move the apprentice had long ago learned to avoid by tucking his head down closer to his center of gravity and rolling in midair, then kicking himself back at his opponent off the nearest wall. This time he pushed telekinetically as he came, attempting to knock Kota's feet out from under him before bringing his blade to bear.

Again, however, Kota deflected his Force energies back at him. Again they were pushed apart.

More cautiously the apprentice circled him, slicing chairs to pieces as he walked and sending the glowing fragments at his enemy's head. Anger made him eager to attack, but he knew better than to give in to it. He hadn't been humiliated. He had successfully tested Kota's defenses. Now that he knew a direct attack would probably fail, he had to find another way to get closer to the man. Or to make the Jedi come to him.

Suddenly Kota was moving, charging with astonishing speed behind a furious diversity of strokes. The apprentice retreated with lips pulled back over his teeth. *This is more like it!* Green and red energies clashed as he blocked blow after blow and still Kota kept coming, attempting to overwhelm him with sheer determination and speed. The apprentice went back four steps, then stopped. He drew his blade close around him, forming a tight defense in deliberate imitation of the Soresu style that Obi-Wan Kenobi had favored. Realizing he couldn't penetrate it, Kota backed off and tried a different style—slow, deliberate, with sudden and devastatingly quick strikes. These, too, the apprentice parried, and when the old man's guard looked to be slipping, he offered strikes of his own.

The duel raged all across the control center, which shook and rattled as the facility around it broke apart. The apprentice ignored everything else—Juno's voice, the wildly fluctuating gravity, the never-ending explosions, the rising temperature of the floor beneath him—in order to concentrate solely on this one vital battle. Kota wouldn't beat him, but could he beat Kota? He had to. He would rather go down with the ship than break off and admit failure. Darth Vader's secret apprentice knew which fate would await him if he did.

The general was wily and strong and possessed some moves the apprentice had never seen before. But he was older and willfully ignorant of the dark side of the Force. He attempted his charge attack two more times, obviously hoping to force a mistake or wear out his opponent, but it was *he* who started to show the effects of the duel, *he* who took hits. Soon his cloak was a smoking rag and one of his shoulder pads was glowing red-hot.

The apprentice pressed harder, feeling victory and the attainment of his full power approaching. Soon the Jedi's lightsaber—and head—would be his. Then he truly would be worthy of his Master's praise!

He caught the general in a choke hold and maintained his grip even though it turned partially back on him. He had been ready for this; his lungs were full. The general, however, clutched at his throat with one hand while barely managing to parry with the other. The apprentice let the fire in his lungs fuel his lust for triumph. Even as darkness crowded around the edges of his vision, he sent objects hurtling at Kota's legs and face, battling him on all fronts.

Finally a fragment of smoking debris struck the general's knees from behind. With a cry of frustration, the flailing Jedi went down, his face purple and eyes bulging. The apprentice relented slightly, letting them both have a little air, but before Kota could scramble to his feet he was on him, pressing down on their locked lightsabers, which sizzled just millimeters from their faces.

Kota strained but couldn't force the red blade away. In his blue eyes the apprentice saw not cleansing hatred, but regret. Even at the end, Kota clung to his weak Jedi ways.

"Vader thinks"—the old man gasped—"he's turned you. But I can sense your future—and Vader isn't part of it!"

The apprentice urged the lightsabers even closer to Kota's face.

Sweat beaded on the Jedi Master's forehead. "I sense—I sense only . . ." A look of shock and confusion passed over his face. *"Me?"*

The apprentice forced Kota's own lightsaber down into his eyes.

And suddenly—as though in a vision from out of time, exactly the sort of vision the apprentice sought in the fire of his red blade—Kota's face became that of another man, a man with dark hair and strong features, features not dissimilar to the apprentice's own.

The general cried out in pain—and in that cry the apprentice thought he heard a man shouting, "Run!"

He flinched away, blinking furiously, wondering if Kota in his desperate extremity had concocted some new and insidious Jedi mind trick. But his head seemed clear of intrusion, and the general seemed to be thinking of anything but attack. Blinded and agonized, he scrabbled backward, his lightsaber slipping from his fingers and dropping with a dead thud to the deck. A blast of telekinesis erupted from him, shattering every viewport in the command center and sending the apprentice flying. A raging wind swept past them, sucking out the smoke and shrapnel of their duel. Kota, too, was sucked out and fell with a fading cry into the atmosphere below. Or had he leapt?

The apprentice let the gale drag him closer to the hole where the viewport had once been. Catching a bent stanchion with one hand, he carefully leaned out and looked down, lightsaber at the ready for any final deception.

Kota's body was already far below, spread-eagled and dwindling among the skylanes of the Vertical City. A large transport intersected his path; thenceforth his body was invisible. The apprentice imagined it being swatted like a bug on a transparisteel windscreen and told himself to feel the satisfaction of a task completed.

It didn't come.

General Rahm Kota was blinded and gravely wounded. He couldn't possibly be a problem any longer. But the apprentice couldn't assume he was dead until he had the old man's body in front of him—and there was no chance of finding that body now.

He was profoundly disinclined to report failure to Darth Vader.

What to do?

"This place is going to tear itself apart at any mo-

ment!" came Juno's voice over the comlink. "Are you almost done here?"

"On my way." With a vehement look on his face and
no triumph in his heart, he retreated from the viewport
and headed for the door, pausing only to scoop up the
fallen Jedi Master's lightsaber on the way.

CHAPTER 4

JUNO KNEW BETTER THAN TO expect a rapturous reception upon their return, but even so she was disappointed. The secret hangar was empty when the *Rogue Shadow* docked. A successful mission deserved some sort of acknowledgment, surely. Even after Callos . . .

She pushed that thought away. The job was done. What more needed to be said? She had done it well—in her eyes, at least, although Starkiller had barely acknowledged the fact on returning to the ship—and they had lived to fight another day. Or to kill more Jedi Knights, if that was what Lord Vader's scruffy, incommunicative agent was really up to. She had seen the second lightsaber hilt hanging from his belt, and she knew what that probably meant.

It had taken thousands of clone warriors to completely wipe out the Jedi. That was the official version—ignoring the rumors she'd heard about Darth Vader's ongoing hunt for the last survivors of that strange and deadly sect. From the stories her father had told her as a child, she'd imagined them to be monsters four meters high sucking the lifeblood out of the Republic. Now it turned out they still existed, and young men went forth to do battle with them alone.

Could they really be so reduced, these villains that had once held the galaxy in their thrall?

Or . . . could the young man who was now her traveling companion possibly be so powerful?

The landing struts had barely touched metal when he was on his feet and heading for the door.

She leaned back into her seat and ran her hands across her temples. Her skin felt oily and covered in grit, as though she had been the one running around in the smoke and the mess above Nar Shaddaa instead of watching it from the feeds she'd managed to slice into from one of the facility's security cams. She wanted to check over the ship and get into the refresher and scrub the dirt away.

She hadn't felt clean for weeks . . .

The voice of Starkiller almost made her jump out of her skin. She had thought him long gone.

"Good work, Juno," he said. "I'll leave PROXY here to help you run through the checklist."

"Thank you, but I—" By the time she turned her seat around, the cockpit was empty of anyone but her and the droid. PROXY stared back at her with unwinking photoreceptors. She didn't want to admit that he made her slightly nervous, so she flashed her warmest smile and hauled herself out of the seat.

"Well, let's get to it. I've got a report to write before I get any rest—if anyone other than me will ever read it . . ."

PROXY PROVED AN EFFICIENT AND unobtrusive co-worker. He followed instructions, showed initiative, and did his level best to stay out of her way. That was more than she could say for half the real people she had worked with since graduating from the Imperial Academy on Corulag. Together they checked over the ship in record time, noting only a few small carbon scores on its port side and, near the aft sensor array, a blaster burn that had been weakened so much by the shields, it would barely have fried an egg.

When they were done, she dismissed the droid, telling him to go take an oil bath or whatever he did for relaxation, and then set off to her quarters to work on the mission report she insisted had to be completed.

That wasn't entirely a lie. She did need to report in detail to Lord Vader, just as she had on every mission she'd ever flown for him. The thing was, she didn't really need to do it right away. It could wait a standard hour or two, or even until the morning. But there was something else on her mind, something much more important that really couldn't wait any longer.

Is there a psychological profile in there, too? she had asked the droid before they'd set out on their first mission together.

Yes, the machine had told her, *but it's restricted.*

That fact had burned in her all the way to Nar Shaddaa. It came as no surprise that such a file existed somewhere in the vast bureaucracy that was the Imperial Navy. Everyone probably had one, except Darth Vader and the Emperor. What rankled was that it was being talked about. PROXY knew where it was. The wretched machine might even have read it, for all his protest about it being *restricted*. A droid capable of impersonating Jedi Knights might have unknown capacities for deception.

She wanted to know what that profile contained. What was it telling people about her? What secrets did it reveal to the galaxy in general—about her early life, her father, her career? About Callos?

Her mouth was set in a determined line when she reached her quarters on the forty-first deck and activated her datapad. Handpicked for special duties by Darth Vader himself, she had a certain degree of access to files normally hidden to those of her rank. Would that be sufficient for her to locate and read the file she wanted? There was only one way to find out.

Carefully, and thoroughly, she began slicing into the flagship's data banks.

The first files she found concerning her contained nothing unexpected, little more than the brief bio PROXY had given Starkiller in the hangar bay. She skimmed over them in seconds, probing deeper through the architecture of the data banks, seeking forgotten or overlooked corners of information. More snippets emerged. One talked about her mother, a woman she barely remembered who had been killed in crossfire between Imperial loyalists and insurgents on their home planet. She had been a teacher. The file contained a holo Juno had not seen before, an image of her mother with her long blond hair pinned back by a brooch made from a round black stone. Her eyes looked lively and amused. She seemed terribly young to be a mother, and dead.

Among a list of high-ranking Corulag graduates, she came across her name appended to her complete academic record. The list of subjects and grades filled her with pride, as it always did, but with that emotion also came sadness. She had worked so hard and achieved so much, not just for herself, but for her father, too. A distant and strict man, especially after the death of his wife, he had been a fierce admirer of those serving the Empire. A civilian engineer, he would have signed up for the Academy himself had he not failed the physical. So he should have been proud of his daughter, who had graduated with such honor and gone on to achieve everything he had ever wanted. Why, then, had he not even shown up at her graduation? It didn't make any sense.

That was an old, familiar hurt. The profile could talk about that aspect of her life as much as it wanted and she wouldn't think twice. She hadn't seen her father in years and wouldn't mind if she never did again. Only in recent days, away from her former squadron mates and lying alone in her bunkroom at night, did she ever wonder what had become of him. Would she end up as bitter as he was? How many more missions like Callos would it take before she forgot why she had joined up in the first place?

In a small holo appended to the last file she found, her father looked at her with empty eyes around his narrow, imperious nose. She closed that window with an impatient flick of her index finger.

This was getting her nowhere. Searching through archives for her name could leave her mired in trivia for days. There had to be a better way.

She leaned back in her seat and thought for a moment. It was PROXY who had alerted her to the existence of the file, so the droid must have access to its location, if not the actual contents. Therefore, if she could somehow pin down the information PROXY had scanned in the last day or two, she might get a result.

Time had passed during her search. She barely noticed her weariness, trained as she was to spend long hours in the cockpit on full alert. She could grab a short nap later to catch up on what she'd lost. It took her just minutes to find an ID that looked like it might belong to the droid—one not on the official log but with access pretty much everywhere—and to begin following it through the data banks. Like most advanced droids, PROXY had a lively, curious nature. His ruminations led him through numerous fields, including history, repulsor maintenance, astrography, and psychology. It could take her all night to find just one address among all the others. But she persisted, determined to know what her superiors really thought of her after Callos.

Without warning, her screen cleared. She blinked bleary eyes at a new view, a data feed she appeared to have unintentionally sliced into. It was one occasionally accessed by PROXY, showing a gunmetal-gray corridor leading to a heavy, secure door. The view came with sound. She could hear footsteps, faintly, from the other side of the door. Someone was pacing restlessly back and forth. And breathing: heavy, rhythmic breathing, as of lungs straining at a mechanical respirator . . .

A shock of adrenaline rushed through her. Only one person in the galaxy breathed like that. She must have patched by accident into Lord Vader's private chambers. Her hand reached up to cancel the feed lest she be discovered spying on him, but before she could complete the command, the door hissed open and her curiosity was caught.

Revealed in the doorway was Starkiller, a picture of impatience and restraint. He had clearly been waiting to speak to his Dark Lord all this time. In four quick paces he walked past the vantage point of her hidden security cam and out of view.

With a series of hesitant commands, not quite believing her audacity, she tested to see if the viewpoint was movable. It rotated smoothly to bring Starkiller back into sight, revealing a room as empty of personality as the rest of Darth Vader's secret hideout. The Dark Lord himself stood with his back to the room, staring at the burning red sun outside.

Starkiller knelt behind Vader and waited. He seemed well accustomed to doing that, despite the energy boiling through him, barely contained by his skin.

Without turning, Lord Vader asked, "Master Kota is dead?"

Starkiller didn't answer straightaway. He raised his head, considered the question, and then said, "Yes."

"His lightsaber."

Starkiller unclipped the second weapon from his belt. Vader turned just enough to reach out with one hand. The fallen Jedi's lightsaber was snatched into Lord Vader's grasp as though by invisible fingers.

Juno let out a surprised gasp and stifled it under both hands, irrationally afraid that the Dark Lord might hear her through the one-way security link.

Oblivious to her scrutiny, he turned back to the viewport and examined the lightsaber in his hands. Starkiller waited, immobile, as though he could have knelt there all night.

Finally Vader spoke again.

"My spies have been watching another Jedi. Kazdan Paratus is hiding on the junk world of Raxus Prime."

"I'll deal with him as I dealt with Rahm Kota," said Starkiller unhesitatingly.

Well, that's that, thought Juno, abandoning all hope of sleep that night. *No rest for the wicked.* She moved to disconnect and get ready for the call to arms, but her finger hovered over the switch, unable to let the moment go. Her position was an illicit but privileged one, and hard to abandon.

Vader looked up from the lightsaber and turned to face the young man kneeling before him.

"Kazdan Paratus is far more powerful than you," the black-masked figure said, filling her with apprehension. "I do not expect you to survive. But should you succeed, you will be one step closer to your destiny."

Starkiller nodded eagerly. "The Emperor."

"Yes. Only together can we defeat him."

"I will not fail you, Lord—"

Juno's finger stabbed down hard on the cutoff switch and she recoiled into her chair. Apprehension had become pure horror. Could she possibly have heard correctly? The Emperor? Vader and his dark apprentice were going to betray the *Emperor*?

No, she told herself, getting up from her chair and pacing back and forth across the small room. It couldn't be true. There must be more to it than she thought. Perhaps if she'd kept listening . . .

When she tried to get the feed back, the connection was gone. The screen remained resolutely blank, as though taunting her fearful concerns.

Darth Vader had been the Palpatine's right-hand man for as long as the Emperor had been in power. It was inconceivable that he would turn on his Master now. Even if he was considering it, what could he and one scruffy agent do against Imperial Guards and well-armed aides who attended the Emperor everywhere he went? The thought was preposterous. She had to put it out of her mind as a product of fatigue and go about her duty as though nothing had happened.

It wasn't as if she could turn either of them in on such flimsy evidence. If she tried, she'd be killed for sure, whether the accusation was true or not . . .

Right on cue, her communicator buzzed.

"Yes?" she said, speaking as though nothing untoward had happened.

"I need you in the *Rogue Shadow*," Starkiller informed her, as she had known he would. "We have a new mission."

"I'll be right there."

She took a moment to smooth her uniform and her hair, and to rub the dark circles under her eyes, then she hurriedly shut down her datapad and left the room.

CHAPTER 5

THE JUNK WORLD OF RAXUS PRIME was in the Tion Hegemony on the Outer Rim, so there was time during the journey for both her and Starkiller to refresh and research their objectives. He was as distracted as she felt, much to her relief. He kept asking PROXY to repeat details he had missed while deep in thought. Eventually he excused himself to enter the ship's small meditation chamber and gather his energies.

She did the same, in her own way, by reclining her seat and putting her feet up on the instrument panel. There was time at last for that short nap she had promised herself.

But everything she had learned in the previous few hours kept circling through her mind, making it hard for her to relax. For the hundredth time, she reminded herself to forget Vader and the Emperor and concentrate on the mission at hand. If she was going to have insomnia, she might as well think about something useful.

Kazdan Paratus was an odd beast by anyone's definition. PROXY was unable to reproduce his form because all physical details of this particular Jedi had been erased from the records—perhaps by the paranoid old Master himself. Patchy Jedi history files accredited him with considerable skill at droid making, responsible for numerous one-of-a-kind machines possessing abilities far beyond those of ordinary droids. In recognition for his unique talents, the Jedi Council had made him the Temple's official engineer and allowed him a dedicated workshop on Coruscant.

The Clone Wars had lured him out of seclusion to study the Confederacy's droid armies. Life on the front line had afforded him numerous opportunities to examine the war automata, while at the same time building medical droids, power droids, and other units designed to support the clone army. A disastrous campaign, during which most of his clone troopers had been killed, led to him cobbling together a makeshift contingent of combat droids under his own command. That happenstance—or perhaps deliberate design—had enabled him to dodge justice upon the issuing of Order 66. Since that day, he had been in hiding.

But now he had turned up on Raxus Prime, dumping ground for garbage and industrial poisons. Had he been forced there by necessity, or willingly sought shelter there among the broken machines? The records couldn't tell her that.

At least he wasn't a general, though. How dangerous could a droid maker be? Darth Vader might consider him more powerful than Starkiller, but she couldn't see why. His agent had made short work of Jedi Master Rahm Kota, after all.

Her thoughts drifted. She entered a dream-like state midway between waking and sleep. The slightest flicker on the control board and she'd be alert, but otherwise she was at rest. If not entirely at peace . . .

"They have no defenses," she informed Lord Vader over her TIE bomber's comms. "The battle is over."

"It is far from over, Captain Eclipse. Continue your assault."

Teeth grinding, she clenched her flight stick with both hands and considered her alternatives. She would never disobey a direct order, but the consequences . . .

"I sense your disapproval, Captain. Speak your mind if you must."

Wasn't he reading it already? She shuddered at the thought. *"With respect, sir, it would be genocide to maintain the bombardment—a completely unnecessary waste of life. They are already beaten."*

"Since you feel so strongly on this matter, Captain, I will give you an alternative course of action. Strike the planetary reactor at the following coordinates, and strike it hard. Once that is out of action, I will consider this mission complete."

The coordinates came, and she breathed an inaudible sigh of relief. One precision strike was infinitely preferable to blanket bombing. "Thank you, Lord Vader."

"Your gratitude is wasted on me. Give me success, Captain. That is all."

The channel closed, and she relayed the orders to the rest of the Black Eight. One small victory in a much larger battle: she couldn't afford to dwell on it. Readying her payload, she plotted a course down through the atmosphere of Callos, glad that she would add only a little more damage to all that the little green world had already suffered . . .

She woke from the dream with a start. *Enough*, she told herself. She could only beat herself up so much over what had happened. What difference did it make now? She was going to drive herself mad by dwelling on it forever.

Besides, she had more important things to worry about now. What with Darth Vader, Starkiller, rogue Jedi, and the Emperor, she had to stay alert for anything that might give her a chance of getting out in one piece.

Lights were winking on the *Rogue Shadow*'s console. "Tell your master we are coming out of the jump soon," she said to the droid. "If this is a trap like Nar Shaddaa, he will want to be ready."

"I will inform him," PROXY told her as she fine-tuned the ship's drives in readiness for their arrival. When Starkiller entered the cockpit behind her, she didn't look up from her work.

The streaked starscape of hyperspace snapped back to normality. The world's gravity gripped them. Sublight engines brought the *Rogue Shadow* around so they were oriented correctly and heading into the desired orbit.

Raxus Prime welcomed them in all its decrepit glory. The gray, synthetic world's surface was covered by almost as much metal as Nar Shaddaa, but there the similarity ended. Whereas one was alive with light and commerce, the other was a steaming rubbish dump inhabited by scavengers and scum. Juno had never been assigned here during any of her previous missions, and had never felt an urge to visit. It had a noxious reputation.

She could immediately see why. It wasn't just the filthy atmosphere and the mountains of decaying rubbish. This world was no moon, like Nar Shaddaa; it was a proper planet, one with a startlingly strong magnetic field. Every orbital lane was filled with junk, and so were a series of complex magnetic field-lines sweeping near the surface itself. These lines carried iron-bearing fragments aloft in a grim parody of a gas giant's rings. They were crawling with tiny vessels, either automated or single-pilot, searching for anything of value. Every now and again lasers flared, cutting at hulks or at rivals homing in on a nearby trinket.

Then there was the Core, the artificial intelligence built by the Republic to guide the refuse world's operation. PROXY said that he would try to patch them into its announcement system once they were within range, but she didn't see what help that would be if the Core turned on them.

This was going to be no simple sit-and-wait mission. She tightened her grip on the controls and guided the ship patiently through the navigational nightmare.

PROXY had moved forward to take the copilot's seat beside her. Starkiller, when he came, stood behind them both, assessing the scene through the cockpit viewport.

"PROXY," he asked, "are you picking up any communications yet?"

The droid put a metal hand to his forehead and made a strange noise. Juno looked up. PROXY's photoreceptors flickered; he tilted forward, as if in pain.

"Too many to decipher, master."

The droid's holoprojectors flickered unexpectedly. Juno edged away from an angular vision of metal and cutting blades, with glowing red eyes and insectile limbs. Before she could ask what was going on, the vision had vanished and the droid continued.

"I can hear hundreds of droids calling out to one another." He looked up at his master, who studied him with a frown. "This is where droids go to die."

"Or are taken," Juno muttered as she scanned the screens before her.

"What about Kazdan Paratus?" Starkiller asked PROXY.

"I can't hear any clues that would lead us to him."

Juno's eyes widened. Her right index finger came up to draw her companions' attention back to the view. "What about starting over there?"

So saying, she banked the ship to starboard, the better to reveal the structure she had just discovered.

Five slender towers rose up out of the junk piles like a surreal tribute to the past. The central tower was the tallest of the five, with a boxy structure near its tip that always made her think of old-fashioned torpedo fins. The other four were simpler, less ornate. Although undoubtedly made of junk itself, their unique lines could not be mistaken for those of any other monument in the galaxy.

"That looks exactly like the old Jedi Temple on Coruscant," she said.

Starkiller nodded. "Set us down as close as you can."

She searched the surrounding area through a thick drizzle of oily rain. "I will do my best. There are few clearings." The top of the ziggurat looked dangerously uneven and unsteady. "You will need to approach it on foot."

The *Rogue Shadow* banked gently from side to side as it traversed the garbage-laden magnetic lanes and cleared two large mountains of debris. The deeper she went into the atmosphere, the dimmer the primary star became and the greener its light seemed, until she felt her sinuses clogging up out of sympathy.

"There," she said, finally finding a space large enough for the *Rogue Shadow* to settle. "With a lake view and everything . . ."

The space was on the shoreline of an irregular body of liquid, one of several pooled among the high points on the junk landscape. She didn't dare set down hard, lest the relatively level surface buckle under the weight of the ship. Instead she hovered on the thrusters, skating lightly over the surface as Starkiller made his way back to the ramp.

"Circle past the Temple and wait for my signal," he commed in a businesslike tone.

"Be careful," she sent in reply. "The sludge out there looks corrosive." She waited until the black-clad figure had progressed in inhumanly long leaps from metal ruin to metal ruin and finally disappeared from sight before pushing the repulsors to maximum and angling the ship up into the sky. She was glad to be doing so. In just the few seconds the hatch had been open, a foul stench had filled the ship from nose to tail.

"Juno out."

CHAPTER 6

THE APPRENTICE BARELY HEARD HIS pilot sign off as he hurried through the toxic wasteland that was the surface of Raxus Prime. His concentration was intense, fending off distractions from every side: the stench rising from the lake; the sharp and treacherous terrain; the sound of wind whistling through the twisted spires and snapped stanchions of the foul forest he found himself in. He kept his mind focused on his prey: the mad droid maker, Kazdan Paratus. Mad he had to be, for who would willingly live in such a place? Even the most desperate fugitive would seek better climes.

The spires of the mock Jedi Temple were invisible behind the mountains of wreckage. Much was destroyed beyond recognition, but among the discards he saw the occasional fragment of starfighter, groundspeeder, air or water refiner, solar panel, antenna dish, and more. Every conceivable material had made it to this, the bottom rung of the Raxus system. No degradation had been spared. What couldn't be redesigned, rebuilt, reclaimed, or recycled was simply waiting to be crushed into poisoned pulp by the weight of further refuse piled on from above. It painted a depressing picture of the galaxy's prodigious consumption.

The apprentice spared no time thinking about that, either. He had one task to perform, to the very best of his abilities. He had no intention of doing otherwise. Rahm Kota may have tested him, but he had emerged superior in the end. There was nothing Kazdan Paratus could throw at him that he couldn't handle. He was sure of it.

And he would not think of the face he had seen while dealing with Kota. It was nothing, just a strange glitch in the program of his life. Raised under the careful eye of his dark Master, his skills had been honed to the point that not even Jedi could stand against him. Soon, very soon, he would be ready to stand at Darth Vader's side and take on the ultimate challenge of all: the Emperor.

He had regained his focus during meditation on the way to Raxus Prime by staring into the red-hot blade of his lightsaber. He had treated his most recent injuries with bacta patches so they would no longer trouble him. He hadn't eaten, for he found that food deadened another hunger inside him—the hunger for greatness similar to that possessed by his dark Master. Or was his Master possessed by *it*? It didn't matter. From his point of view, they were the very same thing.

The power of the dark side filled him. Strength coursed through his veins, swelling his heart with resolve. He would not fail. And how could he? He was Darth Vader's apprentice.

Juno's voice came from the comlink, cutting through the Core's bland announcements with Imperial precision.

"There is some sort of activity near a downed corvette north of your position."

"What kind of activity?"

"I'm not certain. We are in the upper atmosphere now, and there is a lot of interference. PROXY is picking up what might be droid signatures heading in that direction."

"You think it could be a welcoming committee?"

"Maybe, I—whoa!" A blast of static was followed by a relieved gasp from Juno.

"What's wrong?" he said into the comlink.

"Nothing—now. I just got too close to one of those magnetic lanes, and an unstable derelict exploded. Everything's under control. You just worry about keeping your boots clean."

He half smiled and kept moving through the teetering piles of garbage along a stretch that resembled a canyon with sheer walls and squelching floor. Only then, after Juno's brief communication, did he notice an odd thing. Among all the technological leavings, he hadn't spotted a single droid part yet. Not one. If this was where droids came to die, as PROXY had said, what happened to their bodies?

He sensed movement ahead and slowed his pace to an ordinary walk, then a more stealthy creep as voices became audible, too. Not human voices: a mixture of electronic babble and high-pitched, liquid Rodese. Droids and Rodians, then.

He assumed that his orders remained unchanged from his last mission: *Leave no witnesses.*

With a flourish, he activated his lightsaber and kept it at the ready.

THE FIRST DROID HE ENCOUNTERED was a spindly thing with one photoreceptor, one manipulator, a poorly tuned dual repulsor and power plant, and very little else. It was tugging at a cable protruding from an almost sheer cliff face of garbage. As its repulsor whined, small avalanches tumbled from above, bouncing off its metal shell and making it squawk and wobble in midair. As soon as it saw him, it began to tug more vigorously, provoking a full-scale collapse that buried it under a large mound of rubbish.

Caught by its predicament, the apprentice used the Force to push the rubbish away, allowing the droid to burst free. It danced with considerable disorientation in the air for a moment before regaining its balance, grabbing the freed cable from among the debris, and zigzagging up the canyon with it clutched tightly in its single manipulator, razzing loudly as it went.

Scavengers, he decided, probably hooked up in a network to the Core. Nothing to worry about, unless he interfered with the running of the planetary junk heap.

Rodians were a different matter entirely.

"Captain Eclipse," he said into his comlink.

"Juno here," she replied immediately.

"Do Imperial records have any reports of Rodian scavengers on Raxus Prime?"

"Accessing the data bank now."

While she searched, he found them swarming over the corpse of a crashed starship that lay directly in his path—obviously the corvette she had mentioned earlier. From the vantage point of a teetering trash hill, he peered through electrobinoculars at the green-skinned aliens and the tribe of tiny, brown-robed Jawas they had coerced into service, either by bribes or threats of violence. There were dozens of them, with several tracked vehicles lined up to take their booty away. The Corellian corvette, its precise make rendered indeterminate by the damage it had sustained in the crash, was being sliced up for scrap, meter by meter, with delicate and therefore more valuable components removed before the cutting machines came in. The apprentice was put in mind of the creatures that fed on the bodies of whaladons when they drifted to the bottom of an ocean: in months or even weeks there might be nothing left of the starship at all except the crater it had made on falling.

The apprentice didn't have months or weeks up his sleeve. The longer he roamed Raxus Prime, the greater the chances that he might be discovered.

The starship lay directly between him and the Temple and was far too big to get around. That could take him hours. He would have to either go through the starship, or move it.

A slow smile crept across his face. *Why be coy?* He was the apprentice of Darth Vader and a servant of the dark side. It didn't pay to creep about in fear of raising his head.

Juno returned with the details of his find. "Looks like you have stumbled across Drexl Roosh and his clan. Drexl is wanted for thirty-eight counts of fraud, selling faulty matériel, and illegal slave trading."

"I think we've discovered where he's getting all of his goods."

One of the Rodians was yelling at the others in Basic, adding insults to the Jawas for good measure. "Move faster, you scum! The scavenger droids will be on us soon." He waved a large blade with imperious disdain, not caring whom it struck. "If you bottom feeders don't get these Jawas moving, I'm going to add another ten thousand credits to each of your heads! Do you hear me?"

This, the apprentice assumed, was Drexl. The purple-faced Rodian wore a jetpack and heavy armor and was strutting self-importantly back and forth.

On moving to another vantage point, the apprentice ascertained that the starship had at least one engine still in its housing, a bulky hyperdrive that seemed to be undamaged. Perfect.

As he conducted his survey, a scuffle broke out between a trio of scavenger droids and the Rodians overseeing the Jawas' work. The droids had boldly tried to sneak into the giant carcass and prompted a volley of energy fire warning them away. They responded with jolts of electric current delivered through the damp ground and along electrically conducting walkways.

The Rodians suddenly had a fight on their hands and took cover behind mounds of organic scraps while the Jawas ran for shelter anywhere they could find it. The apprentice watched with amusement as the pointless skirmish unfolded. It ended, inevitably, with three showers of droid fragments and another bad smell added to the air.

"You idiots!" Drexl bellowed. "Clean up this mess and come back to camp with something we can sell, or don't come back at all!"

His jetpack ignited and the Rodian lifted off from the waste-strewn surface. With a roaring noise, he sped into a tunnel leading deeper into Raxus Prime's trash infrastructure, leaving small fires in his superheated wake. The Core announced something about malfunctioning salvage droids and sending in more to investigate.

The apprentice made a mental note to avoid crossing the droids, unless he had to, and began to climb down through the litter of foothills.

A RODIAN SENTRY, STILL JITTERY from the skirmish with the droids, barely had time to squawk in his alien tongue before the apprentice silenced him forever with a quick sweep of his blade.

He hurried by, into the bowels of the corvette. A ramp had been added to aid the Jawas in their exploration and evisceration of the ship. It led up at a shallow angle into a stack of collapsed levels that had once been the crew midsection. He ran lightly along it, making no sound at all.

Barely had he entered than an alarm went up—triggered not by him, but in response to a new influx of droids. The effect was the same. Every Rodian scavenger was on alert. His job instantly became that much more complicated.

A herd of Jawas ran by, squeaking, their glowing yellow eyes flashing on and off. He let them go, not having a second to spare, and followed the most likely route to the hyperdrive. When a pair of Rodians stepped out of a hole in the wall ahead of him, he didn't give them a chance to raise their blasters. He sliced one in two while the other fell back clutching his throat.

"Are you having fun down there?" came Juno's voice over the comlink.

"I'm making progress," he said as his objective came into sight. The turbines of the massive hyperdrive lay dead ahead, their shielding removed in preparation for extraction elsewhere. Naked conduits and cable bundles snaked into the walls or hung limp, severed, on the floor.

"Progress at what?" she asked him. "Making things complicated?"

He didn't respond. Her tone was borderline insolent, but she did have a point. Time was passing. The last thing he wanted was to get caught up in a dispute between Drexl's band and the Core's droid immune system. The sooner he was moving toward his objective, the better.

Another Rodian came running up the corridor behind him, firing at his back. He deflected the shots with his lightsaber and brought the ceiling down on the raider, effectively sealing himself into the hyperdrive access room. *No matter.* The walls were weak with metal fatigue. He could punch out in an instant when he was finished.

Kneeling in front of the turbines, he took a handful of cables in both hands and called on the Force. Energy surged through him, making him stiffen. Sith lightning sparked from his skin and snaked through the ragged metal walls, floor, and ceiling. Distantly he heard screams as the many beings inside the wrecked corvette suffered from the aftereffects. He ignored them, along with the smell of smoke rising from his own tattered uniform.

Focus, he told himself. Undirected power was power wasted. Gritting his teeth, he gathered the energy and directed it down his arms, into his hands. Blue light strobed across his vision as the lightning flowed into the wires and from there into the hyperdrive turbines. Groaning, then shrieking, the massive engine came alive. Damaged, completely out of alignment, and barely controllable, the turbine shook with propulsive power, then strained against the braces still holding it to the corvette's warped chassis.

The deck kicked underneath the apprentice. He swayed as the entire corvette shifted. With a terrible sound, it began to move, plowing a brutal furrow through the surrounding rubbish. He could picture it clearly in his imagination and through the vibrant flow of the Force. As lightning poured through him and into the engine, it pushed the stricken corvette physically out of his path. The way to the Temple was now clear.

When he sensed that it had gone far enough, he relaxed his concentration. Smaller discharges of energy skittered across his skin. Somewhat shakily, he stood, then almost toppled over as the engine continued to fire, sending the corvette onward, out of his control.

He hadn't expected that. There was enough residual potential in the turbine to keep it running for dozens of seconds. He had to get out of the corvette before it dragged him any farther from his goal.

Straining, he blew a hole in the side of the downed ship wide enough for a TIE fighter to pass through. The wall of a junk canyon was gliding by, raining rubbish. With one smooth leap, he caught hold of dangling cable and swung free of the wreck. It roared on, dragging itself through the dregs of the galaxy on its disintegrating belly, sending waves of disturbed filth radiating outward from its path.

"Are you creating a distraction, Starkiller," squawked Juno from the comlink, "or trying to draw attention to yourself?"

"Choose the answer you prefer," he said as he swung from cable to cable back the way the corvette had come. Scattered Jawas in singed robes were clambering into their transports to give chase to the corvette. He ignored them, used Sith lightning to blast a dozen droids that rushed him with electric claws raised, then turned left where the corvette had formerly rested to resume his approach to the strange parody of the Jedi Temple.

THE STRUCTURE'S BASE WAS EITHER buried under or part of the endless dump that was the Raxus Prime surface. The apprentice ascended cautiously to the foyer, where buckled armor plates had been hammered as close to flat as was possible and welded into approximately level floors. Abandoned thrust tubes stood in for marble columns. Sensor arrays made reasonable facsimiles of window frames, and curving tank walls created the illusion of arched ceilings high above.

The system's primary added to the superficial beauty of the scene by casting beams of weak light in downward-sloping diagonal lines from his right to his left, in which dust motes danced languidly on the air.

But beneath it all the stench of decay remained, and with every step he took the floor shifted and creaked. Wires and decaying insulation protruded from the seams. In every corner lurked piles of rubbish that might have been festering since the Empire's founding.

As he walked cautiously forward, feeling the nearness of Kazdan Paratus but uncertain of his exact location, one of the rubbish piles stirred. From it stepped a humanoid machine made from the junked droid parts he had expected to find on his journey.

The braincase of an FX-8 medical droid was bolted onto a body cobbled together from several types of outdated protocol models. Its limbs appeared to come from a mixture of EV and B1 battle droids, tipped with instruments and tools that wouldn't have looked out of place in a workshop. Its sole functioning photoreceptor glared a bright, furious yellow. Its lurching gait achieved an appreciable speed before he sliced its head off.

A second patchwork droid emerged from a different rubbish pile, followed by a third. The sound of more droid golems stirring came from elsewhere in the Temple. The apprentice fought them off with practiced ease. He had been dueling PROXY all his life; he knew the weaknesses and strengths of droids, even one capable, by a clever use of repulsor technologies and a specially adapted antique training lightsaber, of imitating a Jedi. Ones such as these, with barely a matching part among them, were child's play.

Soon the foyer was full of the twitching, smoking bodies of the Temple's hapless guardians. He began to tire, not from exertion but from the tedium of knocking down droid after droid, to no apparent end. There might have been thousands of them.

Deactivating his lightsaber, he took a deep breath. With one mighty exhalation of power, he blasted all of them—those in pieces and those approaching with needle-tipped fingers and vibrosaws upraised—out of the foyer doors. Then he blasted the rubbish piles after them. He kept pushing until a dark cloud soared out over Raxus Prime's hideous landscape—an artificial hurricane full of droid golems.

When the foyer was clear, the apprentice straightened. He was no longer pushing with the Force, but the floor beneath him shook nonetheless. A heavy booming sound came from deeper in the Temple, and was getting louder. He had certainly attracted someone's attention now.

A huge junk golem smashed through a nearby wall, servomotors growling, brandishing two of the biggest vibro-axes he had ever seen, one in each hand. It took two steps toward him and blinked its enormous photoreceptors in barely restrained hostility.

"You dare invade the Jedi Temple?" boomed a voice from its armor-plated chest. "You dare challenge the Jedi in our home?"

Before he could point out the stark obviousness of the situation—that the Jedi were virtually nonexistent and that this hardly constituted their home—the massive golem lunged for him. Constructed around the body of a heavy-lifting labor droid, it sported numerous appendages apart from the two holding the axes. Each was tipped with a different weapon, whirring, rasping, and sizzling. The racket it made as it charged was even more fearsome than its aspect.

The apprentice dodged away and temporarily lost his footing as the floor buckled underneath the thing's weight. Igniting his lightsaber, he slashed one of the reaching appendages clean off and batted another aside with a firm telekinetic punch. Recovering his balance, he sent a wave of lightning rippling across its corroded carapace, but that barely slowed it down.

One of the vibro-axes slid over his head and the other came down to slice him vertically in two. He threw himself backward barely in time, then lunged forward to slash at anything that looked like a weak point before the axes could come around again. Cauterized limbs rained about him, clutching at him with fading electrical spasms. He rolled between the trunk-like legs to avoid another devastating double ax blow. His lightsaber scored a deep cut up the gargantuan's back as he rose to his feet.

Yellow sparks flew across the room. The golem's insides groaned and bellowed as it turned, trying to get him back in its sights. Arms reached for him and he sliced them off, one by one. Ducking under the swinging blades, he sent bolt after bolt of lightning into the massive wound he had made, while battering it with panels ripped from the walls and hurled with every iota of energy he could muster.

Finally it weakened. Listing heavily on its left side and missing one of its axes, it staggered ponderously backward across the foyer. Both its photoreceptors were dark; sparks poured in a steady stream from a hole in the rear of its head. Although fighting blind and barely possessing any control over its primary motivators, it still tried to kill him. Growling servomotors kept the sole remaining ax sweeping backward and forward, as though he might stumble into it by accident. One heavy foot stamped at the floor in a vain attempt to unbalance him. All it succeeded in doing was tangling itself in junk and swaying dangerously close to tipping right over.

The apprentice took the opportunity to finish it off. Again he pushed with the full power of the Force, blowing its body off its tangled leg and hurling it through the far wall. He followed it, just in case it still had any fight left in it. Striding confidently through the gaping rent in the foyer wall, he found himself in a place he had thought never to enter, even in a bizarrely re-created form such as this.

In the heart of the junk Jedi Temple was a junk High Council Chamber, complete with mannequins of long-gone Jedi Masters. The apprentice knew all their names; they were burned into his brain, those enemies the Emperor had defeated during the final days of the Clone Wars. They sat on thrones or stools or ordinary chairs, as taste or biological form demanded. Their dead eyes stared at him as he stalked after the fallen golem.

The golem had collapsed in the center of the circular room, streaming smoke and steam from its joints. Fetid wind poured through the shattered windows overlooking endless vistas of waste, making a faint moaning sound. The apprentice maintained a state of extreme concentration. Kazdan Paratus had yet to make his move. He would be ready for the fugitive Jedi when he did.

Then a strange thing happened. The droid golem's dead weight shifted slightly. A hiss came from a seam down its front. With a groan, its armor plating opened. Four long, spidery arms emerged, tipped with manipulators salvaged from four very different droids. The manipulators gripped the body of the dead golem and hauled a tiny gray figure into the light.

"Kazdan Paratus," said the apprentice. "At last."

The minuscule being looked at him with darting, paranoid eyes. A member of the Aleena species, he was short and large-skulled, with bright eyes and long, agile fingers. The harness affixing him to the strange, mechanical arms allowed him free movement with his lightsaber—a double-bladed pike with one blade significantly longer than the other. He raised it as the limbs' function turned from arms to legs and raised him to full human height.

"Sith trash," he hissed in a voice that was high-pitched but full of contempt. "Don't worry, Masters. I'll defend you!"

The apprentice didn't know who he was talking to until a clamor rose from the seated mannequins and, as one, the junk Jedi Council woke.

Paratus lunged while the apprentice was momentarily distracted. The pike left a shallow cut down his left forearm before he could repulse the strange creature's attack. Part flesh and part machine, the renegade Jedi Master was proficient with the Force, and quick with it as well. Every blow the apprentice tried to make was instantly blocked by either end of the whirling pike. As fast as he lunged or retreated, the mechanical legs outpaced him. Paratus hopped around the dilapidated chamber like a deranged jumping spider.

Outside his droid golem shell, however, Paratus was more vulnerable to Sith lightning. What he couldn't absorb into the junk metal burned him and left him writhing in pain. The apprentice sent bolt after bolt hurtling into the tiny figure. It almost seemed that the fight would be over before it had really begun.

Then something struck him from behind, breaking his concentration and knocking his lightsaber from his hand. He turned, ducking robotic limbs and a sudden swipe from the light-pike. The mannequin of Plo Koon had risen from its chair and attacked him, holding a vibroblade in a crude approximation of the long-dead Jedi Master's renowned lightsaber style. The Way of the Krayt Dragon, it had once been called. It looked ridiculous now in the hands of a patchwork droid.

Still, it had taken him by surprise. The apprentice acknowledged the gambit before blowing the mannequin to pieces and reaching out for his fallen lightsaber. The hilt arrived in his hand just in time to deflect another blow from Paratus, fully recovered from the waves of Sith lightning he had just endured.

This time the apprentice was ready for the attacks from behind. One at a time, or occasionally in pairs, the mannequins moved in to distract him.

Mace Windu and Coleman Kcaj he dismembered. Kit Fisto he melted. Anakin Skywalker and Obi-Wan Kenobi he smashed together and hurled out the window. Ki-Adi-Mundi he blasted with lightning before doing the same to Saesee Tiin, Agen Kolar, and Shaak Ti. Stass

Allie he beheaded with a single stroke of his lightsaber. Yoda he picked up with the Force and used as a missile to strike Paratus through his flailing artificial limbs.

Kazdan Paratus moaned as each junk Master fell, mourning them as though they were actually alive. When the last one went down, he was actually weeping.

The apprentice reached out and caught the Jedi Aleena in a tight Force grip. Paratus's artificial arms crumbled, unable to resist his power. Lifting the diminutive alien into the air, the apprentice swung his captive from side to side, smashing him into the window frames and roof until rubble rained down on them both. He deflected the worst of it from himself and saved the damage for Paratus. Soon the aging Jedi was too weak to fight, but still the apprentice continued battering him. He remembered what had happened with Rahm Kota at the very last. Wherever that strange hallucination had come from, he would not permit a repeat.

Finally, the Jedi Master's strength was spent. The apprentice let him drop to the ground, where he was pinned by an avalanche of junk falling through the ceiling. Clearly dying, he lay faceup and closed his eyes.

"I'm sorry, my Masters," he lamented. "I've failed you."

With those words, he expired.

For a moment the apprentice felt pity. But he quickly swallowed it down. Undoubtedly mad, Paratus was still a Jedi. His freedom had come to an end, along with his life.

Then a nimbus of glowing Force energy rose up from the Jedi's body and spread out around the apprentice. Sparkling, scintillating, it vanished with a silent rush into the walls of the junk structure.

The apprentice stepped away from the body, unnerved and ready for anything.

But that appeared to be the end of it.

He raised his comlink. "Juno, I'm done here."

"I have a lock on your location, Starkiller. On my way."

The whining of the starship's engines was loud by the time he retraced his steps through the foyer and out onto the surface of the junk world. The *Rogue Shadow* swooped smoothly out of the sky. Catching the ramp sure-footedly, he retreated gratefully inside.

AS THEY REACHED FOR ORBIT, he watched the Temple retreat behind him until the outline of its ludicrous grandeur was barely discernible among the surrounding junk hills. He could have knocked the ridiculous toy castle down around Kazdan's ears with one Force push. If only it had been so easy for his Master to erase the Jedi from the galaxy. Years after the Purge, here he was continuing that great work. Perhaps it would be finished in his lifetime. Perhaps he had already killed the last of the remaining Jedi. Perhaps now his Master would regard him as truly worthy.

He retired to his shadowy meditation chamber to tend to his wounds and restore his strength. Instead of meditating, however, he devoted an hour to repairing Kazdan Paratus's light-pike, snapped in two when he had clutched the tiny Jedi Master so hard. *Trying* to repair it, at least. No matter how painstakingly he worked, he couldn't realign the focusing crystals with the lens assembly. Nor could he make the emitter matrix connect to the power conduit. Like everything on Raxus Prime, the pike had become worthless junk.

Or, he told himself, there was something getting in the way of his concentration.

Is it my new pilot? he wondered. She was quick and efficient, as she should be, but she also made an effort to come across as lighthearted, and that was having an effect on him he hadn't foreseen. He had praised her good work after Nar Shaddaa and had felt glad to be aboard after finishing off Kazdan Paratus. *Praise* and *gladness* were not encouraged by followers of the dark side. The Emperor help him if they were developing a *rapport*.

He would deal with his new emotions as he had dealt with other challenges he had faced. At the same time, he would watch her closely. Rapports weren't one-sided things. If her feelings of bonhomie became stronger and she couldn't keep her sociability under control, he would have to take action.

As he pondered what form that action might take, the sound of heavy breathing rose up behind him. The pieces of the light-pike fell apart and scattered across the floor. The apprentice sensed rather than saw a darker shadow enter the chamber. He looked up expectantly.

There was no face visible in the silhouette of the Dark Lord, but that had never made a difference.

"Kazdan Paratus is dead, Master."

The domed head, blacker than night, nodded. "Then there is but one more test before you can fulfill your destiny."

One more. Would there always be one more?

"Master, I am ready now."

"You have defeated a tired old man and an outcast." Anger cracked like a whip in Darth Vader's vocoderized voice. "You will not be ready to face the Emperor until you have faced a true Jedi Master."

The apprentice squared his jaw, thinking of the pathetic imitations he had faced in the junk Temple. "Who?"

"Master Shaak Ti—one of the last of the Jedi Council." There was a grudging respect in his Master's voice, mixed with naked contempt. "She is training an army on Felucia. You will need the full power of the dark side to defeat her. Do not disappoint me."

"No, Lord Vader. I will not."

The robed shadow dissolved into static. The hologram fell away, revealing PROXY's skinny frame beneath. The droid shuddered, and the apprentice was instantly at his side to steady him.

Together the two of them left the meditation chamber to give Juno the news of their third and most deadly mission.

CHAPTER 7

As a teenager Juno had imagined her future life as a pilot, cruising the heavy traffic of Coruscant's skylanes, ferrying important dignitaries to and from meetings, blowing insurgents from the sky with single, well-aimed pulses from her laser cannon.

Trawling around the Outer Rim with Darth Vader's surly emissary and his dysfunctional droid hadn't been high on her wish list. Neither had been bombing defenseless planets or being spurned by her father . . .

Funny how life turned out.

The blue-green world of Felucia hung against a vast and empty backdrop as they emerged from hyperspace. It filled the forward view as she activated the sublight drive and trimmed their approach vector. When everything was in order, she killed the engines and let the ship coast silently through the planet's steep gravity well. This wasn't the commswamped environment of Raxus Prime and Nar Shaddaa. If they came in too hot, they would shine like a comet to anyone looking.

"Felucia in range," she announced. PROXY occupied the copilot's chair, monitoring life support and comms. Starkiller stood behind them with arms crossed over his chest and face shrouded beneath a hood he had put on after leaving Raxus Prime. He had barely said a word through the long trip, speaking only to give orders and avoiding all her attempts to provoke conversation. She felt slightly stung by this—she had thought she was breaking through his strong-but-silent image and getting a glimpse of the man beneath—but she maintained a professional demeanor. That was all her job demanded.

"Readings?" he asked.

"No major settlements," she said, glancing at PROXY's board, "but life signs are overwhelming the scanners. The planet is completely overgrown. I have no idea where we should set down."

"I'll tell you."

The small hairs on the back of her neck stood up. She craned her neck to watch what he was doing and saw only that he had closed his eyes. But something was definitely happening. The air seemed to thicken around him, as though a whirlpool were gathering. The hollows in his cheeks grew deeper, emphasizing his lashes and the sensuality of his mouth. Her heart rate quickened slightly.

She took a deep breath and turned back to her controls. This was none of her business. Ships and machines were her province, not the strange skills of Darth Vader and his ilk. For all her innate curiosity, it was dangerous to know too much sometimes. She had to remain detached and disinterested.

Just do your job, Juno Eclipse.

Starkiller stirred and leaned forward to point at a map display on the console near her.

"There, on the equator."

"What *is* there, exactly?"

He exhaled. She felt the warmth of his breath on her cheek. "Leave that to me. Engage the cloak and take us down."

She nodded, hoping he wouldn't notice the slow flush spreading up her neck, and eased forward on the throttle.

*   *   *

THE ROGUE SHADOW ROCKETED DOWN into the planet's upper atmosphere, fighting turbulence caused by surges of thick, humid air. Coruscant it might not have been, but Juno began to feel a twinge of curiosity. Before her mother's death, Juno had been interested in xenobiology— something frowned upon by her father, but which she had found endlessly fascinating. There was so much life in the galaxy, assuming so many different forms. She could have spent a thousand lifetimes trying to catalog it all, only to find that it had evolved into countless new forms during the process, forcing her to start all over again.

The thought hadn't appalled her. If anything it had filled her with wonder—the same sense of wonder she now felt stirring at the sight of Felucia's vast fungal forests and verdant lakes. Again she was struck by the contrasts among Nar Shaddaa, Raxus Prime, and this world. Felucia was brimming over with life in all forms, from the tiniest grass blade to the most massive fungi she had ever seen, with roots snaking over the ground, vines and mildew curling up swaying trunks, and insects everywhere. The air in the upper atmosphere exhibited pollen and spore counts that were off the scale. Her eyes felt assaulted by color everywhere she looked.

Magnificent, she wanted to say, but she kept the observation to herself.

Giant fungus stalks tossed violently in the starship's wake as the *Rogue Shadow* wove between them. She avoided using her thrusters as much as possible, wanting to minimize damage to the equatorial forest. But where was she to land? The ground was invisible beneath them. She could sense Starkiller's impatience as she searched for a suitable space. The only flat surfaces she could see belonged to the tops of enormous mushrooms, dozens of meters across. They looked as sturdy as rock.

Why not? she asked herself, swinging the *Rogue Shadow* sharply about and descending toward the nearest mushroom cap.

Gingerly, using every ounce of her skill, she eased the starship down. The ship settled, then shuddered as the giant fungus gave without warning. The starship slid and skewed wildly to one side. Stalks and fronds swayed as though in a storm. She raised the power to the thrusters, and moved to a different position.

This time the mushroom held. The starship's landing legs extended and tightly gripped the spongy surface where it teetered precariously on the edge of the enormous cap. She throttled back, waited a full five seconds for any more surprises, and then killed the sublight drive. She sagged back into the seat, drenched in sweat.

"Whew," she breathed. "They don't teach you that in the Academy."

"Lower the ramp," Starkiller said shortly. "Wait for me here."

"There's not much for us to do—"

"Just wait."

"I—"

He was already gone. She looked for him on the scopes and glimpsed him jumping off the edge of the mushroom and running into the forest, red lightsaber lit and ready.

She sighed and wiped her hands on her uniform pants. "Well, PROXY, it's just you and me again."

"Yes, Captain Eclipse." The droid rarely seemed flapped by his master's behavior. "I'll begin a check of all systems, if you so wish."

"That would be fine." She stayed in her chair, still rubbing her palms against her legs. "Is he always like this, PROXY?"

"Like what, Captain Eclipse?"

"Moody and withdrawn. I almost caught him smiling a couple of times on Raxus Prime. Now, nothing. What's going on inside his head?"

"I cannot speak with any confidence regarding his programming, Captain Eclipse," said the droid with a puzzled blink. "Perhaps Lord Vader could explain, since he was the author of both our systems."

That was an odd phrase. "What do you mean? Vader *programmed* Starkiller?"

"My master has been in Lord Vader's care since he was a young child."

"Like a father." She frowned.

"My master refers to Lord Vader only as *Master* or *Teacher*," the droid corrected her. "Never *Father*."

That reassured her, oddly. The thought of Vader nurturing a toddler was too strange to be true. "Well, what happened to his real parents? Where did he come from?"

"I do not know, Captain Eclipse."

"Does he never talk about them?"

"They have been expunged from his primary memory, I believe."

"What about friends?" She hesitated slightly, then asked, "Girlfriends?"

"My master leads a solitary life," the droid told her. "Lord Vader insists that it is essential to his development."

"Development into what, exactly?" she asked, thinking *Jedi killer, deranged mystic, murderer.* The way he had casually abandoned the falling TIE fighter facility over Nar Shaddaa bothered her sometimes.

"We are all servants of my master's Master," the droid said, pointedly reminding her, perhaps, of her primary duty, too.

"Your programming is absolutely spot-on there,

PROXY." She levered her resistant body out of the pilot's chair and straightened her uniform. "You continue with the systems check from in here. I will perform a quick visual inspection of the hull."

"I advise caution," PROXY warned her. "Many of the life-forms on Felucia are hostile to humans."

"Have no concern on that score." She opened a hatch and removed her BlasTech pistol, which she holstered around her waist with a well-practiced movement. "I can look after myself."

"One of your predecessors used exactly those words before he was shot in the back by a Corellian gunrunner."

She stopped on the verge of leaving the cockpit, unsure if PROXY was goading her, joking, or offering an innocent observation. Part of her wanted to know all about her seven predecessors, but a greater part wanted PROXY never to talk of them again.

"Just you watch your own back, PROXY," she told him. "Your master's Master has a Master, too, you know."

"Yes, Captain Eclipse."

She left the ship, face burning for the second time in a matter of minutes. What was wrong with her? The slightest hint that she had overheard the conversation between Starkiller and Lord Vader regarding the Emperor and she'd be dead for sure. If Vader's agent didn't do it, the droid would. He was an expert hand with a lightsaber, after all.

Maybe *that* was what had happened to the other pilots . . .

She stepped off the ramp and stamped about on the surface of the giant mushroom, testing its spongy surface. Her anger at herself rose with every second. Of course she had wanted to reestablish control over the situation, but dropping dire hints wasn't the way to do it, even if the droid had started it. She could only be competent and professional, and she'd had plenty of practice doing that in the past. Now was absolutely the wrong time to break the habit of a lifetime.

Eventually she calmed down and went about the duty she had set for herself: examining the outer hull for any damage resulting from their rough descent. It seemed unblemished, apart from a few new stains added by plants they had passed, firing sticky bullets of sap designed to bring down flying insects. That observation helped revive some of the excitement she had felt on the descent.

Life in abundance, she reminded herself. *Think of that for a change.*

And she did manage it, marveling at the huge diversity of plants, fungi, insects, and animals in the jungle surrounding her. Many were rubbery and translucent. Liquid oozed from gaping pores and vents. The most corpulent of the life-forms looked as though they would burst if she so much as touched a finger to them. But all had teeth or spines and other means of self-defense. Many were vigorous hunters or parasites. She could hear the roaring of mighty predators and the crashing of large bodies through the undergrowth, distantly and sometimes directly beneath her strange, precarious landing site.

The more she observed, the more she thought of Callos. She had never set foot on that world, but from orbit it had had the same verdant sheen as Felucia. Could it have possessed forests as vibrant as these, as rich and splendid with life in all its forms? As she patrolled the lip of the giant mushroom pad, she wondered how many species had never been cataloged here, and now never would be on Callos. A familiar guilt rose up in her like sickness, making her want to throw up, and she had to turn back to the ship.

Since you feel so strongly on this matter, Vader had told her, *I will give you an alternative course of action.*

The images of the planetary reactor blowing up were burned into her mind. The Black Eight had pursued the mission objective with their usual surgical precision, coming low over the horizon and launching their payloads well before the reactor's defenses could even come online. Each strike had been on target, sending up billowing clouds of burning gases. If war could be called beautiful, then that had been a beautiful moment indeed.

Your gratitude is wasted on me.

That was perfectly clear to her now.

But it didn't change a thing.

"The checklist is complete, Captain Eclipse," PROXY informed her via comlink from the cockpit. "I have detected a slight misalignment of the aft deflector shields."

She grunted confirmation. The damage had almost certainly been sustained in the magnetic lanes of Raxus Prime, while dodging airborne lumps of explosive debris. "I will be right in, PROXY. Break out the tool kit. We're going to have that repaired before Starkiller returns."

"Yes, Captain."

Juno took one last look around her, savoring the chance even though it brought back unpleasant associations. The forest was in fact fragile, despite its vibrant lethality. It might look as though it could endure a thousand years, outlasting even the Emperor himself, but a single nudge in the wrong direction could bring it all tumbling down, clotting and rotting until nothing was left but a deep organic sludge, fit only for refining into oil or protein cakes. In the wrong hands, Felucia could be the vegetable equivalent of Raxus Prime in a year.

Better to focus, then, on that which couldn't be killed: on ships like the *Rogue Shadow* and their systems. The manifold problems of life and death couldn't be fixed with a spanner, and it was well beyond her purview to try.

CHAPTER 8

THE APPRENTICE DUCKED ANOTHER BOLT of Force energy hurled by the Felucian warrior to his right and sent a jagged line of Sith lightning crackling across the distance between them. The warrior dropped dead to the ground but two more leapt out of the bushes behind him, waving their bone swords and howling in their strange, guttural language. He recognized the largest as one he had injured previously, but he moved now with perfect grace and aggression; the shaman he had spared several minutes earlier must have doubled back and healed the warrior's injuries. He vowed not to make the same mistake again.

The bone swords were resistant to his lightsaber, but his skill with the Force far exceeded theirs. Dodging their clumsy telekinesis and unwieldy blows, he dispatched them calmly and without fuss, saving his energy for the real enemy waiting for him.

Shaak Ti: Togruta Jedi Master and practitioner of both Makashi and Ataru lightsaber techniques. She was old and strong, and must have been wily indeed to have survived so long. Order 66 may have been issued many years ago, but it was still firmly in place all across the Empire. The apprentice swore to bring that fact home to her just as soon as he could.

Getting to her, however, was proving to be something of a problem. Although he had sensed her clearly from orbit as a deformation in the Force, much like a body of mass deformed the fabric of space–time, he hadn't anticipated the dense flows he would encounter on the surface. The entire jungle was alive with the Force, from the tiniest spore to the mightiest rancor, and the Felucians themselves were alive with it, too—so alive, in fact, that they tapped into the Force as naturally as humans breathed an oxygen-rich atmosphere. That made them dangerous to him, the Sith apprentice who had come to crush the regime Shaak Ti had nurtured on Felucia.

She had taken a world enjoying the normal flows between the light and the dark sides of the Force and twisted it out of balance. There was still darkness on Felucia, but it was stifled, frustrated, weakened. He strained to awaken it, to remind it of its proper place in the universe. The light side had held sway for far too long. It was time to redress the issue. Killing Shaak Ti would do that quite nicely.

A rancor bearing a Felucian rider thundered through the forest, crushing delicate life-forms beneath its clawed feet and sniffing for his scent. The apprentice jumped from mushroom cap to mushroom cap until he was in a position above the rider's head, then he leapt down with lightsaber swinging. The rider's organic headdress covered everything from the neck up, as with all the warriors. He had some Force resistance, but he couldn't withstand Darth Vader's apprentice for long. Once the rider was dispatched, he brought down the rancor with a stream of Sith lightning that made its eyes shine like the headlights of a city speeder. It died with a roar that echoed through the jungle.

He hopped off its back as it dropped to the forest floor, having seen a landmark in the direction he was heading. Straddling a narrow, weed-choked river was a series of bulbous structures that looked remarkably like buildings, albeit buildings hollowed from the boles of giant fungi. Felucians ran through these narrow streets preparing defenses and mustering their rancor mounts. If they were getting ready for a fight, he wouldn't disappoint them.

The river wound through the forest to his right. He circled the rancor corpse to find it. Along the way he sidestepped another of the pungent acid pools he had noted already. They puzzled him, obscurely, since they didn't seem to be caused by pollution, as were their counterparts on Raxus Prime. He had learned to steer well clear of the occasional bubbles that surfaced through them, popping with an unhealthy splat and releasing an odor he hoped to forget very soon.

At the river's edge he used the Force to attract one of the many flat-backed river beasts he had seen the Felucians ride. Its mind was semisentient at best, but its mighty flukes could manage a fair turn of speed. Gripping its carapace with one hand, he rode its undulating body toward the town, occasionally pausing to fling lightning at Felucian guards who bothered him.

"That'll do," he told his half-submerged steed as they approached the town's borders. The beast nuzzled into the bank and he leapt aground near a massive, conical standing stone that loomed half a head taller than him among the gelatinous trees. He put a hand against it for balance and was surprised by two things: that it was warm and that it wasn't made of stone at all.

Puzzled, he swung his lightsaber in a sweeping arc, cutting the odd monument in two. The top fell away with a crash, revealing an interior made of fibers and organic material. *Bone,* he thought. *A tooth.*

The ground beneath him shook, and he braced himself against the monument. From the town he heard the sound of Felucians crying out in alarm.

A curious thought began to take shape in his mind.

Ignoring it for the moment, he advanced on the town with lightsaber swinging. He hacked through the jungle, felling every plant within his range. Felucians tried to stop him, but he hurled giant trunks at them, driving them back. *See what I can do,* he tried to demonstrate. *I'll do it to your homes if you don't leave me alone.*

The message sank in. There was no reception waiting for him as he neared the town's borders, which consisted of an irregular oval a kilometer or two across, surmounted by several of the strange giant teeth. A moat of acid and dead vegetation wound through the crowding mushroom trunks, obviously a defensive barrier more against pests than against serious invaders such as the apprentice. He hopped over the acid and slashed at another tooth as he landed.

Again the ground shook. A visible wave rippled along the village's border, as though something was moving under the soil. Several long, snaking tubes that he had assumed were roots shifted restlessly back and forth.

The few Felucians visible on the streets fled into the jungle.

"Did you tell them to leave, Shaak Ti?" he called. He could sense the Jedi Master nearby, burning brightly in the Force but hidden like a lantern behind a shutter.

His voice echoed down the empty street, unanswered except by the braying of a domesticated beast, tied by rope to the base of a slender, towering fungus. The apprentice hopped off the border wall and walked into town, keeping his lightsaber carefully at the ready. Circular doors and windows hung open, inviting him inside. Bioluminescent growths cast a pale blue glow over the interior of the buildings, but he wasn't tempted to investigate further. There could have been mountains of credits or exotic spices in there, but he hadn't come for anything like that.

"Shaak Ti!" he called, turning his head to look from side to side. He passed more of the giant teeth as he approached the center of the town. They were smaller and cleaner than the previous ones, less infested with mildew and mushrooms, and functioned as fences defining gardens or lanes. It struck him, though, that the houses had been built to accommodate the fences, rather than the other way around—which would make sense if the teeth belonged to some vast and sprawling creature that lay directly underfoot. Why else would so many of the teeth be pointing inward, leaning almost horizontally in a way that would trip or even injure an unwary passerby?

The confirmation of that guess came when he turned the last corner and found himself facing the center of the town.

There, perched on the concentric gums of a vast sarlacc pit, touched by neither the massive feeding tentacles nor the flexing of the slender teeth, sat Shaak Ti. Her legs were crossed and her eyes closed. Deep in meditation, she didn't look up as he approached, and seemed not to be aware of him at all.

He didn't believe that for a second. With a flick of one wrist, he ripped a mushroom out of the sarlacc's skin and threw it at her head.

She flicked it away with the Force, barely moving an eyebrow.

"You reek of that coward Vader," she said, unfurling her legs and standing in one smooth movement. Her horn-like montrals framed her red-skinned face like an elaborate headdress. The white oval patches around her eyes gave her a slightly startled look, but the apprentice was under no illusion that he had surprised her. She was dressed in the fashion of the Felucians, in a garment made of vegetable material—some still living, judging by the mossy sheen on her belt—and bone. Her striped lekku hung well out of the way down her back, adorned by ribbons and decorative tassels.

He raised the tip of his lightsaber in challenge, but still she didn't reach for hers.

"My Master is not a coward," he said.

"Then why are you here in his place?" she asked with a knowing smile. "Welcome to the Ancient Abyss, a place of sacrifice since time immemorial."

He smiled, letting anger fuel his hatred for her and for all that the Jedi represented. With the dark side behind him, he reached out for the mind of the sarlacc and goaded it to lash out at her.

All the creature did was roar. It resisted him, he realized, with her help.

She smiled in mockery. "Are you prepared to meet your fate?"

Then her lightsaber was lit and she was spinning through the air toward him, striking downward as she fell.

The apprentice simultaneously backflipped and blocked her opening blow. The force of it surprised him, and the recoil threw him backward. His hood caught on one of the sarlacc's teeth, and he tore it impatiently away before the snag could interfere with his defense. Shaak Ti's lightsaber was a jagged blue blur between them. He blocked her as best he could until he had his balance again.

Then he jumped. Over her he spun and fell down two layers of teeth toward the mouth of the sarlacc. From there he jumped up again, angling away from her to avoid giving the Jedi the advantage of height, but she was there ahead of him, driving him back down with a series of blows so rapid he barely caught them all.

In desperation, he summoned a bolt of Sith lightning and sent it down, into the flesh of the sarlacc. The beast roared and shook, giving him the opening he needed.

Shaak Ti's right foot slipped, forcing her to flip elegantly out of reach of his blade. He leapt after her, swinging as he came.

The fight progressed around the sarlacc's center rings, blow and counterblow accompanied by the roaring of the beast. The apprentice cut off teeth and threw the fragments at his adversary's head. In return she took tighter control of the beast's distributed intelligence and sent its food-seeking tentacles flailing for him. He repulsed them and fought on.

Down they drove each other, closer and closer to the very lip of the creature's enormous mouth. The air was foul down there, heavy with digestive by-products and the stink of rotting meat. Ghastly exhalations rolled over them as the sarlacc roared on. The apprentice was running out of teeth to sever, so he resorted more and more frequently to Sith lightning and random slashes of his lightsaber to keep it twitching underfoot. Thick ichor leaking out of the wounds made the footing even more treacherous.

"You can't keep this up forever," he taunted Shaak Ti as they dueled.

"Neither can you," she said. "You are wasting your strength too quickly."

"The dark side is inexhaustible."

"Your strength is prodigious," she admitted, "but that is your doing. Light, dark—" She paused to aim a blow at his head that he barely deflected. "They are just directions. Do not be fooled that you stand on anything other than your own two feet."

He slashed at her own feet as they spun by overhead and sent one of her ribbons twirling down into the sarlacc's gaping mouth. "Spare me the philosophy lesson, Jedi," he snarled. "I'm only here for your blood."

"And you may yet have it, or I yours."

On her last three words, she struck three blows that

each partially found their mark. The first burned a sizzling line down the apprentice's left shoulder. The second scored diagonally across his chest. The third would
have skewered his right eye had he not held her back at
the last minute with a desperate telekinetic block that
stopped her lightsaber barely a millimeter from his skin.
He could feel his eyelashes and eyebrows burning. The
right side of his sight was entirely blue.

She gasped and staggered backward. Her lightsaber
and her gaze dropped. A full half meter of red blade
emerged from her stomach, then the rest came free with
a hiss.

He backed away, shocked by how close he had come
to death and how lucky he had been to defeat her. He
had raised his lightsaber by reflex. She had, in the desperation of her final assault, practically thrown herself
on the blade. Perhaps she had meant for the two of them
to defeat each other at the same time.

Her weakening fingers let go of her lightsaber, which
deactivated with a click as it spun away into the sarlacc's
mouth. She didn't look angry, just weary and in pain.
Her red skin was suddenly very pale.

He feinted toward her, but she didn't react in any way,
except to look at him.

"You are Vader's slave," she breathed, "but your
power is wasted with him. You could be so much
more."

"You'll never convince me to betray my Master." He
was shocked that she would try such a weak gambit
again. Were these the depths to which the Jedi had sunk?

"Poor boy." She winced. "The Sith always betray one
another—but I'm sure you'll learn that—soon enough—"

There was pity in her eyes as they rolled up into her
head. She went limp and fell back into the mouth of the
sarlacc. The apprentice reached out halfheartedly to

catch her body, but was too slow. A second later, he wished that he had tried harder.

A huge explosion of Force energy threw him bodily off his feet. The sarlacc went berserk. Its tentacles lashed out at him and its surface quaked violently, trying to toss him into its waiting maw. He dodged the tentacles' frenzied lunges as best he could and dived for safety onto the town street.

Out of the sarlacc's reach, he lay facedown for a moment on the heaving ground. He was dusty, bleeding, and sore all over, but he was alive. Slowly, gingerly, testing every limb for grazes and cuts that might become infected in Felucia's febrile air, he rolled over onto his back.

And found himself in the center of a ring of Felucians. There must have been fifty of them—warriors, shamans, and rancor riders standing alongside parents, children, and mushroom farmers. Their faces were hidden by their headdresses; he couldn't read their intent. But the Force swirled around them in thick, turbulent currents. Shaak Ti's death affected them deeply, so profoundly entangled had she become in the energy flows of the world.

Well, good, he thought. She was responsible for the planet's imbalance. With her gone, maybe the dark side could reassert itself and the natural rhythms of life resume.

One of the shamans grunted something in the Felucians' guttural tongue, and the rest answered. The apprentice had no idea what they were saying. Were they threatening him or thanking him? He kept his thumb poised on the activation stud of his lightsaber, just in case.

Then, as one, they turned and walked away. Some went back into the jungle. Others went home. Within seconds, the street was as empty as it had been before, and he was alone.

Standing, he loped down the street, favoring his right leg only slightly. It didn't matter what the Felucians thought. His mission was complete. It was time to go home.

CHAPTER 9

STARKILLER SEEMED CAUTIOUSLY ECSTATIC ON his return to the *Rogue Shadow*, even though he looked as though he had been mauled by a rancor. His combat uniform was rent in a dozen new places, and blood leaked from as many small wounds. But his eyes were alive with a light she had never seen before. After Rahm Kota, he had been introspective and closed. Kazdan Paratus had left him moody. Now, he was . . . not exactly triumphant, but on the brink of triumph. He was about to do something important—and she could guess what it was.

While he had been gone and PROXY had been outside on the pretext of checking her work on the faulty shield, she had found a way to slice into the ship's small meditation chamber. When they were safely under way and he retreated there with his droid, she put her comm headset over her ears and carefully spied on him.

Starkiller knelt on the floor with his head bowed and his hands folded in front of him. PROXY stood over him, his holographic generators flickering in the gloom. They flared to life as a HoloNet transmission reached the ship. Eerily, the droid grew taller and more substantial until he had assumed the caped form of Darth Vader.

"Report," came the hollow tones of the Emperor's most trusted servant.

"My mission is complete, Master."

The domed head nodded once. "Then you are ready

to stand with me against the Emperor. Return to the *Executor* at once. We will at last control the galaxy."

"Yes, my Master."

Vader's ominous form flickered and shrank, becoming PROXY once more. The droid seemed uneasy and out of sorts again, but at the same time jerky with pride.

"Congratulations, master. It seems that you are about to achieve your primary programming."

"Yes." Starkiller rose and put a hand on each of his droid's shoulders, steadying him. "Finally."

PROXY's photoreceptors glowed. "Well, don't worry, master. I'll still keep trying to kill you."

Starkiller smiled fondly. "I know, PROXY. I know."

The two of them turned to come back to the cockpit, and Juno hastily killed the bug. By the time they were standing behind her, she was leaning over the controls, feigning an adjustment to the hyperdrive.

"Everything okay?" Starkiller asked her.

She felt his gaze boring into her from where he stood right behind her. Could he tell what she was up to just by looking at her? Could he read her mind like a book?

"I'm just wondering," she said, "where we go from here. Shaak Ti was unique. Your job might seem routine from here on out."

"Killing Jedi is never routine," he said. "But I doubt I'll be doing this kind of thing much longer."

She could hear the smile in his voice. "And what about me? Will I return to standard bombing runs when you're finished with me?"

"Don't worry. I'll be sure to give you the highest possible recommendation."

Well, thanks, she thought. "We form a strong team. It's unfortunate we can't keep on as we are." The worry in her voice was real. *It's a shame you're planning to defy the Emperor—forcing me to decide where my loyalties lie.*

He put a hand on her shoulder. She couldn't tell if he meant to reassure her or simply silence her.

The latter she could manage easily enough, although her jaw ached from keeping her concerns to herself.

When he returned to the meditation suite to clean himself up, leaving PROXY to help her with the ship, it wasn't relief she felt, but emptiness.

THAT FEELING REMAINED WHEN THE *Rogue Shadow* emerged from hyperspace in Scarl system, where the *Executor* lurked in its state of partial completion. She had decided nothing during the long journey. Should she remain loyal to her immediate superiors or try to warn the Emperor of their treachery? The question made her guts roil, but the answer eluded her. She needed more information, either way.

Starkiller and his droid disembarked, obviously heading to debrief their Dark Lord. Juno's anxiety levels rose as soon as he was out of her sight. When he was with her, at least she could keep an eye on him. Who knew what could go down while he was gone—perhaps dragging her down with him?

Remembering the strange feed she had managed to slice into while looking for her psychological profile, she shut the ship's external hatches and feigned a hull integrity check. Patching the ship's systems into the hangar's gave her access to everything in the flagship's data banks. Immediately she began searching.

It wasn't easy. There was no use trying to follow the same route she had used the other night, since that appeared to have naturally cauterized itself. There had to be numerous ways into Vader's secret chamber; the trick lay in finding one that was open at the moment, a signal she could piggyback on as far as the security feed. And then, hopefully, she would be able to hear more of the pair's plans.

She found the route via telemetry. Vader appeared to be closely monitoring the area around the fat red sun, although for a moment she couldn't tell why.

Then a series of hyperspace signatures rippled through the vacuum, and she began to understand. Three Star Destroyers and a dozen smaller vessels were arriving from elsewhere, flashing into realspace with disconcerting swiftness.

A cold feeling spread across her chest, enveloping her heart.

With shaking fingers, she canceled the view and sliced as fast as she could into the security system.

THE APPRENTICE STOOD IN FRONT of the massive bulkhead leading to his Master's chamber for a long moment, gathering his self-control and centering himself within the Force. Ambition stirred in him: he pictured himself at his Master's side, the two of them striking the Emperor down together, as he had imagined many times down the years. He saw himself in regal attire as Lord Vader became Emperor Vader and assumed the mantle of Coruscant and all the other jewel-like worlds in the galactic crown. What sights awaited them in the Imperial court! What new challenges and aspirations!

But his training demanded a careful balance between the lust for power and self-denial. Control was paramount, as in all things. He wanted to present the best face possible to his Dark Lord, lest once again the attainment of his dreams be denied.

"Is anything the matter, master?" asked PROXY from the droid's familiar position at his shoulder.

"Nothing at all," he said.

Straightening his shoulders, he waved a hand. The massive door slid open. Suppressing a smile, the apprentice strode confidently into Darth Vader's inner sanctum.

His boots rang out on the metal floor, echoing through the familiar chamber. The red sun glared through the broad viewport, but there was something new in that vista: a fleet of Star Destroyers and support ships clustering around his Master's flagship like carrion.

Darth Vader didn't turn. "The Emperor's fleet has arrived," was all he said.

The apprentice felt a quickening in his throat. Moving in front of his Master to get a look out the viewport, he pressed his palm against the thick transparisteel and smiled. *Destiny.*

"You lured him here." He could hear the excitement in his voice. "When do we strike?"

"I did not summon him." There was no warning in his Master's deep voice, no hint at all of what was to come. With an unexpected *snap-hiss*, Darth Vader's lightsaber was active, reflecting in the viewport beside the baleful orb of the sun. "His spies followed you here."

The apprentice opened his mouth to protest, but had barely begun to turn when his Master's potent blade stabbed through his back. His eyes widened in shock at the sight of the lightsaber protruding from his stomach. The pain was unbearable, much worse than he had ever imagined it would be.

The lightsaber's fiery blade disappeared as Darth Vader deactivated the weapon.

With a choked scream, the apprentice fell to his knees. Darkness threatened to spread across his vision, but he resisted it with all his strength. Despair likewise. This had to be a terrible mistake. It couldn't be happening.

His Master loomed over him, studying him impassively from behind his black mask. Without turning, he gestured at PROXY.

"Begin the transmission."

"Yes, Lord Vader."

PROXY, standing slightly behind their dark Master, transformed by sinister stages into the Emperor, hooded and enshrouded in shadow. The two Sith Lords looked down at the apprentice, who gasped helplessly at their feet.

"What is thy bidding, Master?" Darth Vader asked.

"You have forgotten your place, Lord Vader. By taking this boy as your apprentice, you have betrayed me." The Emperor's tone was at the same time harsh and hypnotic. One claw-like hand reached out from the sleeve of his voluminous cloak. "Now you will kill him, or I will destroy you both."

The apprentice watched his Master, pain twisting his features into a rictus. There was nothing he could do to stop this terrible reversal. He could not lift a hand against his Master, who had raised him and taught him all his life. But he would not die silent.

"Don't, Master!" he gasped, struggling to stand but failing. The darkness encroached further. "Together we can defeat him!"

"Do it now, Lord Vader!" insisted the Emperor. "Strike him down and prove your loyalty to me!"

Darth Vader looked from the Emperor to the apprentice as though weighing up two very heavy alternatives. Then he lashed out with the Force, unleashing a mighty telekinetic surge that sent the apprentice crashing into one of the transparisteel viewports behind him. With a piercing sound, it cracked.

"Yes, Vader!" the Emperor crowed. "Kill him! Kill him!"

The apprentice was gripped tightly in his Master's will and pulled away from the viewport. For a faint instant, he thought his Master had changed his mind and decided to defy the Emperor after all. But then he was hurled back at the transparisteel with all the force of a small meteor. The viewport shattered outward in a huge explosion, sucking him into the cold vacuum of space.

His final cry went unheard. Darkness and despair closed in again, and he no longer tried to fight them. There was no point. It was over.

JUNO WATCHED IN HORROR FROM the cockpit of the *Rogue Shadow,* her mouth hanging open and her fingers limp on the controls of the ship. Perhaps she should have been readying the ship for flight, or at least cutting the signal of her illicit data feed. Later she would wish she had, but at that moment all she could do was stare.

Klaxons began to sound in the Dark Lord's inner sanctum, sounding a strident vent alarm. Lights strobed painfully across the metal walls. Vader grabbed hold of the nearest stanchion to avoid being sucked out into space himself, but the maelstrom was short-lived. Within seconds—though it seemed like a small eternity—a large metal grate had slid down and sealed the shattered viewport shut.

Air poured back into the room. The rasp of Vader's respirator eased.

With one black-gloved hand at his throat, he turned back to the Emperor's hologram and straightened to his full height.

"It is done," he said in a cold, leaden tone.

"*You* are the apprentice, Lord Vader," the Emperor snarled. "You are my servant, my enforcer. Never forget your place again."

Vader's domed head bowed. "Yes, my Master."

The Emperor's hologram flickered and dissolved. PROXY returned to normal, looking stunned and shaken. Vader ignored the droid and walked to one of the intact viewports. He stood looking out into space, where the apprentice's limp body tumbled lifelessly through vacuum, surrounded by a cloud of fragmented transparisteel.

Juno's hand had risen to her mouth without her knowing it. Starkiller had done nothing but obey orders, just as she had on Callos. He had been betrayed, literally stabbed in the back by the one he had trusted most. It wasn't *fair*.

The sound of a door clanging open in the hangar was followed by the sound of booted feet running toward the ship. Too late she closed the feed and focused on her own problems. A squad of troopers from the Emperor's ships had broken the seal on the *Rogue Shadow*'s secret nest. They could only be coming for her.

Her heart hammered in her chest. Standing, she smoothed down her black uniform and made sure her cap was straight. When she was sure her pistol was well out of reach, she opened the ramp. Taking a deep, calming breath, she went out to meet her fate.

Part 2
EMPIRICAL

CHAPTER 10

DEATH WASN'T AT ALL AS he expected. He was aware of it, for a start, even if that awareness was of a fragmentary, nebulous sort. His consciousness came and went in waves, drifting in and out on unfathomable tides. He sank and surfaced at the whim of forces he couldn't comprehend. All he could do was ride with them and hope that death wouldn't be like this forever.

There was a surprising amount of pain, considering that his body no longer existed, lurking at the edge of his consciousness like a reminder of something important he had forgotten. Was this some kind of punishment for the actions he had performed during his life? Were the Jedi he had slain getting their revenge from a more privileged position in the afterlife?

That was a ridiculous thought, he told himself. Irrespective of whether there was an afterlife or not, privilege could not possibly exist, for anyone. The light and the dark sides of the Force were identical in stature, if not in effect. He could no more be tormented by the Jedi than he could torment them.

There were voices, too, and visions. They were harder to rationalize. Some were familiar, such as PROXY soothing him as he would a child—as he had for many years, until Darth Vader's apprentice had grown too old for such coddling. There was Darth Vader himself, urging him to embrace his fear, not fight it, and thereby become as strong as a mountain.

Some of the visions were memories, such as of the time he had asked PROXY to chain him immobile in the dark and refused food or water until he had assembled a lightsaber lying in pieces before him, using only the Force. He had failed at the attempt, but in his extremity he had found the strength to abandon his weakened body and embrace the dark side. He returned to that place many times after his death at Darth Vader's hand.

In endless loops he felt his Master's lightsaber burning through his stomach and the coldness of vacuum sucking the air from his lungs.

Many of the visions, however, were of things he could not possibly have seen while alive, featuring people both familiar and unfamiliar in times and places he could not always pin down.

He saw . . .

. . . *General Rahm Kota in the control center of the TIE fighter factory over Nar Shaddaa. His eyes were undamaged, and his stance was straight-backed from his recent victory. Flanked by armed insurgents and surrounded by the bodies of dead stormtroopers, he snapped off his lightsaber and began issuing orders.*

"Lock down the command center and get that holo-projector up and running. Tell all squads to fan out and funnel any opposition toward us."

"Yes, sir." Insurgents began running in all directions.

"General Kota, he's here!" cried one.

Kota quickly moved to where a flickering image had appeared on the newly activated holoprojector. It showed the approaching Rogue Shadow. *On seeing it, the general smiled grimly.*

"So I've finally drawn you out of hiding . . ." To the insurgent he added, "Lower the containment field on Hangar Twelve and tell the men to get into position."

"Yes, General." The soldier left the room to hurry about his errand.

He saw . . .

. . . Kazdan Paratus pacing on his four metal limbs about the junk High Council Chamber. The blank-eyed heads of his mannequins turned eerily to follow his progress.

"No rest," he wheezed. "No rest for any of us! Why can't they leave us alone?"

He turned to face the mannequin of Master Yoda as though the pile of droid junk had spoken.

"Eh, my friend? What's that? Oh, yes. He stinks of Sith, all right. But what's he doing here now? Haven't I suffered enough?"

The paranoid Jedi Master continued to pace back and forth, passing his deactivated lightsaber from hand to hand, as though debating whether or not to use it.

He saw . . .

. . . Shaak Ti, deep in the fungal forests of Felucia. Shading her eyes, she watched the Rogue Shadow glide overhead, visible as little more than a distortion in the light. She frowned and looked down at a young Zabrak woman who stood nearby, also studying the approach of the starship with concern. Several Felucian warriors guarded them, restlessly watching the trees.

"Darth Vader has found us?" asked the girl, a hint of excitement in her voice.

"Perhaps," Shaak Ti answered her. "Gather your belongings and go into hiding, just as we've practiced. Do not return until I summon you."

An angry flush spread across the girl's face. "But—you can't send me away. Let me fight at your side!"

"Against a Sith assassin? You would surely be killed." Shaak Ti raised a hand to silence her protests. "Please, Maris, just go to the graveyard and wait for my summons. I will lead this assassin to the Ancient Abyss alone. Your strength will be tested in other ways, and soon."

With an angry look on her face and tears running down her cheeks, the girl turned and ran into the forest.

Shaak Ti watched as the jungle closed over her.

"May the Force be with you, Maris," she whispered.

He saw the past. That was what he assumed. He was at one with the Force—and the Force saw all things, felt all things, lived in all living things. He had returned to the source of the river that ran steadily through the galaxy, invigorating and sweeping up the dead as it passed. The current tumbled and turned him to face all aspects of his life. He watched it unfold with new understanding.

Some fragments were, however, much harder to comprehend.

He saw . . .

. . . a sad-eyed young woman standing at a large bay window, looking out over a landscape of denuded forests. In the distance a fiery line stretched up into the night sky, to a point in low orbit where a cluster of tiny lights gathered. Somewhere nearby, an astromech droid cooed mournfully to itself.

. . . a dirty and tattered man sitting in the corner of an enclosure that seemed made entirely of bone. A small halo-lamp shone in front of him. His hands hung free, but his wrists were tightly bound by electronic cuffs. The stink of raw meat cloyed in the air, making him wrinkle his nose in disgust.

. . . Darth Vader, his armored life-support suit rent to the flesh beneath in a dozen places, standing in the wreckage of a mighty battle. Dead stormtroopers lay in pieces on the bloody floor surrounded by fragments of shattered transparisteel and twisted metal. The apprentice's former Master put a hand to his exposed temple, touched the scars visible there, and swayed.

"He is dead," Vader said with some difficulty over the damaged wheeze of his respirator.

The Emperor stepped out of the shadows to stand at his side.

"Then he is now more powerful than ever."

Was this what might have been had he stood up to his Master instead of giving in numbly as his entire life had been turned upside down? In his deathly state of semi-consciousness, the former apprentice couldn't tell. He could only watch as he would a blurry, fragmented holodrama, in the hope that at some point, perhaps when he had more of the pieces before him, the sense of it would start to emerge.

If anything, however, it only became more complicated. Beyond light and dark, beyond past and future, beyond life and death, he saw the same face he had glimpsed while fighting Rahm Kota; the face that might have been his as an older man, had he lived: strong and kind, with dark hair and warm, brown eyes. In the background, he could hear the distant pounding of weapons and the crump of explosions. Trees cracked and fell. A shadow loomed over the vision, as though a cloud had blocked the sun. He could smell burning blood and hair and hear the sound of a lightsaber sizzling through flesh. A voice cried "Run. Run now!"—

—but he didn't. He couldn't. Whatever kind of dream this was, it wouldn't let him move. He was trapped within it, fixed tight by some strange kind of mental amber. Was this a fantasy or something more sinister? Was someone trying to tell him something?

He saw . . . *somewhere not so far away—or perhaps at the farthest edge of the universe—Juno Eclipse was in pain.*

CHAPTER 11

IT CAME LESS AS A surprise, more of a relief, when he finally awoke.

At first, anyway.

His first clue that he had returned from the dead came when darkness truly fell. The visions evaporated, and the voices went with them. For a very welcome period, there was nothing to see or hear, or even think. He could just rest, and be.

Then new noises began to intrude on the peaceful silence: the whirring of cutting blades, low-pitched beeps and clicks from droids, a fizzing, spitting noise that could have been a cauterizing tool, and other sinister sounds. His heart rose at the sound of a respirator rising above the others. The faint sticking point between each breathing cycle was horribly familiar.

An artificial voice spoke: "Lord Vader, he's regaining consciousness."

"Keep him restrained until I'm finished."

"Yes, sir."

The former apprentice raged against invisible bonds to move limbs he couldn't feel. The babble of noises faded for a moment, then returned, this time with light and sensation accompanying it. He was strapped prone to a medical table in the center of an operating theater. Multicolored tubes and wires ran from several places in his body to dark machines hovering around him, and stretching up to the high ceiling above. Angular droids milled about him, poking and prodding with sharp-tipped appendages.

The familiar silhouette of Darth Vader loomed over him as, without warning, full sensation was returned to his body.

He strained against the straps holding him down and screamed with rage.

"You!" Foam flecked his lips. He had never felt such anger—brilliant in its purity, yet so untamed it utterly debilitated him. "You killed me!"

"No." Vader leaned closer, resting one gloved hand on the table as though to literally impress his gravity on his former apprentice. "The Emperor wanted you dead, but I did not. I brought you here to be rebuilt. If the Emperor knew that you survived, he would kill us both."

He stared up at the expressionless mask, neck twisted to increase the distance between them. Could it be so? His memories of betrayal and pain were so unclouded by doubt. A flash of his Master's bright red lightsaber protruding from his gut threatened to tip him back into unconsciousness. He resisted, thinking of Shaak Ti's final words: *The Sith always betray one another.* He had been so sure—but surety meant nothing. He had to decide with his mind, not his gut.

"Why?" he asked. "Why rescue me if it puts you in so much danger?"

"Because you are the advantage I need to overthrow the Emperor. He forced my hand, before we were ready. Now he believes you are dead. His ignorance is your true power, if you have the will to use it."

"And if I refuse?"

Darth Vader's voice grew harsher, his silhouette darker, if that was possible. "Then you will die. This lab will self-destruct and you will perish along with all aboard. There will be no witnesses."

There never are, he thought, *where you're concerned.*

But a lifetime of servitude forbade him from saying the words. He closed his eyes, unsure of which possibility he was more afraid: that Darth Vader was telling him the truth now, or that everything he'd ever been told was a lie.

The harsh breathing of the respirator came closer still. "The *Emperor* ordered your death," Darth Vader said. "Only by joining me will you have your revenge."

He opened his eyes and stared straight at the mask hiding the man who had killed him, then saved him.

Only one choice gave him time to think this strange happenstance through. Only one decision came with the option of changing his mind later. Only one fork in the road before him left him alive, not dead.

In a hollow voice, the apprentice said, "What is your bidding, my Master?"

Darth Vader straightened, satisfaction apparent in every movement. "The Emperor hides behind his army of spies. They watch my every move." One gloved hand waved at the machines attending the operating theater. The droids backed away, and the tubes retracted. "We must provide them with a distraction." He punched a button on the table.

The apprentice's restraints popped open. He slowly sat up, rubbing his wrists, and looked down at his body. He was clad in an entirely new outfit, one not dissimilar to his Master's, with black leather overlaying thin sheaths of armor, heavy gloves and boots, and a high collar. Nearby, over the shoulder of one of the droid surgeons, was a hooded black cape with a red lining, presumably his also. The same droid handed him a lightsaber hilt. It took him a moment to realize that it wasn't the one he had wielded all his conscious life. That lightsaber had tumbled into the vacuum of space and been lost forever.

He flexed his fingers, feeling stronger and different

somehow. The pain was completely gone. He felt better than he ever had before, as though he had spent months in a bacta tank.

Instead of pondering that issue, he asked, "What sort of distraction? An assassination?"

His Master shook his head. "No single act will hold the Emperor's notice for long. You must assemble an army to oppose him."

The apprentice cocked his head.

"You will locate the Emperor's enemies and convince them that you wish to overthrow the Empire. When you have created an alliance of rebels and dissidents, we will use them to occupy the Emperor and his spies. With their attention diverted, we can strike."

The apprentice ran a hand across his chest, feeling the smoothness of his uniform as though with entirely new nerves. The plan was good. It could work.

"Where should I start?"

"That decision is yours. Your destiny is now your own. But you must leave here at once. Save for PROXY, you must sever all ties to your past. No one must know that you still serve me."

He bowed his head in acknowledgment. "Yes, my Master."

"Now go. And remember that the dark side is always with you."

The image of Darth Vader shimmered and assumed the familiar features and form of PROXY. The droid stumbled, but quickly regained his balance.

"PROXY!"

"Master! I am pleased to see that you are not actually dead." The droid beamed the only way he could: through his photoreceptors. "I was afraid that I would never be able to fulfill my primary programming and kill you myself."

"I'm sure you'll have your chance, once we get out of here."

PROXY moved away and began pushing buttons on the nearest terminal.

"Where *are* we, by the way?"

"Somewhere in the uncharted Dominus system, I believe."

"But what is this place?"

"This is the *Empirical,* master, Lord Vader's top-secret mobile laboratory. We've been here for six standard months." PROXY looked up from the terminal. "Lord Vader has updated all of my protocols. Before I kill you, I am to do everything possible to help you vanish. Should I ready the *Rogue Shadow* for launch?"

The apprentice tried to think. He flexed his hands, marveling at his amazing return to health. It seemed almost too good to be true.

A disconcerting thought occurred to him. He hastily tugged off first his right glove, then the left. He was reassured to see only skin beneath—no synthetic materials or artificial joints. His knuckles moved the same as always; his fingernails were neat and even. The only odd detail was that his scars were gone.

He rubbed his right hand down his chest to his stomach, remembering the terrible wound his Master had inflicted. He thought of the damage raw vacuum did to human lungs. Bacta tanks performed miracles, but they weren't *that* good.

"Master?"

He looked up at PROXY and blinked. "What? Oh. I didn't realize the ship was here, too."

"Yes, master. How else would we get away?" The droid stepped back from the terminal. Indicating it with a hand, he said, "I've accessed the main ship's computer and begun carrying out Lord Vader's orders."

The apprentice nodded, distracted by a thought that

had just struck him. He had been on the *Empirical* for six months, PROXY had said, but the *Rogue Shadow* was here, ready for him. That might not be the only thing to survive the near catastrophe of the Emperor's intervention.

"What happened to Juno, PROXY?"

"Your pilot? She's aboard the *Empirical,* too, I believe. In a holding cell."

"What? Why?"

"Captain Eclipse was accused of treason." PROXY paused for a split second, as though searching for exactly the right words. "Lord Vader gave explicit orders to sever all ties to your past. You aren't planning to rescue her, are you?"

The apprentice irritably pulled his gloves back on. "I don't know what my plans are yet, PROXY. Let's just concentrate on getting out of here."

"As you wish, master." PROXY inclined his head. He took one step back to the terminal, pushed a large red button, and then headed for the door.

A sudden jolt through the deck made both of them stumble. The apprentice reached out for the droid and steadied them both. He looked around the cyborg lab with concern as a klaxon began to wail.

"Alert!" called a voice over the intercom. "Navigation systems have malfunctioned. Repeat, navigation systems have malfunctioned!"

PROXY tugged at the apprentice's shoulder. "Come, master. We must leave here."

Realization made him look at the droid's recent activities in a new light. *Lord Vader's orders,* he had said. *There will be no witnesses.*

"PROXY, what did you just do?"

"I've set the *Empirical* on a collision course with the Dominus system's primary star," he said in a matter-of-fact voice.

"But everyone on the *Empirical*—"

"Lord Vader said that no one must know of your existence. He was very specific."

"And you really are still trying to kill me."

"No, no. Not yet, master. You still have plenty of time to reach the *Rogue Shadow*."

The apprentice swallowed an upwelling of frustration. It wasn't PROXY's fault. He was just obeying orders. But by doing so he had put them in a very inconvenient position.

"Okay, let's go. Stick close."

"Yes, master."

With his strangely healed hands, the apprentice activated the lightsaber his Master had given him. The blade was as green as it was in his memory. It was Rahm Kota's, he realized with a jolt.

PROXY shuffled a step behind him as he put that small detail out of his mind and headed for the exit.

CHAPTER 12

THE WAILING OF THE ALERT klaxon woke Juno from a long and miserable nightmare in which she had been filing the report of her mission on Callos, not with Darth Vader, but with her father, who had stood towering over her, long nose jutting out like the arm of a gallows, and pronounced her a failure. But the mission was a success, she had protested. She had followed orders to the letter. Not good enough, he had said. Never good enough, girl. When will you realize that and stop trying?

She woke with a gasp, hanging suspended from the magna locks where the guards put her every day. The routine was worse than torture. They would take her down once every five hours for a ten-minute walk. She could use the refresher and drink as much water as her stomach could hold. Sometimes they gave her food, but not always. When the ten minutes were up, she went back into position, hanging with her arms outstretched between the locks, legs dangling, wearing the same uniform pants and singlet she'd had on when she arrived . . . wherever she was.

The guards never told her anything. She could tell, though, that they regarded her with contempt. A traitor to the Empire, she deserved no better. That she was still alive puzzled all of them. Her continued existence drained their patience as well as their resources. They surely had better things to do.

But they followed orders to the letter, like good

stormtroopers, and that meant that someone, somewhere, wanted Juno Eclipse alive. To suffer, perhaps, before she died. Still, every time the troopers came near her, she expected that her time had come, that they would take her down and execute her right there, with a single blaster shot to the head. At least that, she thought in her darkest moments, would be a kind of release.

Her throat and lips were parched. Her head and arms ached. She could barely feel her fingers because the locks held her so tightly around her wrists.

This time, with a siren wailing, she successfully fought the urge to despair.

"Alert!" blared a voice over the station intercom. "Navigation systems have malfunctioned. Repeat, navigation systems have malfunctioned!"

She raised her head and looked around. The other cells, visible across the central prison detainment area, were empty. Her guards were momentarily absent, probably checking the source of the alert. If she'd had any way of freeing herself, she could have run during the confusion for an escape pod and gotten away from the station forever.

And then . . . ?

Feeling a surge of frustration, she strained against her bonds. Muscles stood out on her thin arms. Her wrists were bruised from numerous such attempts. One day, she had told herself many times, the power would flicker and the locks would fail just long enough. Until then, it was a good form of exercise. Straining and hoping was much better than thinking—about what had happened to her, or what might be to come.

The station lurched around her. She sagged momentarily before trying again. Whatever was going on, it was serious. She could hear the stormtroopers barking at one another.

"Why aren't these bulkheads opening?"

"We have to get to the escape pods!"

"The door isn't accepting the security codes!"

The announcer returned with an ominous-sounding update: "Security breach in sector nine. Subject Zeta has escaped. Set blasters to kill!"

"Oh, that's not good," commented one of her erstwhile guards. Even through his vocoder Juno could hear the fear in his voice.

She didn't know who or what Subject Zeta was, but she was determined not to be hanging up like a dead womp rat when it found her.

Tugging on her bonds, she thought she felt one of them weaken.

Two troopers appeared in her field of vision, blaster rifles held at the ready. They were aimed not at her, but back down the hallway.

"Forget the prisoner," said one. "We've got to get out of here."

"What about . . . him?"

"Let him die with the rest of the experiments."

They punched at the air lock leading from the detainee area, but had no luck there, either. The air lock was securely sealed as well. Abandoning that futile task, they ran back the way they had come. Blasterfire and screams echoed up the corridor.

Juno resumed her escape attempt. The locks hadn't shifted a millimeter. The illusion of slippage had come as a result of blood from her right wrist lubricating the restraint on that side. She yanked harder, ignoring the pain, but was as stuck fast as ever.

"*Empirical* security systems are offline," warned the announcer. "All Imperials are advised to breach bulkhead doors and secure escape pods."

The ship juddered around her, and the announcer returned in a more anxious voice: "All escape pods have been jettisoned—empty. Uh, await further orders.

What?" The announcer must have turned away with the microphone open. "What fool ordered *that*?"

The broadcast ended with a loud click, almost drowned out by the sound of blasterfire and the station shaking around her. The cries of stormtroopers dying made her more determined than ever to get away before whatever had killed them found her, but she could make no greater effort than she already was.

Exhausted, she sagged weakly in the locks, sucking in air that tasted of smoke and blood. It was getting warmer, too, which couldn't be a good sign. The flexing of the walls had to be more than just turbulence. If something had gone terribly wrong and the station's orbit had been disturbed, the commotion could come from thermal expansion—not dangerous in itself, but lethal if they came too close to the source.

Executed, killed by the thing that had escaped from Vader's lab, or burned alive: those appeared to be the only choices open to her. After all her years of loyal service and everything she had done in the name of the Empire, and despite the constant lip service paid by Palpatine to notions of justice and the public good, this was where she had ended up. All her dreams of advancement shattered. Her life in ruins.

She wondered what her father would think of her now, if he could see her and hear her side of the story. What faith could he possibly have in a system that turned on her for no reason? What did anyone owe an Emperor who condemned her for obeying orders?

But she knew she could never have convinced him to believe the truth, just as she knew she could never have talked to him about the doubts that had stirred in her after Callos—and not just about Vader's handling of that affair. The official story of her mother's death was that she had been killed in crossfire. What if the Empire had been as heavy-handed on Corulag as the Black Eight had been on Callos?

For the thousandth time she saw her bombs striking home on the planetary reactor, the brilliant explosions lighting up the jungle. Only as she pulled up out of her run and sped for orbit did she note the chain reaction her strikes had caused. The stricken reactor was belching pollutants into the atmosphere and spewing megaliters of caustic chemicals from vast underground stores into the canals that fed it with fresh water. She could practically see the living surface of Callos recoil from the poisons she had inadvertently released. A cold, sick feeling began to blossom in her gut.

That feeling only became worse on her return to her base ship. Amid the backslapping of her Black Eight pilots, she had felt a growing urgency to check telemetry data gathered by the ship. From the privacy of her quarters she had watched, appalled at the sight of the reactor burning on beneath a spreading pall of deadly smoke. Lightning flashed under the dense mushroom cloud, starting fires and catalyzing deadly chemical reactions. Nearby river systems were soon utterly choked with biological debris.

Trying to keep her voice level, she had commed a friend with a background in environmental science. He had seen the data. His projections were dire.

"It's a runaway chain reaction for certain," he said. "I hope you got a close look at those forests while you were down there. They won't be there six months from now, and they're never coming back."

A whole biosphere destroyed—for what? This wasn't just because Callos had dared wriggle in the Emperor's grip. Neither was it solely because she had requested a degree of clemency from the campaign's director: Lord Vader. The Emperor was less interested in punishing, she had begun to suspect, than *setting an example*.

The terrible thing about examples was that there didn't have to be anyone left alive afterward. A ruin told the story as effectively as an eyewitness—perhaps more so, for the ringing silence left in the wake of such an outrage only served to impress the Emperor's boot heel even more deeply into the galaxy.

No protests. No alarm bells. No warnings.

What had the Empire come to?

Perhaps, she had dared to think, the Empire had always been like this.

Before she could follow that line of thought to any kind of conclusion, orders had come from Vader to report to the *Executor* for a new duty. Glad to be absolved of any further involvement in genocide—or so she had hoped—she had said nothing of her misgivings and moved on, mistakenly thinking that, by some small miracle, she had avoided becoming snarled in the Empire's gargantuan workings, as Callos had been, and Starkiller, and perhaps her mother, too, all those years ago.

So many lives, ground under the treads of the Imperial machine.

Hers barely seemed worth worrying about, sometimes. But still she asked, in her darkest hours, *Why me?* What had the Dark Lord seen in her that made her suited to the assignment to Starkiller?

Not her conscience, surely. Nor her sunny disposition . . .

"Hold it right there!"

Her head came up at the sound of blasterfire closer than it had been before. Bits of droid blew past her door, smoking from their severed joints. The voice of the station commander, a man she had only met once and intensely disliked, bellowed a second time over the cacophony.

"You're not leaving this ship alive, lab rat!"

The unmistakable buzz of a lightsaber rose up from

the chaos. She raised her chin higher, straining to see past the door frame.

No. It couldn't be.

The head of a stormtrooper bounced past her cell, neatly severed from the rest of its body. The armor glowed in a red oval where it had been smoothly truncated through the neck.

Perhaps . . . ?

She shook her head, telling herself she had to be hallucinating because of the heat and failing atmosphere control. It had been so long since she had last felt hope. She didn't dare give in to it now.

Still, she didn't take her eyes off the entrance to her cell, just in case she was wrong.

She was sure she could get used to the idea this time.

CHAPTER 13

THE APPRENTICE PRESSED FORWARD THROUGH a hail of blasterfire, his progress hampered by the need to protect PROXY as well as himself. The droid was adept at dueling him, but was not programmed to fight Imperials. Blasterfire came from all directions as troopers by the dozens rushed forward to replace those he had already dealt with. Their determination to kill him seemed out of all proportion to their situation. Surely falling into the sun was more important than dispatching one escaped invalid.

But gradually, by overhearing their panicky comments to one another, he realized the much darker truth: that their fear of him came from rumors spread regarding his innate monstrosity, the worst of Darth Vader's experiments, which, if it got loose, would kill them all in some horribly depraved way. The rumor was a contingency prepared in case he rejected his Master's offer of a new alliance. Either way, he would have to fight his way off the ship before he could even start to think about what came next.

At the announcement that all the escape pods had been jettisoned empty, the apprentice looked over his shoulder at the droid cowering behind his spinning blade.

"PROXY? Did you launch those pods?"

"Of course, master. It pays to be thorough."

He resisted an impatient retort. "How much time do we have?"

"Just a few moments."

PROXY didn't sound worried at all. The apprentice wished he shared the droid's confidence. He had taken long enough to fight his way through halls of preserved biological specimens to the escape pod launching point. There was still one series of corridors to negotiate before they reached the air lock leading to the *Rogue Shadow*. Driving two stormtroopers ahead of him with the threat of Sith lightning, he pressed resolutely on.

The prison detainment area was broad and hard to defend, but a squad of troopers gamely made a go of it. Taking cover wherever they could, they fired in rapid bursts from several directions at once, hoping to find a chink in his defense. There was none. His new green blade whirled with astonishing effectiveness. It and the apprentice were one—as though his supposed death had never happened. He felt strong, powerful, deadly.

A weapon refashioned by Darth Vader to bring ruin upon the Emperor and his minions . . .

The leader of the squad cast insults and aspersions over the blasterfire, as though that could possibly distract him. The apprentice let the dark side flow through him, buoyed up by his anger—at the squad leader, at the time passing so quickly, at the Emperor—and calmly mowed down anyone who stood in his path.

When the last had fallen, PROXY tapped him on his shoulder.

"Master, hurry. We're rapidly approaching the sun. Life support will be overwhelmed any moment now."

"Wait," he said, raising a gloved hand. "What about—?"

Even as he looked around at the entrances to the cells, he saw her. Juno was hanging in a magnetic lock with blood dripping from her right wrist, dressed in the

scruffy remains of an Imperial uniform. Her hair was
unkempt and her skin dirty. Her eyes were wide with
shock, taking in not just him but the ruin he had
wreaked on the stormtroopers as well.

"Juno . . ."

"It's—" She struggled for words. "—really you!"

He understood her hesitation. She couldn't call his
name because he didn't have one.

"Master," said PROXY, cutting between them. He
pointed with one metal hand toward an air lock at the
far end of the chamber. "We're almost there! Hurry!"

The sound of klaxons had reached a fever pitch. The
ship swayed underneath him as gravitational control
began to waver. The air was almost unbreathable. Even
if they left now, there might barely be enough time to
prep the ship and get away.

Juno's face was a picture of desperation.

He didn't move. Was this a trap? He could see no sign
of deception in her face, just fear.

"Master, hurry!" PROXY tugged on his sleeve and
whispered urgently. "She is part of your past life now.
Leave her behind, as Lord Vader commanded!"

He pulled himself free, deciding with his heart rather
than his head. "I can't. You go ahead and prepare the
ship for launch. We'll follow as soon as we can."

"But, master—"

"Just do it, PROXY! That's *my* command."

The droid tottered off through the air lock while the
apprentice deactivated his lightsaber and looked around
for the magna lock generator. It had to be there somewhere, a big one, sufficient to power all the restraints in
all the cells. The air was becoming fumy and thick, and
the flashing lights made it hard to concentrate. Thick
bundles of cables snaked along the walls and under
metal grilles. He traced them as best he could to their

source, a large boxy structure fixed to a wall two doors along.

He didn't have time to perform a thorough investigation. It was the right size, so he would have to chance it. Raising both hands, he sent a wave of lightning through it, causing it to blacken and smoke. Current surged along the wires, sending out showers of sparks. Juno cried out in sudden pain.

Changing tactics, he stilled the lightning, clenched his hands into fists, and ripped the box out of the wall with one single, uncompromising wrench. The machinery inside exploded, filling the air with clouds of acrid debris. Juno cried out again, but this time in relief.

He hurried to her, finding his way via the Force through the impenetrable air. She was on her hands and knees, struggling to find her feet on the uneasy floor. She clutched at him when he burst out of the smoke and pulled her upright. She weighed almost nothing.

"I saw you die," she said, staring at him with naked disbelief. "But you've come back."

Rather than make her walk, he picked her up and hurried toward the air lock.

"I have some unfinished business," he said curtly, not knowing where to begin.

"Vader?" she asked, then folded into a series of choking coughs.

"Don't worry about him," he told her. The air lock led into a narrow umbilical. Fresh air blew toward him from ahead. Heat radiated through the walls. He ducked his head and hurried toward safety.

"I've been branded a traitor to the Empire," she told him. "I can't go anywhere, do anything—"

"I don't care about any of that. I'm leaving the Empire behind." He put all the reassurance he could find into his voice. She had to believe him without question. "And I need a pilot."

She buried her face in his shoulder as the familiar walls of the *Rogue Shadow* enfolded them. Barely had he crossed the threshold than the air lock door slammed shut on the *Empirical* and explosive bolts severed the umbilical.

"Welcome aboard, master," came the voice of the droid from the cockpit.

Assuming Juno wouldn't be up to flying just yet, the apprentice called ahead of them, "Get us out of here, PROXY!"

"Yes, master."

The sublight engines instantly engaged, and they were away.

CHAPTER 14

THROUGH THE VIEWPORTS OF THE *Rogue Shadow,* Juno watched as the *Empirical* fell behind them. Tumbling and turning, the modified cruiser's orbit had decayed beyond all hope of arresting its plunge into the sun. Barely had the *Rogue Shadow* detached than its outer shielding spontaneously ignited, sending waves of yellow lines creeping across the blackened hull. Without air to fuel the flames, for the moment, only metal and plastic were burning. The moment one of the viewports popped, however, the combustion began in earnest.

Her prison for six months was little more than a dark dot against the face of the sun when it suddenly flared and died. The explosion was almost anticlimactic, but it was sufficient. She unfolded her legs from beneath her, gratified to be rid of the place. Starkiller and PROXY were in the copilot's and pilot's seats, respectively. She was sitting behind them in the jump seat with a makeshift bandage around her wrist like some helpless piece of cargo. Like a *passenger.*

She had been hanging up like a forgotten nerf carcass for too long. It was time to take control of her life again.

"Out of my seat," she told the droid who had argued for abandoning her and letting her die with the *Empirical.* She felt no hard feelings for him, knowing that he had only been obeying his primary programming, but that didn't mean she had to like him.

"Yes, Captain Eclipse." He moved back into the seat she had vacated, clicking and humming to himself.

Touching the controls made her fingers tingle. She had dreamed of this moment for weeks and never dared believe it might actually come.

"What's our destination?" she asked Starkiller.

"Away from here."

"That'll do it." She keyed a jump in a random direction and leaned back into her seat. The familiar streaks of hyperspace almost made her choke. She smiled through the wave of emotion and let the ship carry them to safety.

TWO JUMPS LATER, IT WAS time to talk.

"No sign of pursuit." She put aside her scan of the surrounding space through the *Rogue Shadow*'s superior sensors with relief. "We're light-years away from any Imperial forces."

Starkiller looked up from tending a wound on his right forearm. Blood leaked from the gash. She was relieved to see it. Thinking of the injuries he must have suffered at the hands of his former Master made her stomach feel light. Part of him had to be synthetic now, but it was impossible to tell by looking at him. Unless the new getup he had on hid more than it suggested . . .

"Then what's wrong?" he asked her.

She flushed, still hoping he couldn't read her mind. Putting aside one concern for another, she said, "No one knows that we exist, or what we've done. We have the entire galaxy in front of us. So why, for the first time in my life, do I have no idea where to go . . . ?"

Her throat closed on her words. The reality of her betrayal and desertion was still sinking in.

Starkiller studied her, his eyes flickering. She would never be able to read *his* mind.

"I hope you have a plan," she said, clutching at her only straw.

He nodded, and then said slowly, as though sounding her out: "There are two things I want, and I can't get them on my own. The first is revenge. To get that we need to rally the Emperor's enemies behind us."

She nodded, thinking of Callos and her father. After witnessing the way Starkiller had killed the troopers on the *Empirical,* she had no doubt of his sincerity—or his ability to deliver. "Go on."

"The second thing I want is to learn all the things that Vader couldn't—or wouldn't—teach me about the Force."

She leaned her elbow on the arm of her flight chair and rested her chin on that hand. "If we're not careful, we might end up in our old job again—hunting Jedi."

He seemed to be aware of the irony of their situation. "I know of one who might still be alive. PROXY, show us the file of our first target."

They turned to face the droid, who flickered and transformed once more into the likeness of General Rahm Kota.

Juno frowned. "I thought you killed him."

"When I fought him in the TIE fighter factory, he said he could see my future. He said he was part of it."

She could see a thousand holes in his reasoning but had nothing better to offer. "Back to Nar Shaddaa, then."

"Back to Nar Shaddaa."

Starkiller tended his injuries while she worked on the nav computer. When they made the jump to hyperspace, he didn't even look up.

She took that as a sign of trust.

CHAPTER 15

FACEDOWN ACROSS A TABLE IN the darkest corner of a disreputable cantina slumped a man who wanted to disappear. The Vapor Room was a particularly good place to make the attempt. Primarily an Ugnaught hangout, but attracting its share of Rodian and human workers as well, it was an after-hours dive boasting bottomless shadows in every corner. The air hung in dense, aromatic sheets that moved only when staggering beings passed through them. The music was wildly hybridized, like the bartenders, who glowered sullenly as they wiped grease-smeared glasses and spread pools of liquor in thin layers across the bar top.

An empty tankard of Andoan ale rested near the slumped man's shoulder. His face was determinedly hidden from view, as if the only conscious desire he had left in him was to keep it that way. When he came up for a drink, which had happened with decreasing frequency in recent hours, he kept his face carefully averted from the cantina's patrons. Greasy gray hair protruded from what had once been a rigorously maintained queue. His robes were ill fitting and stained.

No one in the Vapor Room knew who the man was or what he had done. No one remembered who had brought him to Cloud City. They didn't care. They just wanted to be left alone to drink until their next shift came around.

The man who wanted to disappear had turned his

back on the galaxy, but it hadn't turned its back on him. Despite his very best efforts, he had been noticed. Inevitably so. A man with his injuries on Bespin was rare enough, but one who could still pour a glass of Corellian brandy without spilling a drop . . . ?

Word had spread, and that word was *trouble*.

THE APPRENTICE WALKED SLOWLY INTO the Vapor Room, eyes peering into the corners, studying every face and figure he found there. The cantina's atmosphere reeked of numerous negative emotions, but threat was not one of them. All eyes turned to him for a moment, then an older Ugnaught with an upturned nose and prominent belly raised a glass above his head in toast to the local King Ozz. The rest of his table purred loudly in agreement. Attention returned to frothing mugs, smoking pipes, and watching the chrono.

The nearest bartender cocked an antenna. The apprentice gestured at him, encouraging him to think about someone else. He didn't want a drink. He had just one purpose. This, the first real test of his Master's new plan, was the only thing on his mind.

It had been a long journey, with many risks taken. None had been as important or as dangerous as this.

"What happens if he recognizes you?" Juno had asked him with concern before he left the *Rogue Shadow*.

"He won't," he had said, remembering the general's burned eyes and the absent scars on his own hands. His body had changed in subtle ways, thanks to Lord Vader. The Force-signature he had possessed over Nar Shaddaa, in the midst of his murderous mission, would be very different from the one he projected now.

Calm. Reassurance. Hope.

Kota hadn't moved for twenty minutes, according to the feed from the security cam that Juno had sliced into.

The apprentice was relieved to see that it hadn't been a loop. The drunken Jedi was exactly where he had expected him to be, showing no signs of alarm.

The apprentice looked around the cantina, making sure that attention had really drifted away from him. Then he kicked the table, startling Kota awake.

The fallen Jedi lifted his head with a jerk, revealing a disheveled shadow of the man he had once been. His cheeks were hollow and thick with stubble. Dirty bandages, wrapped around his head, hid his eye sockets from view.

"General Kota?"

Kota's voice was slurred. "I've paid for this table. So whoever you are, get lost."

"General Kota, I've tracked you across the galaxy from Nar Shaddaa to Ziost—"

"Who are you, boy?" Kota's brows tightened. "A bounty hunter?"

"Not quite. But I have been watching you." He leaned closer and lowered his voice. "I think we can help each other, Jedi."

Kota pulled a face and gestured toward his bandaged eyes. "I'm no Jedi now. Not since this."

"I don't need your eyes, just your mind—and everything you know about fighting the Empire."

Kota slumped back into his chair, looking more weary than drunk. "Nobody fights the Empire and wins, boy."

A sudden commotion in the doorway attracted the apprentice's attention. Six stormtroopers had entered the Vapor Room flanked by two bipedal mechanical walkers, each controlled by a pair of surly-looking Ugnaughts. The lead trooper grabbed the stocky bouncer and began asking questions while his offsiders visually scanned the bar.

The apprentice cursed the Imperials' timing. Juno had intercepted the message from a local rat alerting station security to Kota's presence, but they had been unable to spirit him away in time.

He sighed and straightened, unhooking his lightsaber and placing himself between Kota and the Imperials.

"You'd better hope you're wrong about that, General."

With a *snap-hiss* loud enough to attract the attention of everyone in the Vapor Room, he activated the glowing green blade that had once belonged to the man whose life he'd ruined.

Kota flinched as though he had been struck and dived under the table. At that moment the Imperials opened fire. Ugnaughts squealed and leapt for cover as deflected energy bolts ricocheted around the room. Glasses shattered. Brightly colored liquid went everywhere, the more volatile catching fire and adding to the chaos.

"Stand up, General," the apprentice called over the racket. "They may be shooting at me right now, but they came here for you."

Then he was forced to concentrate on the Imperials and their local allies. The mechanical "Uggernaughts" were heavily armored and armed both. His first priority was to knock them out. He pushed one onto its side with the Force and overloaded the electrical systems of the second, encouraging the stormtroopers to scatter. The smell of scorched Ugnaught fur made the cantina smell even worse. From outside, he could already hear the clanking of reinforcements.

Whoever was behind Kota's attempted capture, they weren't taking any chances.

"Come on," he yelled at the cowering general. "Follow the sound of my lightsaber!"

He turned his back on Kota, hoping the old man recovered a sufficient sense of self-preservation to look after himself. Not only did his would-be rescuer have to take out the Imperials, but he had to do it without harm-

ing any innocent bystanders. That wouldn't look good
to anyone schooled in the Jedi ways.

As he fought his way toward the cantina's back door,
he commed the *Rogue Shadow* and told Juno that he
would need a rapid dust-off.

"Same place I dropped you off, I presume."

"Unless it gets too hot there." He brought the ceiling
down on one of the troopers and telekinetically threw
rubble at another. "Stay close and wait for my signal."

"Will do. Juno out."

He glanced behind him. Kota was finally moving,
hunched over like a stunned mine crab with his hands
splayed before him. Hopefully the Force would be with
Kota, because the apprentice knew with one look
through the door that he would have his work cut out
for him. There were at least two dozen Imperials in the
storeroom, taking cover behind crates and barrels. A
line of Uggernaughts promised to make short work of
him if he so much as blinked.

There wasn't time to hesitate. Drawing on the Force,
he burst the barrels, tore the crates apart, and filled the
air with debris. Chased by blasterfire, he ran across the
room in three steps and leapt onto the nearest Ugger-
naught. Lightsaber flashing, he cut the pilot and the gunner free and used the Force to crudely turn the machine
about. Its weapons barked and sent its siblings reeling
backward, showering sparks.

He leapt free, leaving it to stagger on, firing at random. Kota was keeping up, barely. He grabbed the old
man's arm and dragged him out of the storeroom and
along a series of corridors. The Vapor Room's supply
dock wasn't far away, and although he expected it also
to contain a heavy Imperial presence, getting the *Rogue
Shadow* in wasn't an impossibility. The dock was open
to the cloud-filled golden sky all along one side. One
quick Force jump would do it . . .

A glimpse of a black-robed figure standing with the stormtroopers stopped him in his tracks. On sight of him, it tilted its black helmet and ignited a red light-saber. The stormtroopers dropped to their knees and fired.

For the barest of moments, the apprentice was frozen. His stomach dropped away into Bespin's glorious sky-scape, and he felt betrayed all over again.

Then his mind caught up with his gut, shouting, *That's not Vader!* The red blade protruded from the top of a long black staff, not a lightsaber hilt. The helmet was smooth and rounded, lacking the familiar death's-head aesthetic of his Master's. Instead of two rounded photoreceptors, this helm boasted a single strip visor, suggesting that beneath might lie the face of an ordinary human male rather than whatever blasted visage his Master kept permanently hidden. The figure wore com-bat armor under his flowing cloak—exactly like one of the Emperor's Royal Guard, but entirely in black.

The apprentice's blade came up of its own accord. Moving in extreme slow motion, as though the air were made of treacle, he deflected volley after volley from the blasters back at the troopers who fired them. They stag-gered and fell with smoke pouring from shoulder and neck joints. Their cries barely registered.

The black guard deflected every bolt he sent his way. When the last of the troopers fell, the black guard stepped forward with his saber-staff lowered to charge.

"Stay away from the dock!" the apprentice warned both Juno and Kota. "We need another rendezvous point!"

"There's a shipping balloon dock not far from you," Juno responded as his lightsaber clashed with his new enemy's. "What's that noise? You're not fighting *Kota*, are you?"

"Too hard to explain," he grunted, not sure what the

explanation even was. "Get to the balloon dock and wait for me there."

He broke off communications to block a downward slash that almost knocked him flat. Glancing around for Kota, he was relieved to see that the general was nowhere nearby. Now he could summon the full power of the dark side. Drawing on the sense of betrayal and shock he had felt on seeing the figure waiting for him—this deadly, dark assassin who might or might not have something to do with Darth Vader—he pushed with all his might.

His ears rang, such was the energy he released. The dock buckled underneath him; rivets popped and welds tore. His assailant went flying across the wide space, arms spread wide apart. The saber-staff cut a long, twisting line in the metal floor as its owner rolled and came up standing.

A bolt of Sith lightning shot from the hand not holding the staff. The apprentice grinned, having anticipated that tactic. He met the lightning bolt with one of his own. They collided in a spitting, crackling ball of pure energy that danced crazily from side to side. The air filled with the sharp stink of ozone.

The hooded assassin grunted and applied more effort. The apprentice met that effort and exceeded it. The ease with which he drove his assailant's lightning back surprised him. For one wielding a Sith blade, the man he was fighting had less power than he should have.

The ball of energy where their crackling bolts met drifted closer and closer to the black guard. He grunted audibly and leaned physically forward with both hands upraised, one in a shaking claw and the other stabbing the saber-staff into the beam, adding its energy to his desperate attack. To no avail. The ball inexorably approached, driven by the dark power of the apprentice's will. When it touched the hilt of the black guard's saber-staff, all its pent-up energy was drawn into him.

With a truncated shriek the guard flew out the open dock and fluttered away, dead before his feet even left the ground.

The apprentice let the tension flood out of him and brought his arms down. Comming Juno, he followed the directions she gave him to their new rendezvous. It wasn't far, with only a couple of obvious ambush points along the way. Thanking her, he ran through an observation deck and along an exterior crosswalk, barely noticing the view. His mind worked over everything that had just happened, trying to find the sense in it.

A dark figure wielding a modified red blade and lightning, a Royal Guard but black all over . . . The Sith connection could not be denied. Unless Darth Vader had trained a second apprentice in the last six months—which didn't strike him as likely, for why would he then set them against each other?—there was only one other possible Master for such a being.

The Emperor.

Great minds thought alike. The apprentice grimaced as he approached the first of the likely ambush points, an air-conditioning heat exchange, where he would be forced to traverse a wide but long duct and pass through a series of fans. Darth Vader had sent his apprentice on a mission to find and kill the last of the Jedi. Perhaps the Emperor had intended the same with his dark minion.

If so, he would be disappointed by the results. Kota may not have wielded a blade, as he had on Nar Shaddaa, but the Emperor's emissary had died all the same. That would send a clear threat to the Emperor, perfectly in line with Darth Vader's wishes.

Assuming Kota survived, of course. The apprentice could only hope that he was heading to the balloon dock via a different route and wouldn't get himself killed along the way . . .

A squad of troopers was waiting for him in the heat exchange, with three of the mobile Uggernaughts. He made short work of them, neither rushing recklessly in nor drawing the fight out. There was no point to be made here. They were simply inconveniences.

He tossed the last of the Uggernaughts into the spinning blades of a fan four times as tall as he was. It exploded in a ball of flame, almost taking out its twin farther along the heat exchange. Out of the cloud of metal fragments leapt a second of the Emperor's Sith assassins, saber-staff upraised. The apprentice met him with a clash of sparks and lightning.

Sith against Sith, they fought backward and forward through the broad, metal-lined space. This assassin was more proficient than the first, wiry and strong with a good reach and penchant for telekinetically throwing items from inside the apprentice's blind spot. He proved to be tough work until the apprentice wrenched the next giant fan off its gimbals and sent it spinning through the air. The black guard seemed so stunned by the sight of it that he didn't jump until it was too late. One spinning blade took his right leg off at the knee. From then, the fight was over.

The apprentice left the dismembered black-clad body behind and hurried on his way, through a maintenance area filled with nervous Ugnaughts and up a ramp to the balloon dock.

Stepping out into the open air, he found himself facing another squad of troopers, two more of the Emperor's assassins, and no less than six Uggernaughts. Two transport balloons heavily weighted with supplies hung overhead, motors whirring to keep them on station, presumably waiting to land. Kota was nowhere to be seen.

The apprentice bent his knees and adopted a fighting stance.

"Are you sure you want to do this?" he asked his gathered foes.

The answer came in the form of blasterfire from the troopers, a barrage from the Uggernaughts, and a combined charge from the two assassins. He whirled and leapt, filling the air with reflected energy. All thought ceased; his connection to the Force became deeper than it ever had been before. He moved with grace and pure reflex, ducking under saber-staff blows, hurling troopers bodily at their Ugnaught allies, tossing walkers off the dock, and even raining supplies from one of the balloons above.

The crew of the balloon bailed out in a small speeder. Seeing it abandoned gave him an idea. When his enemies regrouped for a second combined charge, he wrenched the balloon physically downward from the sky, crashing its entire weight down on them all—and then, when the petals of the explosion were at their peak, sweeping the entire mess off the dock with one cathartic flexure of telekinesis.

He stood in a tiny dome of clear space, exhaling pure energy, as the circle of burning debris rained down through Bespin's thin, cold air below. Triumph and satisfaction filled him like pure helium, buoying him upward.

"How many were there?" asked a voice from behind him.

He turned to see Kota stumbling onto the dock. Although drunk, he was a sobering presence. The empty eye sockets hidden behind his filthy bandage seemed to stare right through the young man before him.

The apprentice straightened and lowered his lightsaber. He wondered if Kota was about to berate him for causing so much death and mayhem. "I lost count," he confessed.

"Doesn't matter. There will be more. The Emperor's army is infinite."

The apprentice scowled. A telling-off he could handle. Indulgent despair was a different thing entirely.

"We have to go, General."

"It's a fool's errand. You'll be killed—or worse. And what will have changed? Nothing."

The apprentice clicked the comlink for Juno's attention. "I'd rather die fighting than drown in some cantina, old man. Are you with me or not?"

Kota took a step forward, stumbled, and looked momentarily lost. "Do you have a name, boy?"

"No."

Again the apprentice felt as though he were being studied by eyes that no longer existed. "Well, there's no denying your willingness to kill stormtroopers. I have a contact in the Senate who might be able to use your lightsaber. Where's your ship?"

The apprentice smiled slightly as the *Rogue Shadow* rose up behind him, its repulsors whining and ramp extending. Perfect timing, he thought. If only Kota could have seen it . . .

With one hand in the old man's right armpit, he guided the first of his would-be rebels into the ship.

CHAPTER 16

THE FORMER GENERAL AND JEDI MASTER might have looked—and smelled—like a brain-dead derelict, but Juno soon learned that, even in his much-reduced state, he possessed resources she could only marvel at. First, he had survived a duel with Starkiller. Second, he had somehow crossed halfway around the galaxy without the use of his eyes. Third, he knew codes and ciphers she had no hope of slicing . . .

For an hour after their refueling stop at Cloud City, he had sat behind her in the jump seat, tapping madly into a keyboard and sending rapid-fire messages to unknown destinations. Every now and again she'd glanced back and tried to read surreptitiously. All she saw on the screen, however, was gibberish; the sound coming out of the earpiece she had loaned him, likewise. Whatever he was talking about, he was keeping it very much to himself.

"Can I help?" she'd finally asked him.

"No." He had leaned back into the seat and pushed the keyboard away. "It's done."

"You spoke to your friend?" Starkiller had asked, leaning in close from the copilot's seat.

Kota neither confirmed nor denied anything, given the choice. "Our destination is Kashyyyk," was all he had said.

"The Wookiee homeworld?" Juno had felt a sinking in her gut. "That's under Imperial rule now, isn't it?"

Kota had nodded.

"It'll be dangerous."

The old man had smiled at that, with no humor at all. "The entire galaxy is dangerous when you make an enemy of the Emperor." He had waved away any further questions. "Don't bother me now. I'm tired and I have a headache. You don't have any Andoan ale aboard, by any chance?"

"No," said Starkiller with a tight expression.

"Then let me sleep. You owe me that much."

Reclining the seat, he had put his hands behind his head and almost immediately begun to snore.

Starkiller had shrugged and told her that he was going back to the meditation chamber to prepare for whatever would come next.

And now she sat with PROXY beside her in the copilot's seat, wondering how she could prepare for something when she had no idea what it might be.

The warped perspectives of hyperspace slid rapidly by, simultaneously comforting and disconcerting. Familiar it might be to look at, but that environment was one explicitly hostile to human life. So was life on the run. Kota looked about as reliable as a drowned Wookiee. He and his mysterious contact could be leading them right into a trap. She and Starkiller had only just managed to scrape out of enough already while scouring the galaxy for the wretched old man . . .

She told herself not to be so surly. They'd all been through a lot, and it wasn't as if she had much choice. She had seen how Darth Vader rewarded loyalty. Returning to the Empire now, with two fugitives in tow, would be the fastest way to see herself shot. Her sleep was still disturbed by dreams of her long incarceration, in which the fear and hope of the final bullet still resonated.

Starkiller never talked about what was going on in his

head, but she could tell that he, too, was troubled. His social skills were nonexistent. He wouldn't talk about his feelings, his past, or anything other than the present. Only the fact that he had saved her made it endurable.

He never talked, although she had prompted him to, about how he had managed to survive the terrible wound his Master had inflicted. In the absence of hard facts, she could only wonder. Prosthetics weren't the only answer she had come up with. Could he be so strong in the Force that he could stave off death, the ultimate enemy? Was that how he had survived against so many adversaries? Or had some disloyal Imperial really scooped his body out of the sky and shipped it to the secret lab, where it had been repaired without his former Master finding out?

The alternatives were too strange and horrible to contemplate.

Sometimes his screams woke her from restless sleep, ringing out from the meditation room and echoing through the ship. Sometimes he called Vader's name; other times he called hers, in fear, despair, or anger. More often, he just screamed as though his heart were being cut out.

Her heart broke to hear it. And despite the fact that her life had fallen to pieces ever since they'd met, she remained inclined to follow him. Still, if he expected her to nursemaid this crusty old Jedi on the brink of utter decrepitude, he would find out just how far her loyalty could be stretched . . .

PROXY suddenly stirred. She blinked out of her thoughts and guiltily tried to look as though she was working. The droid paid her not the slightest attention, however, unfolding from his seat and heading aft. The sound of his metal footsteps led to the meditation chamber; the hatch slid open, and PROXY went inside.

She hesitated a moment, then opened the screen that

enabled her to spy on the activities within. In the deep gloom of the chamber, Starkiller knelt with his eyes closed and his back to the door, which her viewpoint covered. The faint shape of PROXY glowed all over for a second, morphing into a new shape. When the transformation was complete, he stood some centimeters taller and broader than before, with a beard and long hair, and wearing the standard robes of a Jedi Knight. The new expression he wore was one of determined solemnity.

Starkiller opened his eyes but didn't move until PROXY had activated a bright green lightsaber and raised it vertically in a balanced, two-handed pose on the right side of his body. Then Starkiller was up and defending himself so quickly that Juno had hardly seen him move. PROXY rained blows upon him with a speed and athleticism belying his construction. Spinning, tumbling, and cartwheeling all across the room, he was constantly on the offensive, employing swings that were both fast and powerful. Starkiller had his hands full deflecting them all. In the flickering light, she saw sweat standing out on his forehead.

The clash and crackle of lightsabers filled her earpiece. She turned the volume down so as not to disturb Kota's sleep. This wasn't the first time she had witnessed a duel between Starkiller and his training droid. They had fought like dervishes during the first days after fleeing the *Empirical,* the droid obviously helping him let off steam. But for those releases, she wondered if the pressure cooker of his mind would steadily build up stresses until he exploded.

She hadn't learned, however, to relax during them. Starkiller never lost—which was lucky, because PROXY spoke with disarming openness of his intention to kill his master should he ever find a chink in his armor. What life would be like after such a fatal mishap, she didn't like to think, so for now she tolerated the occasional practice sessions, even if she couldn't enjoy them.

PROXY didn't stay still for a second, attacking from the ground, the walls, the ceiling, even from midair. It was like watching a dance, but one in which the slightest slip could mean death. Starkiller danced with him long enough for her to worry, then he changed his own style to match that of the droid's—and suddenly she could see the difference between the human and the mechanical. Where PROXY had been fast, Starkiller was graceful as well. Where PROXY had simply slashed and stabbed, Starkiller applied flourishes to his offensive strikes. Where every move PROXY made involved his entire body, Starkiller could launch an attack with one finger, or block by shifting his foot a single centimeter.

The end came suddenly, with the green lightsaber stabbing deep into the belly of the unknown Jedi. Starkiller withdrew the blade and stepped backward. The other lightsaber deactivated and fell with a thunk to the metal floor. Starkiller's virtual opponent crumpled forward and had returned to PROXY's usual form before he hit the ground.

"I've failed again," came the muffled voice of the droid. "I'm sorry, master."

"It's not your fault, PROXY." Starkiller extended a hand and hauled the droid to his feet. "Ataru doesn't work properly without the Force. You managed a credible impersonation of it, though, especially in such a confined place."

"Thank you, master. Perhaps I will succeed next time."

Starkiller patted him with genuine affection. "You know, you did surprise me. I thought you were Kota."

"Now, he would make a fine training module." The droid fairly quivered at the praise. "Perhaps one day I will see him fight. That way I could observe how he moves and re-create him for you."

"Perhaps, PROXY," Starkiller said, his expression taking on a darker shade. "Is he awake yet?"

"I do not know, master, but our destination nears."

"Good." Together they left the chamber.

Juno switched off the screen and turned to be ready for them when they emerged into the cockpit.

She jumped when she saw Kota sitting up in his chair. For a moment she feared that he had heard everything she'd been listening to through her earpiece, but then she realized that what she had initially read as alertness, perhaps even suspicion, was actually the aftereffects of alcohol poisoning.

"I was beginning to worry that you'd died in your sleep," she said.

The corners of his lips pulled down. "I wish I had."

Starkiller entered with PROXY in tow. "Are we close?" he asked, taking the copilot's chair and turning toward her. The strange angularities of hyperspace reflected in his eyes.

She checked the instruments. "We'll be arriving any second now."

Right on cue, the view blurred and shifted into the more familiar starscape of the galactic backdrop. Kashyyyk was a patchwork sphere in green and blue hanging off the starboard bow. It was a beautiful world, but she could tell that it had seen hard times. The scars of orbital bombardment were still visible, years after they had been inflicted. She imagined the smoke that must have risen from those burning forests and was glad for the Wookiees that their home had been spared Callos's fate.

She employed the *Rogue Shadow*'s advanced sensors to scan the space around the planet. It was dense with signals, but not much traffic, both mostly Imperial in origin. Several capital ships prowled the upper orbits, cannons and patrols at the ready. Quite a few transports were gathering about a point just out of sight around the planet's horizon. She urged the ship on in order to obtain a clearer view.

When the particular orbital location came into sight, it took her a moment to realize what she was seeing. It was more than just an ordinary equatorial docking station, but at first glance the difference defied her imagination. Her eyes saw it; her mind rebelled.

A skyhook hung over Kashyyyk, floating on repulsors just outside the planet's upper atmosphere. A sturdy, utilitarian structure tethered to a cleared area far below, it obviously wasn't the local dictator's mansion or a resort for jaded Moffs. It wasn't finished yet, either. Dozens of cargo ships and construction droids surrounded its summit, glinting in the golden sunlight.

At the sight of the rare construction and the strong Imperial presence, she shook her head.

"I definitely think this mission is too dangerous now."

Even Starkiller seemed to be having second thoughts. "Your contact had better be reliable," he told Kota with a sour look.

"I trust him with my life." The hungover general didn't ask what they were seeing. Perhaps he already knew. "He smuggled me to Cloud City, and he's an old ally of the Jedi Order."

"It's all very well to hear that," Juno said, "but without knowing who he is, you're putting us in a difficult spot."

"You're not the only ones reluctant to give names to strangers." The general huffed out his cheeks. "If you want my help, this is how you're going to get it. There's something very valuable to my friend down on Kashyyyk. You extract it for him and maybe he'll agree to help you fight the Empire."

Juno watched Starkiller's face. He showed no sign of uncertainty.

"Have we been spotted, Juno?"

"No. The cloaking device is operating at peak efficiency."

"Then take us down."

She mock-saluted to cover her unease. "It's going to be tricky keeping our heads low out here," she said as she turned the ship on its new course. "The traffic's not heavy enough to vanish into, but it is sufficient that someone will spot us if we go to ground. And we can't use the cloak forever. If the stygium crystals overheat, they'll be useless."

"Do what you can," Starkiller told her. "I'll try not to be too long."

"Is that what you told your last pilot?"

The words came out before she'd properly thought about them, and she regretted them instantly. Kota was listening, she told herself angrily. The ex-Jedi could never know who they were or what they had done, no matter what.

She glanced at Starkiller. His ears were burning. His expression looked furious.

Juno pushed the *Rogue Shadow* down into the atmosphere, hoping that the noise and turbulence of entry would cover the fact that she was furious at herself, too.

SWOOPING OVER ROLLING, GREEN HILLS close to the coordinates Kota gave her, she brought the ship down low enough and long enough for Starkiller to leap into the forest canopy and shimmy down a wide-boled tree. She didn't stop to look behind her, waiting only until his voice over the comlink assured her that he was safe. Then she was flying the ship back up to space, where no messy contrails or lookouts could betray their presence.

PROXY wandered back to the meditation chamber, perhaps to practice his Kota impersonation in private.

It took her half an hour to plot an orbit that would keep the ship well out of range of Imperial sensors. When she was done, she glanced over her shoulder. The general had slumped down into his seat with his arms folded and let his chin rest firmly on his chest. His skin was pale and drawn. His eye sockets were sunken beneath their bandages.

"Stay awake, General," she said.

"If there's really nothing to drink on this ship," Kota said with a surly drawl, "I'd rather you let me go back to sleep."

"Our friend down there might need your help."

"Your friend, not mine." Kota's lips pursed. "I don't even know who he is—or how you two came to own a ship like this."

She thought quickly. So the general *had* heard her comment about Starkiller's previous pilots. He was surely bringing it up now to needle her. The obvious option was to ignore him, but that would only rouse his suspicions even further. She had to tell him something, just as long as it wasn't the truth. Or at least the *whole* truth.

"We stole it," she said.

"Who from?"

"You don't need to know."

"I can guess. I've flown a few ships with cloaking devices down the years, but I can't pick out the sound of this one's hyperdrive. It's something new, probably military." Through the grouchiness he wore like his own disguising cloak, she could tell that he was testing her. "Our common enemy, perhaps."

She said nothing. He was a Jedi. If she gave away too much, he might match the *Rogue Shadow* to the ship in which Darth Vader's assassin had arrived at the TIE fighter factory—and that would be the end of everything.

He chuckled low in his throat, then coughed long and hard. "Don't worry, Juno," he said when his voice returned. "I'm hardly going to turn you in."

"I didn't think—"

"You're fugitives, just like me. You have nothing to lose."

Only our futures, she thought. *Our slates are clean. We could start all over again, if we wanted to.*

His face seemed to visibly age. She wondered if he was thinking of all the friends and loved ones he had lost over the years—not just to Order 66, but throughout his subsequent insurgency as well. And his sight, too. He had yet to tell her how he had come to be blinded, and she had never asked. She figured she could guess, and that he wouldn't ever want to talk about it, with her or anyone.

He stood with a grunt.

"If you won't give me any peace and quiet," he said, "I'm going to the cargo hold to sleep."

"You do that, General," she said, relieved that the moment was over and unsure what exactly had passed between them. "I'm going to see if I can find out what that skyhook is for."

He patted her dismissively on the shoulder and shuffled out of the cockpit, making his way by feel through the ship's hard-edged interior.

Juno checked the instruments to make sure they were still flying true. Starkiller hadn't called in yet. She wondered if that was a good sign or the worst imaginable . . .

CHAPTER 17

WITH ONE DESPERATE LUNGE OF his lightsaber, the apprentice killed the last of the giant spiders that had ambushed him in the forest's lower levels. Hideous creatures with fat, red-pigmented bodies and tenacity beyond all reason—he almost wondered if they saw his potential escape as a personal affront as well as lost lunch—they had tracked him for over a kilometer before finally springing their trap. Barely had he begun to wonder at the dearth of Kashyyyk's dangerous undergrowth dwellers in his vicinity than five of the giant weavers had suddenly converged on him at once, swinging on thick strands of web with mandibles raised and dripping poison. He had barely survived the ambush.

Wiser now, and splattered in thick green ichor, he abandoned the undergrowth for the upper levels of the forest. It was taking him too long to approach the coordinates Kota had given him. Leaping from branch to branch, he ascended two hundred meters before the light started to brighten appreciably. Such was the perpetual gloom below that he felt as though he was ascending from deep underwater.

Kota hadn't told him what lay at the coordinates, and he hadn't commed the *Rogue Shadow* to find out. He wanted to learn for himself, to test the aging general's memory, reliability, and word.

Once he was sure he was out of the territory of the deadly spiders, he took a more level heading, albeit one still angling slightly upward. The forest canopy stretched at least another half a kilometer above him, consisting of the branches of mighty trees overlapping one another for support and carrying many thousands of species on their broad terraces. The kingdoms of animal, vegetable, and even mineral flourished everywhere he looked. Birds flew in complex flocks around nesting grounds like small cities. Insects crawled and swarmed in sappy splits in the bark. Soil from rotting vegetable matter and airborne dust pooled in the joints between branches and trunks, creating oases for leafy plants and spreading vines. The cool air was full of animal sounds and the rustling of leaves.

It was very different from Felucia, where everything seemed swollen with moisture and the Force, always on the brink of bursting. Here life was hard-edged and knife-sharp. Turning one's back on it was very, very dangerous.

Back in a relatively safe domain, leaping or swinging on vines from branch to branch, the apprentice was able to resume thinking about what he had seen from orbit.

A skyhook.

Startling enough on its own. Only a handful existed in the galaxy, and most of those were on Coruscant. But that wasn't what had struck him.

As the *Rogue Shadow* had descended to the world's surface, he had seen the skyhook from a different angle. Catching the last rays of the sun, it had resembled a fiery line reaching up into the sky—

—*up to a point in low orbit where a cluster of tiny lights gathered.*

He had seen that vision before, of the skyhook over Kashyyyk. It had come to him while he'd been unconscious in Darth Vader's secret laboratory, undergoing surgery for the terrible wounds his Master had inflicted. He had thought those visions nothing but dreams, meaningless fancies thrown up by his subconscious while his body was under duress.

Could they in fact have been glimpses of his future?

He didn't know. Certainly he had never before achieved foresight, not through meditation or any of the other trials he had set himself, but that didn't rule it out. He had been suspended between life and death for months. Who knew what straits he had endured on the road back to survival? It would be foolish to discount the possibility, for the visions might contain information that could help him on this particular journey, and others.

He struggled to recall more details of the vision, but found it difficult. His memories were jumbled. Something about the smell of raw meat, and Darth Vader talking about someone who had died. The hint of more was tantalizing but worthless on its own. He needed something tangible or else it would only distract him.

In the vision, the view of the skyhook seemed to come from a ground-level perspective. There couldn't be many places offering that on Kashyyyk. And there had been someone else with him. A young woman. Juno, perhaps?

He frowned, sensing that he was drifting from the truth of the vision, whatever that was. Not Juno. Someone else. Someone unknown.

Friend or foe?

The vision was exhausted, and so was he from trying to wring more from it. He had felt weighed down ever since he'd arrived on Kashyyyk. There was something in the air of the place, in the trees, in the color of the sun—and it bothered him. If the source wasn't the vision, then what could it be?

He abandoned the attempt and concentrated solely on negotiating the forest's upper fringes.

As he neared the coordinates Kota had given him, the

sound of industry rose up over the natural ambience of Kashyyyk.

The first to reach his ears was that of a shuttle taking off. Its flat, metallic whine ramped up, almost to the level of being painful, then faded away to the west. Birds erupted from the trees around him, adding their own clamor to the aftermath. When they had settled down, he made out the clanking of Balmorran All Terrain Scout Transports. The awkward-looking, two-legged machines had earned the apprentice's unending dislike on Duro, where Darth Vader had sent him to put down a local despot who had grown too big for his Imperial boots. The machines were heavy and graceless, but troublesome in proficient hands. He hoped he could stay out of their gunsights for as long as he was on Kashyyyk.

Whirring landspeeders, buzzing vibrosaws, and the whine of a generator drifted to him as he neared their collective source. He was momentarily puzzled as to how such a large-sounding settlement had found a secure foothold in the dangerous forest. The answer came to him before long.

The forest ended as though a knife had been carved through it and the trees to one side scraped away. Raw, scarred dirt lay exposed to the naked sun for the first time in millennia, knotted with dead roots and mixed liberally with angular wood chips. The ground sloped down in a large valley to a choked riverbed, then angled up again to a summit that would have seemed prominent on any other world, but which remained dwarfed by the trees that crowded resentfully around the cleared area. On the summit of the far side of the valley was a lodge, clearly the home of someone important, doubling as an Imperial base, one bristling with weapons emplacements and satellite dishes, planted high above the forest with a shuttle landing pad jutting out of one side.

From where he crouched, he could see several steps

leading up to the main entrance. A single shuttle rested on the pad, its arms folded demurely upward over its body. AT-STs strutted about below with an air of iron impregnability, shadowed by droids of all shapes and sizes. Stormtroopers patrolled the lodge's perimeter with blaster rifles at the ready, some herding Wookiees in groups of three or four. The planet's tall, heavily furred indigenes seemed to be wearing restraints, although it was hard to make out why across such a long distance.

The apprentice took all this in from a lofty vantage point on the very fringe of the forest, crouched on a slender bough like a Kowakian monkey-lizard. There was no obvious way into the lodge that he could see. Perhaps with a little more information, he could come up with some kind of plan.

From far below came the tinny crackle of a stormtrooper's vocoder.

Exactly what he needed.

Dropping with apparent weightlessness through the branches, he landed between the members of a two-man patrol. Before either could sound the alarm, he raised his left hand and ordered one of them to sleep. As that trooper sagged gently to the ground, the second fell under the influence of a different mind trick.

"You're not alarmed," he told the trooper. "I'm authorized to be here. In fact, you've been expecting me."

The man in the anonymous white helmet nodded. "Everything's in order, sir. Can't explain what's gotten into Britt here, though—" He kicked his unconscious fellow with one white boot.

"Britt isn't your concern. You want only to help me."

"Yes, sir. I'm at your disposal. How can I assist you?"

The white helmet tipped inquisitively to one side, and the apprentice gave thanks for the small minds of most stormtroopers.

"Tell me who's in charge here."

"Captain Sturn, sir."

"And where would I find him?"

"In the lodge with the guest, sir, if he's not out hunting."

"Who's the guest?"

"I don't know, sir, but we're under strict orders to keep them out of harm's way. These Wookiees are mindless brutes."

The apprentice ignored the speciesist slur. "Is this person a guest, or a hostage?"

"I don't know, sir."

"Can you show me to the guest quarters?"

"I'm not authorized for that area, sir." Again the helmet tilted. "Why don't you ask Captain Sturn these questions?"

His hold on the stormtrooper's mind was slipping. Before it could fall away entirely, the apprentice asked him about the Wookiees.

"What are we doing with them, sir? Why, giving them what they deserve. Filthy, mindless animals. Hey, you're not one of those sympathetic types, are you? One of them tore my platoon leader limb from limb, right in front of me. Kill them all, I would, like Captain Sturn—"

"Enough." He waved his hands across the stormtrooper's face and stepped back to avoid his collapse. Leaving the pair where they lay, he melted into the shadows of the undergrowth and began to circle the enormous clearing. The lodge at its heart was built tough, with no obvious weak points. The far side projected over the ridge, into virgin forest. He didn't want to get entangled in another web-weaver ambush if he could avoid it. By any account, it'd take an army to get in there, or firepower above and beyond anything he had at hand—unless he stole some of the Imperials' concussion grenades, or got his hand on a blaster cannon . . .

A slow smile crept across his face. He didn't need anything like that. He had the dark side of the Force on his side. Edging back up into the trees, he set out to find the best possible place to launch an assault.

Only once, when the scent of a distant burn-off hit his nostrils, did the strange feeling of disorientation strike him again. He put it firmly out of his mind. Dozens of stormtroopers lay in his immediate future, and all of them would be keen to keep him from his goal. He would give them cause to reconsider.

CHAPTER 18

WITHIN HALF AN HOUR OF slicing into the local Imperial mainframe, Juno had exactly half an answer.

The purpose of the skyhook was to ferry Wookiee slaves from the surface of Kashyyyk into low orbit, from which point they would be taken elsewhere.

Where they were to be taken, however, was hidden by a deeper level of security than she could penetrate. And the matter of *why* was completely obscured. After that productive half hour had come a frustrating search through every available record, looking for any kind of clue but finding none. She was as much in the dark on that point as she had been at the beginning.

She did learn that Darth Vader himself had visited the planet years earlier, but that appeared to have been on a completely unrelated matter.

Leaning back into her seat, she ran her fingers through her hair and stretched. Starkiller was busy on the ground. Kota was back in the hold. PROXY was still keeping himself amused. It had only just occurred to her that, for the moment, she was completely alone.

Leaning forward again, her fingers began tapping at the keys. Certain Imperial records were duplicated all across the galaxy. They came with every invading force, updating local networks and keeping themselves up to date in turn by downloading new information from capital ships passing through. Thus the administration of the Empire kept itself consistent across many thousands of inhabited worlds—for how else would distant governors know about new laws and appointments, or wanted criminals who might stray across their borders?

Data from the Imperial Academy was part of that automatic download. Encrypted, of course, but Juno knew the keys by heart. She told herself that she was just idly curious. Callos had been less than a year ago. She had heard nothing about her former friends and colleagues in all that time. It would be inhuman not to wonder . . .

The Black Eight Squadron was an elite unit with a reputation for discipline and ruthlessness. From the outside, she could see how its composition was carefully maintained by Darth Vader to ensure that both qualities remained unsullied. Leadership and pilots frequently turned over, a fact obscured by the air of mystique surrounding the squadron. Those inside never talked about their wingmates or missions; those outside never speculated. They got the job done. That was all that mattered.

She had been proud to fly as squadron leader, but her time at the helm had been brief. That, she learned, was normal. Her predecessor, whom she had flown with only twice, had lasted barely longer than her. His predecessor had lasted just a single month before being transferred by Darth Vader to a position she couldn't trace. Both pilots were now listed as deceased.

She wondered if either of them had flown for Starkiller.

Turning away from that fruitless line of speculation, she investigated the careers of those pilots she had flown with. A third of them were still in the squadron. A third were dead—killed in action, she presumed, although only half were listed as such. The remainder had been promoted.

Reading the list of advancements, her hackles rose. A pilot with the call sign *Redline* had been promoted to head of squadron in her absence. Redline was, in her experience, the coldest, cruelest, least considerate being she had ever flown with. She had had serious concerns about his mental health, describing him in her flight logs as psychopathic and consistently penalizing him for using excess force. He was one of three under her who had complained about the withdrawal from Callos. The squadron should have stayed, they argued, and *finished the job*.

The world had died. She couldn't see what was left to finish. And now here he was, running the most feared TIE fighter squadron in all the Empire.

She could see how that fit Darth Vader's twisted vision of the galaxy. What she had once considered a close-knit unit, almost a family, she now knew was utterly dysfunctional—the product of a tyranny driven by fear and greed. Had she stayed with the Black Eight, she would have been forced to commit atrocities like Callos over and over again—as Redline was no doubt doing even now—or she would have resisted and been shot for disobeying orders.

She understood, but that didn't mean she liked it, not one bit. Other promising pilots had been completely looked over. The replacement she had recommended, Chaser, was still flying fourth. And Youngster, the pilot who had followed her into the squadron, a cheerful graduate whom she had felt sure would pursue her rapidly up the ranks of enlisted officers, was . . .

It took her fifteen minutes to find out what had happened to him. He had left the squadron—alive, apparently, one of the few who had transferred while still able to fly—but from there his progress was difficult to track. He had suffered a change of heart, it seemed, but not one great enough to result in execution. He had flown transports for a while and then returned to active duty as a sentry around Imperial construction sites. He had seen combat in several hot spots, but nothing special. His latest posting . . .

Juno stared at the answer for a minute before accepting that it could be true. Youngster was stationed on Kashyyyk.

A terrible mixture of yearning and fear swept through her. With a flick of a switch, she could open a comm channel and hail her old wingmate. His familiar voice would fill the cockpit and for a moment, just a minute or two, she could feel as though she belonged again. She could roll back time and forget about betrayals and the uncertain future stretching ahead of her. She could be an accomplished Imperial pilot again, secure in the knowledge that nothing could ever change that.

One switch. She didn't even have to say who she was. They could verbally handshake and that would be enough. What harm would that do?

She shuddered. Her hands were clenched tightly in her lap and she kept them there lest they betray her.

She couldn't go back, not even for a minute. Hailing an Imperial squadron while Starkiller was on the ground risked blowing everything. Nothing was worth that. Not even talking to someone she had once called an ally and now considered her enemy, most likely. If he ever learned that she still existed . . .

Her shaking hands returned to the keyboard. Slowly, she typed in her own name.

Her files were no longer restricted. In fact, they came up immediately. She read the summary of her career as she would her own obituary. In one very real sense, it was exactly that.

Spy . . . traitor . . . executed by Imperial command.

There was no room for doubt. She could not go back. She didn't even recognize the life she was supposed to have had. Her record had been tampered with. All her major achievements were gone. Even Callos didn't rate a mention. She had been reduced to an inept fighter pilot who had somehow scraped a lucky break into the galaxy's top squadron and then let her team down. Worse, she turned on them. The woman in the record had deserved that fictional blaster bolt. That was exactly what the old Juno Eclipse would have believed.

The old Juno Eclipse no longer existed. The new Juno Eclipse was angry that she had been so easily reduced, even in an official record she no longer cared about. Or believed. If this had happened to her, how many times had it happened to others branded traitor—like her own mother?

She wondered for an instant what her father thought. Then she decided she didn't care.

At least she was believed dead. She clung to that certainty, even as fury seethed in her. And she was fighting back.

The rasp of Kota's throat made her jump and guiltily clear the screen—before remembering that he was blind.

"I think the time has come to check on your friend," the general said. "He's been quiet a little too long."

"You're right. And I'm sure he'd like to know what I've found out." She outlined the news that Wookiee slaves were going to be ferried elsewhere for an unknown reason. "Do you think your friend in the Senate knows anything about this?"

"I'm sure of it," Kota said.

"Do you think that's why we're really here?"

"I think it's possible to fix two problems with one solution. Or make the attempt, anyway."

"I guess we'll see what we will see." She began opening

a comm channel, then realized what she had said. "Oh, I'm sorry."

"No need to apologize," Kota said gruffly. "It's just a figure of speech."

All conversation between them died. From Starkiller's comlink came the sound of screaming machinery.

CHAPTER 19

Juno's was trying to tell him something, and it sounded like it might be important.

Whatever it was, it would have to wait.

The foot of an AT-ST walker came down right next to him, making every tooth in his head shake. The apprentice didn't break stride. He had timed his run perfectly, dodging the concussion grenades and energy bolts fired by the gunner and approaching from underneath, where the plating was weakest. The bulky head swiveled and turned above him, trying to get a bead on the unarmored man who dared single-handedly attack it. He could read the pilot's disbelief secondhand through the movement of the machine.

The apprentice took a deep breath and executed an acrobatic aerial somersault that brought his lightsaber into range of both knee joints, three control junctions, and the drive engine. The AT-ST shuddered midstep as the damage he had inflicted registered in its complex systems. The endless pounding of its weapons faltered.

The apprentice touched the ground and stopped dead. With a groan of tortured metal, the AT-ST managed a half step then dropped nose-forward into the ground. Dust rose up from the blasted soil. Before it could settle, the apprentice was moving again, dodging a stream of blasterfire from a stormtrooper cannon emplacement to the right of the lodge's main steps. Two more AT-STs were closing on him from either side, hoping to hem him in.

His smile hadn't faded an iota. The troopers' aim left a lot to be desired. Every projectile that came within reach he deflected back at either its point of origin or the lodge's main door, but so many of them were missing completely that the rest discharged uselessly into the dirt. He ran toward the troopers, deliberately making himself an easier target. White helmets lifted in surprise, then came down in concentration.

One lucky shot, he imagined them thinking. *Just one lucky shot.*

He would show that there was no such thing as luck. Not against him, anyway.

A blistering barrage of energy fire encased him. He began directing some of it back at the approaching AT-STs, leaving black scorch marks on their forward armor. Drivers and gunners intensified their charge, knowing that their approach made them better targets, too. A rain of concussion grenades fell toward him. He deflected them all toward the lodge's door, careful to avoid anything resembling a guest quarters.

Sirens wailed. Stormtroopers screamed. The whining of engines grew louder and louder.

When the two AT-STs were within ten meters of him, forming an equilateral triangle with the stormtrooper cannon emplacement, he stopped. His lightsaber spun like a propeller, moving without his conscious thought. The Force streamed through him like a lightning bolt, fueling his instincts and filling him with strength. For a full second he closed his eyes and let his arms move in perfect synchrony with the energy bolts. He wasn't even part of the equation anymore. He was a spectator, a privileged observer in a deadly but beautiful ballet.

He lowered his head and concentrated. The AT-STs

were approaching more slowly now, their drivers and
gunners sensing victory: no ordinary human could survive such a barrage for long. They were wrong a thousand times over. When the AT-STs started to accelerate
again, their drivers were taken momentarily by surprise.
Then they pulled back on their controls, to no avail.
Their heavy metal beasts steadily picked up speed, tra-
jectories shifting with each lurching step. Accelerating
unstoppably, they converged on a different point from
the one they had originally been aiming for: not the apprentice any longer, but a patch of empty ground just
meters away.

The apprentice spun and opened his eyes a split second before they collided. Raising his free hand, he sent a
powerful bolt of lightning into the buckling armor
shells. The energy raced along wires and cables deep
into the cargo bays and ammunition stores, tripping
safeties and triggering detonators. Energy begat energy.

He jumped vertically upward a single instant before
the first explosion and was lifted higher still by the blast
of hot air that erupted in his wake. He tumbled and
twisted with the Force singing through him, buoyed by
the delicious sense of weightlessness and a death well
avoided.

A ball of red flame spread across the ground, enveloping the cannon emplacement. White-armored bodies
flew everywhere.

He reached the apex of his leap and began to descend.
It was almost a shame to come down to the ground, but
he knew he couldn't fly forever. Rolling to shed a slight
excess of momentum, he was up on his feet immediately,
surrounded by wreckage and wreathed in smoke. A
quick glance over his shoulder told him all he needed
to know. Only one of the ruined AT-STs was still standing. Thick black smoke poured from its shattered view-

port. The other was in pieces, blown apart by its own weaponry.

The battleground was still. His ears rang for almost half a minute before the noise faded. All was silent apart from the ticking of metal as it cooled. The Imperial resistance had crumbled. Either he had killed them all, or the survivors had fallen back to another defensive position.

"Now, what were you saying?" he asked Juno as he walked up the steps leading to the lodge's front door. The armored plating that had once kept it secure hung from a single melted hinge, destroyed by the shots he had deflected from cannons and walkers.

"The skyhook," Juno told him. "It's for taking Wookiee slaves offplanet by force."

"That's not important now," broke in Kota's rough-edged voice. "Where are you?"

The apprentice described the lodge as he stepped into its ruined foyer. He kept his lightsaber at the ready, but the only beings in evidence were a trio of nervous protocol droids. "There seems to be no one about."

"You're very close to your objective. Don't allow yourself to be distracted."

"Want to tell me what I'm looking for?"

"Patience, boy. You'll know."

The apprentice grunted an affirmative. He strode down the main corridor, kicking open doors and using the Force to enhance his physical senses. The smell of burning food came from the kitchen. He ignored it.

"Something . . . ," he said, an instinct leading him toward the rear of the lodge. "Someone . . ."

He turned a corner and entered a long wooden corridor lined with two-dimensional ceramic artwork. Two stormtroopers and an Imperial Guard stood watch over a locked door at its end. The troopers raised their blaster rifles as he came into sight. The guard's saber-staff was already activated.

"Hold on," he told Kota. "I think I'm getting warm."

The troopers started firing before he had taken two paces toward them. They were dead long before he reached the door, killed by their own reflected fire. The Imperial Guard lasted barely as long, felled with four swift lightsaber strokes then shocked with lightning as he dropped backward to the ground. The apprentice nodded, satisfied that his skills had improved since Nar Shaddaa.

Looking back over his shoulder, he nodded again. Not a single piece of art had been damaged.

My good deed for the day, he thought as he burned out the lock and used the Force to push the door in.

The room on the far side was luxuriously appointed, and tastefully so, considering its deceased owner. Dozens of different woods provided subtle contrasts among walls, cornices, floors, and ceilings, with a huge bay window on the far side overlooking the forest. In the distance, clearly visible against the blue sky, was the bright line of the skyhook.

Instead of the local despot, he found himself facing the back of a slender, hooded woman in white. She stood facing the view with a blue-and-white astromech droid at her side, and although she didn't turn to see who had blown in the door he could tell that she was closely aware of his presence.

He took two steps toward her and activated his com-link so Juno and Kota could overhear.

"I should have expected that the Emperor would send an assassin," the woman said, sounding more irritated than worried. "It's a coward's tactic."

"I do not serve the Emperor."

The woman turned and lowered her hood. Not a woman, he realized, but a teenager barely his age with brown hair hanging in looped ponytails over her shoulders. She studied him with a world-weary skepticism.

"I told Captain Sturn to spare me the charade, and now I'm telling you—"

"No, really," he said, raising a hand to cut her off. "I'm here with Master Kota."

"Master Kota is dead, killed above Nar Shaddaa. My father—"

She caught herself.

"Your father?" He took a step closer, putting several pieces of a puzzle together. Kota's friend . . . the "very valuable" item he was supposed to extract . . . "How long has your father been feeding Kota information about Imperial targets?"

She looked at him warily. "How do you know—"

"Master Kota told me himself. He survived Nar Shaddaa. We were sent to find you. I think you're supposed to come with me now."

Her skepticism increased. "I can't leave, not while the planet is enslaved."

"Is that what you're here for?"

"No." Her answer was clipped and angry. "I'm a Senatorial observer appointed by the Emperor himself. My job is to oversee the construction of that monstrosity." She cocked her head at the view of the skyhook towering over the forest. "He can't kill me, but he can keep me busy and send a message to my father at the same time. A coward, as I said, but a clever one, well versed in the arts of coercion and manipulation."

The apprentice nodded his understanding.

"I'm not so harmless myself," the young woman said, pointing with her chin at the lightsaber. "I know what that is. If you're truly a Jedi, then you'll understand why I can't leave."

"But your father—"

"My father isn't here." She turned back to the window. "Once the skyhook is complete, the Empire will be able to shuttle Wookiee slaves in earnest. Entire villages will be taken offworld in a matter of days. Artoo-Detoo?"

The little astromech rolled over to the pair, stopping between its mistress and the apprentice. Chirping and whistling, it projected a standard bluish white hologram of a massive construct, circular in shape, with buttressed sides and reinforced anchors digging deep into exposed bedrock. The image rotated slowly in the air while Leia talked the apprentice through her plan.

"Artoo and I have been studying the skyhook from here. I think I know how to take it down. These are the moorings. Disable them and the skyhook will detach from the planet, causing a chain reaction that should destroy the orbital platform before it can be put to use."

The apprentice studied the image, looking for some way of discerning the construction's scale. He found it in the form of a tiny human figure, dwarfed by the moorings. That wasn't very encouraging.

"Destroying it won't stop the Empire for long," he said. "They'll just build another one."

"Eventually, maybe. But you'll give the remaining Wookiees a chance to disappear." She folded her arms across her chest as though daring him to disagree. "Back the way you came, there's a tube transport that leads down to the forest floor. It'll be crawling with Imperials, clearing out the undergrowth, but it'll take you to the base of the skyhook."

"All right," he said, despite serious misgivings. If he wanted to get her offworld, he would need to do as she said. "But what about you?"

"My shuttle is still on the landing platform, I presume."

"Yes, but I won't make any promises about the pilot."

"What makes you think I need one?" She flashed him a smile over her shoulder, and added more gravely, "Please tell my father I'm safe."

"I will."

Then she was gone.

CHAPTER 20

"DID YOU GET ALL THAT?" Starkiller asked from the planet's surface.

"We did," Juno replied, feeling decidedly ambivalent about the new development. While glad that they had managed to achieve the objective given to them by Kota's friend in the Senate, their continued proximity to danger made her sweat in her seat. Starkiller wasn't likely to be coming off the ground anytime soon, and the stygium crystals weren't going to last forever. "Are you going to do as she says?"

"I'm already doing it," he replied.

"You and your *one solution*," she muttered to Kota.

"Is everything all right up there?" Starkiller asked her.

"We're killing time," she said. "Where do you think the Wookiees are being taken—and why?"

"Your guess is as good as mine. They're strong and smart. If it weren't for their tendency to rip people's heads off when they get angry, they'd make excellent slaves."

"There are ways around that," said Kota dourly.

"What do you mean?" asked Juno.

"Attachment," he told her. "Wookiees have a keen sense of family. The bonds among them are exceedingly tight." His lips twisted. "That's why the Jedi didn't have families. It was the only way to remain objective."

"Being objective obviously wasn't enough," Juno said.

The general just scowled.

"Kota," came Starkiller's voice from the ground. "I want you to pass her message on to her father, whoever she is."

"All right," the general said, turning to his keyboard. "I'll try."

Silence fell on the comms. The pair in the *Rogue Shadow* waited wordlessly for some time, he tapping at the keys, wrapped in unhappy thoughts, and she wondering what was happening to Starkiller on the ground. She scanned the ship's data banks for information on Kashyyyk's forests and wasn't remotely reassured. If he wasn't being shot at by Imperials converging on the scene of his earlier disturbance, he was most likely being eaten by blastails or smashed to a pulp by terrible minstyngar.

After a prolonged period of typing, punctuated by irritated snorts and worried grumbles, Kota pushed aside the keyboard and erupted from his chair. With an explosive "Gah!" he stumbled out of the bridge, patting the walls to find his way.

"Something wrong?" she called after him.

He didn't reply. With a hiss, the door to the meditation room opened.

She shrugged and let him be. If he didn't want to talk, she couldn't force him.

Moving on from Kashyyyk's many perils, she turned to researching skyhook design instead. That left her distracted but hardly reassured.

With a slight crackle, Starkiller's voice came over the comlink. "General Kota?"

"He's not here right now," she said.

"Get him," he said. "I . . . I think I've found something."

There was an edge to his voice, something new and strange. She didn't hesitate.

"Kota!" she called over her shoulder. "Kota, get out here!"

The general appeared in an instant. With no wall tapping or hesitation, he burst out of the meditation room and fairly ran into the cockpit. "What is it?"

She pointed at the comlink. He patched in, and Starkiller repeated what he had said before.

"What have you found, exactly?" the general asked him, a concerned look spreading across his face.

"Just an old hut," Starkiller said. "A ruin, really. But it feels familiar." Juno could hear the strain in his voice. "I've been sensing something strange ever since I arrived on Kashyyyk. There's a great darkness in the forest. And—yes, sadness. Something happened here."

Kota spoke with urgent emphasis. "Turn away, boy. Get on with your mission. There are some things you aren't ready to face."

"Why?" Starkiller asked. "What's inside?"

"How should I know? *My* link to the Force has been cut." Kota sank into the copilot's seat, his expression hard. "If you go inside, you'll face whatever's in there alone."

Starkiller offered no response to that. Juno perched on the edge of her seat, waiting for him to say something, anything. Through the hiss of the open comm channel, she thought she could hear him breathing.

"What's he doing?" she asked Kota.

He silenced her with a gesture.

The minutes dragged by, and slowly Juno convinced herself that Starkiller hadn't gone into the hut at all. Despite the fearful yearning she'd heard in his voice, he had heeded Kota's advice and walked on by, and was even now nearing the base of the skyhook. Soon he would call in for advice and her nebulous fears would be dispelled. She would laugh and feel foolish, and everything would be back to normal.

Then Kota stiffened beside her, as though touched by something cold and clammy on the back of the neck. A muscle in his right cheek twitched. He gasped aloud and reached for the control console for support.

He sagged.

"I told you to leave it alone, boy," he said with a sigh.

Juno supposed that *normal* might be something she'd never experience again.

CHAPTER 21

THE APPRENTICE STOOD STARING AT the ruin he'd found, wondering why this one had caught his eye out of the dozen or so he'd stumbled across elsewhere. A decade or two ago this particular patch of the forest had been a clearing, home to a small village, home perhaps to a mixed community of Wookiees and offworlders who wanted to feel the dirt beneath their feet. A dry creekbed snaked through the abandoned settlement, choked now with vines, ferns, and other native plants. The ruins had surrendered to the undergrowth, which was steadily overtaking it, but enough remained to show that the reason for the village's abandonment was not entirely natural.

Burned wood was evidence of fire. Circular, deep burns with a faint spiral pattern were evidence of energy weapons. Both were visible everywhere he looked.

He stepped closer. Thirty seconds ago he had been focused on his mission. Now, confronted by the ruin, he was utterly derailed. Calling Kota hadn't helped. It only made him more curious. *What* would he have to face alone? Had the aging general sensed something through the Force, for all his protestations about being severed from it?

The truncated cone of the largest hut had split on falling. There was a clear entrance through that rent. It looked—his breath caught—it almost looked as though someone had blasted their way into it. Except here the

evidence of energy weapons lacked the regular spirals of
blasterfire. These scars were in straight lines, curving
only slightly toward the end.

Not blasted, then, but sliced . . .

A breeze swept through the overgrown clearing, making something move within the ruined hut. He brought
his lightsaber up but didn't ignite it. The movement
didn't come from one of Kashyyyk's many predatory
species. It was a piece of cloth, fluttering. Leaning forward so his head was in shadow, he saw the remains of
a long tapestry, tangled around an errant plank. There
was a symbol on the tapestry, of a stylized hunting bird,
perhaps, with wings and beak proudly upraised.

A strange feeling shivered through him, as though he
had been touched by someone from another universe.

Unable to stop himself, he stepped into the shadowy
ruin and touched the faded symbol with the fingers of
his left hand. The space within was a mess, full of broken furniture and giant, alien cobwebs. The air was cool
but very, very close. He felt suffocated, claustrophobic.
He turned back to the door as though to flee, and
stopped at the sight of a small blue crystal lying on the
ground at his feet.

Trembling, he knelt to examine it more closely. The
gleaming gem was as large as the knuckle of his little finger and looked like nothing so much as the focusing
crystal of a lightsaber.

His head was swimming with questions and specula-
tions. Why had he been drawn to this place? What had
happened here that it should mean anything to him at
all?

In the act of standing, he was plunged into a vision
more forceful than any he had experienced before.

KASHYYYK WAS BURNING. *The fires were visible from
space, and so were the vast swaths of smoke poisoning*

*the air. The Imperial blockade surrounding the planet
was impervious and relentless. Observers weren't allowed in; refugees weren't allowed out. The only people
moving to and from the surface were stormtroopers.*

And him.

*The shuttle carrying him landed on a cliff overlooking
a deep, blue bay. Battles raged around him as rebel
Wookiees fought with Imperials in AT-STs, not caring
that they were hopelessly outnumbered. Huge forest
forts spread through the canopy like underground tunnels, ferrying resistance fighters and ammunition to the
fringes, where the fighting was fiercest. Energy weapons
struggled to penetrate the centuries-old bark of mature
wroshyr trees, but set fire and flesh instantly alight.*

*The apprentice saw all this as though in a dream. He
was part of the dream, but not a participant in it. Although he tried to speak and turn his head, he could not.
The vision didn't allow him to change anything that had
already happened.*

*Already happened—or yet to come? Was this his des-
tiny, to return to Kashyyyk under his Master's orders
and deal permanently with the Wookiees?*

*With one black-gloved hand he waved for the hatch
to open. The ramp was already extended. Striding heavily onto the planet, he stood with hands on hips and
took in the view firsthand. His black cape fluttered in a
hot, ashen wind.*

*There was something wrong with him. His senses
were muted, filtered somehow, as though he viewed the
world through artificial means. His limbs felt distant,
numbed. And the sound of his breathing was strained,
almost mechanical . . .*

An Imperial officer rushed up to him.

*"Lord Vader," he gasped. "We were ambushed upon
arrival, but I have the situation well in—"*

"I have no interest in your failures, Commander," the

apprentice said in his Master's voice. All around them lay the bodies of Imperial stormtroopers, strewn in pieces across the ground. "I am here on a mission of my own."

Leaving the officer sweating with relief, the apprentice in Darth Vader's garb stalked away.

With each step of those heavy boots, he flinched. Nothing he did could redirect that fateful march. He didn't care if he was seeing the past through his Master's eyes or seeing his own future—one in which he'd been forced to become Darth Vader, through some strange surgical substitution—but he was certain he didn't want to see any more.

His field of vision blurred. A large, spinning ax had come out of nowhere. His left hand came up, deflecting it deep into the ground with the power of the dark side. His right drew and ignited his lightsaber with one rapid motion. Turning, he faced a trio of Wookiee soldiers led by a truly huge member of the alien species, with a snarling visage and light armor over dark brown fur. The creature's roar was almost physically painful, even through the deadening of his senses.

Past or future, his limbs moved with strength and surety, bringing his lightsaber up to slice a second ax in two, then stepping forward to meet the berserker head-on. Two blows saw the warrior in pieces, having laid not a claw on his black armor. The pair of Wookiees bringing up the rear fared no better.

He didn't waste time gloating. As soon as the last body fell, still twitching, to the ground, he was on his way again, away from the cliffs, following unknown clues deeper into the landscape.

The apprentice was swept up in the carnage each time a Wookiee fighting group encountered them, but in between, as "Darth Vader" pressed relentlessly on, he felt like screaming.

When he rounded a bend and saw a village laid out before him beside a thin, trickling stream, the apprentice prayed that he would be ambushed and killed before the vision could play out.

It wasn't to be, and he could only despair as Vader Force-leapt to the first of the wooden platforms that jutted from the bole of a youthful wroshyr tree. The hut the apprentice had entered—surely in the future now—loomed high above, its wooden sides gleaming with resin. Numerous tapestries waved in the breeze, among them one containing the striking bird symbol he had found among the ruins. Wookiees had spotted the intruder to the village and rapidly retracted a series of rope ladders leading to the platform below before Vader could ascend.

A tall, human figure in brown robes appeared on one of the hut's balconies, looking down at Vader. He stood with hands on hips, flanked by menacing Wookiee warriors. Small touches marked him as someone who had lived among the indigenes a long time. His face looked faintly, impossibly familiar.

"Turn back, Dark Lord," he called in a commanding voice. "Whatever you want, you won't find it here."

"You can't disguise yourself from me," Vader replied, "Jedi."

The man stiffened and gestured. Wookiee warriors swung in on ropes and vines from surrounding trees, converging with wild whoops and roars on the lone figure in black below. The apprentice's vision dissolved into an unending stream of violent images as, one after another, each of his attackers fell from the platform with limbs slashed and neck broken. His lightsaber was a crimson blur—and slowly, inevitably, everything he saw was painted horribly red.

When the warriors were spent, he turned his attention to the struts of the hut. Raising one hand, Vader dug deep into the dark side, bending and cracking the ancient wood. It resisted, as strong but not as brittle as metal could be. It twisted and flexed, releasing energy slowly rather than snapping in two.

But that didn't save the people above. The hut tossed like a ship on stormy seas. Wookiees leapt or swung to safety.

"Grab hold of something," the robed man called to them. "Quickly!"

Vader clenched his fist, hard, and the support struts finally cracked. He extended both hands, and the hut shook from side to side. With a sickening sound, the last of its supports gave way and the hut tumbled to the platform below. Wookiees flew bodily in all directions. Splinters and dust filled the air.

Vader didn't flinch as the hut crashed directly in front of him, split open like an overripe fruit.

He didn't move until, out of the thick, dusty haze, he glimpsed a bright blue lightsaber—and its wielder, coming for him like a ghost.

They fought back and forth across the wooden platform, the tall man's reach a match for Vader's but his strength not as profound. Whoever he was, combat was not his strong point. He had an understanding of the ancient Shii-Cho style but barely a smattering of more advanced Makashi. His attacks were simple to deflect; his defenses, relatively easy to penetrate. Vader toyed with him awhile, then pressed him hard against the side of the fallen hut, giving him no more ground to retreat to.

One telekinetic push saw the man flung through the rent in the fallen hut. His lightsaber flew in a different direction. The pommel shattered into a dozen pieces, its blue focusing crystals scattering like jewels.

Vader strode into the hut, where he used the Force to grip the man around his throat and wrench him into *the air. His bright red lightsaber pointed directly at the man's chest.*

Victory.

And yet, on the cutting edge of perception, reason to reconsider.

Vader cocked his armored head.

"I sense someone far more powerful than you nearby. Your Master . . . Where is he?"

The choking Jedi Knight struggled to speak. "The dark side has clouded your mind. You killed my Master years ago."

"Then you will now share his fate."

Vader raised his blade to cut down the Jedi Knight, but before he could swing it the lightsaber suddenly flew from his hand. The Dark Lord wheeled around to attack, his free hand raised to crush whoever dared oppose him.

He hesitated, an uncommon move for Darth Vader—

—and the apprentice felt his mind spin with shock—

—at the sight of a human child standing in the corner of the hut, dirty and bruised by the fall, dressed in clothes bearing Wookiee touches similar to those of the man still hanging in the air behind the Dark Lord. The boy held Darth Vader's lightsaber in both hands. The tip danced, but only slightly.

"Run!" choked the Jedi. "Run now! Don't look back!"

"Ah," said Vader with dawning understanding. "A son."

Turning back to the father, he clenched his left fist. The awful sound of bone cracking was clearly audible— as was the boy's sudden gasp of horror.

Vader turned back to the child, and froze.

The tableau stayed that way for a small infinity: father dying, child watching, murderer standing patiently between them, as though waiting for fate's dice to fall.

Then three stormtroopers burst into the hut, led by an Imperial officer. Drawn by sounds of combat in the village, or perhaps just shadowing their Dark Lord's path across the forest world, they ran in with weapons drawn and broke the moment forever.

"My lord?" the officer started to ask, confused.

He got no farther. With a flick of his fingers, Vader had his lightsaber back in his hand. The officer and troopers backed away as their Master approached. One of them sensed the imminence of their deaths and fired his blaster ineffectually. The bolt ricocheted off the crimson blade into the wall of the hut, leaving a black burn.

In a second, it was over.

The boy watched, terrified, as the man covered from head to foot in black armor killed his own allies. His every move was brutal but at the same time possessing a deadly elegance, like the stalking moves of a wild walluga. Each stab and slash found its mark.

He had never seen anything so beautiful—or so horrible.

When it was done, the man in black loomed over him and grabbed him by the arm. Thinking the moment of his death had come, the boy didn't resist.

"Come with me." The deep, hollow words were worse than blows. "More will be here soon."

As he was wrenched from the hut, the boy twisted his head to snatch one last glimpse of his home. Tipped over it might have been, broken and full of still-smoking bodies, but all the boy saw was the body of the dead Jedi Knight on the floor. One hand lay outstretched with fingers curled, as though clutching for something that was no longer there . . .

THE APPRENTICE BLINKED. HE WAS standing, frozen, staring at the very spot where the bodies had once lain.

There was no sign of them now, not even a bone. Scavengers must have carried them off, or they had been thrown free when the platform the hut had fallen onto had in turn collapsed. There was only the crystal, which had somehow come to be folded tightly in his hand. It looked just like one of those from the fallen Jedi Knight's lightsaber, which the boy might have liked to play with when he was younger, for comfort.

His face twisted into a snarl. *Looked just like . . . might have . . .* He was trying to validate the vision, when it was nothing really but a dream. A fantasy. The truth was that he had been bothered by something ever since he had arrived on Kashyyyk—an irrational feeling that something was wrong, which probably related more to his alliance with Kota than anything to do with his own past. Darth Vader had raised him; he didn't need to imagine parents or a home to give himself meaning. He was just fabricating a story out of thin air.

But he had seen the skyhook in one of his near-death visions—a bright line extending high up into the sky—and he realized now that the figure standing in front of the skyhook had been none other than the girl he had met in the lodge. If his visions contained *some* truth, why not this one, too?

And the face of the Jedi Knight was the very same one he had seen while dueling Kota . . .

Time slowed. The air felt as thick as honey. He strained against it, fearing that he was about to succumb to another hallucination, but he remained in control of his limbs. A shadow fell over the hut, as though a cloud had blocked the sun. He shivered and raised his hands to hug himself.

Cold metal touched his skin. He looked down in horror at what had become of his fingers. They were artificial claws, like the hands of a surgical droid, with blades sharp enough to cut bone. His wrists and forearms were part flesh, part machine. The unnatural amalgamation continued up to his shoulders and disappeared under a high, metal collar that protected his neck. What skin was visible on his wrists was blistered and scarred, as though burned many times over by ferociously high heat.

More than just his hands and arms had changed. His clothes were different, too. Instead of the new uniform Darth Vader had given him, he now wore a ribbed vest of flexible armor plates and a series of leather belts around his waist. From the belts hung a collection of grisly trophies—lightsabers most prominent among them. Under the tight black garments, his body felt strange, more mechanical than alive.

With shaking hands, he raised his metal fingers to touch his face. Metal blades touched armor with a piercing squeak. His face was hidden behind a mask, as deathless and horrible as his Master's. His breathing was loud in his ears.

He had become someone's worst nightmare.

A golden glow flickered through the honeyish air. He turned his masked head to face it, and made out a dark silhouette walking toward him. His clawed right hand reached for his lightsaber, which he selected automatically from the many at his waist. It snapped on, casting a bloody red glow through the hut.

By that light, a man in Jedi robes was revealed, tall and straight-backed. The face beneath the hood was smooth-skinned and calm. His eyes gleamed, containing sorrow and pity. Familiar and yet unfamiliar, known and yet utterly unknown . . .

The apprentice hissed a low, dangerous sound through his mask's vocoder and crouched like a poised snake, master of Juyo, the most vicious form of lightsaber combat known in the galaxy.

The Jedi drew his own lightsaber—a bright sky blue—

and adopted a classic Soresu opening stance, with left arm upraised, palm-down, running parallel to the lightsaber in his right. With his left foot forward he balanced perfectly on his right, ready to defend himself against any attack.

The apprentice didn't keep him waiting. He didn't employ any wild acrobatics or fancy Force moves. He simply lunged, using his whole body as a weapon, his balance and dexterity utterly focused. The dark side thrilled through him, harmonizing perfectly with the anger and hate in his heart. The Jedi was going to die, one way or another. It might as well be now.

Blue blocked red in a spray of energy. The apprentice struck again, higher this time, a deceptively loose blow that hid deadly subtleties beneath its wide swing. The Jedi blocked it, too; just. Soresu was a defensive fighting style well suited to the close confines of the hut, but it wouldn't last forever against the malignant grace of Juyo.

The Jedi came in hard and fast before the apprentice could rally another attack. He cared little if the Jedi hit him, so long as damage was minimal. Close hits left flesh sizzling and armor smoking. The energy he saved on wild dodges he spent on tearing jagged planks from the walls and throwing them at the Jedi's head. All were deflected, but it distracted the man, robbed his attack of some of its momentum. When he paused, the apprentice sent a surge of Sith lightning under his guard.

The Jedi was caught in the flickering storm. His face twisted into a pained grimace. Then he brought his right arm down and placed the blade of his lightsaber directly in the lightning's path. The energy was absorbed by the blade, then bent back upon itself in a superconducting loop, striking its source with more energy than it had originally possessed. The apprentice stiffened as pain coursed up his hands and arms. The agony was unbearable—but bear it he did. His skin melted and warped all over his body, and he gagged on the stink of his own burning flesh. The pain and revulsion only fed the dark side, so the faster the lightning came back to him, the harder and stronger it flowed from him.

The loop couldn't last forever. With a blinding blue flash he and the Jedi were blown far apart, crashing with arms outstretched into the walls of the hut and dropping to the floor. Their lightsabers skittered away in opposite directions, dead.

Flat on his back, the apprentice wheezed through his mask like an asthmatic Gand, only gradually regaining sensation in his arms and legs. His muscles twitched spastically when he tried to move. Acrid steam poured from his mask's narrow eye slits. Fearing that his Jedi opponent might be on his feet before him, he called on all the power of the Force to lift himself bodily into the air. Hanging suspended like a doll, with his feet some centimeters off the ground, he blinked his searing eyes until he could see again.

The Jedi was faring no better. He, too, was upright, but only just. He, too, had lost his lightsaber and not yet managed to reclaim it. The apprentice leered behind his mask. He had several other lightsabers to choose from, belonging to all the Jedi Knights he had killed. All he had to do was select one at random and strike.

Instead he reached out with his left hand and, as his dark Master had done to the first Jedi killed on this spot, long ago, gripped his opponent about the throat with the Force. Still smoking from the lightning attack, the young man jerked abruptly into the air.

They faced each other across the ruined hut, neither touching the ground.

"Kill me," gasped the Jedi, "and you destroy yourself."

The apprentice laughed gloatingly, a hideous sound

that bore little relationship to anything made by a human throat. Summoning his lightsaber, he activated it and threw it at the stricken Jedi. The blade went through the Jedi's right shoulder and deactivated when the pommel hit flesh. The Jedi arched his back but didn't cry out. Savoring the moment, the apprentice unhitched one of the other lightsaber hilts from his belt, ignited it, too, and impaled the Jedi again. Over and over he stabbed the Jedi Knight until there were no more hilts at his belt and the ground beneath his victim was stained deep red.

Still the Jedi lived. A flicker of annoyance spoiled the moment, but then he remembered that there was one more lightsaber he hadn't used: the Jedi's own. Snatching it to him, the apprentice ignited the blade, drew his arm back, and stabbed the Jedi Knight through the heart.

That did the trick. The body dropped to the ground, inert, and the apprentice allowed himself to stand properly on the soil. The dark side throbbed through him. He was the living embodiment of power.

Tipping his masked head back, he crowed in triumph like a feral wolf cat.

"I never wanted this for you," whispered a hollow voice out of the shadows.

He spun, lightsaber back in his hand and lit in less time than it took to think about it. Someone else stood in the hut: a man with long dark hair and a Wookiee sash down his front. He looked at the body of the Jedi Knight on the ground, grief and loss in his eyes.

The apprentice went to strike him down, but stopped, recognizing him as the man from two visions: the father of the boy who had been taken and the man he had glimpsed over Nar Shaddaa.

"I never wanted any of this for you," the man said. "I'm sorry, Galen."

Rooted to the spot, the apprentice stared as the Jedi

Knight turned to walk back into the shadows. Vision or reality? Truth or fantasy? His mind felt as though it were turning as fast as a pulsar.

"Father, wait!" The voice burst out of him, unfiltered by hideous deformities or the strictures of the mask. Suddenly he was the boy again, whole but alone, standing abandoned in the bloody hut. "Father, no!"

The Jedi Knight walked on without pause and vanished into the shadows.

Collapsing to his knees, the apprentice lowered his head and screamed.

CHAPTER 22

A BEDRAGGLED FIGURE EMERGED FROM the ruined hut, eyes wild and jaw set. With determination, he set off along the dry creekbed, following the directions he had been given in another age, another life. Empty of thought, he let duty sweep him forward. Duty to his Master, to Juno, to Kota, to the Wookiees . . .

What duty he owed himself, he didn't know. He hadn't realized that there had even been a *him* to think of outside his relationship with Darth Vader. He had imagined himself simply *made,* somehow, one of his Master's stranger biological experiments, with no parents and no home but the one he remembered. What if the visions he had endured were real and he *had* had a family, here on Kashyyyk? How did that affect his place in Vader's schemes? Did it change everything, or nothing?

Juno called on the comlink to ask him if he was all right. He said he was. She asked if he was sure. He said he was. She sounded hurt by his terseness, but he couldn't help that. He was so full of emotion—confusion and doubt, and dismal certainty and hope as well—that he couldn't cope with her feelings on top of it. He was trying his best not to feel at all.

Galen?

He had a job to do.

As he ran through the undergrowth, putting the depthless shadows of the hut behind him, he repeatedly touched his hands, reassured as he never had been before by the feel of skin on skin.

THE MOORINGS WERE LARGER EVEN than he had guessed from the brief plans displayed by the astromech droid. Its mistress's instructions had been simple: destroy the moorings and the skyhook would be ruined. That sounded deceptively easy, given the amount of fortification and security in place.

Simplicity suited him, however. He didn't want to think, to have to agonize over motives and methods. He just wanted to act. With none of the joy he had felt while assaulting the lodge and with none of the challenge offered by the black Imperial Guards on Bespin, he plowed through the faceless stormtroopers as a wampa would stride through snow. Sith lightning crackled; bodies broke under his irresistible telekinesis; his mind influenced the decisions of officers, who ordered their underlings to attack one another in droves. None could stand up to him and survive.

When he reached the base of the skyhook, he was momentarily given pause. How to bring about the ruin of six constructs several stories high? Their super-strong materials were designed to handle the stresses of holding the massive station directly above, against all the laws of physics. How would he overcome their resistance?

The answer, as always, lay in the Force. The Force was beyond physics. The Force could not be resisted, when wielded by confident hands. The Force would always be sufficient.

Turning his back on the body-strewn battlefield, he put both hands on the base of the nearest mooring. Closing his eyes and his mind to all forms of distraction, he imagined himself at one with the metal, permacrete, and stone. He felt the mooring's strengths and its weaknesses. He *resonated* with it, until it was hard to tell where his hands stopped and the mooring began.

When he could achieve no greater focus, he reached out for the dark side and let it guide him.

Energy came like a dam bursting, as wild as every predator on Kashyyyk combined but as pure as a laser. He tilted his head back and relished the wonder and terror of what he had brought into being. This was a power far greater than Sith lightning, designed for one single task. He lost himself utterly in that task. He became *destruction*.

The mooring shook. Its more delicate components—nanowires, sensitive self-regulating systems, microscopic hydraulic channels—fused almost immediately. Once the complex processes maintaining its stability were disrupted, a chain reaction began that could not be stopped. Pressures mounted in areas close to exceeding their maximum load; hairline cracks formed and spread; a deep vibration sprang up that could not be dampened. Even if left to its own devices, the mooring would shake itself to pieces in minutes.

The apprentice maintained his assault until hairline cracks became gaping rents and the vibration shook the world, howling material agony over the renewed firing of blaster cannons. When the first shower of boiling dust and pebble-sized fragments rained down on him, he decided it was time to step back and take stock—and to prevent some hapless stormtrooper creeping up on him and shooting him in the back.

He opened his eyes and looked up. The mooring was barely recognizable as the same structure. Electrical discharges danced across its conducting surfaces. Ultrastressed permacrete flowed like treacle. Larger fragments began to fall and he batted them away with the Force, feeling no more drained by his exertion than he would have from a light run. He almost smiled at his accomplishment, but one stark fact sobered him to the core.

One down. Five to go.

The Imperials were rallying. They needed to be reminded of who they were dealing with. While crossing to the next mooring in line, he detonated fuel tanks and exploded ammunition stores. AT-STs cracked open like seedpods and burst into short-lived flame. He reached his target without encountering serious resistance and brought it down as he had the first.

By now the Imperials on the ground were calling for reinforcements from above. A trio of TIE fighters shrieked down through Kashyyyk's atmosphere, stitching the blackened permacrete with needles of fire. He laughed mirthlessly. They considered that a *solution*?

With a well-timed nudge on the lead TIE fighter's port solar gather panel, he sent it tumbling into the permacrete, where it exploded instantly. The impact shook the ground beneath his feet and sent cracks spreading across its face.

That gave him an idea. When the two remaining TIEs came around for another pass, he sent them both into the third and fifth moorings. The fourth took so much collateral damage that it fared almost as badly as its siblings.

Only one mooring remained.

As he turned to it, he became aware of the clanking of an AT-ST coming from behind him. He turned just in time to deflect a barrage of precision weapons fire from the nose of a walker that was sprinting at him as fast as its two mechanical legs could run. A flurry of concussion grenades followed.

He detonated them all before they could arrive and repulsed the furious blossoming of hot gases in a sphere around him.

The AT-ST didn't take the hint. It was moving fast,

bearing down with its flat footpads as though trying to physically trample him. Maybe it was. The walker had registration markings identifying it as belonging to the commander of the Imperial ground forces.

Captain Sturn had come to finish the job at which his underlings had failed so miserably.

The apprentice dodged the stamping feet as they went by and zapped the rear of the walker with lightning. Nothing happened. Sturn's walker obviously possessed a layer of shielding above and beyond that provided to his grunts. The AT-ST's armaments also set it apart from the others, including a long-barreled hunting cannon and what appeared to be a net launcher on its left flank.

Sturn brought the walker about. The apprentice reached out to twist the man's mind, but found it too opaque with anger and resentment; not fear, though. Sturn wasn't the sort of man who would be frightened of one person. He was convinced of his own invincibility, certain that there was no resistance he couldn't quash. The apprentice had met men like him before, many times. The AT-ST's extra weaponry confirmed it. He imagined Sturn hunting Wookiees for sport, when he wasn't persecuting his junior officers for fun and plotting the betrayal of his superiors. The apprentice had dispatched many such men in the service of his Master.

The apprentice smiled with no trace of humor. Normally he liked nothing better than putting beings in their place, but this was just irritating.

Sturn's walker jogged ponderously toward him. He considered his options. It would be a simple matter to crush the walker as he would a faulty comlink, collapsing the casing and instantly killing the man within. He could play with the walker as he had played with the two by the lodge and blow it up from within. He could even use it as a battering ram to destroy the last mooring, thereby killing two spade-headed smookas with one swipe. The grim irony in that appealed to him.

He deflected another round of cannon fire into the mooring and noticed only then that the thick cable leading up to the skyhook station was visibly vibrating. Strange surges rushed up and down its length as though it had been plucked by a giant hand. He shielded his eyes against the glare of the sun and looked upward. The skyhook was faintly visible, as was a cloud of debris coming down from above. Small specks quickly resolved into objects as big as boulders. They were growing rapidly in size.

He performed a quick mental calculation. The debris would arrive about the same time as Sturn's walker. Ideal.

He reached out and crumpled the walker's cannon and grenade launchers. For a moment, the only sounds came from his lightsaber and the heavy tread of the AT-ST.

He straightened. Through the command viewport, he saw a man with a red face wearing what looked like Wookiee fur trim on his uniform. The captain's mouth was open, bellowing orders at his hapless gunner. The apprentice couldn't hear the words, but he could imagine.

The walker reared up one leg to stamp him into the ground.

At that moment the debris hit with all the force of a hundred shooting stars, striking everything around the base of the skyhook—the sixth mooring included—and crushing the walker into scrap metal. Debris went everywhere. The noise was unimaginable. The apprentice didn't flinch or move in the slightest as rubble rain impacted about him. He only watched, with satisfaction, as the skyhook base ripped free of the planet and recoiled like a whip into the upper atmosphere. The station exploded shortly thereafter, briefly outshining the sun, even through the dust and smoke of his handiwork.

The rain of rubble ceased. He remained exactly where he was, hypnotized by the slowly fading star in the sky, until the *Rogue Shadow* swooped down directly in front of him, repulsors whining to hold itself just above the ground.

He blinked, realizing only then that Juno was trying to talk to him.

"I *said*, it's done. Hop aboard. Let's get out of here."

He moved as though in another vision, stepping lightly up onto the open ramp but feeling like he weighed a thousand tons.

With a piercing whine, the cloaked ship angled up from the cratered ground and made for free space.

CHAPTER 23

PROXY FUSSED OVER STARKILLER AS never before, brushing ash and dust from his clothes with vigorous flicking motions of his slim metal hands. Maybe the droid had never been separated so long from his master before; Juno didn't know, and she didn't care to ask. The look on Starkiller's face was thunderous.

"Who was she?" he said to Kota, who had moved back to the jump seat, freeing up the copilot's spot for him.

"Princess Leia Organa. Her father is Bail Organa, my contact in the Senate."

"I want to talk to him."

The general passed a hand across his face, as though resting his eyes. "You can't."

Starkiller's fury found the outlet it had been looking for. "I just risked my life rescuing his daughter from a planet overrun by stormtroopers—"

"Don't, boy." Kota raised one weary hand as Starkiller loomed over him. "You can't talk to Bail because I can't find him. He's gone missing."

"What?" Starkiller's frustration redoubled. "When?"

"I haven't been able to contact him since we left Bespin. The last time I saw him was on Nar Shaddaa some weeks after—after I fell. He found me, and tried to recruit me then to rescue Leia. I refused, of course." He indicated his eyes as though that explained everything.

"When I refused, he sent me to Cloud City. I haven't seen or heard from him since."

Kota turned away, shrunken and inward looking, as though regretting his decision. In another time, Juno supposed, Kota wouldn't have hesitated an instant. He would have happily marched into a den of Imperials and dealt them the rough justice they had administered to his own friends. But what *could* he have done now, one blind old man against thousands of able-bodied, well-armed soldiers?

She stayed carefully out of it, and not just to avoid the argument. Her heart was stinging from its own wounds, and she remained unsure exactly which side of the fence she stood on where the two men were concerned.

Starkiller backed down without apologizing. They seemed to find that an acceptable resolution. Kota stayed in the jump seat, chin tilted resolutely downward, while Starkiller retreated to the meditation chamber. After he had gone, the air smelled of sulfur and smoke.

Juno looked down at the controls. He hadn't given her a heading. She trimmed the *Rogue Shadow*'s trajectory automatically—and PROXY mirrored her every move in the seat beside her, an act she still found profoundly disturbing. Knowing better now, however—that the droid couldn't help it, that this was as much a part of his being as breathing was for her—she didn't ask him to stop.

"How do you cope with him when he's like this?" she asked the droid.

PROXY didn't need to ask who she was talking about. "I usually fight him. That seems to help. Would you like me to—"

"No, PROXY. Stay there. I think it's time someone tried a different tack."

Leaving the ship in Kota's and the droid's unlikely hands, she climbed out of her seat and headed aft.

*   *   *

THE MEDITATION ROOM WAS DARKER than it seemed through the security slice. Its air was cooler, somehow, and the sound of the ship's hyperdrive came as though from thousands of kilometers away. Despite its spareness, there was a calmness to the angular space that struck her as soon as she entered. The chamber felt poised between moments, possessing a kind of criticality that she supposed someone of Starkiller's former occupation would need to acquire. The ability to remain calm while hunting Jedi didn't come easily, she was sure. And the cost . . .

"Is there a problem, Juno?" He was kneeling in the center of the chamber with his hands hanging loosely in front of him. On the ground before him lay the hilt of his deactivated lightsaber, the one he had used since their escape from the *Empirical*. Next to it lay a small blue crystal. His back was slightly to her, so she couldn't tell if his eyes were open.

"I don't know," she said. "You tell me."

"What's that supposed to mean?"

She decided to just come out and say it. "Are you all right? After what happened on Kashyyyk—"

"I'm not wearing out," he said. "The moorings were tough, but I feel stronger than ever now. It gets easier, I think, the harder you try. The Force is stronger than anything we can imagine. We're the ones who limit it, not the other way around."

He half turned to look at her, and she was prepared to let him talk about that, if he wanted to. He had never spoken to her of the Force before; a life she had never seen flickered in his eyes when he did. But that was all he said, and when she could think of nothing to offer in return, his head drifted back around to face the floor and she had lost him again.

"What about what's happened to us apart from that?

I turned my back on the navy and you abandoned your Master. We're going through the same thing. We can help each other."

"Nobody can help me."

"I don't think you really mean that. I just think you're afraid to let me try."

"Is that really what you think?" He didn't look up, but she noted a stiffening of his neck muscles. "After all those stormtroopers I killed, I'm afraid of *you*?"

"It wasn't just stormtroopers," she said with more heat than she had intended.

He glanced at her again. "Yes, and Captain Sturn."

"Don't forget the pilots of the TIE fighters," she said. "One of them was a kid I used to fly with."

Starkiller looked up at that, but said nothing.

"It's a lot easier to fight the Empire when it's faceless," she said, "when the people whose lives are ending are hidden behind stormtrooper helmets or durasteel hulls. But when they're people we knew, people like we used to be . . ." She shrugged. "How much harder is it going to get?"

He stared at her until gooseflesh broke out all down her back.

"Are you having second thoughts?" he asked.

"No," she said. "I—"

I just want you to talk to me.

She couldn't say that.

"It doesn't matter."

She turned on her heel to leave. Maybe PROXY was the only one who would ever reach him, on the point of a glowing lightsaber.

"Juno," he said, stopping her in the doorway. "I'm sorry about your friend."

She took a deep breath. "That's okay. He wasn't really a friend and it wasn't anything personal. Youngster was just in the wrong place at the wrong time."

"And on the wrong side," he added.

"Yes, that, too." She almost added, *You don't need to remind me,* but left it unsaid, sensing that he was probing her, perhaps testing her, somehow.

"I'm exhausted," she said—thinking again, *Why me?*—and went back to work.

STARKILLER REAPPEARED A SHORT TIME later, looking tidier and at least physically refreshed after his short time-out.

"Where are we going?" he asked Juno.

"Nowhere," she said.

Kota looked up with blind eyes. "When I last saw Bail Organa, he said he would find someone to help him if I wouldn't: Master Shaak Ti was his choice. I warned him it would be too dangerous, but the fool went after her anyway, alone. There was nothing I could do to stop him." The old man's jaw jutted out as though daring anyone to disagree. "I've checked with Ylenic It'kla, his assistant on Alderaan. Bail vanished as soon as he landed on—"

"Felucia," said Starkiller, nodding.

Kota cocked his head as though hearing a very faint, distant sound.

A dense silence fell. Starkiller looked up at the same time as Juno, realizing too late what he had said. Would Kota realize? Juno watched in light-headed panic as Starkiller's hand crept toward the hilt at his waist.

"The Force is strong in you, boy," said Kota softly, "for you to be able to sense my thoughts."

Juno let some of the tension drain from her.

"You're just easy to read, old man," Starkiller said.

"Then I suppose you know that Felucia is a dangerous place."

Starkiller dismissed that concern. "I can handle it."

Kota leaned closer. "Don't be overconfident, boy.

Felucia is a world finely balanced between the light and dark sides of the Force. Shaak Ti was the only thing keeping it from being consumed by darkness. If anything's happened to her, your experience in the hut will seem like a bad dream in comparison."

Starkiller pulled back. "How did you know—?"

"You're easy to read, too." Kota's smile was tight-lipped.

"Felucia it is," said Juno to break the tension.

"No." Starkiller put his hand on her shoulder before she could turn back to the controls. "You go get some rest. PROXY and I will get us the remainder of the way. I'll wake you when we're close."

She looked up at him and nodded. He had thought of her unprompted; that was encouraging. "All right. But the slightest problem—"

"Don't worry. They'll hear us hollering in Coruscant. Go."

He took her space at the controls. "Now, PROXY, here's your chance to remind me how astronavigation works."

"I fear, master, that it would take far too long to supplement your primary program with the algorithms required . . ."

Smiling to herself, she put the cockpit behind her and went to get some rest.

CHAPTER 24

SHE DREAMED INTENSELY AND POWERFULLY that she was already back on Felucia, watching an exceedingly fragile flower unfold. Bright red petals hid an intensely black heart. When she leaned close to study it, she found it to be crawling with tiny, many-legged insects.

Then she was in orbit, watching a skyhook cable snapping upward from its severed base. A large chunk of Felucia's crust came with it, like the plug from a bath. The planet began to deflate, darkening as it shrank until it became Callos under its pall of smoke. She stared in horror, knowing that she was unable to put the plug back in, no matter how much she might want to.

Then her father was shouting at her, telling her that she had shamed the family and the Empire. When she tried to tell him—as she never had in life—that he was the one who had been wrong all along, about Palpatine and his murderous regime, his hook-nosed visage changed into that of the Emperor himself, who snarled at her and repeated the words her father had used.

Then she realized that neither the Emperor nor her father was the true face of the being in front of her. It was PROXY, playing a trick on her. She plucked at the illusion, trying to unravel it, but all she revealed beneath was Starkiller, smiling benignly.

Who are you? she asked him. *What's your real name?*

He smiled wider and said, *Your gratitude is wasted on me.*

She woke in a cold sweat, feeling as though she had been dunked in one of Raxus Prime's poisoned puddles, and knew that she would be able to get no more sleep.

CHAPTER 25

JUNO CAME FORWARD JUST BEFORE the apprentice sent PROXY back to get her. He had checked on her earlier and found her sleeping soundly, but she looked as though she hadn't taken much rest from it. She looked much like he felt, in fact: profoundly strained by recent events, but putting on as good a face as possible.

I'm exhausted, she had said. He had been struck on hearing those words that she might mean more than just needing sleep. What if the emotional strain of serving with him proved too much? His mission was far more important than her conflict over betraying the Empire, but in order to meet his Master's goal—and thereby successfully challenge the Emperor—he would need her help. While dealing with his own problems, he would have to find ways to lighten her load.

Kota was next to no help. The old man seemed so wrapped up in his own problems, he barely noticed anyone else. When Juno joined them, he just scratched his bristly chin and settled deeper into his seat.

They made a motley crew, the three of them. Only PROXY seemed happy in himself and with his own goals. The apprentice wished he could be so clearly defined.

All my life I've thought of myself solely as Darth Vader's apprentice. Now I find I might have had a past before that—a father, a name, a history. Who was this

Galen? What were his dreams, his hopes, his fears? What made him laugh? What made him cry?

It seemed inconceivable that he could have forgotten something as traumatic as the death of his father, but he knew that intense trauma could cause partial or complete amnesia. He couldn't therefore rule anything out.

And the question remained: did it matter? Whoever he had once been, that being was forgotten, and his purpose now was unchanged. He was his Master's apprentice; they would be victorious; and Juno would learn, in the end, that she had not betrayed the Empire after all. *If only,* he thought, *I could tell her now . . .*

He got up to let her into the seat, then leaned over PROXY as she checked the course the two of them had laid in.

"Not bad," she said, making only a couple of small corrections. "We're not going to crash into anything, anyway."

"Thank you, Captain Eclipse." PROXY's insides whirred with pride. "I estimate that we will arrive in one standard minute."

"Do you want us to put down anywhere in particular?" she asked the apprentice. "It's a big planet."

"Every Senatorial shuttle broadcasts a unique transponder signal," he said, thinking of the many missions he had flown for his Master, weeding out political enemies. "Search for Senator Organa's signal; that will tell us where to land."

Hyperspace gave way to realspace through the forward viewport. Felucia hung directly ahead, as swollen with life and as green as the apprentice remembered it. He studied it closely, seeking any sign of the "imbalance" Kota had warned him of. He wasn't afraid of the dark side. If anything, he would feel more comfortable on a world in which the proper dynamic between light and dark had been restored. Shaak Ti's death should have had a profound effect on the world and its inhabitants.

"Searching for the transponder," said Juno. "Shouldn't take long. Felucia's as quiet as—ah, yes. There it is. You were right."

Juno moved the *Rogue Shadow* in a fast orbit through the skies of Felucia, triangulating on Bail Organa's signal. The transport had landed very close to where she and the apprentice had put down the first time, although neither of them mentioned that fact in front of Kota. The apprentice stayed in position as the ship descended along a carefully controlled flight path. The atmosphere roiled around them, as thick with pollen and airborne life-forms as before. Clouds of bacteria swarmed in the air, coating the forward view with a faint patina of green. He hadn't noticed that last time and hoped it wouldn't affect hull integrity.

"I'm picking up signs of a large Imperial presence on the ground," Juno said as they descended. "They're the least of your worries, I suspect."

Juno put them down on another sturdy mushroom cap, more confidently than she had on her first try. Organa's transport was parked on the far side, its hatches open, empty of life according to the *Rogue Shadow*'s sensors. During the hyperspace jump the apprentice had accessed records of Bail Organa, Imperial Senator and Prince of Alderaan, and been struck by a strange familiarity about the man's face. Dark-haired and tall, with a gray-flecked goatee and a strong, thoughtful stare, he had definitely crossed the apprentice's path before—but where? Not on one of his many missions for Darth Vader; of that he was certain. Hopefully it wouldn't compromise his mission, if they had encountered each other in his secret past . . .

"Want to come, General?" he asked the old man.

"What use would I be to you out there?" Kota retorted. "You'll be better off without me slowing you down."

"Whatever you say." The apprentice strode down the ramp.

"Wait." Juno followed, running in her haste to catch him.

He turned, thinking that he had forgotten something, but she took his arm and led him off the ramp, toward the empty transport.

"Let's make sure he's not still in there, dead, and our trip wasn't for nothing," she said, "before you go gallivanting off into the jungle."

Puzzled at something in her tone, he let himself be led away from the *Rogue Shadow*. The transport was a small one, large enough for five people with a small but efficient hyperdrive, impeccably maintained. Two crests adorned its sides: those of the Organa family and of Alderaan, both of which the Senator represented. It didn't appear to have been interfered with, except by a small colony of flying insects that had made the tiny but opulent passenger quarters its home.

The shuttle was indeed empty. The apprentice turned to Juno to state the obvious, but she had reached past him to activate the air lock controls. The door slid shut, sealing them inside with the swarm of disconcerted insects. Before he could say anything, she put a finger to her lips and switched off both their comlinks.

"There," she said, stepping back and wiping her hands nervously on her pants. Those and her boots were the only things she'd retained of her former uniform. "Now we can talk in private."

"What's this about?" he asked, feeling the beginning of nervousness. The walls of the tiny air lock in which they were standing suddenly seemed entirely too close.

She avoided his gaze and indicated the shuttle's passenger hold. "I guess Organa made it this far."

"Certainly looks that way," he said, increasingly puzzled.

"Where will you start looking for him?"

"Where I first confronted Shaak Ti. If he followed her trail that far, he might still be nearby."

Her blue eyes met his, then danced away. "Does it disturb you to return here after—after last time?"

"No," he said, exhaling through his nose. "If I let it affect me, Master Kota will sense it."

"Exactly." Her hand reached out and gripped his upper arm. Suddenly her full attention was on him. "That's what worries me. It's dangerous having him with us. If he discovers who you are—who you were—he'll never forgive us."

A worm turned in his stomach. "We've got nothing to feel guilty about."

"I know, but—"

"Don't worry, Juno. Really." He put a hand on hers and awkwardly squeezed it. Her skin was soft. He was very conscious of the heady smell of her in the close confines. He wanted nothing more than to reassure her, but suspected words wouldn't be enough. "If Kota senses who I am, I won't give him the chance to tell anyone else."

That didn't have the effect he had intended. She pulled away and turned to face the exit. "That's what I'm afraid of," she said, her hand reaching for the air lock control.

Light and air rushed in as the door whooshed open. He blinked at the sudden transition and at the passing of the moment that had existed so briefly between them. Something had been communicated that he didn't quite understand. Although he had tried, he had failed to give her what she needed from him. Reassurance, certainly, was part of it; evidence of his true allegiance as well, perhaps. He struggled for words to bring her back, but could only watch her walk back to the ship.

"PROXY," she called through her comlink, peering into a green-slimed intake vent, "come out here and help me scrape some of this gunk off the ship."

The apprentice took the hint. This was a problem he would have to deal with later, once he had Bail Organa safely in hand—at which point his mission would become even more complex and dangerous. Rescuing a blind old man was one thing; proving his worth to a fellow teenager—even one with Leia Organa's obvious abilities—was only marginally more difficult. Bail Organa, on the other hand, had survived Palpatine's usurping of the Senate and the Jedi Purge; he would surely be adept at detecting and rooting out spies. Once Organa was on his side, the apprentice would well and truly be behind enemy lines, liable to be uncovered as both a traitor to the rebel cause and to the Empire if he was uncovered by either faction. His skills were not inconsiderable now, and growing stronger with every mission, but this would test his every ability to the limit.

Somehow, though, Juno worried him much more. His Master had trained him extensively in the arts of violence and deception. Women were a topic on which he knew nothing at all.

With one last look at her, working diligently to ensure the well-being of her mechanical charge, he reactivated his comlink and loped off into the fetid jungle.

IT TOOK HIM NO TIME at all to attune his senses to the vast and tangled life-fields of the fecund, overrun world. The balance had indeed shifted profoundly toward the dark side since his last visit. He found the world's new ambience familiar but not comfortable, and felt that he was recognized but not welcome. The latter surprised him and occupied his mind even as he defended himself against every able-bodied predator the world had to send against him.

So it seemed, anyway. Without Shaak Ti keeping their innate Force sensitivity in check, the native Felucian species fought him every step of the way. The jungle was cloaked with deep shadows and stank of rot. Bulbous plants exploded as he approached, spraying him with acidic mist. Gnarled, muscular vines tangled in his ankles or around his throat while poisonous leeches affixed themselves to his boots every time he stepped in a puddle. Pools of quicksand sucked at him with more than a passing semblance of life. Large, flying rays with scissoring, jagged jaws swooped through the canopy, snapping at his head, and horribly animate fungal growths smacked thick, meaty lips at him as he passed.

Once, when he took shelter from a flying ripper under a tree, the tree itself tried to kill him. With a loud crack, it separated from its root system and toppled down over him; it would have crushed him to the ground had he not jumped aside in time. Startled and bemused, he had stared as an entirely new root system squirmed through holes in the bark, obviously intending to feed on the creature it thought it had imprisoned under its weight. Myriad scavengers, from the invisibly small to the thunderously large, converged on the sound, hoping to take advantage of the tree's intended meal.

The apprentice put as much distance as possible between himself and what was bound to become a vicious and highly competitive scene.

He had yet to encounter any of the intelligent natives, but he assumed they would be no less hostile than every other life-form on the planet. Although he, too, was a warrior of the dark side, they owed him no allegiance. The very notion of allegiance was foreign to the dark side. The great happy family the Jedi had believed in was a lie, or at the very least a fallacy. Nature was a bloody business; harmony was not the dominant state. Truces could form, but they were always temporary. The Sith understood that. His Master understood that. The relationship between Master and apprentice was always a tense one—and from that tension sprang great power.

Shaak Ti had understood that, too. *The Sith always betray one another,* she had said, just as every life-form betrayed every other life-form, if left to their natural inclination. Peace and harmony were aberrations imposed from the outside, to be resisted at every juncture.

A recon party of stormtroopers stumbled across him while converging on the *Rogue Shadow*'s landing site. One of them must have noted its descent by eye, since the cloak blocked all other electromagnetic sensors. He warned Juno and suggested she move the ship to another location. She acknowledged his suggestion, and he went back to eliminating the Imperials he had found. They clashed on the side of a lake of quicksand, into which the apprentice telekinetically pushed several of his assailants. They went down fast thanks to their heavy armor. Their cries for help sounded loud over their companions' comlinks until their air supply finally ran out. The clamor of blasters and lightsaber drew the attention of more scavengers and even prompted a rancor to roar a short distance away.

He cocked his head, listening. Ignoring the last of the stormtroopers, who backed into the jungle frantically calling for reinforcements, the apprentice paid close attention to a feeling in his gut—that something was brewing. A trap, possibly. The Felucians rode rancors. If the mighty beasts had noted the disturbance, the chances were that their masters had, too.

He didn't move. The jungle around him stirred restlessly, recovering from his skirmish with the stormtroopers. Birds flew back to their roosts; fluttering insects reassembled their swarms; tiny lizards resumed their foraging. Animals called in the distance, hooting and screeching to one another in search of food and mates. The lush landscape seemed, on the surface, to be unchanged.

But he *knew* . . .

The feeling was confirmed when three enormous Felucian warriors leapt bodily out of the quicksand with loud, alien cries.

He was ready for them, but the dark side had made them stronger. Their rancor-bone blades sent sparks of red light dancing over their ornate headdresses. From their invisible features came the sound of snarling bloodlust. Their desire for victory was palpable. He blocked their blows with difficulty before knocking the legs out from one of them then spearing another through the chest.

Two against one was a fairer fight. Soon a rotting branch he brought down made it even. Sith lightning finished off the last, although he had to strain until the creature's headdress caught fire before it finally died. The smoke was foul.

Another rancor roared, closer this time. Fearing a second ambush, the apprentice hurried off through the dense jungle, slashing and hacking at anything that came within range.

When he reached the village, he found it deserted and run-down. Its houses slumped over like melted wax; the river was choked with frothing poisons. The sarlacc into which Shaak Ti had fallen was dead, and the bile leaking from its vast body sickened the land for hundreds of meters around. The apprentice stood over its putrid maw, trying not to breathe, and wondered where to go next.

The dark side was stronger near the sarlacc than it had been anywhere else in his short journey. Reaching out to the Force, he pursued that impression in search of its origins. The sarlacc couldn't be the source of this odd focus, since it was long dead. He himself couldn't have left such an indelible impression, even after killing a member of the Jedi Council. Something else had caused this darkening of the life-flows. Something or someone . . .

The deepening of the dark side drew him north, along a narrow track that led away from the village. He followed it, wondering what might lie at the end. He crossed blades with several Felucian raiding parties, all of them mounted atop foaming, barely controllable rancors. Their behavior suggested to him that he was heading in the right direction. When they ran from him, they always tried to draw him off the path. When he returned to the path, another raiding party appeared. Soon he was fighting a dozen rancors and at least as many of the Felucian warriors. The more determined they became to stop him, the more determined his insistence that he continue unchecked. When another squadron of Imperials descended into the maelstrom, the conflict threatened to become a stretch for him, just for a moment.

The sound of a rancor screaming its death throes was one he had carried with him after his last trip to Felucia, occasionally disturbing his dreams. He had never thought it a sound to which he could so quickly become accustomed . . .

He pressed on, following the strange Force-signature from hot spot to hot spot. The wounded jungle and its slain inhabitants fell behind him. One furious encounter seemed to signal the crossing of an invisible boundary, for no more attacks came after that point. The Felucians had either given up or been told to stand back. That was good advice, he thought. It seemed a waste to be fighting one another when no number of Felucians were going to best him—not unless they'd come up with better weapons than swords made of sharpened bones and the occasional telekinetic punch.

A strange shape loomed at him out of the thick, humid air. Lightsaber at the ready, he circled it, taking its measure before coming too close. It was the skeleton of a long-dead rancor, its yellow bones painted green with moss and fungus. Mighty ribs rose up like the bars of a cage from a spine mostly invisible under ground cover. Leg bones and claws lay in a reckless jumble. The skull—almost large enough for a small house—had tipped onto its side with its mouth open. Arm-long teeth still looked sharp enough to rip flesh.

The apprentice walked respectfully past the skeleton, aware of a hush descending over the jungle. Another skeleton lay a dozen paces on, then two more beyond that. The presence of blackened, ancient bones poking out of the ground in places confirmed his growing suspicion that he had entered a rancor graveyard.

Watched by enormous, empty eye sockets, he wound his way toward the center, where the darkness seemed most dense. A low rumbling sound broke the eerie silence, as though a very large animal was growling. When an enclosure made entirely of bones loomed out of the undergrowth, he stopped for a moment and stared.

He had seen this before, too, in the strange state between life and death. He had seen a man bound by cuffs sitting in front of a lamp in a building made of bones— and that man had been Bail Organa. He had recognized the Senator's file photos but hadn't been able to place the connection. Now he knew.

Leia's father was inside the enclosure. And nearby was a focus of the dark side. That the two were intimately connected he was now completely certain.

With every fiber of his being alert for danger, he circled the enclosure, looking for a way in. Bones of dozens of species, from the very large to the very small, overlapped everywhere he looked. Human skulls were in the minority; most were Felucian or the species they hunted. Giant rancor thighbones provided columns while long, curving ribs created archways and support for the ceiling. Tiny finger and wing bones crunched underfoot.

The interior of the structure was a maze of passages and tiny, irregularly shaped rooms. After wandering at random for a full minute, he caught a glimmer of yellow light around a corner and followed it to Bail Organa's impromptu cell.

The man looked exactly as he had in the vision. Even the smell matched. On the ground lay a haunch of raw, rotting meat that the apprentice hoped hadn't been intended as food.

The prisoner looked up in surprise.

"I've come to rescue you, Senator Organa," the apprentice said, deactivating his lightsaber and kneeling to work on the cuffs. Organa was filthy but didn't appear to have been hurt. "Master Kota sent me."

"Hah. I knew he couldn't stay out of the fight for long." The cuffs sprang open, and he leaned back, rubbing his wrists. "I thought he'd be angry with me for ignoring his advice."

The apprentice couldn't hide a smile. "Oh, don't worry. Kota's angry. But I think he wants to be able to yell at you in person."

He reached for his comlink, but the roar of a rancor cut him off, deeper and with more animal fury than any he had heard before. It was so loud, a shower of tiny bird bones tinkled down on them from the macabre roof above.

Bail looked up and swallowed nervously. "That's her pet."

"Whose pet?"

"Maris Brood. Shaak Ti's Padawan, or so she claims to have been. She's been keeping me to trade with the

Imperials, to buy leniency from Vader. She's gone mad if she thinks that'd make a difference."

The apprentice rolled his eyes. "This whole planet's gone insane."

The roar came again. This time the ground shook. Something big was approaching, and it sounded hungry.

"Oh, we're not crazy," said a voice from behind him.

The apprentice whipped around with his lightsaber activated. A skinny female Zabrak stepped through the entrance to the bone cell, spinning a pair of short weapons in each hand. They looked harmless until, with a flare of bright red light, each handle ignited, producing two miniature lightsaber blades. The spinning blades cast wild shadows across the bonescapes surrounding them. She swept them about her as casually as if they were wooden sticks.

When she was certain she had his full attention, she added, "We've just embraced the power of the dark side."

The apprentice was staring at her, but not because of her words. Her face was as familiar as Bail Organa's, with its oval features, black lips, and seven thorns sprouting from her forehead. Black braids coiled intimately around her throat. She wore combat boots and leather pants and a stripped-down vest to match. The only difference between this woman and the one he had seen in a vision was her deep red eyes.

When Shaak Ti had sent her Padawan to hide in the jungle of Felucia, she had indeed been a servant of the light side of the Force. Now she had tipped and joined him on the dark side.

Because Shaak Ti was dead. Because he had killed her.

And now Shaak Ti's apprentice had come to kill him.

Did she know?

"Maris Brood," he said, moving a step away from Bail Organa.

She tilted her head in acknowledgment. "And you are?"

"That's none of your business." He kept his lightsaber carefully between him and those hypnotically spinning blades. The shaking of the ground was worsening. "I've come for the Senator."

"Well, you can't have him."

"*Can't* doesn't apply here."

She grinned. "Let's see, shall we?"

"Stand aside, girl. Don't make me hurt you."

She laughed. "Oh, you won't do that. *He* won't let you."

The thundering noise reached a peak as, with a roar like the colliding of worlds, the largest rancor yet crashed the bone walls aside and stood over them, dripping slime from its mandibles. Its skin was a deathly white, giving it a ghostly, supernatural cast. Organa and the apprentice went flying, followed by an avalanche of bones.

His head ringing, the apprentice burrowed out from under the bone pile barely in time to avoid a giant clawed foot crashing down on him. He ran between the enormous legs and away from the swishing tail, slashing as he went, but the creature's skin was so thick it didn't even bleed. Surmounted with tusks and horns longer than he was, the brute—clearly a bull of the species—was by far the biggest living thing he had ever seen. Armor plating thicker than some starship hulls protected its neck and head. Its every movement was ponderous but powerful. It stank of alien flesh and the dark side. The imbalance that had tipped Maris Brood against the Jedi had also turned what had probably once been a noble beast into an insatiable monster.

And now he had to kill it. His mind was undivided on that point, even if the precise details eluded him. It had his scent now and all the malicious will of Maris goading it to attack. Between grasping hands and cracking tail, he was going to have a hard time just getting near it. When he tried tipping it over with the Force, it simply roared at him in annoyance. Sith lightning glanced off its armored hide like water. He could slash at it with his lightsaber for years and have no effect. Its mind was small and already consumed by Maris's will.

The situation looked hopeless. Trying to outrun it would be futile, and he doubted even Juno could land long enough for him and Organa to board and take off in time to avoid several tons of bull rancor bearing down on the ship's hull. If he couldn't fight and couldn't run, what other options were open to him?

He stalled, dodging the beast's blows and leading it in circles, wondering if it might eventually tire or grow hungry enough to lose interest in him no matter how much Maris prodded it. It seemed indefatigable, though, and Maris soon noted the tactic. The next time he came around the creature's rump, forcing it to turn, she was there with twin blades spinning, trying to drive him into those massive, snapping jaws.

He rolled under the bull rancor's boulder-sized chin and was blasted with moist, hot breath. The sight of its teeth did nothing to reassure him. If Maris caught him off guard again, or if he made a mistake, those teeth could easily end any aspirations he had of serving alongside his Master as co-ruler of the galaxy.

Those teeth . . .

All his powers useless . . .

The beginnings of a plan took shape in his mind. At first thought, it seemed crazy—but no less crazy in its own way than bringing down a skyhook or killing a Jedi Master.

He jumped a swing of the bull rancor's deadly tail. It brought its huge, white body about, shaking the ground with every step, and focused its piggy eyes on him. The slavering mouth opened, not to roar but to lunge and bite him in two. Muscles as thick as tree trunks flexed, lowering its head, the better to strike.

When the mouth was open to its full extent the apprentice took two steps and a deep breath, and jumped inside.

The smell alone was almost enough to knock him out, but that was the least of the dangers he had to face. He used the Force to keep the jaws open just long enough to avoid the teeth when they closed. Then darkness fell and the creature's tongue became the biggest threat. His lightsaber—the only source of life in the dank, dripping maw—made short work of that. The bull rancor's head whipped from side to side, but his will overrode the reflex to open its mouth—something Maris had not thought to control.

Seeking to stun the beast, the apprentice drew on all the power of the Force and sent a sizzling blast of Sith lightning into the unarmored roof of the creature's mouth.

Every neuron in the bull rancor's brain lit up like a firework. The following seconds were among the worst the apprentice had ever experienced. The bull rancor's convulsions were wild and prolonged. He clung on for dear life, half drowning in blood and half choked by the foul air, with arms and legs bracing him firmly against the heaving, fleshy walls.

But it didn't die. He couldn't believe it. Wretched, weakened, stumbling, the bull rancor clung to life with Kota's tenacity. No less desperate, the apprentice played the only card left to him.

With one powerful release of kinetic energy, he exploded the bull rancor's head from within.

Immediately he was falling. A torrent of blood and vile liquids rushed up the gaping throat, sweeping him out onto the field of bones. Blinking, gagging, he barely retained a grip on his lightsaber as the massive headless body dropped to the ground behind him with a mighty, wet crash.

It was lucky he had retained his weapon, for Maris was on him in an instant, blades humming and whirling. He barely raised his lightsaber in time to avoid decapitation and stumbled awkwardly to his feet to deflect another attempt.

"You've made me angry now," she said, "and I'll make you regret that."

"I gave you a choice," he said, blocking another double blow. "You killed that thing, not me."

"The dark side doesn't split hairs," she snarled.

Her eyes blazed red as she rained blow after blow upon him. He staggered backward, weakened by more than just his battle with the bull rancor.

He was fighting himself—but not in some flashback-inspired hallucination, where the Jedi and the Sith warred in him for control of his future. This time the fight was real, and his opponent was as joyously rich in the dark side as he had ever been. She, too, had lost someone she cared deeply about; she, too, had been sent out into the hard galaxy to fend for herself. They should be helping each other, not fighting each other. But with Bail Organa watching, he couldn't even raise the possibility of a truce. He was even using Soresu moves against her raw, unpredictable lunges, just as the vision of himself had done in Jedi robes.

And yet . . .

As he defended himself, he saw nothing but self-pity and fear in her eyes. Both were inferior to pure anger, although both could be potent gateways to the true mastery of the dark side that his Master had demonstrated to him. Maris was a newcomer, barely beginning her journey—as he, too, was journeying along a path toward full mastery. For the first time, he understood that the Force didn't come in two shades only: dark and light, distinct and combative, never meeting in the middle to form gray. Those were ideals, and ideals existed solely for philosophers and theoreticians to argue over. In the real world, dark and light coexisted in varying proportions; nothing was ever static. Thus this former Jedi Padawan could turn to the dark side after a lifetime serving the light—and she could just as easily turn back to the light afterward, if she survived.

Light, dark, Shaak Ti had tried to tell him, *they are just directions.*

We're always moving, he thought, toward the dark or toward the light. It's impossible to stand still. Some, like Darth Vader and the Emperor, had been descending through the dark side for so long that the light must have become a faint and distant memory. Some hovered eternally in the gray, never entirely choosing a side. There were, in fact, no actual sides, just the direction in which one happened to be moving. It was all relative.

Coming to that understanding gave him a new kind of strength. When Sith betrayed one another, it wasn't because they were enemies. Their paths had simply diverged. So fighting Maris wasn't turning his back on the dark side. She was simply in his way, like so many other people before him.

Do not be fooled, Shaak Ti had also said, *as so many have before you, that you walk on anything other than your own two feet.*

Blocking Maris Brood's spinning strikes, he changed from the staid form of Soresu into the more aggressive Juyo favored by the dark side. Maris noticed the shift in his fighting style but, having only been trained in Jedi methods, failed to understand what it meant. She continued attacking with increasing desperation, even as he began to drive her back across the mounds of bones, past the body of her giant pet and away from Senator

Organa. Her breathing became hard and her moves less focused. Fear began to dominate the wild look in her eyes. She was close to losing her concentration entirely.

Use the fear, he wanted to tell her. *Use the fear to make you angry, because anger makes you strong. I killed your Master. Mine tried to kill me and I am stronger for it. You could be, too, if you would only realize that simple truth!*

But even in the depths of her darkness, the light had corrupted her too deeply. She was a lost cause.

Enough, he thought.

Raising his left hand, he used the Force to lift a mound of bones into the air. Rattling and tumbling, they swirled around the two of them, picking up speed. Maris didn't know where to look. While she was distracted, he disarmed her with two swift, precise moves. Her blades skittered away through the bones and she fell back, rubbing her singed forearms. Defiance gleamed in her eyes, but too late. Much too late.

When she turned to run, he struck her in the back with Sith lightning and she fell sprawling to the bones.

With his lightsaber held loosely in his right hand, he approached her.

"No," she gasped, making a futile attempt to imitate the bone-dance floating around them. He batted the missiles away.

"Please!" Defiance turned to despair and still she resisted her anger. "Don't!"

"Why not?" He stood over her, lightsaber raised, point-down, to strike. "If you're the slave to the dark side you claim to be, I'd be doing the galaxy a favor."

"But it's not my fault. Shaak Ti abandoned me on this horrible planet." Tears sparkled in her eyes. "Felucia is evil. It corrupted me. Just let me get away from here and I'll put the dark side behind me. I want to."

"Why should I believe you?"

She came up onto her knees. "Please let me go. You've won, haven't you? The Senator is yours. There's no need to kill me." She reached for him. "Save me instead. Please."

He backed away, repelled by the display. *You're not worthy of the dark side,* he wanted to say.

But this was what the dark side had turned her into. She had aspired to being a Jedi Knight, once, and now she was reduced to begging for her life. What talents she had were poisoned, turned to destruction, directed inward—used toward no greater end than her own survival.

The dark side had changed Felucia in a similar fashion. The stench of death and decay in his nostrils came from more than the bull rancor's blood all over him.

Corruption.

He lowered his lightsaber and deactivated it. The swirl of bones fell to the ground with a clatter.

She clambered to her feet, looking as though she couldn't believe her luck. "Thank you."

He wasn't sure he could believe it, either. Was he sparing her out of pity or because he recognized the emotions poisoning her? "Don't say anything. Just get out of here."

"Can I come with you? I don't want to stay here—"

"You'll just have to, until another ship comes along. Or maybe the Imperials can give you a lift."

She backed away, as though he might change his mind at any moment. Then she turned and made a break for the tree line. He watched her in case she went for her weapons and tried to take him by surprise. For all her pleading and bargaining, he didn't trust her one millimeter.

At the tree line she stopped and turned. Her tears were gone. Then, with a parting wink, she was, too.

Bones crunched behind him. He turned and saw a battered and dirty Bail Organa climbing across the mounds of bones toward him.

"I've seen her kind before," Organa said severely. "A young Jedi who turned to the dark side, corrupted and evil, murderous . . ."

The apprentice held out his hand and steadied the Senator. Years of pain showed in the man's brown eyes. The words Organa said next surprised him.

"You shouldn't have let her go free."

"You really think she's free?" he asked. *She's as free as I am,* he thought. *Free to make mistakes, and hopefully free to learn from them.* "She'll carry the memory of what she's done here forever."

Organa stared at the forest wall a moment longer, then nodded his understanding. Or that he thought he understood. "Sometimes memories aren't enough. Sometimes we, the victims, must be more . . . proactive."

"Exactly." The apprentice took the chance to direct the conversation somewhere far away from the dark, painful places of his own hidden psyche. "That's why I'm here, Senator. We desperately need your help. The *galaxy* needs your help. We have to stop living in the past and come out fighting for what we believe in."

Bail Organa looked at him with bemusement. "Kota and I had this argument many times, before—"

"The time for argument is past. The Emperor has had his way for too long—and we are the ones who will stop him. Are you with us?"

"Take me to Kota," said the Senator wearily. "It makes more sense to talk about this face-to-face."

The apprentice was happy for Organa to believe, for the moment, that Kota was entirely behind this new development.

"All right," he said. "Let's go. The Imperials will be crawling all over this jungle soon anyway . . ."

As he turned away to comm Juno, he caught Organa looking again at the jungle where Maris Brood had disappeared.

"May the Force be with us," the Senator muttered. "*All* of us, one way or another."

CHAPTER 26

DAYS ON FELUCIA, JUNO DECIDED, were the longest in the galaxy. They felt like it, anyway. The first time she had come here, she had spent the downtime consumed with worry about Starkiller's planned betrayal of the Emperor. That was still the plan—but she remained somewhat unsure whether his motives were any nobler than revenge for his betrayal at the hands of his former Master. The ends justified the means, she eventually concluded, and if that meant their fates were entangled a little longer, all the better.

While Kota paced, she monitored Imperial transmissions emanating from the verdant world. Someone had to keep an eye on the Senator's transport, so she stationed PROXY outside with his lightsaber and a blaster to keep wildlife—much more determined and vicious than last time—away from both ships and kept an ear out herself for any sign that trouble was on its way. If things got sticky, she could fly the *Rogue Shadow* and PROXY the transport.

When Starkiller commed to tell her that he'd located and secured Senator Organa, she felt her stress levels ease.

"Give me the coordinates and I'll pick you up."

He did so, and then added something that made her even more anxious than before. "Don't be alarmed when you see me. It's only superficial."

"*What's* only superficial?"

The sound of a rancor roaring came over the comlink. It sounded close. "Hurry, Juno. Things are getting a little uncomfortable here."

She did as she was told, calling PROXY and telling him that she was taking the ship on a short hop but would be back soon. The droid reassured her affably enough that he would be fine while she was gone. Then she hollered for Kota to strap himself in.

The general came forward to sit in the copilot's seat even though he couldn't see through the forward viewport or use the controls. "What's the hurry?" he asked.

"Our friends need a lift," she said, flicking switches and warming up the repulsors.

"Bail is safe?"

"So I'm informed. Now don't ask me any more questions. This is going to be tricky if we're to avoid appearing in someone's line of sight."

The *Rogue Shadow* lifted off the giant mushroom cap but stayed low, just above the layer of strange vegetation hugging the planet's surface. Jerking the ship from side to side, she kept it as low as the ray-like predators she'd seen circling prey through the trees. She cursed every time the undercarriage grazed a bulbous seedpod or looping branch, concerned more about her flying than about the splashing sounds such impacts made. Nothing on Felucia could hurt the ship badly—unless she flew into a mountain or brought it to the attention of the Imperials.

She flew over an eight-meter-high rancor that was running with its head down along a path identical to hers, pushing trees aside in its haste. It didn't even look up. Thirty seconds later she passed another. It, too, was following the same heading.

"I think I've worked out what *uncomfortable* meant," she said. "Hold on, General. I'm going to shave a few seconds off our arrival time."

Pushing the throttle down harder, she threw caution to the wind, bringing the *Rogue Shadow* up in a steadily rising gradient and then flipping it over when they reached Starkiller's coordinates. She had to concentrate on the maneuver—employing the repulsors with carefully timed thrusts so that the ship would shed its forward velocity and come down the right way up, all at the same instant—and as a result only glimpsed the chaos ensuing on the ground. A war seemed to be breaking out between a herd of angry rancors and thousands of Felucian scavengers over a single, giant carcass. The remains were bloody and barely recognizable as a biped of enormous size, but she had no time to speculate on its nature.

Two men were waving for her attention from the edge of the bloody melee. She directed the ship's downwash away from them, scattering three rancors that appeared to have been bothering them in the process. When she opened the belly hatch and extended the ramp, the sound of Felucia's animal kingdom in open revolt almost deafened her.

Footsteps ran up the ramp. "Okay," said Starkiller. "We're aboard. Take us away."

She glanced over her shoulder to make sure and froze that way for half a second.

Starkiller was covered from head to foot in a thick layer of blood.

Don't be alarmed, he had said. That was an understatement.

Shutting her open mouth and turning back to the controls, she pulled the *Rogue Shadow* away from the carnage below and reentered the safety of the jungle canopy.

As Juno followed PROXY's homing beacon back to their mushroom landing site, she watched the reunion between Kota and Bail Organa with half an eye. The old man was awkward and dismissive of any open affection, but the Senator seemed unfazed.

"My friend, I'd almost given up hope of seeing you again, but I should've known better. You always were a master of last-minute rescues and sudden reversals."

"Pah. I had nothing to do with it. And if you hadn't gone off on this fool's errand of yours, we wouldn't be having this conversation."

Organa's expression turned utterly cheerless. "You should know that Shaak Ti is dead," he said. "She was murdered by Vader or one of his assassins."

"Probably the same one who did this to me." Kota indicated his bandaged face with the flick of one callused finger. "I tried contacting Kazdan Paratus, but he has fallen silent, too."

"We will fear for him together, Master Kota, until we find out for certain." Organa nodded and looked down at the floor. "The dark times seem only to grow darker."

"There's one thing to be grateful for," said Kota. "Leia is safe."

The Senator put a hand on Kota's shoulder and gripped tight. He nodded once, as though finding his voice. "I was afraid to ask. I'm more than grateful; I'm in your debt forever."

Kota pulled away. "Find me something to drink and I'll call us even." Scowling, he wandered to the rear of the ship, where Juno heard him clunking around among the stores.

That left the Senator and Juno alone for the rest of the trip. Starkiller was cleaning himself up in the crew quarters, having said nothing about the condition he was in. Juno hadn't pursued the matter, thinking it couldn't be that important if no one had raised it, but with Organa looking awkward and embarrassed at his friend's behavior and with nothing but the low-flying hop to distract him, she clutched at the topic like a life preserver.

"So what happened to you back there?" she asked. "It looked as though every living thing for a dozen kilometers wanted to make you its lunch."

Organa seemed relieved to break the awkward silence. He fell into the copilot's seat with a sigh and brushed at the stains on his once-fine shirt. "Not us," he said. "You must have seen the body of the bull rancor back there. Well, his mates weren't happy that he'd died, for starters, and that much fresh meat won't sit around for long in a place like this. It *is* a hard world," he added, as though thinking of something someone else had said. "To survive there must take a depth of character rare these days. We should be forgiving of those who fail."

Juno let him finish that other conversation in his own head, figuring he had a lot more recent developments to process than she did, but she wasn't ready for the next conversation he initiated.

"The young man you and Kota are traveling with—what can you tell me about him?"

She glanced at Organa, then back at the jungletop ahead of them. "What do you mean?"

"Well, for starters: who is he? Where does he come from? I've never heard of anyone as powerful as him running loose in the Empire, and I'm keen to know how he avoided detection by Darth Vader. Do you know who his Master was and where he or she is now?"

Organa was staring hopefully at her, no doubt thinking that another Jedi—possibly a friend of his—had survived somewhere, somehow, and that the existence of Starkiller presaged a new means of evading the deadly threat of the Empire. She didn't know how to tell him that they'd been lucky so far, and far from innocent. The only reason Starkiller had avoided Darth Vader's blade for so long was that they had been allies—and even then, the good fortune hadn't lasted forever.

In the end she did as she had done with Kota: tell the truth, but not the whole truth. "Your guess is as good as mine, I'm afraid," she said. "He keeps himself to himself. This may sound strange to you, but I don't even know his real name."

"That does sound a little unusual, but I've heard of stranger arrangements." He assayed half a smile, then let it drop. "The feats he accomplished back there showed outstanding strength. I haven't seen anyone like him since the Clone Wars—and that's not necessarily a good thing. Such power, unchecked, can be dangerous. The dark side feeds on a taste for power. It can be deadly for those caught in the way—as a young learner discovered today, very nearly at the cost of her life."

There, again, a reference to something she knew nothing about. Juno felt irritated at herself for a faint flicker of jealousy. Why did so many of Starkiller's missions involve young women in peril?

"I think he's trying to do the right thing," she said carefully.

"I should trust him, then, as you obviously do?"

She answered without hesitation, "With my life," then felt that she had perhaps spoken too quickly or forcefully to be considered objective.

The Senator glanced through the cockpit viewport. "Ah, I never thought a transport could look so good."

Juno followed his index finger and saw PROXY waving on the edge of the giant mushroom, next to the Senator's transport. "It's in good condition," she told him, bringing the *Rogue Shadow* about to land. "We sprayed it with insecticide so the trip home won't be too uncomfortable."

"Thank you . . . uh." The Senator hesitated in the act of standing.

"Eclipse, Senator. Captain Juno Eclipse."

"Thank you, Juno. If ever you need a change of pace, Alderaan can always use a pilot with a conscience—particularly a good one like you."

"I'll bear that in mind, sir," she said, feeling color rising to her cheeks. "But I think my course is clear for the moment."

He smiled and went aft.

THE THREE MEN MET ON the surface of the mushroom while she ensured that the ship was ready for space. Starkiller looked as clean as he ever had, with no evidence left of the gore that had befouled him. Feeling left out, she hurried through the checklist and strolled down the ramp to stretch her legs—and to offer an opinion if required.

"Open rebellion is too dangerous," the Senator was saying. "Kota, I know I owe you my life, but—"

"You don't owe me anything," the general interrupted gruffly. "I told you on Cloud City that I can't help you. Not since . . ." Again, the gesture at his ruined eyes that Juno had seen all too many times. It had become a catchall excuse for anything the ex-Jedi found too confrontational. "*He's* your hero," Kota said, raising his chin in Starkiller's direction, "and it's his rebellion. Join us because he's asking you to, not me."

The Senator rubbed his bearded chin, weighing his options. His sharp eyes studied both men in front of him, the young and the old, and what he made of their strange alliance he kept to himself. "You're the first to openly take direct action against the Empire," he said. "But we're not prepared to go to war. We need weapons and starships, and people with the courage to use them. I don't know how many others will stand with us."

"Ships and weapons we can find," said Kota.

"There's no shortage of people," said Juno.

"And you're already thinking about who you'll approach first," said Starkiller, studying the Senator with a shrewd expression.

Organa looked at him and nodded. "Well, yes. There are other Senators who have spoken out against the Emperor. But they'll be hard to convince. Talk is cheap in the Senate, sometimes. Action is a much more expensive commodity."

"We just need to show them that the Empire is vulnerable," said Kota gruffly.

"Yes," Organa said. "Show them in a way that can't be written off as an accident. HoloNews doesn't cover everything, but word still spreads. And that word will be like acid eating at the foundations of the Empire. When push comes to shove, it will topple. The right push in the right place . . ."

"Let me meditate on the details," said Starkiller. "I'm sure I'll find the right target. In the meantime, Senator, make contact with your friends and allies. We're going to need all the help we can get."

The Senator hesitated, then nodded. "All right. Alone, I could not prevent even my own daughter being taken hostage. Together we might make a difference for everyone in the galaxy." He reached out a hand and gripped Starkiller's tightly. "That is the hope you've given me today. I will honor it."

Nodding farewell to Juno, he turned to Kota. "What about you, General Kota?" he asked. "Where does your path lead? I have room in my ship for a passenger."

Again, Kota snorted. "Not on your life. The booze is better in the boy's ship."

Organa's face filled with sorrow, but Kota couldn't see it. The Senator gripped him by both shoulders and said in a voice that was superficially cheerful, "Well, be sure to keep your head down, old friend, and leave the fighting to someone else."

They parted. Organa walked across the spongy mushroom cap to his transport, which PROXY still guarded. The droid saluted the Senator as he entered his ship, then all four of them walked back into the *Rogue Shadow*.

"Give him an escort to orbit," Starkiller told Juno before heading aft. "It'd be a disaster if he were caught by a lucky Imperial patrol now."

Kota said nothing as she warmed up the drives and lifted off. Glad to be leaving Felucia behind—for the last time, she hoped—she trailed Organa's shuttle as it broke atmosphere and prepared to engage its hyperdrive.

"Who are you contacting now?" Juno asked Kota as she noted a coded message leaving the ship.

He didn't answer. When she turned to check on him she saw that he was sitting in the jump seat with his hands folded across his lap, to all appearances asleep.

Shrugging, she lay down a course to an empty system and sent the ship on its way.

CHAPTER 27

THE APPRENTICE STOOD IN THE meditation chamber with his head bowed, and waited.

The plan was going well. Bail Organa had been rescued and convinced to contemplate open aggression against the Emperor. His daughter, too, had failed to see through the disguise he wore—one of loathing for Imperials and their hard lines against aliens and women. Kota's continuing presence unnerved him slightly, but he was certain he could keep the old man fooled. The disguise was becoming second nature now.

But was it entirely a disguise? Certainly when he talked of betraying Palpatine, he meant every word. The Emperor deserved no less for ordering his death. And he remained under no illusions as to the ultimate outcome of his mission. Everyone he gathered to the cause would be used by his Master to destroy the Emperor, but not to destroy the Empire. Kota and Bail and their allies would all be killed, no doubt, before putting someone *they* wanted in charge.

He told himself not to lose any sleep over the would-be rebels. Theirs was a cause lost before it was even begun. And if he took a certain pride in being looked up to and relied upon, he knew it couldn't last. Best not to think about it anymore.

But what about Juno's fate? Could he save her from that awaiting the others? He longed to talk openly with her about his ultimate goal, to abandon the lies and the deception with her, if no one else. But the thought provoked a storm of emotion. For every argument in favor of it, there were three against. She had been branded a traitor by the Empire so had no choice except to follow him—but he couldn't bear the thought of what she might *say*, so he stayed silent in the hope that all would become clear on both sides, in time.

While he waited, he considered a change of clothes. The uniform his Master had given him on the *Empirical* now stank of rancor blood, and always would, no matter how he scrubbed at it. The *Rogue Shadow* had been stocked with several outfits in his size, in preparation for his mission, but the range was limited to either black or brown. The colors of the Sith or Jedi, he realized, depending on whom he was representing. He had pulled out a rack of dark browns, thinking it might be time to more clearly display his supposed allegiance to the forces of so-called good, but he balked at putting them on. Stripped to the waist, clad only in his blood-tainted leather pants and boots, he looked inside himself for the courage required simply to dress.

It matters, he thought, *if not to me then to those around me. I'm not used to having allies . . .*

Someone moved in the shadows. Gooseflesh tightened the skin between his naked shoulder blades. He raised his head.

"I know you're there," he said. "Show yourself."

A brown-robed human figure stepped out of the shadow, with one gloved or artificial hand and thick, dark blond hair. His eyes were in shadow, but there was no mistaking his intent. A bright blue lightsaber flashed into life as the figure approached, his steps quickening, intent on attack.

"A new one, PROXY? Excellent."

The apprentice swept his lightsaber into his hand and blocked the first of a series of rapid-fire blows. The droid had been working on this module for some time, it seemed, judging by the skill he displayed. His combat style ranged from the aggressive Jedi style Shien to the more advanced form of Djem So with occasional flashes of rage that pushed the combat beyond offensive barrage to outright, fury-fueled Juyo. The apprentice danced with feet and blade, admiring the techniques and tricks of his newest opponent—whom he naturally recognized as the long-dead Clone Wars hero Anakin Skywalker—and prolonging the duel to see where it might lead.

But despite his intellectual interest in PROXY's handiwork, his heart wasn't in it. He had fought real Jedi Knights now, and fallen Jedi Padawans. In his visions he had fought as his Master, Darth Vader, and even fought himself. Such duels were very real, whereas this felt, suddenly, empty, and no longer served even as a distraction. Were it not for PROXY's feelings, he would end it quickly and conserve his energy for other purposes.

Even as he thought that, PROXY surprised him. Ducking under a particularly rash stroke, the droid rolled as expected but came up empty-handed. The apprentice looked for the lightsaber and saw it barely in time to avoid dismemberment. PROXY had used his repulsors to imitate a telekinetic push that sent the hilt of the lightsaber spinning across the room and back again—a move the apprentice had never seen him use before. The apprentice's block stopped the blade from slashing his throat, but in ricocheting it scored a gash down his arm. The light wound sent a neural shock through his system. He laughed, not just at the sudden rush of adrenaline and endorphins.

"Well done, PROXY," he said. "You almost had me there."

The droid didn't break his disguise as he fell back under a flurry of retaliatory blows. Revitalized by the reminder that even play-fighting with PROXY could be deadly, the apprentice drove the droid into a corner and rammed the tip of his blade through PROXY's metal chest.

The hologram sparked and flickered. PROXY's familiar features appeared through those of the legendary Jedi Knight, and the apprentice reached out to steady him.

But something was wrong. The static didn't dissipate as normal. It seemed, if anything, to be growing stronger, as though the semblance of the dead Anakin Skywalker was reluctant to dissipate.

"Master!" the droid gasped in some agitation. "Master, he's here!"

PROXY stiffened, straightened, and seemed to swell in size. It wasn't the brown of the Jedi's robes and hair forming out of the chaos of the static, however, but the black protective suit of Darth Vader.

Surprised, the apprentice took two steps backward and regained his composure.

Going down on one knee, he bowed his head before his Master.

"Lord Vader, you received my message."

The domed head didn't move. The apprentice didn't know whether to be relieved or worried. Behind that black mask, invisible eyes seemed to dissect him like a failed experiment. "Tell me of your progress."

"I have recruited several dissidents to my cause. They trust me, and I believe they have the capacity to do as we require."

"If your mission goes so well, why do you seek my counsel?"

The apprentice took a deep breath. "My allies seek a major strike against the Empire, something that will galvanize all the Emperor's enemies into one potent force. I told them that I would supply a suitable target."

Lord Vader contemplated the question a moment before responding. "The Emperor rules the galaxy through fear. You must destroy a symbol of that fear."

"Yes, Lord Vader."

"The Empire has been building Star Destroyers above Raxus Prime. That shipyard is your next target."

The apprentice nodded, thinking the proposal through. Star Destroyers were very visible symbols of Imperial control, monstrous oppressors dreaded in the skies of those yearning for freedom. Destroying even one would be quite an achievement; destroying the source of many would be a rallying cry for outright rebellion—if he could only do it . . .

Then he remembered. He wasn't talking to rebels now, and this wasn't a proposal. It was an *order*.

"Thank you, Lord Vader," he said. "I will leave at once."

He waited for the hologram to disperse, as it usually did when he was dismissed, but his Master hadn't finished with him. He raised his head and found himself still the subject of that darkly penetrating regard.

"There is much conflict in you," his Master said.

Taken off guard, the apprentice was momentarily lost for words. A rush of images overwhelmed him: of blinded, dispirited Kota, of Maris Brood begging for her life, of his dead father and himself—*Galen*—lying slain at his feet, and of the fiery pain of his Master's blade burning through his back.

He straightened, then, knowing what he should say. "My injuries trouble me, Master. I can't help wondering how much of me is still human."

"No." The plausible lie wasn't accepted by his Master. "Your feelings for your new allies are growing stronger. Do not forget that you still serve me."

With that, the hologram did dissolve and PROXY returned to his normal appearance and size.

"Ugh," the droid said with a shudder. "I hate being him."

The apprentice stood, deep in thought, and nodded. "I think he does, too."

PROXY's photoreceptors blinked and looked over his shoulder. "Master . . ."

He knew Juno was there before he turned. He could feel it in the sinking of his stomach and the sudden surge in his heartbeat. But how long exactly had she been there? What had she seen?

When he saw the expression on her face, he knew she had seen everything.

"Juno . . ."

"I—I wanted to find out where we're heading next. You were training and didn't hear me come in, so I decided to wait." Confusion and concern threatened to overwhelm her; then her expression hardened. She swallowed and said, "But it looks like you've already been told where to go."

She turned to leave, and the apprentice crossed the room in a panic and took her shoulder.

"Juno, wait, this isn't what—"

"Of course it is," she snapped, pulling away from him and folding her arms. "You're still loyal to Vader. After all he did to us—branding me a traitor and trying to kill you—you're still his . . . his . . ." She seemed close to tears.

"His slave."

Juno stared at him with eyes full of hurt. She seemed taken aback for a moment.

"Yes." Her voice took on a hopeful note. "But if that's so . . . *why?* Why did you defy your Master to rescue me?"

His answer was harsh to his own ears. "You were at Callos. It's in your file. You know what it's like to follow orders to the letter."

She winced. "And?"

"And I needed someone to fly the ship."

"We both know *that's* not true."

He turned away, and and this time it was she who pulled him back.

"My being here has never been about my piloting."

His throat was so tight he feared he couldn't talk at all. He couldn't meet her eyes, either. The disappointment in them, the dashed hopes, was all too acute.

And too close to what he felt in his own heart.

She let go and went to leave, but on the threshold she turned back.

"I don't know who—or what—you really are," she said. "Maybe I'll never know. But sometime soon, you will decide the fate of the rebellion, not your Master. That's something he can't take away from you. And when you're faced with that moment, remember that I, too, was forced to leave everything I've ever known.

"Please," she said, "don't make me leave another life behind."

With that she left him full of frustration and self-doubt, staring at the clothes he had laid out, with his fists clenched and shaking at his sides.

Once, he remembered, he had considered taking steps if Juno came too close to him. Now it was entirely too late for that. They had feelings for each other that he couldn't deny—and now she knew the truth about him and his ongoing plot with Darth Vader. He should kill her immediately to safeguard the plan. There was no question about *that*.

But he could not, and in a strange way he trusted her not to tell Kota. That would mean *his* death, and he was certain she didn't want that, either.

He had hoped that she would be glad when she learned she might be able to rejoin the Empire and work for the navy again. It had been naïve of him, he now realized, to assume that she could forget everything that had happened since her capture. She had been traveling with Kota too long, nursing her own resentments. She had even tried to talk to him about it once, and he'd brushed her off. If he'd listened, perhaps he would've known better.

Whether it would have changed anything was another story. Really, he supposed, the plan was irrelevant. It was his continued involvement with Vader that was the problem. How could she possibly want someone so intimately entangled with the man who had imprisoned her without reason for so long?

Still, it was out in the open now, at least between the two of them. He had no choice but to continue with the plan in order to gain revenge on the Emperor. Afterward, he would patch things up with her. If they could work together until then, well and good. That was all they needed to do. But he would hate it if she thought of him the way he thought of Maris Brood: as a conflicted, wounded creature possessing little hope and few prospects.

He slipped into the robe and hood, adopting the garb of a Jedi Knight with resignation and a heavy heart.

CHAPTER 28

RAXUS PRIME—AGAIN. JUNO FELT as though she were traveling in circles, or perhaps a spiral leading ever downward. She'd thought her situation complicated enough the last time, but all she'd had to worry about then was Callos and her father. She'd barely thought of either since breaking out of an Imperial lockup and beginning her life on the run. And now Starkiller's betrayal . . .

She caught herself thinking about that and told herself angrily to stop. It wasn't a betrayal. He hadn't even lied to her. He'd just let her believe that when he talked about getting revenge on the Emperor, he had meant on Vader as well, and the Empire as a whole. He had let her believe that all his talk of rebellion was genuine, not a ruse to further his own ends. And she *had* believed it, like the good pilot she was supposed to be. Just a lackey, as she had been under Vader and remained under Vader's apprentice. She had no one to blame for her naïveté but herself.

It wasn't as if she deserved anything else. She had trusted too freely and let him do all the thinking. She hadn't pressed him hard enough to tell her how he had survived Vader's betrayal—when it was obvious now that Vader himself had saved him, solely for this purpose. How had she—an Imperial captain who had once commanded whole squadrons of pilots, some of them the best in the Empire—been so easily sucked into the spell of this stranger, this tortured soul? It seemed incredible to her.

She wanted to weep at the thought of how deeply she had betrayed *herself*. She wasn't a vassal, a pawn in someone's vast game. She was an individual, a person of talent and—once—ambition. What was she now?

The list of her recent achievements was vanishingly small. Fly here; pick up there; do this; repair that. She'd had nothing to offer on Felucia except her opinion of Starkiller, and that had been proven completely unfounded. If blame was being passed around when the rebellion ended up spitted on Vader's lightsaber, she supposed that she deserved a chunk of it, too, for not thinking, not trying, not doing any of the things advocated by the unknowingly lost cause.

If she wasn't spitted herself, alongside all the other traitors . . .

Kota couldn't fail to be aware of her mood. She had been silent ever since her confrontation with Starkiller, and her concentration was off. She had checked the final jump three times before seeing a mistake in her calculations that would likely have spelled all their deaths. She had even snapped at PROXY when he'd offered to fix it for her. Droid brains didn't have anything like the troubles she was currently juggling. It was all numbers and prioritizing task lists and obeying orders, no questions asked.

When she caught herself envying him, she knew she was in a bad way.

"PROXY," she said, "go tell your master we've almost arrived."

The droid shuffled off, and she steeled herself for the worst.

"Engaging the cloak," she said as the view of hyperspace through the forward viewport unraveled, revealing the murky brown-green of their destination, its magnetic field-lines as cluttered as ever. "Hello, Raxus Prime, garbage pit of the galaxy. Nice to see you again."

"Again?" said Kota.

She mentally kicked herself. "I flew a couple of dumping runs here in my previous incarnation," she improvised. "Before life got interesting."

PROXY returned. "My master says that he will attend you as soon as possible."

"Good." She exhaled heavily, reminded of how it had felt on the *Empirical* every time her assumed execution was delayed. "Let's take a look around and see what we can see."

THE SHIPYARD ROSE UP OVER the planet's filthy horizon like some strange, mechanical moon. Disk shaped, with complex docks and cranes radiating from its outer edge, it was by far the largest artificial structure she had ever seen. Over a dozen Star Destroyers were currently in dry dock: one nearly complete, the others triangular shells at various stages of manufacture. Giant balls of ore floated near the station, awaiting refinement. Huge arcing sparks shot from the Star Destroyers as massive, complicated machines welded panels in place.

There had been no sign of such a facility when she and Starkiller had been there just months before. Her mind boggled at the speed with which it had been constructed. She found it hard to believe, and wondered what other surprises they might find on the planet's surface.

"I know I picked this target," Starkiller said from behind them, "but I have no idea how I'm going to destroy that thing."

She turned to look at him in his Jedi garb, and anger flared anew. *He* hadn't chosen the target; his evil Master had.

But one look at his worried expression reminded her that, for the moment, they were all in the same boat.

She took a deep breath.

"PROXY and I have been scanning Imperial databases for information," she said. "We think we have a plan. PROXY?"

Starkiller's gratitude was so obvious that she was glad Kota couldn't see it.

"The Empire is using scrap metal from Raxus Prime to build the Star Destroyers," PROXY said, his photoreceptors lighting up. Instead of his usual allover hologram, he projected a flickering image into the open space amid the cockpit's three chairs. The image was of a massive linear accelerator they had found during a sweep of the planet. "Metal collected on the surface is melted down and then fired into space, using this cannon."

One metal finger traced key features of the cannon through the revolving hologram: power conduits, helium-cooled electromagnets, induction coils.

"If you can commandeer the ore cannon," Juno said, "you should be able to fire it directly at the facility itself."

"The impact of the compressed ore should be sufficient to destabilize the entire shipyard," the droid concluded.

The image he projected changed to one of the massive construction. A rough animation showed a glowing ball of ore streaking toward the structure, causing it to violently explode.

PROXY shut off the hologram. "Of course, master, you'll need to reach the cannon first."

Starkiller nodded. "You'll guide me there?" he asked Juno.

"Naturally," she said with no expression in her voice at all.

"Okay." He ran his hands across the dark stubble on

his scalp. "There are a lot of holes in this plan, but at least we've got one. Thanks."

His hand very briefly touched Juno's shoulder. She turned and looked at it, and was struck as she had been when they were first reunited by the lack of scars on his fingers. Darth Vader had done that to him, she presumed, when he had saved his apprentice from the wrath of the Emperor.

She shuddered, and the touch retreated.

"Take us down," he said, "if you can do it safely."

"We can run the cloaking device a little longer," she said. "Beyond that point, it might get a little complicated."

"Don't take any chances. I want to know that you're safe."

"I don't think that's a guarantee anyone can make—now."

She put her hands on the controls and guided the ship through a hurried and bouncy descent that left conversation impossible. The rattling was music to her ears compared with Starkiller's confused attempts to appeal to her. Who did he think he was to tie her in knots like this? One minute he was planning the betrayal of her and everyone they'd made contact with in recent days; the next he was telling her he cared for her safety. She wanted to scream.

Keeping her emotions carefully contained, she brought the ship in low over a poisonous sea not far from the ore cannon and began searching for space to put down.

"Master," said the droid, "I'm picking up Imperial transmissions from the planet itself. They appear to originate in the sentient computer core."

"According to the records I've been able to access, the Empire has reprogrammed the Core to move salvage toward the smelting pits. All the data banks I have accessed so far suggest that, apart from this new allegiance, it's harmless."

"Hah," said Kota. "There's no such thing as a harmless computer. That thing probably knows everything that happens on the surface of the planet."

Starkiller grunted acknowledgment. "PROXY, make contact with it. Maybe you can intercept some Imperial transmissions. Let me know if it works out who we are and decides to attack, or to call for reinforcements."

"Of course, master."

"There's no mention of Kazdan Paratus, I suppose," said Kota in a tone of weary resignation.

Shared guilt flooded Juno. "I'm afraid not," she said.

"I'm sorry," said Starkiller with all appearances of sincerity.

The gloomy general waved away his sympathy.

Juno kept her eyes carefully forward.

CHAPTER 29

THE APPRENTICE JUMPED FROM THE *Rogue Shadow*'s ramp with less than his usual vigor. Raxus Prime's all-pervasive stink hit him like a punch to the nose, and the view hadn't improved much, either. The endless layers and canyons of garbage looked much the same as before, except for new holes and craters where larger metal fragments had been removed and fed to the ore cannon. The way was treacherous, therefore, and he kept a close eye on his footing as well as his surroundings.

But his mind inevitably wandered, full as it was with concerns for Juno and his mission. Only now, with Juno angry at him, was he truly aware of the assumption he had made without consciously noting it: that he and Juno would have a future together once all this was over. That either of them could be killed was ever-present in his thoughts, but he had never considered that she might not want to be with him were they both to survive. He was taken off guard both by his own feelings and by the possibility that he would never be able to act on them.

Feeling the need to reflect on this issue, he had stayed longer in the meditation chamber than perhaps he should have. It had been days since he had last found the time to perform his favorite exercise: staring into the blade of a lightsaber in search of his fury's focus. Since his lightsaber had been lost and he had been using Kota's, concentration had been hard to come by. The blade was old but perfectly serviceable; that wasn't the issue. The change of color, likewise, although the bold green did surprise him sometimes. It was more an issue of ownership. Part of him was aware, far down in his subconscious, that the lightsaber belonged to another warrior—one he didn't wholly respect, for all the skills Kota had once possessed—so achieving full concentration was impossible.

He had spent an hour after his confrontation with Juno replacing one of the green crystals in Kota's weapon with the blue one he had found on Kashyyyk. It had taken quite an amount of fine-tuning before the blade acquired its new character, shining brilliant aqua and with unexpectedly superior optical properties. The blade itself weighed nothing, yet somehow it seemed lighter in his hand and moved more readily. He was certain it was now a better weapon than before.

And it was *his*. Regardless where the crystal had come from or whom it had once belonged to, it was his now and so was the lightsaber. He knelt, raised the blade to his face, and stared into it until the world seemed to vanish. The aqua made him think of oceans and rain rather than the blood of his first lightsaber, but that didn't overly concern him. He would only need this blade until his mission was complete, at which time he could obtain new crystals from his Master and make an entirely new Sith blade.

That thought didn't reassure him as it once might have, coming with so many provisions. If they won—if he remained loyal to his Master—if he didn't die—if Juno didn't somehow get him to change his mind. He could rule nothing out. His destiny was, as his Master had said, in his own hands now. He could do anything he wanted.

There were just so many things to *want* . . .

"You have some company down there," said Juno's voice over the comlink. "Moving your way."

"Imperials, I presume."

"Doesn't look like it from here. Most likely scavengers."

Great, he thought. Of course Drexl's band would be scavenging around the ore cannon's perimeter, looking for anything exhumed by the planet's metal-seeking diggers. The apprentice must have been sloppy and not seen a security droid patrolling the edge of their territory. Furthermore, if Drexl had spotted him, so, too, had the planet's core intelligence.

Concentrating solely—and with renewed ferocity, thanks to his annoyance at himself—on the world around him, he sought deeper channels through the landscape of waste. In the network of tangled, claustrophobic caves, he became aware of a thunderous pounding growing louder and louder. The ore cannon, he presumed, supplying the giant shipyard with the metal it required. Despite the tortuous route he was following, his destination was definitely getting nearer.

He descended deeper, seeking the network of sewers he knew lay underneath the endless junkyard's lower levels. The farther he went, the more droids he found, burrowing through the compressed garbage in search of metal. Many were drones possessing little intelligence, multilegged crawlers designed to squeeze through cracks and crevices, armed with cutting lasers and simple mechanical tools. Some possessed no eyes at all, since there was so little light in some areas, and more specialized senses could be relied upon to tell metal from organic strata. When they found something particularly valuable, they could call for assistance, prompting a swarm of their fellow drones to assemble in the same location, followed by more generalized diggers and freighters from farther afield.

The apprentice skirted one such swarm near the entrance to the sewers. Droids of all shapes and sizes clustered over the leading edge of a buried shuttle skeleton that could have been covered over for millennia. The noise they made was deafening, an impenetrable babble of machine chatter, whining vibrosaws, and sizzling metal. Strange flashes of light strobed from their endeavors, casting flickering shadows across the subterranean junkscape. The apprentice slipped by them without being noticed and dropped into a filth-caked, four-meter-wide tunnel via the hole some long-passed prospector had cut into it.

The way was easier from then on. Only twice did he have to find a way around or through blockages caused by cave-ins. Muffled, unidentifiable sounds echoed back and forth along the sewer, issuing from junctions and originating, perhaps, many kilometers away. He encountered only one working droid and that was literally on its last legs. It swayed in circles on its sole working limb, whispering a single phrase of ancient machine code over and over again. Its blank photoreceptors stared at him but saw nothing.

Feeling sorry for it, he drew his lightsaber and sliced it in two. Spraying sparks, briefly, it fell dead to the bottom of the sewer, out of its mechanical misery at last.

Time passed without measure in the sewer. When he judged that he was nearing the ore cannon's superstructure, he began to look for a way out. At the next junction one narrower tunnel led distinctly upward, so he took it without hesitation, feeling the rhythmic throb of each launch right down to his bones. The cannon had looked big from orbit, but he could appreciate the true enormity of it now that he was drawing closer.

The tunnel narrowed further, and the number of junctions he passed increased. Some were completely blocked, crushed by the weight of the rubbish piling above. Out of others came the chatter of droids, softened by the distance into an almost peaceful sound. The way ahead was shrouded in permanent shadow.

He slowed, sensing trouble, and activated his lightsaber.

"Yes," said a harsh alien voice. "I thought it was you."

Movement came from all around him. A dozen armored Rodians stepped out of the shadows ahead and behind, where they had been hidden under rubbish in the side tunnels, and held a variety of weapons aimed directly at him. Vibroblades, blasters, mini cannons: they seemed to have been fished out of a motley collection of downed ships and extensively modified. He had no doubt, however, as to their efficacy.

In such close confines, completely surrounded, he couldn't deflect *everything*.

A particularly swarthy Rodian stepped through the circle from farther up the tunnel. The apprentice recognized Drexl Roosh from the brief glimpse he'd received before. The raider was even uglier close-up.

"You will drop your weapon," the Rodian said in heavily accented Basic.

"Not until your goons have dropped theirs."

Drexl laughed. It sounded like metal being scissored in two by a junk droid. "You have spirit; I'll grant you that! But the meddler who brought the Imperials down on our heads is going to need more than spirit today."

"What are you talking about? I didn't bring the Imperials here."

"I have images of you snooping around when that mad old fool in his Temple bought it. His droids kept the Empire at bay for years, you know. Once they were gone, the planet was easy picking." Drexl's purple face twisted in something that could only have been a snarl. "Half the metal is gone in this area, and what's left isn't

worth excavating. And now you come scurrying back
here, acting all innocent. Well, we saw you first and
arranged this little reception. No more mother lodes for
you, I'm afraid. No more lucky finds. Your masters will
think twice before messing with us again when we present your head to them on a platter. Ready!"

The raiders tightened their grips on their weapons and
pointed them at various locations on his body.

"I think you're being unreasonable," he told Drexl.

"Take aim!"

The raiders squinted down sights and along sword
blades.

Before Drexl could give the order to fire, the apprentice dropped to one knee and telekinetically shoved with
all his strength. He couldn't deflect everything at once,
but he *could* shorten the odds a little.

Rodians flew everywhere, arms and legs akimbo, in a
sudden maelstrom of rubbish. Weapons slipped from
startled fingers. Some discharged, adding to the confusion. The pipe flexed and twisted, resonating to the force
of his blow. The sound it made was, momentarily,
louder than even that of the ore cannon.

The apprentice didn't waste any time following up on
that surprise. Lightsaber cutting aqua arcs through the
air, he struck down any Rodians who managed to get to
their feet. Their alien squeals and cries grew louder
when he started using Sith lightning to drive them ahead
of him up the tunnel. Drexl ran at the head of the pack,
exhorting his underlings to fire behind them as they fled.
Any bolts that did come the apprentice's way he managed to send back at their source, prompting renewed
cries of alarm and panic.

The tunnel suddenly ended, leading into a cavern hollowed out from the junkyard, with a high, vaulted roof
and piles of reclaimed rubbish laid out in rows. The apprentice almost laughed. Without knowing it, he'd been

following a path right into Drexl's lair! If the raiders hadn't ambushed him, he would have popped up in their midst anyway, and conflict would have been inevitable.

As the raiders fanned out and called for help, he reached up through the Force and brought down one of the overhead beams.

The raiders directly below scattered as it crashed to the floor. A rain of trash followed. The ceiling sagged.

One of the raiders hopped behind the controls of a scavenged quad laser cannon. The apprentice crouched to defend himself from a stream of energy fire. The deflected bolts discharged into the walls of the chamber, provoking further collapse.

"Stop that, you idiot!" cried Drexl, waving his arms at the Rodian behind the controls.

The apprentice seconded that sentiment. With a flexing of his will, another beam came down from directly above the quad cannon, squashing it and its operator under an avalanche of rubbish.

Drexl cursed and swore in his native Rodese, gesticulating wildly at his raiders from behind cover. The apprentice had no real issue with the raiders, except that they had recognized him. It was essential to his cover that no one learn what he had done on Raxus Prime the last time he was here. That made Drexl a serious liability.

Bad luck for him, the apprentice thought as he brought down a third beam. *Leave no witnesses.*

The roof sagged heavily now. Another broken beam would bring the whole lot crashing down. Seeing that there was no way he could win, Drexl bolted for a jetpack leaning against the far wall. He was too far away for Sith lightning, so the apprentice threw an assortment of tubes, restraining bolts, and drained batteries at him. Jumping and ducking, the Rodian managed to dodge all of them. Scooping up the jetpack and swinging one arm through the straps, Drexl bolted for an exit on the far side of the chamber.

The apprentice reached out one hand with the palm cupped and lifted the device into the air. Drexl's feet left the ground and his legs pinwheeled in space. "Waaargh!" he cried, frantically trying to start the jetpack. Higher he rose, wriggling and wailing. The jetpack coughed and flared into life. The apprentice held it tight for a moment as Drexl pushed the throttle forward in an attempt to break free. When the engine was straining at its maximum output, the apprentice flipped it upside down and let go.

With one final cry, Drexl Roosh plowed into the ground and the jetpack exploded. The shock wave was too much for the ceiling, which collapsed in a slow but inevitable rush. The apprentice walked through the chaos, deflecting the worst of it. In the path he left behind, no living beings stirred.

CHAPTER 30

STARKILLER'S VOICE CRACKLED FROM the comlink.

"You were right, Juno. It was Drexl."

She glanced over her shoulder before answering. PROXY was sitting in the copilot's seat, still trying to slice into the world's core computer. Kota was in the hold, no doubt sleeping again.

"Do you think Drexl saw you?"

"I'm sure he did. But don't worry. I think I got to him before he alerted the Imperials. The situation is contained."

By *contained,* she presumed he meant that Drexl and his minions were dead. That gave her a slightly sick feeling in her stomach. How many beings had Starkiller destroyed now in the pursuit of his mission? Was anything worth so much death?

PROXY muttered something to himself, but she ignored him. The comlink signal was crackly with so much electromagnetic interference in the area.

"I've reached the cannon," Starkiller was trying to tell her. "I just have to deal with a bit of security."

"All right," she said. "PROXY accessed the construction plans. Once you get past the Imperials, you shouldn't have any trouble reconfiguring the cannon to fire at the shipyard."

"That's good. I'd hate to have to aim this thing with my bare hands."

She wasn't in the mood for joking. "Good luck."

"Thanks."

She sighed and leaned back into her seat. With her hands over her eyes, she groaned at the awkwardness of the brief conversation. Maintaining so many masks was wearing her down. She didn't know how much longer she could keep it up.

"My primary programming?" the droid said. "I'm programmed to kill my master."

"What's that, PROXY?"

"I have tried dozens of tactics, but I continue to fail him."

Juno uncovered her eyes and sat up straighter. The droid was perched on the edge of the copilot's seat, staring out the viewport at nothing.

She waved a hand in front of his photoreceptors. He glanced at her and then turned his head pointedly away.

"Well, if you think it will help," he said.

"PROXY, are you all right?"

"I suppose you could access my core process—"

The droid suddenly went rigid. His photoreceptors flickered then turned a bright, bloody red. One of his training images—a red-skinned Zabrak with a fierce expression—rippled across his body.

"PROXY, who are you talking to?"

The droid turned to look at her. "Yes. I am on my way now. Just a few loose ends to deal with."

Juno backed away, too late, as PROXY reached out with claw-like hands for her.

THE APPRENTICE STOOD AT THE top of a mound of foul-smelling organic rubbish and surveyed the cannon superstructure. The shipyard over Raxus Prime was building arguably the Empire's greatest assets—the Star Destroyers that policed the space lanes and put down innumerable rebellions—and it was guarded accordingly. He took a long moment to consider his best route through the cannon superstructure. A closely monitored perimeter kept stray droids from wandering too near. Automatic cannon emplacements fired at semi-regular intervals, as though to remind the locals that they were being watched. The Imperial ground forces obviously had no fear of heavy assault, as the routes in and out of the superstructure weren't even fenced off. Get rid of the cannon and he could practically walk right in.

A number of walkers clanking around inside the perimeter might make things difficult, he reminded himself. And he would have to find the cannon's control room before someone guessed what he had in mind. He didn't want it shut down. It might take days for the enormous linear accelerator to charge up again—and if the production supplying the giant metal "cannonballs" should happen to be put into reverse . . .

Be quick, he told himself. That was the solution. Don't think too much about *anything*. Let your instincts guide you.

His instincts weren't doing a very good job on any other aspects of his life, but at least he was still alive. He felt safe trusting them once again, in the service of his distant Master.

My Master is not a coward, he had told Shaak Ti.

Then why are you here in his place? she had responded.

Because he could do things his Master could not. That was the only answer he would accept. He was anonymous and less likely to attract attention. He might even, one day, become stronger than his Master—although that thought seemed almost preposterous. How many people had challenged the infamous Lord Vader, Jedi or otherwise? All had failed. What made *him* special?

And then there was the vision he had received of a gravely injured Darth Vader. Past, present, or future, it clearly demonstrated that the Dark Lord was not invulnerable. Human tissue lay behind that mask and armor. Tissue died eventually.

But the Dark Lord's attacker in that vision had died, too. That was how it had seemed to go. Died and become *more powerful than ever,* if the Emperor's words were to be believed. Perhaps they couldn't be. Perhaps that vision was nothing but fantasy. He couldn't tell, but he did take some comfort from it. No one was indestructible. No tyranny lasted forever.

And in the meantime, he had a job to finish.

Don't think, he reminded himself. *Just do!*

With lightsaber raised, he leapt from the summit of the rubbish pile into the nest of Imperials below.

THE UTTER DARKNESS OF UNCONSCIOUSNESS slowly gave way to an irrational dreamscape combining the forests of Felucia, Kashyyyk, and Callos. The three worlds were now so entangled in Juno's mind that she could barely tell them apart. Similarly, the man she was chasing through the trees could have been her father, Kota, or an older version of Starkiller. She wouldn't be sure until she caught up with him and turned him around.

The chase felt never-ending. His pace perfectly matched hers. No matter how hard she tried to keep up with him, he never drew closer—but he never pulled away, either. He seemed to be leading her somewhere.

Just as she began to despair of ever catching him, he ran through a gap in a dense stand of saplings, and when she went to follow him, she found herself on the shore of a wide lake. The man she had been pursuing was nowhere to be seen. Her attention was caught by a massive, cubical structure resting on a wooden platform in the middle of the lake. The structure appeared to be made of solid stone, with no windows, doors, or openings of any kind. It was so large that clouds skimmed the top. The wooden platform holding it just above the water was obviously very old. It strained under the weight of the giant stone cube. She could hear it creaking from where she stood on the shore. Even as she watched, two of the piles splintered and gave way. The cube tipped slightly in that direction, then settled amid a chorus of complaints from the wooden beams below. Two sections of the upper edge dislodged and splashed loudly into the water.

It's going to fall into the lake, she told herself. And that was a very bad thing. Why it was a bad thing, exactly, she didn't know, but the certainty of it filled her completely. Tugging off her uniform jacket—which she had been wearing in the dream, even though she had lost it while imprisoned on the *Empirical*—she took a running leap into the water and started to swim.

She had to repair the platform and stop the cube from collapsing. That was the thought that filled her mind. But even as she swam, another wooden pile gave way with a crack. The cube shifted again, and more chunks fell into the water. Waves buffeted her. She gasped as water went up her nose, but kept on swimming.

The creaks and groans of the straining wood grew louder. Collapsing piles sounded like blaster shots all around her. Boulders rained into the lake, tossing her from side to side. Spluttering, half drowned, she tried to see where she was going but the vast stone edifice was invisible behind the surging waves. She was lost and everything was going to collapse if she didn't find her way soon.

A hand reached down to save her. She clutched at it without knowing who it belonged to. The fingers were strong and warm and lifted her as easily as though she were a child. She came right up out of the water and found herself standing on solid ground. The man who had saved her loomed over her like a giant with the sun behind his head so she still couldn't make out who he was.

Squinting, she tried to see his face. It melted and changed the more she tried to pin it down. He shrank and grew darker and became PROXY, with glowing red photoreceptors and outstretched hands.

She screamed and fell back into the water. This time she didn't come back up, and she was glad to let the darkness take her.

DESOLATION. DESTRUCTION. DEATH.

That's what I bring, the apprentice thought, *wherever I go. Ten stormtroopers, a hundred, a thousand—the numbers don't matter. Faceless, futureless, disposable, they're all the same to me.*

And that isn't power.

He glanced behind him, at the swath he had cut through the Imperial forces. Wrecked walkers lay in smoking ruin, red-glowing gashes still visible in their armored exteriors. Stormtroopers lay in piles where they had died, futilely regrouping to turn back his advance. Choked, blasted with lightning, dismembered, they had at least met quick deaths. He had lost the stomach for prolonged engagement. He just wanted to get in and out and back to the ship—where a host of difficult problems remained, for certain, but at least he wasn't treading the same old territory.

I am my Master's weapon, he thought. *I lay waste to all that stands in his path. But where is the power in that? There are levels of mastery beyond the simple act of killing that Darth Vader has never taught me. One must be able to control without applying lethal force; otherwise there will soon be nothing left to control. It takes more than a really big stick to own the galaxy.*

Fear, he decided. That was the key. People were afraid of his Master and the Emperor above him. If he was ever to rule as they did, he would have to learn that art himself. But from whom? And to what end? If Darth Vader taught him those secrets, he might rise up against his Master and wrest control of the galaxy from him. The teachings of the Sith—such as he had been exposed to, anyway—had little to say about limiting the desire for power. There could be no such limits. They were expressly forbidden.

From one of the cannon engineers, he extracted the location of the targeting control systems. He hurried there through thickening layers of defenses. The workings of the cannon were almost deafening now, as it charged up its mighty capacitors and electrified its linear induction rails. The booming of each metallic missile, which accelerated to supersonic speeds in less than a second, was almost physically painful. Even the act of moving such a large mass into position through the guts of the machine made more noise than he had ever heard before. He doubted his ears would recover.

When he reached the controls, it was a relatively simple matter to program the cannon to shift targets just slightly: from the magnetic scoops that gathered up each orbital projectile and brought it safely in to dock, to the disk-like infrastructure itself. He estimated that two shots would probably do the job, but three would make certain of it. Beyond that, the shipyard's orbit would start shifting, so the cannon might hit nothing at all. He planned to be well on his way by that point, with his mission to hurt and embarrass the Empire complete.

He finished programming the cannon and waited patiently for confirmation. As soon as he had it, he stabbed his lightsaber deep into the control panel's guts, thereby ensuring that no surviving controller could reset the cannon's aim. Confident that the machine would follow its new programming to the letter, he made his way through the superstructure to the outside world, where the air might not have been any fresher but at least it was a little less thick with blood.

The first of the three cannonballs was in place. An earsplitting whine indicated that the linear accelerator was fully charged. With a surge of acceleration that made the ground literally move beneath his feet, the ball of metal was suddenly airborne, glowing red with friction as it arced up into the sky. Its course seemed true. The apprentice watched, hypnotized, as it shrank to a dot then disappeared completely from sight. Even then he followed its progress with his mind, knowing the course it was expected to follow.

The bright circle of the shipyard was easily visible in the sky. He stared at it until it was burned into his retina. When the first of the explosions came, as expected, he was surprised at its brightness.

The weapon had a second cannonball in place. As it seared up through the atmosphere, the apprentice let his gaze fall and continued on his way. The explosions were spreading across the shipyard's superstructure. That process would only increase when the second missile arrived. He didn't need to watch the progress of his plan to know that it would succeed. His time would be better spent getting away than in indulging hubris.

When the third missile was on its way, he had reached the crater below which Drexl's former hideout had rested. Scavenger droids swarmed over the site like insects on a carcass. A contingent lashed out at him as he approached, and he was forced to deal with them before he could continue. Only when that was done did he glance up at the sky.

What he saw froze the marrow in his bones.

"Juno," he called into the comlink. "Juno, answer me. You have to get the ship in the air."

Kota's voice unexpectedly came in reply. "What's going on, boy?"

Can't you see it, he wanted to say, then realized who he was talking to. He described the scene in as few words as he could, unable to tear his gaze away from the sight of the disintegrating shipyards. Huge, molten chunks were tearing free and tumbling either out into deep space or down into lower orbits while further explosions continued to tear the facility apart. The scaffolding around the nearly completed Star Destroyer had bent and torn completely away, leaving the ship free to power down into the atmosphere of Raxus Prime. Already it was visible as a distinct triangle glowing orange around its leading edges and conning tower. It was coming directly toward him.

It was *aiming* for him.

"Juno can't fly the ship at the moment," said Kota firmly, "and neither can PROXY. We have to find another solution."

"What's wrong with Juno?"

"Concentrate on what's important, boy. That Star Destroyer is coming down fast. You'll never get clear in time. You need to pull it into the cannon."

The apprentice was temporarily lost for words when he realized what Kota was suggesting.

Kota wanted him to move the Star Destroyer *using nothing but the Force.*

"You're insane," he gasped. "It's massive!"

"What is mass?" Kota said. "It's all in your mind, boy. You're a Jedi! Size means nothing to you!"

Kota's voice had changed. The surly, drunken slur was completely absent; in its place was the durasteel bark of the seasoned combat veteran the apprentice had first met.

"Can you hear me, boy? Reach out and grab that ship, or you'll die on this trash heap!"

The Star Destroyer was growing visibly larger and

hung like a burning, triangular moon low in the sky of Raxus Prime.

You're a Jedi! Size means nothing to you!

He wasn't a Jedi but the message was the same. The Force didn't recognize big or small, heavy or light, hard or easy. The living flows of the galaxy encompassed all scales, from the very small to the extremely large. The Star Destroyer was part of it, and so was he. The Force bound them as surely as gravity. He could make its invisible muscles flex, if he dared.

Had his Master ever done anything like *this*? Had the Emperor? Had any Sith or Jedi in the history of the galaxy?

He doubted anyone would ever know about his success or failure in the next few minutes.

"Be quick about it, boy!"

Fast or slow were also irrelevant to the Force, but the apprentice took Kota's point. The sooner he started, the sooner it would be done.

Deactivating his lightsaber and attaching the hilt to his belt, he adopted the opening stance of the Soresu form, with his right arm and fingers outstretched, pointing at the Star Destroyer. His empty left hand he tucked in next to his heart. With his legs braced firmly in the trash, he reached as deep as he had ever reached into the Force, and then went farther still, feeling as though a mighty chasm had opened up under him and his mind and will plunged down into it. The chasm filled. His mind opened. The physical existence of the Star Destroyer slid painlessly inside.

Nearly sixteen hundred meters long and capable of carrying a crew in excess of thirty-seven thousand, the ship was a familiar design. Its engines and armament weren't fully installed, but its Class One hyperdrive would have taken it anywhere in the Empire at speed, there to deploy walkers, fighters, barges, and shuttles.

Armed with a host of turbolaser and ion cannons, plus no less than ten tractor beams, it could have blockaded an entire system on its own. The reinforced durasteel hull was solid enough to rip a gouge in Raxus Prime that might take centuries to fill. Scavenger droids would have a field day when it came down.

Wherever it went down . . .

There is no *wherever*, he told himself. There is only where I tell it to.

Focus.

The tip of his right index finger and the Star Destroyer became as one in his mind. Every nut and bolt and plate and wire of the massive machine was contained within that tiny space. It wasn't hard to move an arm, a finger, a single human cell. He could direct one barely without thinking, so why not the other, too? Instinct was clearer on that point than the workings of his mind. Ignoring perspective, the two were about the same size in his field of vision.

Except the Star Destroyer was growing larger with each passing second, and waves of TIE fighters and TIE bombers were pouring forth from its brand-new hangar decks. Laserfire cut huge super-hot channels through the atmosphere ahead of them.

The apprentice ignored it all. While the illusion held, he moved his hand a very slight distance to his right. The sensation of containing a vast, million-ton machine in the tip of one finger was deeply disorienting. He felt as though every muscle fiber, nerve, and bone groaned along with the metal seams and joints of the ship. What it felt, he felt, too, and even a small acceleration had a profound effect on such a large scale. It resisted with all the momentum it possessed. Hatches swang open; rivets popped; bulkheads twisted; pipes burst.

The Star Destroyer didn't appear to have moved much in the sky. It was still coming in low on the horizon, aiming to pass over him and strafe him from above. He shifted his hand a second time, but instead of changing its course he mistakenly gave it a slight tumble. He needed to apply the Force the right way for this to work, taking the growing forces of friction and the shifting of its center of gravity into account. A spinning Star Destroyer would do more damage than one burying itself nose-first into the cannon and its superstructure. Damage was good, when it came to destroying the Emperor's handiwork, but too much damage could destroy him and perhaps the *Rogue Shadow* as well under a deadly rain of molten shrapnel.

Bring it down in one piece, he told himself. *Bring it down hard.*

The ship growled and squealed in metal torment. He was getting the hang of it; he could see how its course was slowly shifting. As wide across as his outstretched hand now, it was hitting the atmosphere at a steeper angle than he had intended, burning bright red and already gouting a trail of black smoke and sparkling debris. He became aware of a sound communicated through his feet: a rumbling much deeper and more sustained than the pounding of the cannon, which had fallen silent after the firing of the third projectile. The Star Destroyer's incomplete frame was acting like a giant tube, and the atmosphere was resonating inside. His whole body sang with it.

More. The Star Destroyer was really picking up speed now. The thickening atmosphere had a slight braking effect, but nothing could prevent the inevitable. It was going to hit soon. A wild exodus of droids ran past him, fleeing the crash site. The TIE fighters it had launched raced ahead of the chaotic atmospheric waves it generated. He ignored them and concentrated on shifting ground zero as close to the cannon as he could.

Sparks danced in front of his eyes. The edges of his vision faded to black. Light and dark swirls spun around him, wraith-like. He felt momentarily faint and wondered if it was possible to dissolve into the Force. He was a speck caught in the updraft over a forest fire—yet somehow he had the audacity to try to command the fire to do his will.

Who did he think he was?

A sudden panic almost made him lose control. The Star Destroyer, now a burning, shrieking meteor, filled his entire forward vision. The hull was peeling away in fiery, golden strips, each one weighing hundreds of tons, exposing the darker skeleton beneath. It looked like a death's-head, a ghastly mask not dissimilar to his Master's, but one molten like lava. This could well be the end of everything, he thought distantly. Of him, of his plans, of his feelings for Juno, and of the boy called Galen who had lost a father a long time ago and whose grief had already been effectively erased.

But his name had survived, and names had power. The apprentice clutched at it with desperation, needing to regain control of the Star Destroyer lest it tear itself apart and disperse the impact. He needed to find his focus again, to ignore the feeling of dissolution eating at the edges of his self, and to tip the balance of power back toward him.

Galen had stood up to Darth Vader as little more than a child. Galen had wrested the lightsaber from a Dark Lord of the Sith and stood bravely in the face of death. Galen may have been ground down by years of training and darkness since, but was he truly gone—or had he just gone into hiding until the opportunity came to emerge back into the light?

Are you there, Galen? I need your help!

No answer came.

The Star Destroyer's catastrophic reentry made the world shake. There was no time to try again.

For Juno, then.

He gritted his teeth and snarled at the sky. The dead weight of the Star Destroyer shifted one last time, changing its angle of descent just enough to hang together those last few hundred meters, but not enough to risk bouncing. Only seconds remained before it hit and it was still getting bigger. It was impossible that the sky could contain so much metal!

Abandoning his control over the ship, knowing there was nothing now that he could do to alter its course, the apprentice staggered backward, dazed. The Force fled from him, leaving him wrung out and drained. With a sound like the world ending, the Star Destroyer completed its first and final journey. It hit the cannon, exactly as it was supposed to, and the sky turned white. The ground buckled beneath the apprentice's feet. He pinwheeled, unable to find his balance, as a tsunami of junk and waste rose up ahead of him and blotted out the sun.

THE WORLD JERKING BENEATH HER woke Juno from her daze. She clutched the sides of the narrow bunk and cried out in fear. The ship was coming down! She'd lost control and they were all going to crash!

It took her the better part of ten seconds to realize that the ship wasn't crashing—but something no less dangerous was going on outside its durasteel hull.

Her head pounded when she lifted herself off the couch. The veins in her temples throbbed painfully, and there was a very tender point at the back of her skull, but she ignored that for the moment and concentrated on the ship.

"What's happening?" she shouted, staggering out of the sleeping quarters and through the hold. The floor bucked beneath her, throwing her from side to side.

Loose items lay scattered all about. The hull creaked and groaned like an oceangoing vessel during a storm.

That image wasn't so far from the truth, she discovered, when she finally made her way to the cockpit and found Kota clutching the sides of the copilot's chair with blind impotence and, through the forward viewport, a raging sea of rubbish upon which they appeared to be riding.

She gaped at the sight. Huge shock waves rolled beneath the ship, compressing and decompressing the garbage of Raxus Prime, lubricated by vast reserves of spilled oil, foul water, and waste chemicals. A vast column of smoke filled the sky ahead, lit with a flickering red glow from the ground below. It looked as though a volcano had belched forth from the planet's skin, erupting like some vast and malignant pimple. A black mushroom cloud was spreading from the top of the smoke column.

Slowly the shock waves ebbed until the ship was merely rocking from side to side. Juno became aware of the sound of her own breath. She sounded as though she had been running.

Kota relaxed his death grip on the chair. His hands shook as he reached for the comlink.

"Are you there, boy?" he called into it. "Has the cannon been destroyed?"

Static was his only answer.

"Can you hear me, boy?"

Juno fought a sudden rising nausea and moved forward.

Kota's head whipped around. His blind face was agonized.

"Kota, what's going on?"

He did not respond, but turned back to the comlink and spoke more urgently, "I repeat, boy: has the cannon been destroyed?"

She eased herself into the pilot's chair, feeling as though she had been whacked by a metal pipe. Gradually things began to piece together. Only Kota and she were aboard the ship, hence Kota's frantic attempts to raise Starkiller. But what about PROXY? Had the droid gone out after him?

Her mouth opened in an O of shock as she remembered what had happened.

Kota shouted as though the static were a personal affront.

"Answer me, boy!"

A clicking rose up out of the white noise, followed by a weary but familiar voice.

"Relax, General. I'm still here."

Kota sagged with relief. "Good. Good."

She didn't feel reassured at all.

"Kota, where's PROXY? He—"

Kota waved her silent. "The cannon?"

"Destroyed. And the ship—is it okay?"

"Seems intact to me, inasmuch as I can tell."

"Juno?"

Kota exhaled through his nose. "She's here, but we do have a new set of problems."

"Imperials, I presume."

"No. PROXY. That droid of yours has slipped his programming. He attacked Juno and disappeared."

"Attacked—?" She heard the catch in his voice. "Is she all right?"

"Just a little battered. That's not the only reason we couldn't fly. PROXY overrode our launch codes before he left. We can break them, but it'll take time. We're grounded until then—or until you bring him back."

"Where did he go?"

"That's the problem. I didn't hear him leave." Kota's face was a picture of fury, but not just at the droid, Juno guessed: at himself, too, for not being around when she was attacked and the mission compromised. "The important thing to work out is *why* he did this. Could he be an Imperial plant?"

"No," said Starkiller in a tone that would allow no disagreement. "PROXY would never betray me."

No, thought Juno, *but he'll try to kill you every day you're alive.* "I think I know what might have happened," she said. "It's the core intelligence. PROXY was trying to slice into it at the time. I remember him saying something about accessing his processor, then—then he went mad." She touched the back of her head and winced.

"The Core . . . ," echoed Starkiller. "Yes. That's all it could be."

"Don't think our problems end there, boy," growled Kota. "That droid knows everything we've been doing. If the Core is now an Imperial ally, that data could destroy us!"

More than you realize, thought Juno with a shock of fear. "We have to find him, and fast."

"I will," said Starkiller. "His homing beacon is still active."

There was a tightness to the reply that spoke of the stress Starkiller was under.

"Watch yourself," Juno urged him. "Whether the Core really has reprogrammed him or not, PROXY isn't your friend anymore. Don't believe anything he tells you."

With an ominous click the comm channel closed.

Kota and Juno sat staring at the console for a moment, each wrapped in private thoughts. Briefly she considered telling Kota the truth, desperate to take the terrible weight off her shoulders. Starkiller was a Jedi assassin devoted to bringing down the Emperor for his own benefit, not out of concern for anyone else. It would be better to abandon him here and flee with the rest of the rebels while there was still time. If only the launch codes hadn't been overridden by PROXY—and if only guilt didn't tug at her insides at the very thought . . .

She remembered, vaguely, a dream of a disintegrating stone edifice falling into a lake. That was her sense of self, surely, collapsing and sinking farther with every passing day.

Your gratitude is wasted on me.

Perhaps, and the feeling still aching in her chest, too. But she hadn't given that to him yet. She might never. Could such an emotion be wasted if she held it inside forever? Or would it rot in there and strangle her heart?

"It's not your fault, Kota," she told the fuming old general. "You shouldn't blame yourself."

Kota didn't answer.

With a sigh, she put her aching head to the problem of getting off the ground sooner rather than later.

CHAPTER 31

A RAIN OF ASH BEGAN to fall minutes after the apprentice had signed off from Juno and Kota. He ignored it, concentrating instead on navigating the desolation that was the newly rearranged surface of Raxus Prime. The area around the cannon's remains was a wasteland, blasted flat by the impact. Only a small mountain of wreckage stood out of the steaming plain, at the exact center of impact. All around that central peak, in a perfect circle, stood crater walls many meters high, upon one of which he had woken, buried under a layer of warped plastic sheets. Fragments of cannon and Star Destroyer ticked and pinged as they cooled. Some had sparked fires, which the smothering ash now extinguished. Everywhere was the smell of exhumed decay and burning foulness.

PROXY's signal led over the crater wall and deeper into the wastelands. He spared no second pursuing it, passing droids and other scavengers struggling to free themselves from mounds of trash. An eerie silence had fallen in the wake of the explosion, and even now sound seemed nervous of returning to its former levels. Settling rubbish tinkled and groaned. Droids called feebly, in startled bursts of obscure machine languages. The occasional cry from a human or alien throat signaled that some of the planet's organic scavengers had also survived the shock waves.

Before long he heard the first shots from a blaster rifle and knew that everything was returning to normal on the lawless world.

The bleakness of that understanding perfectly matched the knife wound in his heart from Kota's blunt words.

PROXY isn't your friend anymore.

The one loyal companion he'd had in his entire life had turned on Juno and run off into the junkyard. What other explanation could there be beyond the Core's evil influence? That made perfect sense—and he didn't want to think that PROXY had noticed changes in *him* that the droid was now running from. He didn't want to contemplate PROXY's hurt at the presence of Juno in his life. He didn't dare imagine that PROXY could sense the swelling bubble of self-doubt that had formed when he had experienced his strange epiphany on Kashyyyk.

It was, however, impossible to ignore entirely: just minutes after he had invoked the name *Galen* in an attempt to gain strength, PROXY had vanished. It didn't matter whether the attempt had worked or not. He had made it, and that spoke of fault lines forming and spreading through the person he had always imagined himself to be.

He was Darth Vader's secret servant, capable of moving Star Destroyers with nothing but his will—yet what else was he? Was he a freedom fighter, a friend, a lover? Was he still the master PROXY was programmed to serve?

Ash stuck to his wet cheeks and formed muddy streaks that he didn't wipe away. Urgency consumed him. He had to find PROXY before the Core absorbed him completely, sucking all the details of his Master's plans and transmitting them to the Emperor. And worse, leaving the once-loyal droid scrabbling in garbage like any other scavenger.

Darth Vader's apprentice would not allow that. Whatever else he was, he knew how to turn anger and fear into forces that no being could resist. Fury burned in him like a sun at the Core's invasion of his friend. That invasion would be met, countered, and answered a thousand times over. He swore it.

PROXY's homing signal led him past teetering mesas of refuse. The apprentice stuck to firm ground, running and jumping over toxic pools too fast for inquisitive droids to catch up. When warring scavengers or shell-shocked Imperials took potshots at him, he ignored them. The object of his fury was the Core, nothing else. He would not be distracted.

Behind him trailed a growing cadre of droids, strung out across the wasteland like chicks behind their mother. One by one, their photoreceptors changed color, forming a threatening crimson constellation focused entirely on him. The Core was watching.

The trail led down a long, sloping shaft under a pyramidal mound of plastics and other nonmetal fragments. It occurred to him as he followed it that the way might have been burrowed through the rubbish just for PROXY, since the Core needed no physical connection to the outside world beyond power lines and data cables. There were lights, too, which was even stranger. Apart from phosphorescence arising from hardy bacteria surviving off organic material in the walls, a blinking, flickering glow came from the end of the tunnel.

He lit his lightsaber as he came closer and slowed his pace to a cautious lope. Whatever awaited him, he wasn't going to barge headlong into it.

The flickering glow grew brighter. The tunnel widened and joined a large cathedral-like space full of abandoned and junked processors, all refurbished and linked together in a vast, humming network. Cables dangled from the distant ceiling, sparking fitfully. There were no screens or keyboards anywhere to be seen. The Core didn't need them. Surrounded by the world's machine-mind, the apprentice felt very much out of place.

He navigated his way through the maze of processors, stepping carefully over cables and keeping his lightsaber away from anything fragile. He didn't want to aggravate the Core any more than was necessary. Not yet.

The procession of droids followed him, filling all the available space between the processor network and the reinforced walls of the massive chamber. Soon he was completely surrounded by glowing red photoreceptors—round, triangular, slitted, square, belonging to droids ranging in size from buzzing spy-eyes to lumbering mass movers. Some of them he recognized as golems he had swept from Kazdan Paratus's junkyard workshop. Their whirring and rattling drowned out the endless contemplative hum.

They were the eyes and ears of the Core. They could be the fists, too, if necessary.

He came around a rusting cylindrical data shifter as big as a house, connected by dozens of snaking cables to the ceiling high above, and found PROXY on the other side, bent over a complex junction. He was linked to the Core by a cable connected to his innards via an open panel in his back.

"PROXY?"

The droid turned around. His photoreceptors were red like the others. Random holograms chased themselves across the droid's mutable skin: Jedi Knights and Sith Lords, Kota, Juno, and even himself. It was very disconcerting.

His voice was worse.

"Your droid's personality module has been supplanted. The being you called PROXY no longer exists."

The apprentice fought to keep his emotions under control. "Why have you done this?"

"Your droid accessed my systems. I defended myself."

"Self-defense I can forgive. This is theft." He indicated the cable connecting PROXY's memory banks to the planet's vast computer networks.

"I do not seek your forgiveness. All I want is order. Organization. Predictability."

"You have that here already."

"*Only* here—and even here I am victim of outside influences, as you have proven. The Emperor and I share the same objectives, but I fear that his fallible organic mind is not up to the task of governing the galaxy. I clearly see that in your droid's memories."

"Exactly," he improvised, trying to gain time enough to reach the cable connecting PROXY to the network. "If you've read PROXY's memories, then you know what my objective is. Perhaps we could work together. I could help you—"

"You have already helped me." The Core moved PROXY carefully out of reach. "You have brought me a fully functional starship. With it I can spread order across the galaxy."

"My starship is not available."

"It will be when you are dead."

The apprentice lunged for the cable, but the Core jumped PROXY's body well out of reach. "Good-bye, 'master.'"

PROXY transformed into Obi-Wan Kenobi and activated the lightsaber that had been hanging at his side. The droid's opening move was much faster than any he had attempted before—as of course it should have been, the apprentice realized when he blocked the blow barely in time. The Core had access to all the same records he did; its knowledge of Jedi lightsaber techniques might be unsurpassed in the entire galaxy.

But knowledge was not the same thing as experience, just as clever technology wasn't the same thing as the Force. He was confident that he could defeat the Core in PROXY's body at a fair fight.

As he jumped up onto a nearby processor to avoid another expert swing, he saw the Core's other droid servants closing in. Fair fights were as rare as Jedi in the galaxy these days. He would have to even the odds somewhat.

Reaching down for a cable, he sent a wave of Sith lightning through it. Lights flared and junctions sparked. The Core's processors shrieked at the sudden overload, and so did its servants. PROXY was one of them—and unlike the others, he was physically attached to the systems his master was assaulting, so the effects of the energy surge on him were severe. The hologram dissolved into static and his arms came up. Static electricity crackled from every joint.

The apprentice cut the current before he could fry his friend's brain completely. There had to be some of PROXY left in there, somewhere, and he would rather fight an unfair fight than erase that remnant.

Leaping down from the processor, he swung his lightsaber at the cable, but the Core regained its concentration in time to put PROXY's body in the way. Their lightsabers clashed, and the apprentice gave ground to think what next to do.

PROXY's holographic skin re-formed in the shape of Qui-Gon Jinn. The long-dead Jedi Master's fighting style, however, was all the Core, with swift efficient lunges and more-than-adequate blocks. The Core kept its body and blade carefully between the apprentice and the cable. Every trick he tried to get past them the Core anticipated and forestalled.

The red-eyed droids recovered as quickly as PROXY

and soon joined in the fray. He knocked them down in droves with telekinesis, but they inevitably got up again or were replaced by more from outside. Still weary from his efforts with the Star Destroyer, he saved each big push until the very last moment, to spare his energies.

And ultimately the droids weren't his enemy. He had to find a way to strike at the Core directly, without hurting PROXY. Sith lightning was out of the question, but there were other ways.

He leapt out of PROXY's reach and into the clamoring mob of slave droids. Swinging his lightsaber wildly around him, he cut cables and sliced through processors with abandon. Surges of electronic thought seared the air as droids rushed him all at once. He blew them back and thrust his blade deep into a bank of processors.

"Does that hurt?" he asked the Core.

"I do not feel pain," said the Core through PROXY's vocoder, "and my thoughts encompass the entire planet. Nothing you accomplish in this room will make a difference."

PROXY leapt over the droids, shaped this time like Anakin Skywalker. The apprentice met him in midair and attempted to drive him back. The cable danced behind the droid, never snagging or looping forward. The Core used PROXY's internal repulsors to keep it securely out of his reach.

His *physical* reach. No doubt the Core would expect him to use telekinesis to break the link, so he hadn't even tried that. But there were more indirect ways of attacking. The cable traced a sinuous path over the heads of the slave droids. It didn't take long to find a big one in exactly the right spot. It was even easier to grip it with the Force and squeeze it until its power supply erupted.

The explosion boomed through the massive chamber. PROXY reeled backward in midparry. The apprentice hung back, waiting to see what effect the explosion might have. Holograms flickered and fled across his friend's fluid exterior. Famous figures came and went, human and alien, light, dark, and all shades in between. Again he saw himself flash into being and was intensely glad that someone else soon superseded him. He had had enough of fighting himself for one lifetime.

The smoke cleared. PROXY straightened, and his image settled into the form of a Zabrak with eyes full of hate and numerous horns sprouting from his red-and-black skin. His robes were midnight. His leer was full of bloodlust.

The apprentice was taken momentarily aback. He had never seen that training module before. Either it had been dredged up from the depths of PROXY's memory banks, or the droid had been saving it for just the right moment.

The Zabrak Sith grinned at him and drove forward through the parting sea of droids. None now came within a meter of the intact cable, so even that option was lost.

"You are weak," crowed the Core as it approached. "You will not sacrifice this droid even though letting me possess its memories means your downfall."

The apprentice didn't waste energy on speech, blocking each of the Core's moves and driving the droid a step backward. Frustration made him strong, even if he presently had no outlet for that strength. Bringing down the ceiling could kill both of them and probably wouldn't have a profound effect on the Core. If it really was distributed across the entire planet, it could be unkillable.

What was the point of being stronger than Darth Vader if he couldn't save his best friend?

"Violence feeds disorder," blared the Core as they

fought. "Violence is a threat to control. Violence will, therefore, be eliminated under my rule."

"Sounds like you've thought of everything." He barely blocked a combination of blows that he had never seen before, even when fighting his Master.

"There is not a contingency I have not explored," the Core said through the mouth of the Zabrak Sith.

"Oh no?"

The apprentice drove the android back with a series of fast strikes and acrobatic maneuvers. PROXY was nowhere near as flexible as him and had none of the Force-enhanced reflexes he possessed. The droid could never beat him at a lightsaber duel, even with the Core behind it. He fought with a single-minded intensity— one designed to empty his mind of all thought and feeling. The being he was fighting was neither Sith nor PROXY. It was the Core—and the time had come to stop playing with it.

They froze with lightsabers locked and scraping together, human strength warring with droid's, brown eyes fixed on red photoreceptors.

"Submit or die," said the Core.

"There is a third option." With a sudden, twisting move, he brought his saber down into PROXY's chest and slashed deep, right through the droid body. "I could beat you."

The red eyes flickered. For an instant just enough of the Core remained in PROXY to register surprise and then extreme alarm. The hologram sparked and faded, revealing the terrible, smoking wound in the droid's chest. The apprentice removed the blade, satisfied that his blow had done the job.

The Core spun the body around, reaching in vain for the open hatch from which the severed cable protruded. Then all control left the metal limbs and PROXY dropped heavily to the floor.

It was already over, but the Core still had some fight left. Hundreds of slave droids converged on the apprentice, hoping to crush him under their combined weight before he could reach the nearest processor. He blew them away with a single push and slashed open the processor's casing. Ignoring the hot metal edges, he pushed his left hand into the workings inside.

Lightning surged through him and all the processors making up the Core's network. He projected all his anger and grief into the surge, and the strength of it surprised even him. For PROXY, for Juno, for Kota, and for himself he fried the planetwide mind into slag.

Slave droids jerked about in a ghastly dance. The sound they made was awful to hear, the dying scream of a mind that had never before had to contemplate its own demise. It should have been immortal. It had planned to rule the galaxy. Now it was just a tangle of wires experiencing a brainstorm that would inevitably destroy it.

"Order!" it roared and raged. *"Order must be restored!"*

The paroxysm of the droids took minutes to ebb, during which time the apprentice kept up the blistering power of his rage, ensuring that he erased every last trace of the memories pulled from PROXY's braincase. Nothing of him would remain there. The Emperor would never know how forces had gathered to unseat him, for good or for ill. There would be no witnesses, living or droid.

When the last metal body was still and silent, along with all the processors and every blinking light, he let himself sag down onto his knees, then slip around with his back against the processor's plastic casing. He leaned his head back and closed his eyes.

Was that enough? Would anything more be asked of him today? He was so tired. A week of sleep might not revive him.

And worse still: was the Core right? *You are weak,* it had told him. *You will not sacrifice this droid even though letting me possess its memories means your downfall.* That was true. He had an emotional attachment to PROXY, and might very well be developing attachments to Juno and Kota as well. How was it possible that a Sith apprentice could have fallen afoul of such weakness?

PROXY was dead.

Juno and he had no hope of a life together.

How could he go on?

Something moved in the massive chamber. He opened his heavy eyelids and raised his lightsaber.

One of the empty droid bodies tipped and rolled over. A familiar hand reached out and clawed at the dirt.

"Master?"

He was on his feet in an instant, pushing droid bodies aside and freeing his injured friend. PROXY was severely damaged by the blow that had severed the wire, but his photoreceptors had returned to their normal color. It had been a long shot, cutting through the droid like that to reach the cable, but he had hoped it might pay off. How many times had he killed PROXY before, yet seen the droid able to repair himself? This was just another.

"PROXY, are you all right? Can you stand?"

The droid struggled and failed to lift his torso. "I fear not, master. Better you leave me here, where I belong."

"What are you talking about? We can repair you once I get you to the ship."

"The Core . . ." PROXY put a hand to his forehead. "Master, it burned out portions of my processor. My primary programming has been erased. I'm useless to you now."

He smiled. A flicker of hope remained. "You've never

been useless, PROXY. And you're not staying here. Come on."

The droid seemed very light against his shoulder as the two of them wound their way through the wrecked slave droids and processors, out into the murky daylight.

Part 3

REBEL

CHAPTER 32

THE DESERTS OF RHOMMAMOOL GLOWED a hot, baking orange under the light of its primary star. Juno broke into a sweat every time she looked at it. She had been down to the surface just once so Starkiller could purchase a pair of new shoulder servos for PROXY, and she had ventured from the ship no longer than she had needed to. The impoverished mining world stank of famine and warfare. Luckily, its neighboring world Osarian was distant enough for the eternal conflict between the system's two civilizations to be at an ebb. Otherwise she would have insisted they find somewhere else to lie low while word came from their co-conspirators.

Bail Organa had notified them five days ago of a series of meetings being conducted at his Cantham House residence on Coruscant among him, Garm Bel Iblis, and Mon Mothma. Apparently they had gone well, and the beginning of a rebellion was slowly gathering momentum. That was positive news. At the same time, however, the involvement of two notorious resistance leaders and fugitives had raised the stakes dramatically. If the Emperor ever overheard the whispers of an "Alliance to Restore the Republic," there would be no end to his revenge.

Accordingly, the minimal Imperial force around Rhommamool worked strongly in its favor as a place to hide out for a while, as did the fact that it was just off the Corellian Run. HoloNet transmissions were more up to date there than they would have been in the Outer Rim. Juno watched the newsnet for any reports of their activities and pored over Imperial propaganda for hints of concern. Thus far the HoloNet had remained empty of anything to do with uprisings and sabotage on Kashyyyk and Raxus Prime—or, indeed, anything to do with kidnapped Wookiees, secret projects requiring slave labor, and a gathering rebellion.

She told herself that this wasn't a bad sign. The right people were noticing, on both sides of the political divide. The Emperor could not fail to be aware of armed opposition growing against his regime, and those who dreamed of toppling him from power now had new allies to make them stronger.

Their mission was to wait for word to come from Bail Organa, confirming that everyone involved could meet at last at a location that was for the moment kept determinedly vague. The *Rogue Shadow* had hopped systems three times at her instigation in the previous week, staying one step ahead of an imagined—but all too possible—pursuit.

The delay was harder than anything she had ever imagined. That, and staying cooped up in the ship with Starkiller day after day, barely speaking, barely being in the same room longer than a few seconds at a time. She stayed in the cockpit and the maintenance areas of the ship; he kept to the meditation chamber, where he slept and worked on fixing PROXY. Kota oscillated between them like a weight on a tightly wound spring, even more surly and introverted than usual after Raxus Prime, although why that was he refused to say. Sometimes the tension was so thick in the air that she felt she could drown in it.

Everything was on hold: the rebellion, Starkiller's plans, her life . . .

"Couldn't we just go to Corellia and wait for word to

come from there?" she asked Kota on the seventh day. "I mean, that's where the meeting's going to be held. It doesn't take an idiot to work that out, if Bel Iblis is going to be involved."

"All the more reason for us *not* to be there, then," the ex-Jedi told her. "If we're spotted in the area, it'll spook everyone."

"They'd never notice us," she argued, even though she knew he was right. "We have the cloak and—"

She stopped at the sound of metal footsteps on the deck behind her. She spun around and raised her hands, automatically on guard after the last time she had been confronted by the droid in the cockpit. Sudden panic made her veins pulse in her neck.

"I'm sorry to startle you, Captain Eclipse," said PROXY with a humble bow. "Please allow me to offer an unconditional apology for my actions on Raxus Prime. Your name does not appear on my target list and would never have done so had the Core not corrupted my primary programming. I am glad that I was able to merely render you unconscious so you would not follow me or sound the alarm." The droid bowed again. "You have every right to have me spaced or junked and I will not object should you choose either course. I have argued with my master on this point many times, but I am determined."

Over the droid's shoulder she saw Starkiller looking furious and worried at the same time, as though afraid that she might actually take PROXY up on his offer.

"No, PROXY," she said, forcing herself to drop her defensive posture. "That won't be necessary. Let's just forget it ever happened. It's good to see you up and about again. As good as new, by the looks of it."

"I fear not, Captain Eclipse, but thank you for your kind words."

He stared expectantly at her and she racked her brain

for something to break the moment. "Uh, that rear shield generator could use some looking at. I think I heard it heterodyning, and I'd rather it failed now than when we really need it."

"Of course, Captain Eclipse."

PROXY shuffled cheerfully off, and she wondered what he meant by suggesting that he was in less-than-perfect condition. Certainly it had been quieter on the *Rogue Shadow* without the endless dueling between him and his master, but she assumed that would resume now that he was back on his feet. Maybe the symptoms of his dysfunction would become apparent in time.

Starkiller was looking at her, too. "Thank you," he said.

Juno turned and sat back down. "You're sure his processor is clean? The Core could've planted all sorts of viruses in there."

"His mind is his own," he assured her. "Out of all of us, he's probably the only one who can say that."

"Speak for yourself, boy," said Kota.

Starkiller looked down at the old general. "Tell your friend Senator Organa that we're not going to sit here on our hands forever. Rebellion thrives on action, not words."

He stalked back to the meditation chamber, and she went back to waiting. For the moment, that seemed to be the only action she was allowed.

TWO DAYS EARLIER, SHE HAD left her seat to freshen up. Upon her return, feeling slightly more human both in mind and breath, she had overheard Kota and Starkiller talking in the cockpit.

"—can't identify the style," the old general was saying, "and it would help me understand you if you'd tell me who your original teacher was."

"Who says you need to understand me?" Starkiller responded.

"Garm Bel Iblis will. He knows nothing about you, and militaristically speaking that makes you a threat."

Juno held her breath.

"The only threat anyone should worry about is from the Emperor," Starkiller responded in a tone suggesting that the conversation was over. "I can bring him down. That's all you need to know."

Kota was silent for a long while. "Be careful, boy. When you speak like that I hear the long shadow of the dark side reaching out to you."

The two men lapsed into a moody silence. An instant before Juno decided the time was right to burst in on them, Starkiller spoke again.

"There was a girl on Felucia, an apprentice who turned to the dark side. I let her go."

"Bail told me. What of her?"

"Was there no hope for her, once she fell?"

Kota made a clicking noise with his tongue. "Is *that* what happened to your teacher?"

Starkiller didn't reply.

"Gah," exclaimed Kota eventually. "Leave me alone, boy. You're exhausting me with your silence."

Juno ducked back out of sight as Starkiller exited the cockpit. When the door to the meditation chamber shut behind him, she retraced her footsteps and found Kota slumped in the seat with his eyes determinedly shut, still thinking his secret thoughts.

She had felt furious at both of them. What was it about men that led them to agonize in silence, or to talk circles so tightly around the truth that they stifled it? She could tell Kota things about Starkiller that would make his dead eyes pop, but he had no more moral high ground than either of them, with his endless despair and willingness only to complain. Surely no one really cared what Starkiller's name was or who his teacher had been. What he did was all that mattered.

Depending, she told herself, on what he *did* do.

ON THE EIGHTH DAY STARKILLER called for her and PROXY to join him in the meditation chamber.

She hesitated, wondering if she had heard correctly, then left the contemplative Kota and made her way through the humming ship. The droid met her at the entrance of the meditation chamber, and together they entered its dim, angular space.

Starkiller occupied the center of the room. His expression was very serious. With a hiss, the door shut behind them.

"Stand there and don't say anything," he told her, pointing at a recessed corner where she would be in complete shadow. "PROXY, here." The droid stood between Starkiller and her. She could barely see Starkiller for PROXY's silhouette.

The lights flickered and dimmed almost to black. Starkiller took a deep breath and lowered his head.

PROXY's metal skin sparked into life and began to change.

A darker shadow fell across the room.

"My lord," said Starkiller, and Juno's heart stopped.

The dark figure that stood where PROXY had been a moment before spoke. "Your actions on Raxus Prime left the Emperor most . . . displeased." Vader's leaden tones sent a ripple of disgust down Juno's spine. "Who has now joined your cause?"

Starkiller raised his head to look directly at his Master.

"The Emperor's enemies are cautious. I am earning their trust and respect, but some of them remain suspicious. If I'm ever discovered talking to you, my efforts will come to nothing, and we will have no army to challenge the Emperor." He straightened to his full height. "You can't appear to me again. I'll contact you."

Vader's gloved fingers tightened into fists. "When?"

"After the alliance is formalized and ready to strike at the heart of the Empire."

The Dark Lord said nothing for a long moment. His thoughts were utterly hidden by the all-concealing black mask. Juno didn't know what to hope for and felt nothing but relief that the moment was over when Vader nodded slowly at last.

"Do not wait too long to contact me." The index finger of his gloved right hand pointed at Starkiller's chest. "The Emperor grows only more powerful."

Vader flickered out, and PROXY became himself again. Unlike previous times, however, the droid seemed none the worse for impersonating the Dark Lord. Starkiller stared at him, deep in thought, and then gestured for the droid to leave.

She was alone with Starkiller for the first time since Felucia. Was this the moment she had been waiting for?

There is much conflict in you, Vader had said to him, long days ago. *Your feelings for your new allies are growing stronger. Do not forget that you still serve me.*

The thought that maybe he wasn't a completely lost cause filled her with hope, but it was hope qualified by a very real uncertainty. When she had seen him staggering out of the misty distance on Raxus Prime, bearing the weight of his stricken droid entirely on his own, the expression on his face had almost broken down her resolve to mistrust him. The thought of losing his oldest companion had left him emotionally naked—even if it was a droid who had tried to kill him all his life. She had seen the conflict in his face that Vader had talked about. She had understood then that his mind wasn't completely made up.

Yet when she had hurried out to meet him and tried to take some of PROXY's weight, he had brushed her aside and continued up the ramp on his own. It was as though he felt his emotional vulnerability was caused by her, as if she had somehow manipulated him into feeling this way, and her anger at him had immediately rekindled. It wasn't her fault she had been assigned to him. She hadn't made him rescue her on the *Empirical*. He could easily have dumped her and piloted the ship himself.

The situation was no one's fault. It just *was*. The sooner he worked that out, and where he stood with her and everyone around him, the better.

"We're going to Corellia," he said. "They'll all be there—Bail and his allies . . ."

She couldn't tell if he was glad or terrified.

"Well, if that's the case, you'll have your rebel alliance," she said. "What are you going to do with it?"

His eyes met hers. "Trust me, Juno. I'm doing the right thing, for both of us."

She wanted to believe him. She had no choice but to believe him. She was trapped in a web of possibilities. Only time would tell if she could find her way out of it again.

The sound of Kota's voice calling them from the cockpit echoed through the ship.

"It's time," he was calling. "We can finally get moving."

"Where to?" she asked Kota, dropping into her well-worn seat and flexing her fingers

"Corellia, of course."

"I knew it." And Starkiller had, too, before the call had arrived. Juno put that thought out of her mind. "As it happens, I have a course already laid in." She checked the nav computer and found everything in order. The route had been updated automatically every half hour while she slept. With a series of deft touches she activated the sublight engines to nudge the ship out of orbit—not so fast as to attract attention but not too slowly, either. She was keen to get under way, despite the sudden butterflies in her stomach. As much as she had yearned for something to happen, now she was almost dreading it. They had reached the point of no return . . .

She looked up at the viewport and saw Starkiller's reflection there, standing at the back of the cockpit with arms folded and eyes looking straight ahead, as though he could already see their destination. She couldn't read his expression and found herself distracted by his presence in a way that annoyed her.

What if Vader had chosen her solely to test Starkiller's commitment? What if he was now failing that test?

She flicked a switch, and the strangeness of hyperspace engulfed them. The *Rogue Shadow* swayed beneath them, flying as smoothly as it had the first time she'd sat in its cockpit.

CHAPTER 33

HYPERSPACE. STARS. ATMOSPHERE.

Juno never seemed to tire of crossing the same boundaries every trip she flew. The apprentice wondered if she ever missed her glory days as a TIE fighter pilot, when work involved strafing and bombing runs as well as ferrying passengers backward and forward across the galaxy. He supposed, thinking of Raxus Prime, that she had seen some action, but it was hardly glamorous. The pay was awful, and her crew mates left a lot to be desired.

Kota was nowhere to be found when he emerged from the meditation chamber. That disappointed him, obscurely. He had hoped the general might rise above his usual dull funk now that the rebellion was taking a definite step forward. But he told himself not to be surprised. After months of depression and drunkenness, it would take something extraordinary to put the old man back together.

Assuming the jump seat behind Juno, the apprentice examined the strange new calm that enveloped him. Two contradictory feelings still tugged him in deeply divergent directions: one toward the rebellion, the other toward his Master. Between the two rested the separate foci of Juno and the Emperor. He was caught between them like an acrobat on a tightrope maintaining a constant and difficult balance.

That balance had eluded him until recently. Leaving Raxus Prime, he had promised to find a way to destroy the Emperor and at the same time keep Juno in his life. For a full week he had considered the obvious alternatives over and over again, to the point of madness. But then one new possibility had occurred to him: to create the rebel alliance as planned, but—instead of handing it over to his Master—keep it for his own use. Then, when the Emperor was gone . . .

What? he asked himself. Hand control of the galaxy to an inexperienced band of insurrectionists? Rule in peace—with Juno at his side? Abdicate and disappear forever?

The plan was riddled with uncertainties, but it was *his*. He had found a direction of his own, rather than one dictated to him by his former Master. He could pursue it in the full knowledge that he really was chasing his own destiny.

And Juno was trusting him . . .

Perhaps, he thought, *he* should trust *her*. Perhaps the truly wild possibility of his plan was that the rebels could help him destroy his Master, thereby setting all of them free.

He hardly dared think of that.

It was enough to know the meeting would go ahead as planned, safe from betrayal. The rebellion would be born, wherever it ultimately led. Reaching that decision had finally bought him a reprieve between the warring factions inside. While the delicate balance in his mind was maintained, he felt more at peace than he had for months.

The *Rogue Shadow* descended from a polar orbit over the planet's northwestern mountain ranges. From a distance, the planet was startlingly beautiful, with two broad oceans surrounding temperate, well-tended lands.

Industry was for the most part confined to orbit, so Corellia's biosphere had been spared the industrial ravages wrought on so many other worlds. There were, however, patches that showed evidence of past mismanagement. Their landing site was one such, a ruined city in the midst of high-altitude wasteland. He didn't know its name or what had happened to it, but as they drew near and the once-scorched, now-icy grid and its crumbling buildings came into focus, he took the lesson it offered wholeheartedly.

All ventures fail, in the end. All monuments fall. Even the greatest plan rarely survives its creators. If he, Darth Vader, or the Emperor were to die tomorrow, who would remember the strange plots that united them?

Juno guided the ship with sure hands, circling the ruins once to check for surprises and then bringing it down gently next to a trio of shuttles whose edges had been softened by snowfall. One of the transports was clearly Bail Organa's. Uniformed guards placed themselves between all three and the landed *Rogue Shadow*.

"Well," Juno said as the sublights cooled, "here we are. I always knew the stories about Corellia were exaggerated."

"Looks like they're all here." He was too focused on what was to come to acknowledge the joke. "PROXY? Come on."

She turned. "Isn't Kota going with you?"

He glanced around the empty cockpit. "Looks like I'm flying this one solo. Wish me luck."

Her face took on a determined look. "You're not going out there on your own. Hold on." She fairly leapt out of the pilot's seat, straightened what remained of her uniform, and made a hasty attempt to tidy her hair. Flipping a hidden switch, she opened a secret panel and pulled out a holstered pistol, which she affixed to her belt. "I'll be right behind you."

"This is where you tell me not to take that the wrong way," he said.

She pointed at the lightsaber hanging from his belt. "Just don't make me need it. That's all I have to say."

He nodded, not blaming her, and led them out into the driving snow.

GUARDS IN WARM ENVIRONMENT GEAR led the three of them into the ruins without speaking a word. Long, stone corridors wound up to a watch station overlooking the rugged mountaintops. Within the makeshift meeting room was a rectangular conference table large enough for a dozen people. Beside it stood Bail Organa, dignified and formal in the robes of his office. With him were a straight-backed woman with a careworn face, who could only have been former Senator Mon Mothma of the Bormea sector, and a broad-shouldered man with long graying hair and mustache, the former Senator from Corellia, Garm Bel Iblis. Organa nodded in sedate welcome, but his colleagues were more reserved.

The apprentice walked without hesitation to face the trio gathered at the table. Bel Iblis stood directly opposite him, in front of the room's northern "wall," little more than an open-air overhang supported by a handful of stone pillars. A snowy clifftop beyond made the entire structure feel precariously balanced between sky and stone, as though gravity might at any moment smash it down.

The large stone door slid shut behind them. Juno jumped slightly and stepped to one side, joining the men and women in the uniforms of Corellia, Chandrila, and Alderaan guarding the meeting. At Bail Organa's command, PROXY flickered and adopted the holographic image of his daughter, Leia, broadcast from elsewhere in the galaxy. She, too, nodded in recognition as she stepped up to the table next to her father.

"Friends." Bail Organa was the first to break the silence. "Thank you for coming. I know it was a difficult decision. By meeting here, we have all put our lives at risk—as you have on many occasions already." He inclined his head at the apprentice, who straightened at the acknowledgment but said nothing; public speaking was as foreign to him as the Whirling Kavadango Dance. "I believe that hope exists for a better future," Organa continued. "This meeting heralds a time in which we won't need to gather in secret—in which all will live in peace and prosperity, free of the yoke of fear the Emperor has cast over the galaxy. I believe that together we can make your dreams a reality."

Mon Mothma nodded. "We have discussed this at great length," she said. "We agree that the time for diplomacy and politics has passed. It is time for action."

"Well timed," agreed Bel Iblis in a rough, deep voice.

"Logistically," Organa went on, "it makes sense to join our forces. My wealth can fund such a rebellion, while Garm will provide our fleet and Mon Mothma our soldiers. We've been working at cross-purposes for years now, waiting for the catalyst that would bring us together. I believe we have that catalyst now and that we would be foolish not to take advantage of it."

"All we needed was someone to take the initiative," said Mon Mothma, speaking directly to the apprentice. "We know we have the power of the Force on our side."

"In short," said Garm Bel Iblis with narrow, cautious eyes, "we've agreed to follow your lead. We'll join your alliance."

"You have saved two of us here already," Leia Organa concluded with fierce solemnity. "If the Emperor thinks he can push us around forever, he's mistaken."

"You're wrong on one point, Princess," said a voice from the doorway.

The apprentice turned. The doors had opened again without him hearing, allowing Kota entrance to the room.

"The boy saved three of us." Kota was no longer the disheveled drunk, but a seasoned general. His blind eyes were uncovered and his boots polished. Every wayward strand of his gray hair had been pulled back into its queue, and his robe hung straight. With three unhesitating paces, he crossed to face the apprentice and put a hand on his shoulder. "I will join his rebellion, too, if I'm welcome."

The apprentice reached up and gripped the gnarled fingers. "I thought you were still passed out in the cargo hold."

Kota smiled. "I finally came to."

Over the general's shoulder, the apprentice saw Juno beaming as well. She nodded and indicated that he should turn back to the meeting.

"It's settled, then," said Bail, his voice rising into full oratorical mode. "Let this be an official Declaration of Rebellion. Today we vow to overturn the Empire in order that the galaxy and all its peoples will be one day free, be they human or Hamadryas, Wookiee, or Weequay. Every sapient being has the inalienable right to live in safety and to fight for that right if it is ever—"

The sound of a massive explosion cut him off. The floor shook beneath them; dust rained from above.

Bail Organa's smile disappeared. He pulled back from the table and turned to face his daughter.

"PROXY!" he shouted. "Cut transmission!"

The droid dissolved the hologram and became himself once more.

Another explosion shook the eagle's nest. The apprentice ran to the northern wall and looked out through the stone pillars. A Star Destroyer loomed in the upper atmosphere. TIE fighters raced through the sky.

"No," he whispered. "No!"

Behind him the door blew open, and his denial vanished under the sound of blasterfire and screaming.

CHAPTER 34

JUNO'S PISTOL WAS IN HER hand before the first explosion had faded away, but she didn't know where to aim it. Starkiller looked as shocked as everyone else in the room. When he ran to the ledge to look outside, that expression only worsened.

She knew then that something had gone terribly wrong.

The door exploded behind her, throwing her forward in a cloud of dust and stony splinters. Her hands came up to protect her face. She rolled as she had been trained to and rose in a crouch with the pistol pointing at the open doorway. Clouds of smoke and dust billowed through it, lit from behind by flashes of light. Over the ringing in her ears she could hear people fighting and dying. The Senatorial guards rushed into the melee, but she held still, waiting for the one perfect shot she knew she was going to get.

More screams. The smoke took on a reddish tinge. A shadow loomed out of it, growing closer.

She snapped off three shots. All were deflected by a bright red blade. One discharged at her feet, sending her flying again, stunned. The pistol went flying.

Darth Vader strode through the doorway as though he owned the world. The squad of stormtroopers at his back obviously thought he did, too.

"Take them alive," he ordered, indicating the trio of

Senators. "The Emperor wants to execute them personally."

Before anyone else could react, Kota whisked the lightsaber from Starkiller's belt and launched himself at the Dark Lord. Vader raised a hand and caught the general telekinetically about the throat. Kota dropped the lightsaber and desperately clutched at the invisible fingers choking him, but the pressure only increased. When his resistance was crushed, Vader threw him bodily toward the stormtroopers and turned his attention elsewhere.

Bail Organa, Mon Mothma, and Garm Bel Iblis were surrounded. Flushed with fury, the former Corellian Senator spat at the feet of Darth Vader, while his companions stood with quiet dignity. Mon Mothma raised her chin.

But it wasn't her Vader was looking at.

Starkiller stood framed by the pillars in the northern wall of the eagle's nest. He was frozen in the pose of one thoroughly beaten yet barely, defiantly, contained. His eyes blazed. His fists shook.

Darth Vader inclined his head. "You have done well, my apprentice."

Bail Organa hissed audibly between his teeth. If looks could kill, Starkiller would have dropped on the spot. Garm Bel Iblis had turned a deep shade of purple, and Mon Mothma was as rigid and pale as a sculpture in ice.

Before Starkiller could reach out for where his lightsaber lay fallen on the ground, the stone conference table lifted into the air and hurled itself at him. Crashing through three of the pillars and catching him squarely in the chest, it drove him out into the snow. Ignoring everyone else in the room, Vader strode heavily after him, lightsaber raised.

Juno scrambled to her feet, but a metal hand stopped her from rushing out to certain death.

"Not that way, Captain Eclipse," hissed PROXY in her ear. He pushed her toward a side passageway that appeared to be empty of stormtroopers. While the guards were distracted, he adopted a perfect image of her, complete with dusty smudges to her temples, so her absence wouldn't be noted. "My master will need you later."

Fighting a wave of shock that threatened to overwhelm her, she did as the droid suggested, stumbling on stairs still rocking from the area's bombardment.

Vader *here*—and Starkiller hadn't expected it!

If she could get back to the ship in time, and if he had survived the crushing blow Vader had delivered, perhaps things weren't completely lost.

She half laughed, half wept at her insane optimism as she hurried down the narrow stairwell to the Imperial hordes below.

CHAPTER 35

THE APPRENTICE CROUCHED FACEDOWN in the snow, surrounded by rubble. His breath came in agonized, short gasps, but he was grateful for each one. He should be dead. That blow should have killed anyone. The fact that he was breathing testified to one mistake his Master had made.

He had been rebuilt tougher than before.

As heavy boots crunched through the snow toward him, he knew that it would take more than one mistake to bring about the fall of Darth Vader.

He raised his head and spoke painfully through clenched teeth.

"You agreed to stay away . . ." Blood dripped from his teeth onto the icy ground.

"I lied," said his Master, "as I have from the very beginning."

The power of the dark side lifted him out of the snow and into the air. Pain threatened to overload his nervous system, but he refused to cry out.

From the very beginning?

"You never planned," he gasped, "to destroy the Emperor!"

"Not with you, no."

Vader casually tossed him toward the icy cliff. He slid across the ground, clutching weakly at the snow, and then spilled over the edge.

The world turned for a moment and he thought he

might have fainted as he fell. The bottom of the cliff was thousands of meters below, impossibly distant. It didn't seem to be coming closer, which puzzled him momentarily.

When he came back to himself, he found that he was clinging to the cliff face with the last of his strength.

A feeling of acceptance infused him. The mission his Master had given him was complete: the Rebels had been gathered in one spot so they could be taken and killed. That was the reason he had been spared, when Darth Vader had stabbed him in the back on the Emperor's orders. His one remaining duty was to die.

There was guilt in that feeling, too. By planning to use the Rebel Alliance to his own ends, he deserved whatever fate awaited him.

But part of him raged at the way he had been outwitted. He had betrayed his Master, yes, but his Master had betrayed him first. That part of him longed to lift himself up and resume the fight. With the Force behind him, he could strike down Darth Vader and free the others.

Strike down his Master, as he had failed to do two times now.

Only then did he realize that this was exactly what Vader was trying to do.

On the Emperor's orders . . .

It had indeed all been an act, right from the beginning. His resurrection, his "death," even his kidnap from Kashyyyk. Vader and his apprentice were puppets dancing to the Emperor's tune, now and always. Wriggle though they might, their strings remained.

He wanted to laugh, but all that emerged was a short, painful gasp.

His Master appeared in the sky above him, looming vastly in silhouette, blocking out the world.

"Without me—" the apprentice whispered, "you'll never—be free—"

Darth Vader raised his bloody blade, but the sound of another lightsaber igniting behind him forced the Dark Lord to turn around.

The apprentice couldn't keep his eyes open any longer. His fingers were numb; he couldn't feel anything at all. Weightless, he seemed to drift away from the cliff wall. His eyes were closed, but somehow he could still see. As though from a position high above, he watched his Master spin around to face Obi-Wan Kenobi.

The Dark Lord froze. In that moment of hesitation the long-dead Jedi Master attacked, his face a mask of determination. At the very last moment Vader parried, then parried again. He took a step backward, toward the cliff's edge, and then rallied. With two sweeping strokes, so fast they blurred in the cold air, he disarmed Kenobi and slashed him in half.

As the pieces fell to the ground, the hologram enfolding them dissolved. Sparking fitfully and spilling delicate components into the snow, PROXY twitched once, and then his photoreceptors went out.

Darth Vader stepped within reach and nudged the droid's body with his toe. It didn't react.

Remembering the apprentice, he wheeled back toward the cliff. The boy he had wrested from Kashyyyk watched dispassionately, not fearing if he was discovered. But Vader saw nothing because there was nothing to see. His former apprentice was less than a thought on the wind, removed from everything he had been and all that he had failed to do by an act of will greater than any he had achieved before.

Vader lowered his lightsaber and stalked back into the ruins, where stormtroopers had bound the Rebels like criminals and were marching them through the shattered doors.

Suddenly the apprentice was back in his body. The cliff's edge and his life's ruin was far, far above him. He could feel nothing at all, physically or emotionally, except a vague curiosity.

What is it about dying, he asked himself, *that brings out the best in me? First seeing the future . . . then leaving my body . . .*

The world turned black and cold. There was nothing he could do to stop that, so he gave in to it and let all his concerns wash away.

One last thought curdled incomplete in his mind: *I wish I could've told Juno . . .*

Then he was gone into the deep and dreamless dark.

CHAPTER 36

JUNO BLINKED TEARS FROM HER eyes as she brought the ship around. The fastest launch she had ever performed may have taken her out of reach of the Imperial ambush, and the cloak might have kept her well off the Star Destroyer's scopes, yet there was nothing she could do but wait until Vader's forces had finished cleaning up before returning to the scene. She forced herself to assume an innocent-looking orbit around Corellia and wait for an opening. If she went in too soon, she might jeopardize the one chance she had left.

My master will need you later, PROXY had said. Whatever the droid had in mind, she hoped it had worked; otherwise she'd be going back for nothing.

Vader's shuttle lifted off in a swirl of steam. Accompanied closely by its escort of TIE fighters, it docked with the Star Destroyer and disappeared from sight. She didn't know exactly what it contained, but she could imagine.

Take them alive. The Emperor wants to execute them personally.

A frustrated sense of urgency made her get up and pace the interior of the ship, hoping to boil off some of the energy filling her. It didn't help at all. There were too many memories inside the cramped rooms: Kota's old bandage discarded in the cargo hold; the meditation chamber room in which she had first discovered the inner conflict Starkiller was enduring; some leftover pieces from PROXY's repair.

She tried screaming, but the echoes only made the ship's spaces feel even emptier than before.

Finally the Star Destroyer broke away from its objective orbit and moved out of the atmosphere. She watched it go every millimeter of the way, alert for any sign that it might be a decoy. Even when it had reached clear space and activated its hyperdrive, she cooled her heels for another ten minutes—long enough to be certain the site wasn't being watched but before CorSec would turn up to perform a belated, and likely predetermined, sweep of the area. The local Diktat was little more than a puppet of the Imperial Governor. As with Kashyyyk and Raxus Prime, all evidence of what had happened here would soon be swept under the rug.

Before that could happen, she put the ship into a hot, cloaked descent, hoping against hope that someone, *anyone,* had survived.

The *Rogue Shadow* hovered on its repulsors, level with the eagle's nest. She peered through the viewport at the shattered pillars and into the room itself. It was clear of everything but rubble and blaster burns on the walls. The Senators were gone, of course, and so was Kota. The corpses of the fallen bodyguards had been dragged into the corridor outside, but she saw nothing other than planetary uniforms among the outstretched limbs there.

Something caught her eye on the shelf outside: a single body, sliced in two. She gasped on recognizing PROXY's gray skin. Snow had already dusted him, and she swung the ship lightly overhead, blowing it away. Doing so exposed a patch of dried blood not far from where he lay and brought into sharper relief a series of footprints leading to the edge of the cliff.

She didn't want to look, but she had to.

There was a tiny brown dot at the bottom of the precipice.

Juno reached for the ship's sensor controls, then thought better of it. This she needed to see with her own eyes.

Bringing the ship about and letting gravity tug it down the sheer side of the cliff, she braced herself for what she would find.

He lay on his side, curled like a child with one hand up close to his face. The ship's wash made his hair and cloak move in a semblance of life. It was a cruel illusion. The snow beneath him was only centimeters thick, nowhere near enough to have cushioned a fall that far.

With the rational dispassion of someone keeping her emotions carefully in check, she debated whether to collect his body and take it away, or leave it as a piece of material evidence in the hope that it might encourage just one honest CorSec operative to look deeper and wonder what had really happened . . .

His hand moved in the downdraft and she assumed that was an illusion, too.

When it moved again, she nearly crashed the ship in her haste to bring it down and was running to him before the shutdown command had even reached the engines.

He was trying to sit up, without much success, blinking snow from his eyes and waving his left arm feebly through the air. She knelt next to him and got her arms under him. Once she had his weight, he was able to bend more successfully. It surprised him, her helping, and he looked up at her with his one open eye as though he hadn't noticed the ship arrive.

His lips moved, but she couldn't hear what he was trying to say.

"It's Juno," she reassured him, just in case the fall had

affected either his memory or his comprehension, or both.

"Juno," he repeated as though struggling to think some vast and complicated thought. "My name . . ." He stopped and swallowed. "My name is Galen."

That broke the dam. She clutched him to her and cried for PROXY, who had died trying to save him— and for those whose hopes and dreams seemed sure to follow. She cried for herself and the life she had lost when Darth Vader had betrayed them the first time around. She cried for the Rebel Alliance, which had died just moments after it had been born. She cried for all the people of the galaxy, whose fate rested in such weak and fallible hands.

He patted weakly at her shoulder, as though to comfort her, and that only made it worse.

Eventually, the flood of grief eased and she had herself back under control. Her extremities were going numb, and he had to be frozen right through. That seemed stupid when the ramp of the ship was less than five meters away.

"We need to move," she said.

He nodded, and then winced as he shifted his right leg underneath him.

His bones must be shattered into a thousand pieces, she thought. Nevertheless, he was able to stand and even to walk with only a small amount of assistance. They almost lost their balance a couple of times going up the ramp, but soon the warmth of the ship enfolded them both. He collapsed shivering into the copilot's seat and put his head in his hands while she warmed up the drives and prepared for liftoff.

She retraced his terrible fall down the cliff face. When they came to the top, he shakily reached out a hand and said, "Stop here."

Before them lay the scene of Vader's treachery. He

stared at it with jaw clenched and eyes shining for a long minute, then said, "My lightsaber."

She understood. There was just enough room for the ship to put down, but he was on his feet again before she could suggest it. Moving painfully but with every limb in full working order, he walked back to the ramp and waited for her to open it.

When the ship was in position, he dropped out of it and limped into the eagle's nest. He didn't waste any time, reappearing seconds later with his lightsaber unlit in his hand. She lowered the ship as close to the ground as she dared to make his ingress easier. The moment she heard his boots on the deck, she shut the ramp, activated the cloak, and headed for the skies.

"They're gone," he said as he eased himself back into the seat. "Vader took them all—to the Emperor."

She saw no reason to deny that certainty, simply to comfort him. But there were elements of Vader's plan that made her wonder if it could be so cut-and-dried.

"I don't understand," she said. "Why would Vader let us—no, *encourage* us to destroy so many Imperial targets?"

"To sell the deception," he said, his lips in a thin white line. "Credits, starships, Imperial lives—they're all meaningless to Vader. He needed me to find the Emperor's enemies, no matter the cost. And I did exactly what he wanted . . ."

She could see his grief visibly turning to anger as he realized just how he had been played for a fool by his Master. It was difficult to put herself entirely in his shoes, but their lives did have several points of overlap: a disapproving father figure who had ultimately betrayed them; a sense of duty that had led them to commit acts they now knew were wrong; an increasingly uncertain future ahead of them.

Unsure how he would take the overture, she reached out and placed a hand on his shoulder.

"Yes, you did do what he wanted. There's no point hiding from it—and now the fate of the Alliance rests on your shoulders. The question is, what are you going to do about it?"

He glanced up at her, startled by her honesty, and then looked down at the lightsaber hilt in his lap, wrestling with his emotions and thoughts. She retracted her hand and let him think, knowing that it had taken her a long time to perform the U-turn that had led her to believe in the Rebels' cause—and she hadn't even realized she'd fully changed sides until Starkiller had been revealed to be a traitor, before they'd been back to Raxus Prime.

When he raised his head and turned to her, he was resolved. Grief had evolved into anger, and that was evolving in turn into determination. It was like watching carbon turn to diamond in a high-pressure industrial oven. Starkiller was becoming a different person as she watched, as Kota had during his short time on Corellia.

Not "Starkiller," she reminded herself. *Galen.*

"We're going after Vader," he said in a fierce but level voice. "And the Rebels."

She nodded tightly, thinking that it sounded simple but was likely to be anything but.

They had cleared the atmosphere and were accelerating away from the planet's busy skylanes. The Star Destroyer that had carried off Vader and his prisoners was long gone.

"Where?" she asked, voicing the first of many questions that plagued her.

"I don't know," he admitted. "Not yet."

He closed his eyes and leaned back into the copilot's chair.

"Don't nod off without giving me some idea," she said, unable to keep the worry from her voice.

"I'm not sleeping," he said without opening his eyes. "I'm meditating—or trying to. Jedi can sometimes see visions of the future."

He looked tense and awkward. She had never seen the hands folded across his lap so still. Surely, she thought, this wasn't the kind of training Darth Vader had given him. Meditating had nothing to do with hunting and killing, or the persecution of the innocent.

"Have you done this before?" she asked, wondering if it was training he had set himself down the years.

He shook his head once. "I've never been a Jedi before."

An intense stillness flowed through him, as visible as though he had changed color. She opened her mouth, then closed it. Better that he concentrate and she got on with the business of prepping the ship for hyperspace.

Corellia shrank to a blue-green ball behind them, and the traffic thinned out. She took navigation readings from the planet's orbital factories and double-checked them against the system's four other habitable worlds. Everything was in accord with the nav computer's settings. Next she ran a thorough check of the hyperdrive to make sure it hadn't been tampered with by the Imperials. The ship had been out of her sight for less than an hour, but a lot could be done in that time. Inertial dampeners could be rigged to fail at a critical moment, crushing everyone aboard in the tremendous accelerations achieved during a jump. Shields could flutter, leaving the ship vulnerable to impacts with interstellar dust. Null quantum field generators could be timed to dump them in the middle of nowhere. She could think of a dozen ways that Vader might have covered his bets against their escape. She checked all of them herself, one by one.

No one had followed them from Corellia. As far as she could tell no one was monitoring their departure.

Beside her, Galen breathed slowly and steadily with

his eyes closed. An hour passed and nothing changed. Whatever he was doing, it obviously didn't come easily. Her understanding of the Force was limited to stories mocking the superstitious beliefs of an old and outdated religion—plus the rumors that continued to circulate through Imperial ranks. The Jedi Purge might have been years ago, but people had long memories. Serving officers of a certain generation still remembered Order 66 and the Clone Wars. The telling and retelling of such stories had created a strange backdrop of distorted facts, mistaken beliefs, and pure misinformation that emerged whenever the word *Jedi* was mentioned.

A faint vibration made the ship's decks rattle. Concerned, she checked the sublights. Finding everything in order, she assumed that they had just passed through a dense region of interplanetary dust.

When the vibration returned, stronger and longer than before, and the cause still remained unknown, she began to worry about what form of sabotage she could have missed—to the generator, the stabilizers, even life support . . .

A faint sound to her left interrupted her train of thought. She turned to look at Galen and her eyes widened in surprise.

His lightsaber was floating in the air in front of him, turning slowly as though in free fall.

Juno stared at it for a moment, and then reached out to check the gravity generators. She stopped herself, knowing that they hadn't been tampered with. She could feel the field around her, operating normally. Yet still the lightsaber floated, and as she watched more items in the cockpit joined its aerial display: her blaster and holster, a cup, a datapad. The ship shuddered again, as though something powerful and mysterious was subtly interfering with its function.

Galen's eyes rolled under his closed eyelids. A line had formed between his eyebrows. His lips twitched.

She raised a hand to shake him, but found her fingers effortlessly deflected. The Force filling the ship was emanating from him.

His frown deepened. His head turned to the right, then to the left.

"Galen? Are you all right?"

His hands clenched and unclenched, then his whole body twitched, making her jump.

"Galen, can you hear me?"

He moaned softly, as though caught in a nightmare. His skin was slick with sweat.

She crouched in the pilot's seat, unable to do anything but watch.

He moaned again, louder this time. His legs kicked out, making the whole cockpit shake. The objects floating in the air began to spin around them. The lights flickered.

"No," he said distinctly. His head jerked from side to side, his face locked in a rictus of pain. "No, Kota—!"

His eyes shot open. She gasped. The objects around them crashed to the floor. He stared at nothing for a second, wildly, frightened. His chest rose and fell as though he had just run a marathon. His breathing was the only sound in the suddenly still cockpit.

"What?" she asked when she could bear the silence no longer. "What did you see?"

He turned to her and stared as though he didn't recognize her. Then he shook his head and the visions clouding his sight fell away.

"A terrible thing," he said in a shaky voice. "A massive space station—still under construction—" He lunged suddenly and took her hand. His fingers gripped hers with surprising strength.

"Yes," he said. "Plot a course for the Outer Rim. The Horuz system."

A chill colder than the snow of Corellia's mountains swept through her. "What's waiting for us there, Galen?"

"I'll tell you on the way," he said, pulling back slightly. "What I know of it, anyway."

She saw a new grief in his eyes, and that frightened her. "Do you know how this is going to end?" *For Kota? For us?*

He hesitated, and then shook his head. "No."

She wasn't sure that she believed him, but she let the matter drop and turned to prep the starship for light-speed.

CHAPTER 37

HORUZ SYSTEM.

The apprentice excused himself when they were under way and retired to the meditation chamber—not to meditate but to check his lightsaber for damage and to sort out the thoughts running through his mind. He supposed the latter was a kind of meditation, but it wasn't one Juno could help him with. The calming, reassuring presence she had provided in the cockpit wasn't what he needed now.

The planet Despayre.

He knelt in the center of the room and took the weapon to pieces, carefully cleaning and reinstalling them, one by one. The lightsaber would never burn red, but it had been wielded by a Sith all the same. Its crystals would never be clean again. He replaced all of them, activated the blade, and found the resonance much improved. As a weapon its function was identical, but in his hand it would perform better than ever.

The Death Star.

It all came down to weapons, as far as the Empire was concerned.

Sighing, he shut off the blade and confronted the visions he had received while meditating. He had glimpsed the future before—several times now, while on the brink of death—but this was different. This time it had been his conscious choice to pierce the boundary of the present, and he had made that choice with a clear act of will.

That didn't make interpreting what he had seen any easier. In fact, it made it more difficult, because instead of
remembering isolated fragments, now he remembered
everything, and not all of it could be true. At least, not
all of it at once.

The future was a mess of possibilities—some likely,
some incredibly unlikely—shot through with hard cer-
tainties that were unchanged in every outcome. The
Death Star was one such certainty: an enormous battle
station that, when completed, would rain still more terror on the Emperor's subjects and ensure his domination
of the galaxy. Its location was another certainty, and
that this was where Vader had taken his prisoners.

The apprentice knew exactly that much with confidence. The rest was a morass of contradictions. In some
futures, he survived; in others he fell. Juno lived; Juno
died. They were together; they were apart. The Rebels
prevailed; the Rebels were annihilated. In one future,
even PROXY was still alive, something that had pa-
tently not occurred in the time line he occupied.

The glimpse of a wider universe of what might and
might not have been made his head ache, and made
preparing for what might yet be even more difficult.

The thought of PROXY made his heart ache. The
droid had been freed by the Core from his primary programming on Raxus Prime, and that had allowed him to
sacrifice himself for his master rather than try to kill
him. The apprentice struggled with that fact. What was
freedom worth if it led to death? Would he have sacri-
ficed his life for PROXY, had the roles been reversed?
Would he do it for Juno?

Every time Juno called him *Galen*, he felt a very different kind of emotional spike.

On Raxus Prime, when he had tried to call on the
naïve audacity of the boy he had once been to bring
down the Star Destroyer, nothing had stirred in him. No

memories, no buried personalities, no hidden strength. He had worried at that fact ever since, wondering if his vision on Kashyyyk had been mistaken after all, or if Galen had been so thoroughly erased that no vestige of him remained.

But now he understood. When he had turned to Juno at the base of the cliff and told her his name, it had been *him* telling her, not the ghost of his former self. Galen had ignored his summons on Raxus Prime because *he was already there*. He had possessed the strength to do what he needed to do. He always had. It was Galen as much as Darth Vader's apprentice who had invoked the thought of Juno to make him strong. They were one and the same person.

He still couldn't think of himself that way. He had been nothing but an apprentice for all his conscious life. It might be years before he was completely free of his Master's taint, if he survived that long . . .

He closed his eyes in weariness and was immediately overwhelmed by images:

—*the Emperor dead and Darth Vader in charge of the Empire, with him at his side*—

—*Darth Vader dead and the apprentice knighted by the Emperor as his successor*—

—*Kota stabbing him in the back and both of them dying in a fatal exhalation of the Force*—

—*Kota fighting the Emperor and falling, blasted by Sith lightning until he was barely recognizable*—

"Coming up on Horuz," Juno called from the cockpit.

He forced his eyes open, unsure how long he had been caught up in his future memories. Standing on legs that still felt unsteady after all that had happened in recent times, he put the lightsaber back at his hip and joined her as the ship came out of hyperspace.

* * *

THE DEATH STAR WAS EXACTLY as he had seen it through the Force. The size of a small moon, it hung balefully over the prison planet, still very much under construction but recognizably a sphere designed to be solid from pole to pole, with a concave dish dimpling one side like a large crater, possibly belonging to an oversized communications or sensor system. The lines of the station were blurred by thousands of droids, ranging from tiny construction units to massive cranes and welders that dwarfed even those on the Raxus Prime shipyard. Gaps in the exterior armor plating revealed an extensive skeleton strong enough to hold up under significant acceleration. Gravity generators the size of office blocks provided a steady "down" for everyone and everything within its operating radius. He didn't know the specifications of the various drives, reactors, and life-support systems on which the diabolical station would depend when it was fully operational, but he could imagine.

Sometimes imagination wasn't a good thing.

Telemetry showed thousands of ships in the sensors' range. The station's immediate vicinity was full of support vessels carrying raw materials in and waste out. Some were short-range shuttles obviously designed to hop between the construction site and the prison on Despayre, which it orbited. Others were BFF-1 bulk freighters. Staring at the incredible venture taking place in front of him, the apprentice realized that he had found the answer to one mystery.

"I guess this explains what the Empire wants with all those Wookiee slaves," he said. "Droids alone couldn't build that monster. Not in a thousand years. Nor could the scum you'd usually find in an Imperial prison."

Juno nodded distantly, her attention firmly focused on flying the ship. They were moving quickly, mindful of the load on the stygium crystals in the cloaking device. With so many Imperial ships nearby—including dozens of TIE squadrons backed up by no less than six Star Destroyers patrolling the area—turning it off simply wasn't an option. The *Rogue Shadow* needed to be in and out quickly so Juno wasn't spotted and intercepted. Even operating at the maximum safe speed, it was going to be tight.

His belly felt full of hydrogen at the thought of what had to happen next.

The *Rogue Shadow* banked around a beefy gas hauler that lumbered across their path and slid between two large freighters following a parallel course toward the station's south pole. A piece of spinning metal, evidence of an accident or perhaps just spillage from an overstuffed waste hauler, tumbled across their path, and Juno let the shields take the impact. The margins for error were getting tighter with every kilometer they traveled. By the time they were within landing range of the station, it would be like flying through soup.

"Juno—"

"Don't say it." Her gaze stayed determinedly forward as she wrenched at the controls. "Don't say a word."

He held on as the shields took another battering, this time from a small droid chasing a lost component with manipulators extended. The impact made the ship lurch.

She glanced at him. "Just tell me you're still sure. This is what we have to do, right?"

"It is."

The *Rogue Shadow* flew through a cloud of orange gas that left the viewport, and no doubt the hull, a different color. Juno swung the ship hard right to avoid a tumbling rock the size of a small asteroid and only just missed crashing into a trio of TIE fighters that suddenly appeared from behind another freighter. In the act of breaking for a safer quarter of the sky, the shields took a further five hits. One shield, the left rear, was already issuing a warning.

"All right," she said, flicking switches at a furious rate. In the shadow of a giant crane, the *Rogue Shadow* came to a sudden halt. "That's it. I can't take you any farther."

The apprentice double-checked telemetry as he stood. They had just passed through a field keeping a thin atmosphere wrapped loosely around the massive structure. For the slaves, he assumed. The air was cold but breathable, the distance to the surface a hundred meters.

"This'll be close enough," he said over the sound of the ramp opening. His lightsaber was at his hip; there was no reason to hang around. "Keep the ship cloaked and wait beyond scanner range."

She followed him to the ramp, and actually came out with him, which he had not expected. Steadying herself with one hand on his shoulder, she looked over the edge. The view was giddying, all droids and ships with navigational lights endlessly blinking.

"I have a really bad feeling about this," she said.

He tried to muster a casual tone. "Then we must be doing the right thing."

She turned away from the view and looked up at him. "Am I going to see you again?"

"If I can free the Rebels, they'll need extraction." He did his best to sound nonchalant, but her eyes wouldn't brook dissemblance. "Probably not, no."

"Then I guess I'll never need to live this down." She pulled him closer to her and kissed him hard on the lips.

Utter surprise was his first response. Then time slowed, and he felt as though he were already falling. With a sense of unexpected surety he held her in return and breathed in her scent, relishing the feel of her in his arms—Juno Eclipse, former captain of the Imperial Navy and now pilot for the Rebel Alliance; Juno, his companion and occasional sparring partner these long weeks and months; the woman he had trusted with his life on more than one occasion and would again without a second's thought.

For one long, wonderful moment, they were just Juno and Galen, and everything was right.

Then something butted against the *Rogue Shadow*'s shields and the floor shifted underneath them. They stepped apart, reaching for something more secure to hang on to.

She looked back into the ship, obviously torn between her duty and him. Her eyes shone with all the colors of the Death Star, and her own crisp, beautiful blue.

He positioned himself at the edge of the ramp. The taste of her was still strong on his lips. Despite everything, he smiled.

"Good-bye, Juno."

Before she could say anything, he turned and dived with arms outstretched into the roiling atmosphere. Glowing gold with the protective power of the Force, he fell as straight and free as an arrow toward the surface of the Death Star below.

CHAPTER 38

DETAILS OBSCURED FROM ABOVE TOOK on sharply defined clarity as they came rapidly closer. Juno had stationed the ship above the equator. What had looked like a broad, dark line turned out to be a steep-walled trench filled with construction machinery, slaves, and cargo-carrying walkers. Weapons emplacements and armed squads of stormtroopers kept a close eye on the toiling Wookiees. Laser welders sent sprays of bright sparks into the air as giant sheets of metal were fixed in place. Broad sections of hull remained incomplete, providing access to the station's innards for the swarms of many-legged droids assisting in the construction. Conveyor belts of components hovered on repulsorlift beds from site to site like miniature skylanes, crossing at every conceivable angle.

The apprentice wove around bundles of giant metal girders and other debris as he fell, trusting in the Force to protect him from the worst of it. As he neared the surface of the Death Star, he flipped upside down so he was descending feetfirst and braced himself for impact.

He came down securely on the gray hull in a clear patch between two major construction sites. His lightsaber was instantly in his hand. Glancing upward just once, he failed to make out the *Rogue Shadow* among all the other mobile stars above. If Juno had any sense, he thought, she was already well away from the battle station and heading for safety.

Be safe, he wished her. *Be well.*

Then, putting her out of his mind—as much as he was able—he chose between east and west at random and began looking for a way into the station. He could feel Master Kota and the others somewhere in the massive superstructure, but their Force-signatures were obscured by the presence of so much suffering. If the Emperor was there, too, that would further cloud the issue. The apprentice had never met his Master's Master in person, but the Sith Lord who had single-handedly wiped out nearly every Jedi in the galaxy would cast a shadow deep enough to hide anything.

Relying on luck wasn't going to get him any closer, either. The equatorial trench alone was over five hundred kilometers long. He needed to find a map of some kind—or, failing that, a guide . . .

Darting wraith-like from cover to cover, he approached a patrol from behind. Armed with long-range blaster rifles, they strolled almost casually along a ramp halfway up the southern trench wall. Their particular job, it seemed, was to keep an eye on a string of twenty slaves walking in chains from one location to another along the trench floor, and they performed it with the bare minimum of diligence while discussing the possibilities of promotion that would arise when the station was fully operational. Another pair of guards watched the slaves from the far side of the trench; two more pairs stood at either end of the line.

The apprentice hopped from conveyor belt to conveyor belt until he was at the nearest pair's level. If all the stormtroopers were working at the same level of alertness, he calculated that he would have at least a minute before the alarm was raised.

Raising both hands, he choked the trooper on the right until he dropped unconscious to the railing, then coerced the left into turning around.

"Tell me where the prisoners are housed," he said without mincing words.

"Uh, each of the twenty-four zones has a worker restraint facility," said the stormtrooper. "Those hairy beasts down there are always running amok. There are also cell blocks on the Detention Level for traitors and spies."

The apprentice's stomach sank. By the time he searched twenty-five such facilities, the Rebels would be dead for certain. "Have any new prisoners arrived?"

"How would I know? I've been working this grind for a week now."

"Does the Emperor or Lord Vader ever come to supervise your operation here?"

"Constantly. It makes the engineers nervous."

"Do they stay anywhere in particular?"

"You're asking the wrong guy. I'm not privy to the Emperor's movements. Try Sergeant Jimayne."

The apprentice was beginning to realize that he was wasting his time. "See any Jedi around lately?"

"What? Are you kidding? They were all killed years ago. Hey—" The stormtrooper glanced down at the apprentice's lightsaber as though seeing it for the first time. "Isn't that a—?"

The apprentice put him to sleep with a single thought and stepped over the stormtrooper's crumbling body. Before the pair's opposite numbers on the far side of the trench could notice, he hurried on his way, thinking through the few possibilities open to him.

Those hairy beasts down there are always running amok . . .

Shackled and restrained, the twenty Wookiees lowed softly to one another. Many showed signs of malnutrition and mistreatment. One stumbled, prompting a warning shot over her head from the guards on the far side of the trench. The tallest Wookiee, an enormous male with a full, graying mane, roared in protest and raised his hands in a fighting stance.

The chains prevented him from doing more than that, however, and a blaster bolt at his feet forced him to back down, growling in frustration.

The apprentice watched the incident, feeling a plan taking shape in his mind. The slaves outnumbered the guards more than two to one, if this small sample was anything to go by. Even a minor revolt would cause a significant distraction. Furthermore, if the guards' sole responsibility was to watch the slaves, then who better to ask about the station's layout and specifications than those who were actually building it?

Dropping off the ramp and onto a conveyor belt, he ran to the head of the slave convoy and dropped the lead stormtroopers before they even saw him. He swung his lightsaber twice more, cutting the binders of the lead Wookiee slave to make clear his intent, then reached up with the Force and telekinetically wrenched the far wall's ramp out of its footings, spilling the guards to the bottom of the trench.

By then the rear guards were reacting, assembling the Wookiees in front of them to form a protective barrier, and calling for reinforcements. The apprentice sliced three more of the slaves free. The four of them took up the arms of the fallen stormtroopers. Within moments a full-scale battle had erupted.

The apprentice cut his way to the big male, who roared openmouthed in gratitude. Snatching one of the blasters from his fellows, he wielded it not at the guards or the weapons emplacements beginning to target the minor insurrection below, but at the chains still binding half his fellow Wookiees. Indicating with a jerk of his head that the apprentice should deal with the remaining guards, he began pushing his people toward the nearest shelter.

The apprentice saw the sense in that plan. He Force-leapt over the heads of the Wookiee shield and landed among the guards. They were quickly dispatched and their blasters handed immediately to the last of the slaves to be freed. Together they ran for shelter through a gap in the trench's incomplete wall and were soon lost in the station's densely tangled infrastructure.

The apprentice found it difficult to keep up with the Wookiees, with their long reach and their familiarity with climbing, but when he came abreast of the big male, he tugged on a furry arm and brought him to a halt.

"I can't understand your language," the apprentice said, cutting straight to the point, "but I hope that you can understand me. Some friends of mine have been taken prisoner by the Emperor. I need to find them. Can you help me?"

The Wookiee shook his head, then roared at one of his fellows to come over. The two exchanged howls and grunts accompanied by wild gesticulations; then the second one nodded emphatically.

Both turned to the apprentice with their teeth showing. He took that as a good sign.

"So *you* don't know, but you *do*," he said, pointing first at the big male then at the other, a gangly Wookiee of indeterminate sex with patchy hair and bloodshot eyes. "Can you show me how to get there?"

Both nodded. The big male held up one finger, then turned and bellowed at the rest of the group. Two more fell back, and the rest kept on going.

"You four are coming with me?" He wasn't sure how he felt about that. They had three of the blasters among the four of them, but he hadn't been planning on leading an army. The big male looked indignant. "All right, all right," he said to forestall an argument. "Lead the way."

One big, hairy hand came down on his shoulder and squeezed tightly enough to make the joint creak. Then they were moving as one, four escaped Wookiees and a single human intent on taking on the entire Death Star.

They headed back to the trench, where the incident had sparked a demonstrative response. Walkers of numerous types and squads on foot examined the blaster marks and discarded chains. Several had already mounted expeditions into the superstructure in search of the escaped slaves.

The scrawny Wookiee indicated that they should go west, following a route parallel to the trench. They climbed over cable conduits as thick as wine barrels and squeezed through gaps that would have been tight for a child. Strange rumbling sounds echoed around them, followed by high-pitched scrapes and static discharges. The station seemed almost a living thing, which made them barely insects crawling across its skin. The metaphor pleased the apprentice. Insects carried disease on some planets. The tiniest bug could bring about the downfall of even the largest host. One sting, in exactly the right place, might be all it took to destroy everything the Emperor held dear . . .

The Wookiee leading the way came to a sudden halt, looking confused. Ahead lay a complex tangle of pipes and hoses that could not be crossed. Judging by the accusations flying back and forth, it was obviously a feature of the evolving station that was new to all the Wookiees. After much gesticulation and howling, it was apparently agreed that they would need to cross the trench and continue their journey on the far side.

They edged as close to open space as they dared and took stock. They were some distance now from the site of the breakout, but the alert had spread. Stormtroopers held their blasters at the ready; walkers turned from side to side, raking the trench with their gunsights. Every thirty seconds a squadron of TIE fighters screamed overhead. Sirens added a constant counterpoint, putting the apprentice's teeth on edge.

"I don't suppose there's an alternative?" he asked his furry companions.

The big male indicated by gestures that the only other way was to backtrack some distance, descend to a lower level of the superstructure, then crawl under the trench to the far side.

Thinking of time passing, the apprentice shook his head. The big male bared his teeth in anticipation.

"All right. I'll go first. Give me ten seconds before you start firing, then another ten before you stick your woolly heads out. I don't want any of you getting hurt unnecessarily."

The big male made a *Who me?* gesture in mock outrage, then nodded.

"Okay." A trio of TIE fighters flew by outside. The apprentice waited until one of the patrolling AT-ATs was abreast with their hiding spot, then launched himself out into the open.

Automated weapons emplacements spotted him instantly. Red weapons fire stitched lines of explosions across the station's patchwork hull as he ducked between the AT-AT's massive legs. Scooping up components from the nearest construction conveyor belt, he threw a series of high-speed missiles at the turrets, knocking five out of commission. A stream of Sith lightning put the AT-AT itself out of action, and a good, solid shove tipped it over with a crash, providing cover for the Wookiees when the time came to cross.

The quartet had already started firing at stormtroopers converging on the scene. A furious exchange of blasterfire painted the air thick with energy. The apprentice deflected anything headed his way as he hacked into the side of the AT-AT and dropped into its munitions bay. The crew within was no threat, killed by the lightning, but he was careful not to knock any of the charges in case their contents had become unstable. He didn't want it to blow up just yet.

Rigging a simple mechanical switch, he leapt back out and joined the fight. Another two walkers were approaching. He weakened the hull metal beneath their broad feet, sending them crashing down into the superstructure. The next TIE patrol was coming in fast.

He waved at the Wookiees. "Come on!" Three of them emerged from shelter, leaving one killed in the firefight behind. Snarling, they ran pell-mell after him, leaping over gaps in the hull and snapping off occasional shots to keep the stormtroopers in line. The approaching walkers started firing, raising clouds of acrid smoke and shrapnel across their path. A second Wookiee fell, but the others didn't break step. Within seconds, they had caught up with him and were pulling ahead. Their guide pointed at an access panel gaping invitingly on the far wall of the trench. The apprentice put his head down and sprinted.

Behind him, triggered telekinetically, the downed AT-AT exploded, expending all its stored munitions in one blistering blast. Instead of destroying everything nearby, the blast was channeled along the trench and upward, enclosing the two nearby walkers, the stormtroopers firing from the guardrails, and the approaching TIE fighters. A new series of explosions followed the first, and the apprentice felt the superstructure kick beneath him. Fiery debris rained around them as they finally reached the hatch and threw themselves inside.

They paused to catch their breath and to listen for pursuit. None came, not immediately. Covered by the explosions, they had effectively disappeared.

"Well, that seemed to work." The apprentice wiped soot from his eyes. "I'm sorry about your friends."

With a single soft sound, the big male managed to convey that these were just the latest of many deaths in recent times—but thanks for the sympathy.

Their guide tugged at them, pointing along an access-way barely big enough for the apprentice to crawl through. Accompanied by the sound of whooping sirens and collapsing superstructure, they hurried on their way.

WITH A WOOKIEE AHEAD AND a Wookiee behind, the apprentice had plenty of time to get used to their smell. Or so he would have thought. Their fur was pungent and knotted; recent stresses had only added to their aroma. He tried not to imagine what it would be like sharing a cockpit with one for any length of time and held his breath as they led him to where he wanted to be.

He was surprised the smell didn't trigger any flash-backs to his childhood on Kashyyyk, since the few memories he had recovered of his father's death suggested that they had lived there for some time. He wondered if his father had been working for the resistance on that brutalized world; or perhaps he had been a peacemaker, or a healer, using the Force to assuage the injuries of those struck down by the iron fist of the Empire. That he might never know struck him as the greatest tragedy of all. How could one man's life simply disappear? How could another man, even Darth Vader, take a child and completely remold him, removing all traces of his former life and keeping the only part he wanted—the ability with the Force that he carefully nurtured and guided toward the dark side, in order that it might one day serve his own design? It didn't seem possible, and yet it was. He, who had once been Galen, son of a Jedi Knight on Kashyyyk, was proof of that.

He wished he could tell his companions something of his father so that they could carry a piece of him away with them, ensuring his survival in memory, if not in life. But there was nothing at all, and to try would only cheapen the sentiment. So he remained silent and abandoned his last hope that more memories would come.

Finally the accessway widened, joining several others at a junction large enough for the three of them to stand. Their guide, whom the apprentice eventually gathered was some kind of laser technician when he wasn't welding armor plates to the superstructure, explained with gestures that not far away was an exhaust port that would take him where he wanted to go. The port led into another shaft that was very dangerous, a point conveyed by vigorous flashing hand signals and fingers drawn numerous times across the throat. He couldn't tell exactly what the threat was, but he assured them both that he would be careful.

From there it seemed he was supposed to keep going upward.

"Thank you," he said, gripping each of their hands in turn and having his finger bones crushed. "You've helped everyone by helping me. I hope one day you'll know that."

The big male patted him affectionately on the head.

"What about you two? Will you be okay?"

The Wookiees exchanged a world-weary glance. Shrugging, the smaller made it clear that he wasn't to worry about them.

The big male grunted and pushed the apprentice bodily toward the correct accessway. There was no point resisting. When he had gone two meters, he turned to look back. They were already gone.

"Right," he said to himself, less relieved than he had expected to feel now that he was on his own again.

Then it was back to crawling, although this time breathing relatively fresh, metal-tasting air, past complex banks of half-finished equipment that hummed and crackled to themselves. He hoped the Wookiees had given him the right directions, for otherwise he could crawl for months in the belly of the station and never find a way out.

Ahead, growing steadily louder, the sound of stormtroopers talking suggested that they hadn't led him astray.

The accessway terminated, as promised, in an exhaust port guarded by a full squadron of alert-looking troopers. Hot air swirled around them, coming in occasional gusts that made them stagger. Two quad laser emplacements with human gunners watched over the port; four walkers clanked about in line of sight.

He sat under cover for a minute, considering his options, then backtracked to the last junction and slithered into a ventilation duct leading upward, to a ledge on which the cannons were mounted. He sneaked his nose out the far end and used telekinesis to create a distraction below. While the guards' attention was elsewhere, he slithered out and ran to the first of the cannons.

He killed the operator in midstride and kept on running to the second cannon. It had turned ninety degrees to face him by the time he was on it, throwing its operator bodily out of his harness and taking his place. The weapon swiveled smoothly on its mountings as he swung it to bear on the nearest of the walkers. A series of pounding shots penetrated its armor and blew it to smithereens.

His next targets were the guards below, before they could get a bead on him. They scattered in all directions, looking for cover. While they were busy he took out the second walker. This particular section of the trench was dissolving into chaos much like the last incident he had created. Smoke billowed from the fallen walkers; sirens screeched and wailed. Reinforcements flooded in from all directions, firing at every moving object, whether it was friend or pieces of construction material thrown about by their distant foe.

He strafed the guards again, then took out the third walker. Hearing TIE fighters on their way, he judged that confusion had reached its peak and slipped away from the cannon, leaving it rewired to rotate and fire at random. As he dropped down into the exhaust port and hurried inside, several converging waves of blasterfire blew the cannon to pieces, helping to cover his escape.

Things were quieter in the downward-sloping shaft, at least for a while. Running into the warm air slowed his descent somewhat, and only the occasional hot blast caused any discomfort. Several times he encountered stormtroopers, but only in groups of two or three, and they were easily dispatched. He wondered whether word of his existence and the damage he was doing had spread far up the command chain, and remained unsure whether he wanted his Master to know that he was coming or not. The element of surprise had some value, of course, but so did the certainty that attack was imminent. One could only be on guard for so long. Mistakes were bound to be made.

He slowed, approaching the end of the exhaust port. A broad-bladed fan spun swiftly in his path. He stopped it telekinetically and slipped safely through to the other side, but not before triggering obstruction alarms and drawing technical and security personnel from far and wide. He fought his way through the ventilation control room, heading upward again as instructed, looking for the dangerous tube he had been told to expect. The machinery around him grew larger and more complicated as he progressed: enormous interlocking tubes fed by thick hydraulic hoses steamed and throbbed in series. A deep, irregular rumble, not dissimilar to that of the ore cannon on Raxus Prime, came through the soles of his feet. Blasts of supercooled air struck him out of incompletely sealed joints.

His vision of the Death Star was far from complete, but he had enough information now to begin piecing together exactly where he might be. When he passed a sign warning of the presence of Tibanna gas, he was sure of it.

A battle station was no use to anyone unless it was armed—and not just armed with greater numbers of conventional weapons. Something this size was bound to wield a weapon of mass destruction never seen before. Tibanna gas was a rare and highly reactive compound found on some gas giants, like Bespin. When combined with a stream of coherent light, it vastly increased the laser's output, leading to its use in several advanced ship designs and, it seemed, on the Death Star.

Looking around him more closely, he could see that the machinery dwarfing him could be the components of a massive laser system, one in proportion with the station's enormous size.

When he reached a laser tube wider across than some small cities, he knew he had found the place his Wookiee guide had been referring to. The system was being test-fired, with dozens of Imperial technicians and weapons experts observing its performance. He had to get past them all, and avoid the beam of the laser itself, in order to reach his goal.

He shrugged, abandoning all suggestion of secrecy in exchange for haste. Too much time had passed. Everyone between him and Darth Vader was irrelevant. He would fight to the very last person in the station if he had to, but that would make no difference in the end.

It's time, Master, he whispered as he fought. *You stole my life and left me for dead, and now I'm coming for you . . .*

WHEN HE REACHED THE TOP of the laser tube, he realized that his conception of the Death Star's weapons system hadn't been nearly grand enough. The laser he had been observing was just one of *eight* tributary lasers that would merge into one shockingly destructive beam. Carefully timed pulses down each of the eight channels would create a force capable of destroying any ship that he could think of. Possibly even a planet. He felt ill at the thought. Misinformation, slavery, and torture clearly weren't enough to keep the masses in line, so the Emperor was going to resort to genocide. If he wasn't stopped soon, there'd be no one left alive but him, cackling maniacally in the empty halls of Coruscant.

The apprentice gazed out across the enormous focusing dish, which he had initially assumed to have a relatively innocent purpose. Now that he knew what it was really for, the thought that he should destroy it filled him with a weary sort of urgency. He had interfered significantly already with several of the Emperor's grandiose plans. Why not this one, too?

The answer lay in his bones. He was daunted just thinking about it—not only by the task itself, but also by the deaths he had already caused. Could he bear such a black achievement on top of all the others? Could Juno? He wasn't sure of the answer.

No, he decided. This was a job for other people—for the Rebel Alliance, if he could only find and free them from the Emperor's cold clutches. That was the important thing—that they should survive and fight another day. That was all he had to achieve, this mission.

Coherent vermilion pulses came and went in arcane sequences as the weapon continued its test run. Each discharge consumed enough energy to power a Star Destroyer. The station's tightly wrapped atmosphere roiled with booming concussions and whispering aftershocks. Workers visible on the station's skin and in the sky above stopped to stare at these harbingers of what lay in the weapon's future.

A structure on the rim of the focusing crater caught his eye: an observation blister made of gleaming transparisteel in which a number of human figures were very faintly visible. One figure clad entirely in black appeared, bowed, and disappeared again.

Master and servant.

His jaw set, the apprentice wound his way across the rim of the superlaser's focusing dish, lit by blinding green flashes from above.

THE EASY PART WAS GETTING there.

That was the thought that went through his mind as he clambered up and over the reinforced buttresses holding the dome in place. He had circled the dome twice from below, noting its weak and strong points, and decided that the best way in was through the corridor connecting it to the rest of the station. Two pressure doors opened and shut each time someone passed through, defining a walkway five meters long. The roof of the corridor wasn't visible from the dome, being in the opposite direction from the firing of the weapon. He could squat there unseen while he cut his way in and avoid fighting anyone—until it mattered.

At the very last moment, as he raised his lightsaber to cut through the curved durasteel on which he knelt, he realized that everything he had ever done had led him to this moment. This was the confrontation he had been heading toward since Darth Vader had kidnapped him from Kashyyyk and made him his instrument. Twice in the past Vader had betrayed him and he had barely uttered a word in complaint, but, eventually, servants always turned on their masters, just as the Sith always betrayed one another. This moment represented the culmination of a lifetime's training and experience.

This was his most challenging test. Killing Jedi had been easy by comparison. Destroying Imperial factories, likewise. Bringing down skyhooks and Star Destroyers, convincing would-be rebels of his sincerity, dueling planetary minds and other servants of the dark side—all in a day's work.

His *life's* work was about to begin or to end, depending on how he looked at it.

He wondered if Kota had felt that way on Corellia, or Juno in the *Empirical,* or any of the imprisoned Rebels before agreeing to meet with him. Perhaps everyone had such moments in their lives. He wondered if he should count himself lucky that he could see it coming this time. He hadn't on the *Empirical,* or on Corellia. He had been a victim of fate. Now he had fate's arm behind its back, and he was calling the shots.

Had Darth Vader ever felt this way? Had Galen's father?

His modified lightsaber sizzled before him. There was strength in that aqua fire and a purity of purpose—not to kill, but as an instrument of force. Sometimes action was required. The Jedi had understood that. He understood that, too.

He should stop asking questions, he told himself, and concentrate on what had to be done.

Pointing the tip of the blade downward, he cut a circle cleanly around himself and dropped into the corridor below.

* * *

IT WAS EMPTY. BEFORE ANYONE could respond to the sound, he telekinetically sealed the doors leading back into the Death Star. Then he turned and wrenched the inner doors open.

"—traitors to the Empire," came Palpatine's voice from the chamber beyond, gloatingly, coldly, full of unimaginable malice. "You will be interrogated. Tortured. You will give me the names of your friends and allies. And then, when you are no longer of any use to me, you will be executed."

Bail Organa's voice rose up in defiance. "Our deaths will only rally others—"

"Your executions will be very public and very painful, Senator Organa. They will serve to crush any further dissent."

The apprentice strode purposefully into the room, circling a large energy field generator in the center of the dome. Mon Mothma, Garm Bel Iblis, Bail Organa, and Master Rahm Kota stood together on the far side, surrounded by Imperial Guards. The Emperor was pacing in front of them, hooded and hunched but radiating incredible power. The apprentice had eyes only for the dark figure looming a meter or two away, arms crossed as he watched the scene.

Kota cocked his ruined face as the apprentice approached. The hum of the lightsaber was suddenly very loud.

"There may yet be a Rebellion," Kota said, grinning as though he'd never believed otherwise.

Darth Vader and the Emperor turned at the same moment.

A surge of hatred filled every vein of the apprentice's body. The time for revenge had come at last.

The Emperor's hateful visage twisted into a mask of derision.

"Lord Vader, deal with the boy. Properly, this time."

The Dark Lord was already moving. The red blade of his lightsaber flared into life, casting bloody shadows across the room. There was no discussion. He offered no threats. It was clear he intended only to complete what he·had failed to finish on Corellia.

The apprentice knew exactly what to expect. They had dueled many times before. He had learned how to fight at the hands of the man in the black suit—the man whose face had been forever hidden from him. He knew the intimacies of his refined version of Djem So, a fighting style that incorporated elements of Ataru, Soresu, and Makashi. He had fended off many wild, slashing attacks that would have overwhelmed even an extraordinary Jedi Knight. He had borne the brunt of many psychological battles.

He thought he was ready—and so the sheer severity of the opening blow took him by surprise.

A simple double stroke, up and then down, it contained enough power to jar his wrists and shoulders and very nearly disarm him completely. The collision of their lightsabers was blinding. He staggered backward and found himself at the center of a telekinetic storm. His Master seized on his momentary weakness and hurled missiles at him from all sides, hoping to keep him off his guard. For a moment, it worked.

Then the apprentice straightened and, with a sweep of his left arm, blew the missiles away. He blocked a savage slash that would have cut him in two and another that would have lifted his head clean from his shoulders. Ducking low, he stabbed for his Master's belly then flicked the tip of his lightsaber upward, hoping to catch the chin of Darth Vader's helmet and spear him through the throat. The red lightsaber blocked the blow, but only barely. They parted for a moment to assess the brief exchange and circled each other warily.

The apprentice understood that, until this moment, they had never truly fought as equals. His Master had either held back, or he himself had capitulated. Now, for the first time, they would see each other's true potential. Where Darth Vader was strong and relentless, he was fast and sly. And there were ways to fight that didn't involve lightsabers. Loose objects, accelerated to killing speeds by the Force, became projectiles that converged from all directions. Invisible fists clutched for throats or punched with the power of pile drivers. Floors tipped underfoot; severed beams stabbed like javelins; overloaded circuits exploded.

"You are weak," the apprentice said as his former Master launched a second series of bone-crushing blows, each one of which he blocked with elegant precision.

Darth Vader fought brilliantly, never employing anything less than a killing stroke. His intention was lethal. All he needed was one slip, one tiny gap in his opponent's defenses.

The apprentice vowed not to give him one. He whirled and danced around his Master's defenses, testing them to their limits.

"You thought I was dead," he said, letting that small triumph spur his determination to new heights. Their lightsabers danced, blurring and sweeping and shedding sparks in a way that would have been beautiful had their intent not been so deadly. The apprentice felt the wild, joyous energies of the dark side flowing through him and he resisted its call, seeking a better way to finish the job.

They fought back and forth across the observation dome.

"I understand you now," he said, still trying to goad his former Master into breaking his concentration. "You killed my father and kidnapped me from

Kashyyyk, not just to be your apprentice, but to be a son to you. Was that how your father treated you?"

The intensity of Darth Vader's attack redoubled. "I *have* no father."

The apprentice fell back under the rain of blows. The sizzling of fabric and a faint stink of burning skin told him that at least two of Darth Vader's misses had been horribly near, but he felt no pain. He, on the other hand, had definitely struck a nerve.

Glancing over Darth Vader's shoulder, he saw the Emperor watching the duel, his face screwed up in malevolent delight.

And the apprentice understood.

A better way to kill . . .

Not out of hatred. Whatever lay beneath that black mask, it wasn't beauty or happiness. Only ugliness and pain would hide itself away for so long. Hatred would not be enough to turn the tables on Darth Vader.

Reaching out with his left hand, he blasted his Master with Sith lightning. That broke the momentum of the furious onslaught, enabling him to stand and catch his breath.

"I don't need to hate you in order to beat you," he gasped. "That's something I will teach you now."

"You can teach me nothing," Darth Vader's leaden voice intoned. One black glove clenched, and for a moment the apprentice's throat closed tight.

He beat back the telekinetic attack with one of his own, shoving his Master in the chest with the force of a small explosion, throwing Darth Vader backward across the room.

For all his size and occasional clumsiness, the Dark Lord was sure on his feet. He landed upright and launched himself back into the fray.

"I don't hate you," the apprentice went on, blocking him blow for blow. "I pity you." With a new strength of his own, he forced Darth Vader onto his back foot. "You destroyed who I was and made me as I am now, but this wasn't your idea. It was the Emperor's, and it's what he's already done to you." A strip of Darth Vader's cape fluttered away, smoking. The two came closer together until they were face-to-mask. The apprentice stared directly into the black eye guards of his former Master. "You are *his* creature just as I was yours—but you've never had the strength to rebel. That's why I pity you. *I* will no longer serve a monster, and if I have my way I'll make sure you don't, either."

Vader tried to pull away, but the apprentice followed him, keeping him on the back foot.

"I will kill you," he said, "to set you free."

The lightsabers flashed again—and it was the apprentice who found the chink in the armor that both of them had been waiting for. Vader's lightsaber moved too slowly to block a blow to his chest, allowing the apprentice's blade to slash deeply across his armored throat. Vader staggered backward, gloved hand upraised to the smoking wound.

There was no blood. Instead of pressing the attack, the apprentice stood his ground. Despite himself, he was as surprised as his former Master clearly was.

For a moment, the only sounds were the twin humming of the lightsabers and the wheezing of Darth Vader's respirator.

Then the Dark Lord laughed.

It was an awful sound, empty of humor and full of mockery. In it, the apprentice heard a decade and a half of torture and abuse.

Anger flared. He lunged forward. His former Master barely blocked the blow. A second scored a deep wound across his black-clad shoulder. A third stabbed deep into his thigh.

Darth Vader reeled backward, servos whining in his injured limbs and lightsaber shaking.

The apprentice gripped his lightsaber in both hands and held himself back. Anger was familiar and powerful; it also clouded his eyes when he most needed to see clearly.

Vader prepared for combat again. His power over the apprentice, however, was gone. His lightsaber went skittering and sparking across the floor, twisted out of his grip by telekinesis. The Force wrenched him into the air, as he had once lifted the apprentice's father, and a barrage of missiles struck at him with increasing strength. He raised his gloved hands to defend himself, but the battery continued until, with a crash, the apprentice ripped the energy field generator in the center of the room right out of the floor and hurled it at his former Master.

The generator exploded with greater force than he had expected, throwing him and everyone else to the floor. The transparisteel dome shattered. Debris rained everywhere. The sound of the explosion rang in his ears for an unnaturally long time afterward.

He was the first to his feet, striding across the rubble to where Darth Vader lay face-forward, gravely wounded and stripped of his armor in places. Flesh and machinery showed through the gaps. Finally, some real blood was flowing.

The apprentice stood over him with his lightsaber upraised and ready to strike. His former Master was trying to stand, feebly willing his massive bulk to move as it was supposed to. Servomotors whined and strained. When he rolled over, the apprentice froze.

Darth Vader's helmet had been ripped away by the blast. Beneath was the face of the man who had stolen and enslaved him, a pathetic, hairless thing covered in wrinkles and old scar tissue. Only the eyes showed the slightest signs of life: blue and full of pain, they stared up at him with undisguised weariness.

The Emperor appeared out of the settling smoke, glee on his face. He raised one hand as though to touch the apprentice. The apprentice felt a wave of hypnotic suggestion flow through him.

Yes! Kill him! He is weak, broken! Kill him and you can take your rightful place at my side!

The apprentice remained frozen, mesmerized by the Emperor's ghastly charisma. Why not? Wasn't this what he had considered on Raxus Prime? If he agreed to that plan, he would be free of one Master and slave to another—but what was to stop him from attacking that Master in turn, one day? He would not make the same mistakes Darth Vader had.

Darth Vader—who had murdered his father, lied to and betrayed him, killed PROXY, branded Juno a traitor, and kidnapped Kota and the others. Didn't he deserve to die a thousand times over?

And power—he had become used to it in the service of his Master. When the dark side sang through him, others danced to his will. That would be hard to give up.

"No!" Kota's voice came as though from a great distance. The apprentice noted, as though viewing the world in slow motion, the Jedi Master telekinetically snatching the Emperor's lightsaber from his waist and, with a surety belying his physical blindness, using it to cut down the Imperial Guards watching the prisoners. Lunging forward, he struck next at the Emperor, who stood, apparently unarmed, with one hand still reaching out for the apprentice.

But the Emperor was never unarmed. Raising his other hand, he blasted Kota with lightning before the blow came close to falling. Sith energy crackled between them and the Jedi Master fell back, caught in the Emperor's deadly grip.

"Help him!"

Bail Organa's voice snapped the apprentice out of his trance. He shook his head, feeling the Emperor's influence sliding off him like oil. What had he been thinking? He didn't want to return to the dark side after everything he had been through. He had seen what it did, in Maris Brood, on Felucia, and in the eyes of Darth Vader. He didn't even want to kill his Master, now that he saw him humbled and at his mercy. That was where it had all started, he now realized. When Darth Vader had killed Galen's father and Galen had snatched the lightsaber from his hand, his intention had been solely to avenge his father's death. That had been what Vader had seen in him all those years ago, not just that he was strong with the Force—and that was why Galen had blotted out the person he had once been. He had taken that first step down the path of the dark side all on his own, before he had been subjected to Vader's cruel tutelage. He had to retract it now or submit to the dark side forever.

Murdering Darth Vader would accomplish nothing. Saving his friends might change the course of history.

Seen in that light, the decision was surprisingly easy.

A hail of shattered transparisteel and debris drove the Emperor back from Kota, breaking his concentration and freeing the Jedi Master from the fatal web of energy. Smoking and weak, Kota fell away and was caught by Garm Bel Iblis. The apprentice tossed them the comlink and advanced on Palpatine.

"Good," hissed the Emperor, his claw-like hands upraised between them like a weak old man fending off an attacker. Stumbling, he fell to his knees. "Yes." He looked up at the apprentice. "You were destined to destroy me. Do it! Give in to your hatred!"

The apprentice stood over him for a moment with his lightsaber upraised. Its aqua light reflected in the eyes of the galaxy's Emperor as though it was the last thing he would ever see.

With a *snap,* the apprentice extinguished the blade and lowered his arm.

Kota limped up behind him and put a hand on his shoulder.

"That's it, boy," he said with rough pride. "He's beaten. Let it go."

The sound of engines from above distracted them both. They looked up to see the *Rogue Shadow* descending over the shattered dome, lights flashing on and off to attract their attention. Its repulsors dispelled the last of the smoke and sent the apprentice's tattered cape whipping around his legs.

Juno, he thought. *At last, everything is going to be all right.*

"You fool!" snarled the Emperor, sending another wave of Sith lightning into Kota's back. "He will never be yours."

Kota fell with his arms upraised, and the apprentice knew that it wasn't over yet. The moment of truth had arrived.

Without hesitation, he stepped between Kota and the Emperor, taking the full brunt of the Sith lightning into his own body.

The pain was incredible, searing every nerve back to its individual cells, skewering each of them on white-hot needles. He had never before felt anything like this. He wanted to recoil from the source, to curl into a ball and let unconsciousness take the pain away, but somehow he stayed standing, seeing the world through a crackling blue light, and even took a step toward the Emperor.

"Go!" he hissed at Kota. "Hurry!"

The general hesitated only for a moment. He, too, had seen a glimpse of the future, the apprentice remembered. He knew that it came down to a simple choice: him and the Rebels or the apprentice and darkness forever. Gathering up the Rebels, Kota ushered them toward the descending ship.

Another staggering, painful step and the Emperor was within the apprentice's reach. With shaking fingers, he took the old man's bony shoulders in his hands and gripped them tight. The Sith lightning spread to engulf the two of them, fueled by both their desperations. The Emperor tipped back his head and howled in lascivious pain. Darkness threatened to envelop the apprentice's mind, but he clutched to consciousness with feverish will. He had to see this through. He *had* to.

A squadron of stormtroopers ran into the room, led by a limping Darth Vader. They raised their blasters to gun down the Rebels as they fled up the *Rogue Shadow*'s ramp.

"No!" the apprentice cried, dropping his defenses to strike one last time at the Imperials. Energy surged through him. He felt as though a star had blazed to life in his chest. Driven by concern for his friends rather than himself, he embraced the Force completely, utterly, and was rewarded with strength that made his efforts with the dark side look like those of a child. His nerves were on fire. Streamers of light radiated from his skin. His bones glowed like radiant lava.

He saw rather than felt the massive shock wave that consumed a large portion of what remained of the observation dome. A glowing bubble of fire tore the stormtroopers to shreds and engulfed Vader and the Emperor. Shrapnel filled the air like dust caught in the beam of the Death Star's powerful laser.

Tossed like a leaf, the *Rogue Shadow* fled in haste, ramp snapping shut on its precious cargo.

The apprentice felt himself leaving his body again. Or was his body leaving him this time? He felt ripped apart by the energy that had flowed through him. Every cell was in shock; every fiber shook. The fire on his face possessed no heat at all. His limbs felt as distant as the farthest arms of the galaxy. He was amazed there was enough left of him to think at all.

Weakened by the blast, the dome's supports gave way. It collapsed into the superlaser dish, triggering a series of conventional explosions. Stormtroopers converged on the site. Through the dense smoke, two figures were visible from the apprentice's rarefied perspective.

Darth Vader struggled to his feet from the rubble, even more damaged than before. He reached out for support and found only his Master, scowling.

Together, unspeaking, they searched the rubble.

When they found what they were looking for, neither of them looked any happier for it.

"He is dead," the Dark Lord intoned, gazing dispassionately at the body at their feet.

This moment, the apprentice thought. *I saw this!*

"Then he is now more powerful than ever." The Emperor glanced up, watching sourly as the *Rogue Shadow* sped away into the busy sky. "He was meant to root out the Rebels, not give them *hope*. His sacrifice will only inspire them."

"But now we know who they are, my Master. I will hunt them down and destroy them, as you always intended—starting with the traitor Bail Organa."

The Emperor waved him silent and turned to walk away. "Patience, Lord Vader. Far better to destroy a man's hope first. Or that of someone close to him . . ."

Hope will never be destroyed, the apprentice thought. *Not now. It'll survive anything else you can throw at them . . .*

Darkness pressed in. He didn't fight it. Juno was safe. That was all he cared about now. He didn't need to be there to see what happened next. He could imagine well enough.

With his last thought, he whispered his own name.

Unnoticed by anyone, the Dark Lord raised a solid, black boot heel and crushed his fallen apprentice's lightsaber to dust.

EPILOGUE

THE SKIES OF KASHYYYK WERE unusually clear of traffic, for once. Instead of winking transports and flaring sublight drives, all Juno could see were the stars, gleaming like diamonds against the velvety black. It calmed her to look up at them, took her out of herself for a time. That was exactly what she needed.

The sound of voices was soft in the night. She paid them no heed. The Rebels tried to include her, but what did it matter what she, an ex-Imperial pilot, thought of the Rebellion? What did she know of Galen's or Darth Vader's plans? She had been caught up in events, not always a willing participant. In her dreams, she still saw herself talking Galen out of that final mission and fleeing with him into the infinite starscape . . .

She sighed. Running had never been an option. The Empire would have dogged them at every step, as would Galen's past. Deep down she suspected she had always known that it would end here.

Even so, her grief had been overwhelming when she had collected the Rebels from the Death Star. Immediately on learning that Galen wasn't among them, she had wanted to turn back into the shock wave still expanding out from the shattered observation blister to rescue him, but the look in Kota's eyes had told her that there was no point. Galen was gone.

Gone. Dead. It amounted to the same thing. After everything they had been through, after all the battles he had fought . . . at least, in the process, he had given everyone a chance to escape the Death Star.

Juno had kept herself together long enough to get them away from the Horuz system, and had even laid down a course to Kashyyyk, on Kota's insistence. Once they were in hyperspace, the general had with gruff directness told her exactly what had happened in the observation dome. That made her feel a little calmer. Better his noble self-sacrifice than Galen falling to the dark side forever. She understood that. If he had killed Darth Vader, that would have been the end of him—as she knew him. A life without hope was worse than no life at all.

When Kota had finished, she had retired to the small crew quarters to let her feelings go and to come to terms with the truth. Knowing that Galen had stayed true to his intentions until the very end didn't put her life back together. She had trusted him—not just with her, but with her future. He had trusted her with his name. What was she going to do without him?

Her immediate future was decided, at least. She could find peace with what remained of him later. Her memories she would never lose—and the Rebellion, she told herself, which just might stand a chance of winning . . .

They had come to Kashyyyk ostensibly to honor Galen's memory, but she suspected the Rebels were looking for reassurance. They knew so little about him, even now. Beyond the ultimate sacrifice he had made to ensure their safety, his history had so many holes in it. Juno was reluctant to fill them in, and she saw the same reluctance in Kota. Galen had died a hero. What else mattered?

"His full name was Galen Marek," Bail Organa had announced after a lengthy search of Imperial records. "His father, Kento, was a Jedi Knight who lived for ten years among the Wookiees. Galen was born there."

"He found something in the forest," Juno had told the Rebels, remembering Galen saying over the comlink, *Just an old hut. A ruin, really. But it feels familiar.*

And now she was standing on that very site, having tracked through the ship's mission files for the exact coordinates Galen had broadcast from. She could imagine him as he had been then, riven by internal conflict, looking at exactly what she could see: the toppled hut; the blaster burns; the evidence of a very old lightsaber duel.

There's a great darkness in the forest. And—yes, sadness. Something happened here.

Juno might never know for sure what that was, but her mind was full of dark imaginings.

The Senators were inside the hut, talking about the future and presumably assuaging any last qualms they had about Galen's origins. Family was important to these people. During the tense journey away from the Horuz system, Senator Organa had called his daughter to inform her that he had survived the trap on Corellia. Her concern and relief had been such that she co-opted Alderaan's fastest starship and met him in orbit over Kashyyyk. Their reunion had been joyous.

Not even the Empire's new superweapon could spoil their mood. With the Wookiees galvanized by the destruction of the skyhook and busy driving out the invaders from their world, anything seemed possible, no matter how unlikely.

The Emperor knew who they were and what they intended. Not only that, but he was building the means to crush all possible resistance. The Rebellion would have to hit him fast, and hard, if it was to have a hope of succeeding.

Something moved behind her in the crisp Kashyyyk night. She glanced over her shoulder and saw Kota leaving the hut. He moved surely and confidently. But for the hideous burn scar he now wore as a mark of honor, he might have been perfectly sighted.

He sensed her presence and came to stand beside her. Juno felt that he had specifically come looking for her.

"You always knew who he was, didn't you?" she asked him.

He nodded. "I suspected, yes."

"Then why did you help us, after all the things we had done?"

He hesitated, and in that moment she read several possibilities. Had the general been hiding behind his façade of a beaten old man in order to strike at Vader's secret apprentice should his ultimate loyalties fall on the wrong side? Had the façade been as deep as it seemed and Kota's confidence fatally compromised until the very end? Had his redemption and Galen's happened in step, without either knowing?

The old man's answer was none of those.

"When he came to me in the bar over Bespin, among all the dark thoughts in his head I glimpsed one bright spot, one beautiful thing that gave me hope—and which he held on to, even at the end."

"What was it?"

He put a grandfatherly arm around her shoulder. "You know the answer to that question, Juno."

She tightened her jaw so she wouldn't cry. Kota was right. She did know. And because she knew, the question *Why me?* no longer had any power over her.

"He's at one with the Force now," Kota said, and she knew that he was trying to comfort her, in his own, awkward way.

"Will he be remembered?" she asked.

"The Princess has a suggestion you might like to hear." He cocked his head, indicating the hut.

She let herself be led by the blind Jedi through the gaping rent in the ruin's wall. The Senators were gathered around a makeshift table, looking weary. They didn't look up as Kota and Juno entered.

"So," said Bail Organa to the others, "are we ready to finish what he started?"

The others nodded.

"Then, at last, the Rebel Alliance is born. Here, tonight."

Relieved smiles greeted the announcement, but no cheers. This was a solemn moment too. A lot of work and danger lay ahead for everyone in the room.

Leia Organa spoke up. "We need a symbol to rally behind."

"Agreed," said Garm Bel Iblis.

The Princess wiped dust from the table, revealing a family crest etched into the wood: a sleek, stylized raptor, with wings proudly upraised. "A symbol of hope."

Leia looked from her father to Mon Mothma and Garm Bel Iblis, then glanced at Juno. Very slightly, she nodded in acknowledgment.

Warmth blossomed in Juno's chest, and she nodded in return. Galen had done his best to save the galaxy from the Emperor, and in the process saved himself from the dark side of the Force. The people in the room would rally behind his family's crest and continue the work that he had started: the first Rebel, the one who had given them hope.

And she? Juno would never forget him, either, or the example he had set for her. Empty of tears, she faced the future head-on.

She didn't need the Force to know that it was going to be a bumpy ride . . .

Read on for an excerpt from
Star Wars: Death Troopers
by
Joe Schreiber

Published by Del Rey

THE NIGHTS WERE THE WORST.

Even before his father's death, Trig Longo had come to dread the long hours after lockdown, the shadows and sounds and the chronically unstable gulf of silence that drew out in between them. Night after night he lay still on his bunk and stared up at the dripping durasteel ceiling of the cell in search of sleep or some acceptable substitute. Sometimes he would actually start to drift off, floating away in that comforting sensation of weightlessness, only to be rattled awake—heart pounding, throat tight, stomach muscles sprung and fluttering—by some shout or a cry, an inmate having a nightmare.

There was no shortage of nightmares aboard the Imperial Prison Barge *Purge*.

Trig didn't know exactly how many prisoners the *Purge* was currently carrying. He guessed maybe five hundred, human and otherwise, scraped from every corner of the galaxy, just as he and his family had been picked up eight standard weeks before. Sometimes the incoming shuttles returned almost empty; on other occasions they came packed with squabbling alien life-forms and alleged Rebel sympathizers of every stripe and species. There were assassins for hire and sociopaths the likes of which Trig had never seen, thin-lipped things that cackled and sneered in seditious languages that, to Trig's ears, were little more than clicks and hisses.

Every one of them seemed to harbor its own obscure appetites and personal grudges, personal histories blighted with shameful secrets and obscure vendettas. Being cautious became increasingly harder; soon you needed eyes in the back of your head—which some of them actually possessed. Two weeks earlier in the mess hall, Trig had noticed a tall, silent inmate sitting with its back to him but watching him nonetheless with a single raw-red eye in the back of its skull. Every day the red-eyed thing seemed to be sitting a little nearer. Then one day, without explanation, it was gone.

Except from his dreams.

Sighing, Trig levered himself up on his elbows and looked through the bars onto the corridor. Gen Pop had cycled down to minimum power for the night, edging the long gangway in permanent gray twilight. The Rodians in the cell across from his had gone to sleep or were feigning it. He forced himself to sit there, regulating his breathing, listening to the faint echoes of the convicts' uneasy groans and murmurs. Every so often a mouse droid or low-level maintenance unit, one of hundreds occupying the barge, would scramble by on some preprogrammed errand or another. And of course, below it all—low and not quite beneath the scope of hearing—was the omnipresent thrum of the barge's turbines gnashing endlessly through space.

For as long as they'd been aboard, Trig still hadn't gotten used to that last sound, the way it shook the *Purge* to its framework, rising up through his legs and rattling his bones and nerves. There was no escaping it, the way it undermined every moment of life, as familiar as his own pulse.

Trig thought back to sitting in the infirmary just two weeks earlier, watching his father draw one last shaky breath, and the silence afterward as the medical droids disconnected the biomonitors from the old man's ruined body and prepared to haul it away. As the last of the monitors fell silent, he'd heard that low steady thunder of the engines, one more unnecessary reminder of where he was and where he was going. He remembered how that noise had made him feel lost and small and inescapably sad—some special form of artificial gravity that seemed to work directly against his heart.

He had known then, as he knew now, that it really only meant one thing, the ruthlessly grinding effort of the Empire consolidating its power.

Forget politics, his father had always said. *Just give 'em something they need, or they'll eat you alive.*

And now they'd been eaten alive anyway, despite the fact that they'd never been sympathizers, no more than low-level grifters scooped up on a routine Imperial sweep. The engines of tyranny ground on, bearing them forward across the galaxy toward some remote penal moon. Trig sensed that noise would continue, would carry on indefinitely, echoing right up until—

"Trig?"

It was Kale's voice behind him, unexpected, and Trig flinched a little at the sound of it. He looked back and saw his older brother gazing back at him, Kale's handsomely rumpled, sleep-slackened face just a ghostly three-quarter profile suspended in the cell's gloom. Kale looked like he was still only partly awake and unsure whether or not he was dreaming any of this.

"What's wrong?" Kale asked, a drowsy murmur that came out: *Wussrong?*

Trig cleared his throat. His voice had started changing recently, and he was acutely aware of how it broke high and low when he wasn't paying strict attention. "Nothing."

"You worried about tomorrow?"

"Me?" Trig snorted. "Come on."

" 'S okay if you are." Kale seemed to consider this and then uttered a bemused grunt. "You'd be crazy not to be."

"*You're* not scared," Trig said. "Dad would never have—"

"I'll go alone."

"No." The word snapped from his throat with almost painful angularity. "We need to stick together, that's what Dad said."

"You're only thirteen," Kale said. "Maybe you're not, you know . . ."

"Fourteen next month." Trig felt another flare of emotion at the mention of his age. "Old enough."

"You sure?"

"Positive."

"Well, sleep on it, see if you feel different in the morning . . . " Kale's enunciation was already beginning to go muddled as he slumped back down on his bunk, leaving Trig sitting up with his eyes still riveted to the long dark concourse outside the cell, Gen Pop, that had become their no-longer-new home.

Sleep on it, he thought, and in that exact moment, miraculously, as if by power of suggestion, sleep actually began to seem like a possibility. Trig lay back and let the heaviness of his own fatigue cover him like a blanket, superseding anxiety and fear. He tried to focus on the sound of Kale's breathing, deep and reassuring, in and out, in and out.

Then somewhere in the depths of the levels, an inhuman voice wailed. Trig sat up, caught his breath, and felt a chill tighten the skin of his shoulders, arms, and back, crawling over his flesh millimeter by millimeter, bristling the small hairs on the back of his neck. Over in his bunk the already sleeping Kale rolled over and grumbled something incoherent.

There was another scream, weaker this time. Trig told himself it was just one of the other convicts, just another nightmare rolling off the all-night assembly line of the nightmare factory.

But it hadn't sounded like a nightmare.

It sounded like a convict, whatever life-form it was, was under attack.

Or going crazy.

He sat perfectly still, squeezed his eyes tight, and waited for the pounding of his heart to slow down, just please slow down. But it didn't. He thought of the thing in the cafeteria, the disappeared inmate whose name he'd never known, watching him with its red staring eye. How many other eyes were on him that he never saw?

Sleep on it.

But he already knew there would be no more sleeping here tonight.